D0665407

A CUP OF STARS

Printed in the USA.

Cover Design and Interior Format

A CUP OF STARS

STORIES *by*

JOSEPH MONNINGER

This collection is dedicated to the many editors with whom I have worked over the years. Thank you for your kindnesses, your wisdom, your sharp pencils. You offered encouragement, understanding, and that most precious of gifts, attention to another human.

ACKNOWLEDGMENTS

A few stories in this collection appeared in the following publications, some under different titles:

Story. “Figure 8,” “Lunch” “Dry Strike”
Victory Park, “Secondary Virginity”
Fiction, “That Line Where Water Meets the Land” “Hunger Moon”
Playboy, “A Man’s Guide to Divorce”
Nerve, “Girls,” “The Moth’s Desire for the Stars”
Ellery Queen, “Python,” “Vampire”

CONTENTS

What is a man anyhow? what am I? what are you?
~Walt Whitman, Song of Myself

THE LAND OVER SEA

O world invisible, we view thee,
O world intangible, we touch thee,
Oh world unknowable, we know thee.
~ Francis Thompson 1859-1907

Time takes all and gives all.
~Giordano Bruno 1548-1600

My friend, judge not me,
Thou seest I judge not thee.
Betwixt the stirrup and the ground
Mercy I asked, and mercy found.
~William Camden 1551-162

1

HIS NAME WAS THOMAS DOUGHERTY, and he was an Irishman in his heart, but a native of Maine just the same. At nineteen he had gone to war. He had fought the Germans in World War I, and he had been twice wounded, and had twice killed with a certainty that would flavor his dreams. In his quiet moments, and on his return in the belly of a transport ship called the *Britannia,* he pictured the boys he had killed, their faces holding surprise where an instant before there had been aggression and fear. He wondered sometimes if his own face possessed those expressions, and what he had looked like an instant before the bullets had found him – once in the right shoulder, and once in the heavy meat of his left thigh – and if he, too, had shown surprise at his own mortality.

He landed in Boston and took the train up to Portland, Maine, where he disembarked and met with his father and mother and his brother, Sean. His father was a schoolmaster; his mother kept house and ran the St. Mathew's choral society, a church singing group that had thrice won the Maine chorale singing competition, held in various parishes across the state. His parents were well-educated for that time and place, and Sean, his older brother, had halved their interests, joining the seminary to study for the priesthood. Sean had not gone to war. He was consumptive, a child who failed to thrive, and one felt, watching him, that his hold on the world was tentative at best.

What should have been a glorious homecoming, for he had served admirably, had received commendations and two Purple Hearts, was undermined by the uneasiness Thomas felt in his heart. He was not the first soldier to find it difficult to reacquaint himself with civilian life. His parents, and his brother Sean, who travelled from Millinocket to spend a few days with his soldier brother, did not know how to tread. On one hand, they did not want to ask impertinent questions. They were conscious of the pain of war, though they had not experienced it themselves, and they were sufficiently sensitive to avoid long discussions of what it must have been like. At the other end of their cautiousness, they guessed, correctly, that their own histories, what they had done or felt or attempted during his absence, might madden him by its featurelessness. How to talk about chorale competitions, or the Portland Academy's academic policies, or even the beauty and majesty of the Lord, without inadvertently offending their beloved child and brother?

They did their best. They took Thomas on social rounds, reintroduced him to a few lovely young women whom he had known before the war, but they knew him well enough to see he had been sickened by his time away. His wounds bothered him and he walked with a limp; his shoulder, when he reached for something quickly, snapped out in a painful spasm that he answered with a tight grimace and closed eyes. They whispered about him and the whispers entered the walls, and though Thomas did not overhear them precisely, he knew he had come home, but that home could no longer enter him.

In time he travelled north into logging country. It was for the best. His parents did not say as much, but they were relieved that he had found a purpose, however temporary, to engage him. His brother Sean wrote him a long letter about the mercy of God, because he felt – his brother this is – that what Thomas required more than anything else was the quiet heart that came with forgiveness.

In Thomas's own mind, he yearned for silence. He may not have had a word for it, nothing quite as tidy as silence, but he had always loved the waters and woods, and often, while stranded in the muddy trenches of World War I, had dreamed of Maine's pristine lakes and forests. He remembered, in particular, a canoe trip he had made down the St. Croix River, the lovely band of black water filled with bass and trout, and the gentle rapids that lifted his heart. He had taken that trip with his friend, Joe, and Joe had not come back from the war. Still, in his memory of the canoe trip Joe yet lived, and Thomas yearned to visit the river once more, though he was also afraid it would not match the memory in his head. He would not be able to stand that, he felt. He could not squander his memory of Joe, and so he kept the trip as a harbor in his heart, and he visited it often in moments of trouble or anguish.

He worked in the logging camps for a year. He was not particularly suited to the work because he did not like to destroy the trees, nor did he care much for the jocular kidding that accompanied the work. It was healthy labor, he granted, but only when it was not killing you. He wondered, as he worked through the winter, guiding the great Percherons that pulled the logs through the deep snow, whether it was possible to fall in love with trees. It was not an academic question in his mind. In the months of working, he found occasion to leave the camp and travel into the deepest parts of the forest alone. His fellow workers, many of them French Canadian, joked that he was *loup garoux*, a werewolf, and his silence unsettled them.

He wrote to his brother about these feelings, confiding in him that he only felt God's presence in the forest, and his brother answered by sending him a volume of Thoreau. Thomas read it exhaustively, and wrote to ask for more, and for anything else that spoke to the need for the sanctity of the northern forest. His priest brother took on the pleasure of sending books and criticisms, and they engaged in a sincere correspondence, one that was more important to Thomas than his brother may have guessed.

Thomas, in his bunk at night, read and was aware of being lost. It was not a romantic position, he did not fashion himself a poet, or a philosopher, someone for whom alienation was attractive. He felt his heart had hardened, or had been stabbed by the vision of those two German soldiers falling, the delight – yes, it had been momentary delight – that it had been them and not him. It disgusted him to recall that pleasure, the exaltation that came with blood-letting. It made him doubt the good of humanity, and made him wonder at his own soul, the barbed thing that provoked him to accept war as a necessary proposition.

In spring he grew restless. He contemplated travelling more, going deeper into the woods, when a letter arrived from his father telling him that Uncle Julius had died and had left a small farm to their family. It was not much of a farm, mostly apple trees and a few pigs and chickens, but it was theirs, deed and all, and his father offered it to Thomas. Sean did not need it, of course, and his parents were too old to embark on a new life, and so, before selling it, his father inquired if Thomas would find it useful.

Thomas equivocated. Secretly, he held great hopes for the property, not as a commercial venture, but as a refuge. It gladdened him to think of it, though he knew of Uncle Julius – his father's brother – only slightly. But his father enclosed a surveyor's map and Thomas saw the property ran to the sea; that it backed up into the land in a large wedge, like a bear's bottom as it tried to pull its head from a barrel. Mostly pine, his father reported, and the nearest town was ten miles away. His father said that he was not sure Thomas would want such isolation, but it was his for the asking.

What did he fear, then? He worried that his father had made the gesture as a means to give him direction; that his father sensed his inner turmoil, had perhaps heard about it from Sean, and that his offer of the farm, however well-meaning, was a concession to Thomas's inability to stand firm. It was a cloudy thought, something he felt more in his stomach than in his head, but when his brother wrote and said, selfishly, he hoped Thomas would settle on the farm so that he, Sean, might someday visit, Thomas wrote to his father and accepted the bequest. In the stroke of a few inked lines, he became the owner of forty-three acres of land near Machais, Maine, in Washington County.

He left the logging camp at ice-out and determined to hike to his new home, a copy of Thoreau in his backpack, his bedroll covered in sealskin to keep it dry. He hiked in a kind of wonder, though that is not to say he did not suffer from privation. It was hard going; often no sustained path pointed the way, and he understood, before long, why many of the early French *voyageurs* had traveled by canoe rather than on foot. Fortunately he had saved money while working at the logging camp, and somewhere in the middle of his trip he purchased a bright, well-rendered canoe from a farm family. He did not paddle the canoe, but poled it near the shoreline instead, standing in the center of the boat while using the pole for leverage. He made good time in this fashion, and soon became a skilled canoeist. By using the pole he could even work his way up a rapid, if necessary, but in general he followed the water to the sea and rode it as surely as rain will run down the nearest river.

The canoe made travel easier, and he spent languid days moving gracefully across the ponds and lakes, his heart emptied of some of the anguish it had carried since the war. At night he slept out beneath the stars beside a smudge fire lit to keep the bugs down. In bad weather, which closed about him frequently, he slept beneath the canoe, his volume of Thoreau held close to his nose in the dimness. At those moments he felt he had turned into a turtle, a slow, quiet creature, the canoe a carapace. Yes, he was part animal, it seemed, and he took pleasure in the sensations of life: he swam twice a day when the weather was good, and he let the sun rest on his skin until he became dark brown and handsome. He welcomed the sight of bears and moose, the wary deer that crept beside his campsite at times, the eagles and thrushes that watched him from branches. He had a sense that he was slowly turning inside out; like a sock with a bothersome seam, he felt that nature might turn him slowly right side around, and he composed many letters to his brother in his head, outlining this impression.

He encountered only three human groups on his trip. First, the farm family that had sold him the canoe. Twice he ran into trappers who lived filthy existences, their bodies and small habitations stinking of blood and gristle and skins. He did his best to avoid them. He saw from their examples that it was possible to be several ways in nature, and that to plunder it brought something raw and unholy into the world, and he vowed that he would be an advocate of good husbandry. He did not kill more animals than he needed in order to survive. He discovered he could eat berries and nuts, and his body felt lighter for doing so, and his mind seemed clearer.

It was late summer by the time he arrived in Machais, Maine, a small settlement built beside the embouchement of the Machais River. He knew in a general sense that Machais was the scene of the Revolutionary War's first naval engagement. It was a rich fishing community, abundant with cod and mackerel, but beyond those bare facts, the land was new to him. After spending so much time among the trees and waters in his passage, and learning to live quietly while keeping to himself, he found even this small village difficult to endure. He wondered if he had not become too solitary, had not somehow broken an unspoken bond with the community of men, that in the silence he had sought he had become trapped unwittingly.

He bought supplies in the general store and hired a wagon to take him to his land. It was, as his father had promised, nearly ten miles outside of town along a road rutted and almost impassable in places. The road was known as the Jorgenson Road, and the grim young man who drove him out recounted the story of old man Jorgenson, a town founder, who had died by felling a tree on himself and laying undiscovered for several days until a rescue party tracked him down. The tree had flattened Jorgenson, and he lay beneath it as a sheet of paper rests beneath a book, only his hands visible where they extended beyond the tree bole. The tree, from all the accounts, had jumped nearly sideways to trap old man Jorgenson, which was a lesson about the life in trees, the boy said, and about the danger of cutting them.

Thomas listened with only half his attention. The scenery absorbed him; it proved more stunning than he had dare hoped. On the seaward side of the road, he caught great vistas of the ocean, its heavy fragrance thick and perfect. Everywhere yellow tansy and Queen Anne's lace nodded and bent with the land breeze, and, as the surveyor's map had promised, a great tract of pine extended into the mainland, its fragrance a match for the sea's scent. It was beautiful land, and he felt his heart calm as he realized he had made the correct choice. He felt welcome here, and at peace, and when the boy drove him up the bumpy path that led to his Uncle Julius' farm, it did not surprise him that the farm rested in the palm of the land, settled and comfortable, no more or less than it needed to be.

He unloaded the wagon and paid the young man, and then stood quietly until the wagon had disappeared. He did not want to enter the house while the grim boy watched. To pass the moment while the boy pulled away, he studied the farmhouse and let its shape, and dimensions and feeling sink into him. It was not lavish, and the weather had certainly worn it down, but he found its outline and form comforting. He said a silent prayer of thanks to Uncle Julius, a man he did not know in any genuine sense except as a reflection of his father. The farm rested, Thomas felt, like a ship at the top of a wave, a moment perched between land and sea, and the sense of it pleased him. For the first time in many months the image of the German boys did not insist on recognition. Yes, he realized, the farm could be a refuge, and for that he was grateful.

He performed the rites of moving in, as anyone would do: he swept the building thoroughly, dusted it, and did his best to rid it of cobwebs and mouse droppings. He took pleasure in the work; he left the front door open and he sometimes smelled the sea beckoning, or heard the titter of chickadees as they found the pinecones in the forest behind him. His mind remained neutral. It did not travel back to the war, nor did it remind him of his injuries. He felt if he could keep his hands busy, concentrate on the things directly in front of him, he might one day forget the stain of battle.

In cleaning Thomas gathered a sense of his uncle. From the family history, he knew his uncle had been in the mills for a time, had worked as a logger, too, and had even spent time on shipboard as a fisherman. Julius was not a reader, his father said, and in truth Thomas found no evidence of scholarship. But he was a man who possessed a sense of order, Thomas felt, because the few sticks of furniture that served him, the simple basin for a sink, spoke to purpose and not ornamentation. It reminded him of the little he knew of Shakers, the simplicity of line that bespoke humility in the face of the divine. The farmhouse was solidly built, and except for a few broken windowpanes, and an obvious hole in the corner of the roof where a raccoon had gnawed its way inside, he felt satisfied that the house would suit him.

He ate jerky and two boiled potatoes for dinner, and then slept on the tick mattress in the single room off the parlor. The world rushed after him; for a time in the darkness he experienced the war again, and all of his travel, even moments from the logging camps and his boyhood with Sean, and he closed his eyes tightly, trying in equal parts to remember and shun the sweep of emotions his recollections brought. Was life always this way for men, he wondered? Why had no one written about this, or told him what could occur in a man's life to bring this pain and emotion? Did all men and women live in such peril, feel this seep of life drifting past and through them?

He slept a long time. When he woke it was middle morning and he felt guilty that he had squandered the purest part of the day. It didn't matter, though, and after eating a corner of bread and a quarter of cheese, he walked toward the sea, eager to see it again. It did not disappoint. It required that he climb down a fairly sheer cliff face, but in time he stood twenty feet above the ocean on a bluff pointing directly east. The sun held him. Yes, he could live here, he thought. The sea rolled and twisted in its summer leisure, and he smelled that the air cleaned itself on the rocks and sand, and that his lungs felt tender and moist in breathing it.

In the afternoon he wrote letters to his brother and to his parents. He told his parents the facts for which they would hunger: that he had found Uncle Julius' farmhouse and that it was in good repair, that he felt he could live here and do work, or simply exist, and he thanked them again for providing this opportunity. To his brother he wrote his strongest feelings: what was the purpose of man, and how did one seal off the calamitous emotions that life carried with it? He did not filter his thoughts, though he was careful not to alarm his brother. He told his brother about the long hike and canoe trip from the logging camp, how he had felt in the forest, and what it had seemed to mean, and he asked his brother about his readings, and what they could tell him. He sealed both letters with candle wax and promised he would walk to town the next day to post them and to arrange for his canoe to be brought from the lake where he had left it.

That night he slept soundly, but woke in the center of the darkness to feel another's presence. It alarmed him. He sat up in bed and lit a lantern, but the darkness was too impenetrable.

It might have been anything, he told himself, and besides, he was not a man easily frightened. He had been to war, after all, and he had travelled through the Maine wilderness, so it was not likely that he would succumb to fear in this small farmhouse overlooking the Atlantic.

Before he could walk to town the next day, fever covered him and kept him in his bed. It approached him violently, storming his vertebrae and making him shiver. This, then, he realized, was the source of the presence he had felt. It had been nothing more than a turn of blood, a virus, an ailment of unspecified origin. He recovered slowly and spent most of two days sitting in the sunlight, dodging into the house only when rain passed over the forest.

He swam in the sea to rid himself of the last of the fever. He felt an invalid's weakness and disgust at his own condition, and he bathed in the water naked, glad to feel the salt rough his skin. He had played in the sea as a boy, and he found he remembered what it felt like, why he had loved it. The waves came in gently; his beach, he discovered, was more rock than sand, and he enjoyed the sound the water made as it rasped through the stones on its journey. When he left the water he stood a long time in the sunlight, his health returned.

In the village he posted his letters and received a package of books from his brother. He described at length the location of his canoe, hoping to get the grim boy with his wagon to fetch it, but it was difficult to make himself understood. Thomas suffered, he knew now, from a social distance he had imposed on himself. He wondered what his brother would say about his sense of isolation, the distance he felt from his fellow man or woman? The words he spoke seemed pried from something deep inside him; he spoke only as much as he needed, and then haltingly. He had changed, he knew, and whether that change was for good or ill, he could not say for certain. He longed to be by himself and he concluded his transaction with the grim boy and walked back the dirt road toward his farmhouse in the last of the summer twilight.

On the road he met a woman. It surprised him to encounter her. She led an old white mule on Jorgenson Road and he could not imagine where she had come from; she smiled and held the mule's lead in her right hand. He smiled in return. Gazing at her as she approached, he wondered how he had forgotten about women. Obviously, no man ever entirely forgets about women, but he had shut the door on their possibility, had seen no room in his life for one, and now, incomprehensibly, a woman's beauty softened him. He felt shy. He felt, too, that a woman might see his vulnerability, and that made him nervous. He tried to pass by her silently, but she stopped and plainly desired conversation.

"You must be Thomas, the man they're talking about in the village," she said.

"I am."

"You're living in Julius's farm house?"

He nodded. His tongue felt thick and stupid in his mouth.

"And you share his last name? Dougherty?"

He nodded again. How beautiful she was! He felt uncomfortable in her presence because it evoked in him feelings he had thought long dead. He wished he had sufficient ease to speak normally to her, but he had lost that knack, if he had ever possessed it, and he touched his forehead in salute to say goodbye.

"I wondered if you might do me a favor?" she asked before he could get away. "This mule is without a home. It's a long story, but I would take it as a favor if you would let him reside at your farmhouse for the time being. Your uncle Julius occasionally did me such favors. You have a barn, I know."

"Did you know Julius well?" he asked.

"Not well. But we had an understanding. You might find the mule useful in any case. His name is Willy."

Try as he might, Thomas could see no reason to refuse her. The house did have a small barn set to the north, and there were two stalls inside. Feed would not be an issue, at least until winter, and water was easy enough to provide. Nevertheless, it was an unusual request to make of a stranger. He wanted to ask her many questions, but his eyes happened to fall into hers and he felt confused and cloudy.

"What's your name?" he asked finally.

"Kathleen."

"I'll watch your mule for a time," he said, hoping to give himself latitude to end the arrangement eventually. "Where do you live in town?"

"Not so close, and not so far," she said. "I'll find you, never worry. Willy won't give you any trouble, I promise. You may take a liking to him. He has some work left in him if you need it."

She handed him the lead. His hand touched hers in passing and she smiled again and he thought she was the most beautiful woman he had ever seen. Her coloring was red and her eyes were green. She was of Irish ancestry, he felt certain, and her voice – what little of it he had heard – contained the burr of a brogue. He gave Willy a pat on the shoulder; he had always loved animals and Willy seemed like an even-tempered creature, happy to go wherever he was led. He had drowsy eyes and a look of comic understanding in his expression.

"I must be getting on," she said, "but I'll come to see you soon. I'm grateful for your help."

Then she left. He turned with the white mule and began walking toward home. He turned frequently to see her, and when she had all but disappeared in the evening light, on the curve of road, she glanced back and waved, and his hand, almost on its own, rose to the air and waved to her.

2

HE LIKED THE MULE. IT was, as he had first noted, a wise animal, happy to oblige, intuitive and centered. It provided good company. In the mornings he opened the stall gate and let the mule out, and for the first week or so he kept it tethered so that it would not wander off. But the mule showed no inclination to leave; it lingered by the farmhouse, its head sometimes appearing in the doorway. Thomas gathered apples for it from a grove of overgrown trees set back and away from the sea, and the mule enjoyed these, devouring them against Thomas's open palm, its hairy lips tickling and playful as it ate.

Thomas did not work the animal, but he rode it occasionally, and the mule seemed happy to have him aboard. He rode bareback, his legs jingling beside the animal's ribs, the halter rope his bridle. Autumn had begun on the highest peaks behind the house, and Thomas rode to meet it, letting Willy pick his way through the trees, content to let the animal graze on beechnuts and grasses when it needed rest. He rode the borders of his property and saw that someone, likely Julius, had set out stone cairns at each corner. Gradually Thomas felt the land entering him, and he felt himself at home.

He was curious, of course, about Kathleen. When the grim boy brought his canoe – he had found it from Thomas's description, a remarkable thing altogether – Thomas asked about the woman's identity, but the boy pleaded ignorance. Whether the boy knew anything or not was difficult to gauge; he was, Thomas determined, a piggish, stealthy boy, who masqueraded in the world as a dolt, but lived by his cunning just the same. He said little and watched much, and soon Thomas gave up asking the boy about the woman Kathleen, which was not to say he did not believe the boy might have provided answers if he felt inclined to do so.

Still, Thomas was glad to have his canoe and he hung it in the rafters of the barn, out of the weather and ready for the following spring. He longed to take it out – he had discovered a small pond on his property, its waters filled with trout and perch – but he had become aware of winter's approach and the need for cordwood and provisions. He set about making himself ready for the season of "cups and spoons" as the loggers called it, a season of soups and beans and the impenetrable chill of northern Maine.

In the evenings, however, when he had made a fire in the hearth and had pulled a chair close to read and be warmed, he thought often of Kathleen. He remembered her beauty and the sweetness of her voice; he recalled the direct way her eyes had journeyed into his, and how, in her soft expression, he had seen something like merriment. Who was she? And where did she live? Twice he rode Willy into town to get provisions and post letters, but his questions concerning Kathleen were always met with evasiveness. People changed the topic or pled ignorance. Thomas sensed that the woman trailed a story behind her, but what the story could be, or why the villagers did not readily know her, he couldn't fathom.

She visited him again on a soft October afternoon. Willy detected her first. She came from the direction of the sea, as if she had been out walking the beach, and Willy made a hiccup of braying at her approach. Thomas had been sawing wood; he found the job contemplative and pleasant, and he liked the scent of sawdust and the slow rasp of the teeth over fiber. He had been thinking of Sean, his brother, and of his brother's latest ruminations about God and sin and virtue. Mixed in his brother's words was his own loneliness, his own doubt, his worry that the path he had chosen to bring him to God was false and unnecessary. His brother had begun to envy Thomas his simple life, and he wrote with longing about joining him someday when his work was finished, and that they could live overlooking the sea and have time, finally time, for all the long conversations they had promised one another.

And then, miraculously, Kathleen appeared. He watched her

walk up the long path toward the farmhouse, and he found he could not suppress a smile, nor the nervous flutter in his stomach. She was as beautiful as he remembered. She walked with a light foot; she wore a jerkin-styled jacket over an emerald blouse, and the color of her shirt picked up the bright green of her eyes. She seemed impossibly elegant for Washington County, Maine. The few women he encountered on his forays into Machais had been either stout, rough women or mere girls. Kathleen was a figure and form different from these others. Even Willy seemed to understand, because the old mule trotted a few steps toward her, apparently happy to see his owner.

"You're going along all right then?" she asked by way of greeting. "You find such a quiet life to your liking?"

"It's not always so quiet," he said, hanging the bow saw on the nail where it was kept. She rubbed the mule's ears and Willy bent to give her greater access.

"I've missed you, boy," she said to Willy. "Have you two been getting along?"

"I've enjoyed his company."

"He's a lovely creature, as I said."

"Have you come to take him?"

"No," she said, "I've come for you."

It was a queer thing to say and for a moment Thomas did not know how to respond. What had she meant? He felt a small stir of misgiving. He stepped a little to one side and tried to see her better. The late afternoon sun had begun to soften, though it was still a beautiful afternoon, sweet and fragrant with the sea.

"I can offer you tea and little more," he said, "although I have a good fireplace here."

"I know that fireplace," she said. "I spent many evenings talking to your uncle Julius beside it. I'm sorry he's gone. I miss his company."

"Where are you from?" he asked. "I've asked in the village….."

Then he knew. He knew deep down in his gut, but he could not accept such an outlandish possibility. He had no certain name for her: a fairy woman, a ban-sidhe, as the Irish called it, a woman of the mound or mist. It was absurd, naturally, and yet she simply smiled as his mind clicked the facts into place. As soon as he reached that conclusion, however, he overturned it. Surely other explanations fit the facts more securely. He smiled and saw the humor in it. He had gone a little strange from living by himself. His brother, Sean, had warned him of it; it was a problem for priests and monks, and that, in the end, was also Thomas's calling.

He invited her inside and as if playing with him, she asked him to repeat his invitation.

"Are you inviting me in yourself, of free will and spirit?" she inquired.

"Why shouldn't I?"

"These things matter," she said.

"Yes, I am inviting you in of my own free will."

"Then I accept your invitation."

How peculiar it all was suddenly. And yet at the same time, as Thomas opened the door for her and let her pass into the center of the house, he could not dispute how lovely it felt to have company, and a beautiful woman at that. He had never been skilled with women. He knew a little of what was required of him in social situations, but often he felt tongue-tied and clumsy. The presence of a woman usually increased that uneasiness, but with Kathleen he felt the possibility of comfort. She moved easily in the house, not shy in the least, but happy, it seemed, to be out of the last of the afternoon daylight. She even knew where to find the teakettle and how to set it to boil on the small stove in the kitchen.

"How long did you know my uncle?" Thomas asked as they waited for the kettle.

He stirred up the embers in the fireplace and fed it a few sticks of pine to get it going. She immediately sat in front of the flames and held out her hands.

"I knew him in his last years," she said. "He was a kind, good man. He liked to hear my stories and he paid with gossip from the town. And he gave me cinnamon, which has always been a favorite taste of mine."

"Plain cinnamon?" Thomas asked, surprised again.

"Oh, yes, in a pinch. But he usually cooked something with it. It's a sure way of attracting me."

"Cinnamon rolls and the like?"

"Yes, exactly. I like sweets. I think the tea water is nearly ready."

And it was. He fussed with cups and saucers, grateful now that his uncle had bothered with such things, and he set them out as handily as he could. Kathleen did not wait on ceremony. She seemed hungry for heat, for the fire and hot tea, and she held the cup in her hands, sipping it happily, her eyes glazed with firelight.

It was, altogether, an improbable moment in Thomas's life. What made it even more improbable was the sensation that he knew it was remarkable even while he experienced it. He wished heartily that he might have his brother beside him. Then the thought of his brother made him wary: who or what was this woman, after all, and were her intentions good or evil? But she did not feel menacing. He glanced at her frequently to see her profile. Yes, she was exceedingly beautiful, a rare, vibrant thing, but the circumstances of her arrival, her lack of substance in the town, made him wary. On the other hand, she delighted him. How pleasant it was to sit beside a fire with a beautiful woman, to feel her happiness everywhere, to sense that something good had started in his life and that he could follow it in interesting ways.

"Do you need to take Willy away?" he asked, although he knew he had already asked something of the sort. "I've grown fond of him, so he's more than welcome to stay."

"He is fond of you as well," she said. "He's happy here for the time being."

"I'm glad to hear that. I wasn't aware I was being studied by a mule."

"Well, of course you were. And you've been satisfactory in every way. If I leave Willy with you too long he will grow fat and lazy."

"Does he have a job to do then?"

"Many jobs. But keep feeding him apples when you can. That's his weakness."

"And if I prepare a cinnamon apple I will have you both."

"As easy as that."

She did not stay much longer. It perplexed him, however, to not know where she meant to go. Back to the town? It was ten miles in near darkness that way and the road was poor. But where else could she go? He did not think she had a house nearby; he had ridden far enough on Willy to know the environs and he had come across nothing like a shelter. He thought to offer her a place to stay, but that was, he admitted, a forward thing to suggest to a woman. As he thought these things, his earlier formulation returned to him. Had he been visited by a fairy woman? Was that the most logical explanation after all? But certainly one did not sit and have tea with a ban-sidhe, or talk about mules, or about cinnamon rolls and apples.

She kissed his cheek on the way out and told him they would be great friends. And then she walked into the gloaming, disappearing down the path. Willy trotted beside her for part of the way, and he saw her kiss the white mule and whisper into his ear, and then the mule returned to the house, its clopping hooves sending a small echo into the forest beyond.

Her visit made him yearn for her company, but she did not return immediately. On his next trip into the village he purchased cinnamon, a fair-sized bottle of it, and he tucked it carefully into his supplies for the ride home. He also received a letter from his father telling him that illness had come to his school, and that it had been quarantined until Thanksgiving, and he hoped to visit Thomas soon with his suddenly won freedom. The communication jarred him, not because his father planned a visit, but that such a visit was possible. It had not occurred to him that he might get on a train and simply travel to visit his family. They were not so far away, after all, and he wrote back immediately to his father and invited him to come and stay as long as he liked.

He grew cautious, however, about Kathleen. What had seemed an exciting possibility, her visits a thing to ease the long progress toward winter, now, upon reflection, worried him. He could shape no explanation for her provenance. His careful inquiries in the village, his growing familiarity with the shopkeepers and grocers, made him suspicious. Clearly, she was not *from* the village, and in time he stopped asking about her altogether, mindful that people who lived by the sea tended to be a superstitious lot. And why shouldn't they be? He himself could not arrive at a satisfactory explanation for the woman's visits, so why should they? He longed to write to his brother in order to make a clean breast of it, but he hesitated and filled his letters with details to delight his brother's sense of homesteading instead, giving his brother a romantic narrative of life on the farm, one that would bring his brother comfort.

Before he sorted his thoughts to any conclusion, his father arrived, brought to him by the same wagon and the same grim boy who had delivered Thomas to the farm. Immediately Thomas's heart felt clean and good and he embraced his father, glad to see him in robust health, though older, certainly, and now entirely gray. After the wagon and the boy left, Thomas gave his father a tour of the farm and its grounds, seeing as he did so the farm in a different light. It was a humble place; Thomas had understood that before, but seeing it from his father's perspective, it seemed more so. Nevertheless, his father took everything in with delight, piecing together things he recalled from his brother Julius, and they ended the tour at the sea. His father linked his arm in Thomas's and watched the water for a long time.

"I worried about you alone out here," his father said, his eyes still on the horizon. "A man can travel too far into himself, you know? But now that I see you, I'm satisfied that you are on a safe course. I can assure your mother that you are sound and engaged with life."

"I'm sorry if I worried you."

"The war and what it did to you worried us, Thomas. You came back a different man. Your eyes had changed and your mother said you seemed haunted."

"I was."

"Are you still?"

"Not as much."

"There's work to keep you busy here. Do you have enough

money?"

"For the time being, I do, but I am running out and I will have to come up with a plan. There is work at the harbor and I can always return to the logging camps."

His father nodded. It was good to stand with his father and watch the sea.

His father stayed three days and each day they took long walks, often staying close to the sea. His father had always been a great walker, and Thomas had everything he could do to stay up with him. Thomas detected a hunger for the outdoors in his father, and together they spotted birds and passing sea life, and they returned to the farmhouse each evening happily fatigued. They ate well, consuming some of the food sent by Thomas's mother, and they talked beside the fire of things they had been reading. They talked fondly of Thomas's brother, Sean, and of the priesthood that both pleasured him and made him feel a captive at times, and they both spoke of their love for Thomas's mother. It was the best time Thomas had ever spent with his father, and when the boy and the wagon returned for him, Thomas told his father that he loved him and that he hoped he would visit again soon, perhaps with his mother next time, and they parted reluctantly. He had seen his father as a man – not merely as a father – and it made him happy to recall their days together, and he wrote to his brother about the visit, and said they were fortunate to have such a man as their father and that, in the end, nothing counted for half so much in life as the accident of one's birth to loving parents.

3

AT FIRST SNOW HE BAKED cinnamon rolls. He felt ridiculous for doing so, though the cinnamon made the house smell wonderful. While they baked, he curried the old mule and made sure Willy had sufficient hay and a few apples to eat. Willy did not like the cold, it seemed, and even when Thomas left the barn door open, he seldom ventured out into the increasing winds.

He followed an old recipe, one he vaguely remembered from his mother, and he was not sure if the rolls would turn-out. He checked them often, wondering, as he did so, how Julius had baked his offerings, and what Kathleen had thought of them. When the oven had them bubbling slightly on the top, he removed them and set them to cool near the window. He felt absurd doing so, but this is what she requested, and he fanned the door at them several times to let the scent travel into the air, then set about making tea.

She did not come. He felt ridiculous sitting beside the fire, the tea ready and waiting, and the cinnamon buns turning to hard biscuits in the soft evening light. What had he expected, he wondered? Did he really believe she was a ban-sidhe, a fairy woman who rose out of the water at the smell of cinnamon buns? The notion disturbed him; he wondered what had become of his mind if he allowed it to believe such things. In a sort of penance, he sat down and wrote a long letter to his brother, outlining some of his feelings about Kathleen, but he committed the letter to the fire before he could think seriously about posting it.

At dusk, however, something strange happened. He heard Willy trotting down the path to the sea and he hurried to the window to look out. It was too dark to see clearly, so he quickly pulled on his hat and coat and followed Willy's tracks in the new snow. A bright half moon made the path clear, but the woods on either side of the path hung dark and shadowed. He called for Willy several times, in part annoyed with the animal for leaving, and in a second part worried that something had spooked the gentle old creature and that he might come to injury. He remembered, too, how Kathleen had whispered in Willy's ear, and that thought made him hurry more.

When he came to the cliff leading down to the sea, Willy's tracks went directly over the edge. Thomas stopped and stared a long time at what he saw. His breath came in shuddery pulls and he watched the white cloud of his exhalations rise into the air and then snap away. For a moment nothing calculated. How had a balky old mule run away to begin with, and then how had it left its hoof prints next to the tight trail down to the sea? Moving carefully for the ice and snow, Thomas leaned over the edge of the cliff, fearing he would see Willy's shattered body broken on the beach. But in the near darkness, he could not see clearly. In fact, the only thing he could make out was a single smear of snow and mud near the tidal zone. He did not let his mind make the final addition: it looked, he admitted, as though Willy had jumped free from the cliff and had run, full force, into the waiting waves.

Thomas stepped backward, shaken. His mind reached for a more satisfactory answer, but his eyes could not dismiss the evidence. Slowly, his face turned to the ground and he followed Willy's trail back toward the barn. Bending carefully over the frozen tracks, he saw something that he had not noticed in his rush to follow the mule. The measure between the tracks, the stretch of the legs, became wider as the mule gained distance from the barn. He did not rely simply on his eyesight to determine this. He carefully placed one foot in front of the other, measuring with his toes and heels, until he accepted completely the inescapable truth. Willy had run with great bounds as he approached the cliff, and he had been at full gallop, Thomas guessed, when he went over the edge.

His fever returned that night. It seemed to him to be a small, stealthy animal that waited in the recesses of his body, biding its time until it might have maximum effect. It was possible, too, that the fever had been brought on by the crazed thoughts swirling in his head. He endured a difficult night, waking and sleeping, at times stumbling out to vomit in the bright snow-light. On his return to bed, the German soldiers waited. He thought he had them under control, but now they scaled back into his fevered brain, and he saw them, the younger first, then the older, shape their faces in a bright O of surprise, then fall to the earth like sacks tossed out on a breeze. All night he heard the crack and whistle of the wind, and when the pines behind his house began to bend and shake, he returned in spirit to the logging camp and watched as trees uprooted and bent with gravity, their sparkling bark flashing as they speeded to the ground. He saw boys running with spiked boots across the tree trunks, and at times the trunks turned into whale backs, and at times the trees turned and rose and revealed a face that showed a remarkable similarity to a lone photograph of uncle Julius that he remembered as a boy.

He could not rise in the morning. He stayed in bed all day and the fire went out and the house became cold and brittle. He wanted desperately to go and search the beach for Willy, but he could not summon the strength. He fell asleep in the afternoon and did not wake until he heard the strike of a match, the sound of a chair pulled free from a table.

A moment later, Kathleen came to him.

She did not speak. She brought a damp cloth and cleaned him. He fell asleep under her hands, and when he woke again the house was warm and the fire, he smelled, burned brightly in the hearth. Thomas knew without asking that Willy had returned. He confirmed it when he finally stood beside his bed, his legs weak, his throat parched.

"Is he back?" he asked simply and Kathleen answered that he was.

He went and sat beside the fire. She gave him tea and broth. He ate it slowly and let his stomach warm to it. He felt he had returned from a great distance.

"What are you?" he asked finally.

"What do you think I am?"

"No more games, please. I must know."

"I think you know already."

"Such things don't exist."

In place of more talk, she kissed him. He returned her kiss and for a long time he kept his forehead against hers, the firelight throwing their shadows on the wall. She smelled of the sea, he thought, and of cinnamon burned slightly on the stove.

At last he was at peace. He felt he had arrived in a safe harbor after a long time at sea. His heart grew solid with love of her and he followed her tread, her scent, even the sound of her breathing as she moved about the house. Did it matter what she was? At times he believed he had invented her; at other times, he thought surely she was a woman from the village, and he had simply imbued her with supernatural abilities. He desired her and she him, and they lived in their bed as if on an island. Afterward they washed with warm cloths soaked in seawater and they dried themselves beside the fire, naked and lustful, and he lived for her kisses and for the quiet of her voice as she spoke softly to him.

She was beautiful, more beautiful than he could have imagined. At times he felt unworthy, that her natural grace and loveliness was so much greater than his that she must surely wake one day and see him for what he was. On that day, he imagined, he would lose her, and he could not say for certain if he could endure such pain.

Winter surrounded the house in full force, but he did not care. He worked in the barn at times, sawing wood and splitting it for the fires she loved, and when he worked he spoke to Willy, singing to him and telling him how his heart felt. Occasionally she was gone when he returned, but he did not mind. He baked cinnamon rolls for her, amending the recipe slightly at her request, and she ate them with great appetite, her mouth greedy for them. They did not speak of her true nature, for what was there to say? It did not matter to him what she was, or what fate had in mind when it brought her to him. He lived to see her and he was content as he had never been before.

Only one thing troubled him: time did not seem to touch

them. It took him many days to test his theory. He measured time passing by the height of the woodpile, but try as he might he could not determine if they had burned one stack of old apple wood, or five stacks. It was a slippery problem. Each time he felt he had measured things accurately, she would kiss him and he would be once more confused. Moreover, try as he might, he could not recall replenishing simple things: food, for instance, or water. Each day brought renewed resolve to track things properly, but in her presence he forgot his intent almost immediately.

"What's happening to me?" he asked her one afternoon as they lay in bed together, their limbs entwined, their appetites sated.

"What do you mean?" she asked.

"I can't remember doing simple things. When did we get more food? And when did I last write to my brother?"

"Only yesterday. Don't you remember?"

But he did not. His mind failed to recall the necessary steps he must have taken to write and post a letter. He did not believe she knew herself when he had last posted a letter to his brother, but even that thought passed quickly and he did not bring it up again.

At night, in certain weather, they rode on the sea.

This was the greatest revelation of all. After they had done so, he no longer doubted what she was. The first time he accompanied her, the night had turned bitter cold but still. He heard the tree sap cracking in the pines and the pond behind the house groaned in its bed. The moon had come up and lay like a broken thing on the lip of the sea. And Kathleen could not calm herself.

"What is it?" he asked her.

"I must go," she said.

"Where?"

She looked at him. How fond he was now of her! He knew each expression on her face, each light of her eyes.

"Dress warmly," she said.

"Where are we going?"

"You'll see."

He wore a heavy mackinaw and a fur hat and thick mittens, but she did not bother with extra clothes. Nearly before he could dress, she opened the door and Thomas saw Willy standing, waiting. Beside him stood another mule, a dark, gray animal, with larger ears than Willy's and a longer face.

"That's Johnny," Kathleen said. "My own dear."

"What does it mean?"

"Follow me. And trust your mount."

Except to ride Willy to town, Thomas had not been on horseback for many years. But when Kathleen climbed on Johnny's back – so quickly! So nimbly! – he climbed on Willy's. Immediately Willy turned and bolted toward the sea, but even he was not fast enough to catch Johnny. Thomas remembered the tracks left in the snow many nights before, and he hunched over Willy's neck and clung to him. This was not a mule! In three strides Thomas knew that much. With each long reach of his legs, the dobby animal known as Willy gave way to something grander. Thomas understood it in his heart, and as he felt them approach the cliff edge, Willy's galloping freer and wilder than anything he had ever experienced, he felt something like joy. All of this had been inside the old animal, and when Willy sprung from the cliff edge Thomas shuddered but trusted him. For a moment, nothing. Then Thomas grew aware of their flight, of the sea reaching up to meet them, of the fog that covered the headlands, of the stars that had just begun to poke through the night sky. Ahead he saw Johnny land and continue running onto the flat surface of the sea, and he heard a wild shriek, something beautiful and unearthly come from Kathleen. And all his life he had been waiting for this one glorious instant, and when Willy landed and ran onto the surface of the sea, Thomas tried to copy Kathleen's cry of joy. His voice blended with hers, though it could not match it, and his eyes opened wider at the sensation of running on the sea. Yes, she had waited for a night like this one, flat and cold and still. And fog shrouded them, but now and then they broke free, and Thomas saw Kathleen bent over Johnny's neck, goading him to more speed, asking for everything. And Johnny – what a marvel! He was no longer a tired old mule, but the most magnificent creature Thomas had ever seen. His muscles ran in cords along his neck, and his hooves flashed like pearls by candlelight. He ran wildly, recklessly, his feet causing the water to slip and splash up and then mend itself immediately.

How long did they ride? And to what purpose? Thomas understood only that to ride was everything. He felt it in his soul, in the deep shove of muscles and Willy ran harder and harder toward the horizon, toward the shattered moon, and for once Thomas's mind asked no question and anticipated no answer. It was sufficient to ride, to feel the sea heaving and moving beneath them, and to watch the moonlight play on Johnny's fierce eyes, and to see Kathleen's hair streak behind her like a memory partially recalled.

4

THE QUESTION OF TIME TROUBLED him, but he did not permit it to spoil the pleasure of her company. He was in a spell; he knew that. He would forsake anything to remain with her, and she seemed to understand this as well. At times he noticed that something had changed. The seasons, for instance, came and went without the usual rise and decline. Winter was a brief, fierce moment, and spring a passing nightfall. He did the work necessary to sustain them, but even that, he suspected, did not follow the usual laws of the universe.

Johnny lived beside Willy in the second stall, and they rode out often, taking to the sea, or at times up onto the wooded hills behind the farmhouse. The horses lived for speed and wild abandon, but Thomas learned they could also walk with complete silence near the homes of his neighbors. They blended with the night, and fog, too, seemed to follow them and give them cover. Leaning across Willy's great ribs, he kissed Kathleen and felt her shiver at his touch, then they would move deeper into the forest, finding the places where the deer congregated at night, where the coyotes ran with fired-eyes over the autumn hills. On certain nights he wondered if he was still mortal; he wondered if he had passed over a line, a line he could never see nor detect, to join her in this second world. That was the name he gave it. He had entered a second world, and Kathleen was the sun of that universe, the source of light and energy and peace.

At night he combed her hair by the fire. Her hair's luster did not diminish, he noticed, and that observation, too, troubled him when it passed through his mind. His own reflection, when he caught a glimpse of it in a bucket of water, seemed unchanged. How could such a thing be possible? He understood he had struck a bargain, but what that bargain entailed, what its terms might be, unsettled him. One night when he had finished brushing her hair, he asked her.

"Will we ever grow older?" he asked.

She touched his hand where it rested on her shoulder.

"No," she answered.

"Will the people we loved grow older without us?"

She nodded.

"Are you not happy here with me?" she asked.

"You know I am."

"You are not missed in the way you might think. By the others, your family and friends. They are not sure where you have gone, but you live in their memories."

"Do they imagine I'm dead?"

"No, merely gone."

"It's the same in the end, isn't it?"

"That's not for us to say."

"Can I travel back to see them?"

She waited a long time before she answered.

"You may," she said. "But not without risk."

He did not pursue the question at that point. He saw that it upset her to think about it. In his own mind, he tried to understand what he felt. He was contented with Kathleen. He loved her as he had never loved anyone else on earth. But what of his parents, his brother, Sean? Was time taking them? And what had happened to the world he had known, to the country for which he had fought? Was time more important than he had known? Without its measure, what weight did things hold? It is the weight of time that makes a flower beautiful, the knowledge that its glory lasts mere days at most.

That night in bed Kathleen wept. When he asked her what it was that upset her, she shook her head and cried into his shoulder. He did not ask her again, because he knew the answer. She understood that she could not keep this lone thing from him, that in their joy the seed of his discontent had been planted. He kissed her back to happiness, but now the world they inhabited had been punctured, and she could not seal it closed again.

One night a storm came and Kathleen brought the horses to the door. A wind blew from the north. On land it was a hard blow, but out at sea, Thomas imagined, the waves would be massive and treacherous. It was autumn and the trees had already gone over, but the wind resurrected the leaves and threw them into the air, as if somehow they could return to the tree limbs and grow once more.

There was a ship, Kathleen said. And it would not last out the storm.

Thomas felt afraid. The sea was too high, but the two mules, aching and snorting to go, could not stand the wait. No sooner had Thomas mounted, then Willy charged to the cliff and launched himself into the raw air. Johnny came behind them, and then they set out across the sea, the waves enormous and hungry, the clouds scuttling and moving like a dark thing searching a drawer. Thomas had never ridden on such a wild night and he felt himself nearly slip away several times, and he realized, with a sudden horror, that Kathleen did not understand his mortality. Yes, she knew he had physical limits, and that he was merely a man, but now, in the hunger of the chase, she had forgotten him. This, at last, was her purpose, was the reason for her being, and her passion precluded him. Of course she loved him, but the dangerous waves, the fierce wind, brought her alive as he had never seen her.

They found ship a mile to sea, two miles – who could say? – foundering in the palm of the storm. The sight struck Thomas's heart with dread. He remembered, with remarkable clarity, his transport ship, the *Britannia,* and how it had felt on the crossing, the waves slapping his ship and turning it on its nose and tail. But this was greater and direr. It was a fishing trawler, wide-beamed and hefty, but the storm had taken it and the men called out in fear and prayer. Thomas saw them; he believed they saw him. Willy ran in wild circles around the ship, springing from wave to wave, and Thomas lost track of Kathleen until he heard her cry.

It was the call of the banshee, escorting the men to their deaths.

He saw the men stop and listen. And it might have been the wind, for all any of them knew, but then Thomas spotted Kathleen. She had grown in vividness, if such a thing were possible. Johnny ran with great, powerful strides, and Kathleen called to the men, matching her voice to the wind, and the ship began going sideways to the waves, and then down.

Thomas buried his face in Willy's mane, appalled. Did her voice soothe the men, or carry them downward in greater terror? He could not say. Her voice went under his skin, a sound unlike any cry a mortal woman could make, and he rode hard after her until he could grab Johnny's mane in his fist.

"Stop!" he screamed, trying to halt the horse and Kathleen at once.

But she shook free of him and galloped harder, her cry rising until he saw the men on board drop like ripe plums into the sea. The boat wallowed; its aft corner dipped down and accepted the ocean water, and then, for a moment, the world was silent. And then he heard Kathleen's true call. The men in their agony heard it, too, and their faces lost all fear or worry. Thomas watched them closely, riding near to see, and when the sea finally sucked them under, the note of her voice went with them, as if it were a provision needed for another world. It was a gift she gave them; he understood it finally, and yet it frightened him with its wavering insistence, with the wild expression it brought to his true love's face.

The storm calmed on their return. They did not stay to watch the boat sink finally beneath the waves. It rolled like a spoon in a dry batter, then disappeared into the hazy light of the ocean. Thomas rode Willy like a demon back toward land, his ears ringing with the sound of her voice, the memory of how it had pierced the air. Willy felt his urgency and ran on the waves as if on a flat strand of packed sand. Thomas gained the land before Kathleen and Johnny, and it was with wonder that he realized he could not tell for certain if he had reached the solid ground of Maine, or if, as he suspected, they now inhabited an island cloaked by mist.

"You fear me," were the first words she said to him when at last the two mounts stood side by side. "I have taken you too far and shown you too much."

"I love you, Kathleen."

"But now you want to go," she said. "And my heart knows it and I will have eternity to remember you."

"If I go, I'll return."

She nodded. And her eyes did not believe him.

She was wise not to believe him, because in the days that followed – were they days? he wondered – the memory of the night on the wild sea would not diminish. Indeed, it grew until he could think of little else. He realized that he had surrendered himself to a dream, and that the dream had robbed him of the full measure of his life. But was that true? He still loved her. He loved her more than ever, and he showed her greater tenderness now than before. At night he held her close and whispered to her of how she had saved him and brought him happiness, but a barrier had grown between them, and neither one of them could surmount it.

Once his mind opened to questions, they would not cease. The German soldiers returned to haunt him and with alarm he recalled his dear brother, Sean. Where had he gone? Where was his beloved brother now, and how had Thomas permitted such time to pass between their communications? He thought of his kind father, and their last visit together, and for the first time in many sunrises he began to wonder if his parents still lived, and what became of them.

Kathleen, he understood, detected the change in him. When he went out to perform his chores, she kissed him as if he intended to be gone a century, and when he returned she held his hand and kept it near. Her heart was breaking, he knew, but he was powerless to prevent it. Twice they rode out to the sea again to let their mounts have their wild freedom, but it had changed now, and Thomas knew he had corrupted its purity.

"You will not like what you will see," she said to him one night beside the fire. "The world has gone on without you and I can do nothing to prevent that pain."

"How do I go?" he asked simply.

"Willy will take you. But there is a condition."

He waited for her to go on. He reached across the small distance and held her hand.

"You may not touch your foot to ground or the age you have escaped will return to you at once. Do you understand? You must not leave Willy's back and I will not be able to save you if you do. You will be banished from the island forever."

He nodded.

"I understand."

They sat for a long time in silence.

"My heart is here," he said, his eyes on the firelight. "I am not leaving you, but returning to others I love."

"This moment began the first time we met."

That night she wept and he could not console her. When he woke she was gone and Willy, once more a quiet, steady mule, stood by the doorway, waiting for him to cross to land.

5

IN AN INSTANT, HE RETURNED. He felt solid earth under Willy's hooves and he turned to gaze back at the sea. Fog covered the island. It was gone. Mist closed it away from him and he looked back with longing and wondered why he had come. For a long time he remained on the beach, caught between two worlds. He might easily return; it was not too late. He rubbed Willy's ears and came close to telling him to run, run like mad back to the island. Nothing remained for him on land except his past and he did not trust what he might find, nor how it might wound him.

But he rationalized that he need not stay long; if he were cautious and prudent, he might make his visit and then return to Kathleen. The thought made him bolder and happier. It did not have to be one thing or the other. It could be both, and he kicked Willy softly in the ribs to get him moving.

He went first to his farmhouse and found it deserted, its disrepair a crude reminder of the passage of time. He wanted dearly to go inside, but he remembered that he could not leave Willy's back. Time had taken the building. Without paint or hands to patch the roof, the building had sought to return to the earth. The barn had collapsed and small oak saplings grew in what used to be the center of the stalls. The sight of the house and the broken barn made him wonder how much time had actually passed. He knew the story of Rip Van Winkle and he felt that character's predicament.

He nearly returned to the island in that moment. The building's disrepair should serve as a warning, he thought, and he sat for a long time regarding the growth of trees around the site, the persistent brambles that had marched like infantry from the safety of the forest. Dark thoughts assailed him. Were all men doomed to lose their past? Why could he not stay with Kathleen in joy and tranquility forever? What was it about human nature that made them thirst for more even when what they had was sufficient?

He bent close to Willy and put his arms around the old mule's neck. Then he kicked him gently and asked him to move on. He whispered that he would like to see his parents, and asked Willy to bring him there.

It took time. Thomas lived on horseback, not fatigued or sore, but able to ride beyond human endurance. The changes of the world assaulted him. A second war waited on the horizon, Thomas learned, and when he listened to people speak about it they claimed it was inevitable. He wanted to intervene, to tell them that war did not have to occur, that the knowledge that it would one day pass was proof enough that war was unnecessary. But he held his tongue. He began to make a list of the marvels and alterations he found, thinking it might interest Kathleen, but in time he abandoned that endeavor. The world changed, certainly, but the heart did not, and he urged Willy forward to bring him to his parents.

He found what he expected and what he feared: his parents were dead and the house that he had known as a child had been sold to new people. They had taken care of the building; it was not like his collapsing farmhouse. In fact, Portland appeared prosperous and progressive and routinely Thomas found himself the source of strange glances. A man on horseback! Now automobiles hogged the roads and the sight of a horse, he realized, had become rare. Children laughed and pointed at him. When he happened to catch his reflection in a pane of glass, it astonished him to see a man well past middle-age looking back at him.

He paid a visit to his parents' grave. He found them buried side by side, the dates of their existences bracketing human lives. His mother had outlived his father by a mere eight months. He wanted desperately to dismount and kneel beside their graves, but he recalled Kathleen's warning and he eventually kicked Willy to push onward.

He went to find Sean, his brother, his heart choked with fear.

Sean might still be alive, he calculated, but what good could come of seeing him? What was he doing on Willy's broad back, resurrecting the past that had already become memory? He followed countless false leads, asking for information from people who regarded him as curious relic. Frequently blank expressions met his questions. Even to his own ears, his questions sounded arcane and impossible to answer. He searched for a thread, one small piece of string that might lead to another, and in the end he found it.

It was worth everything to see his brother once more. He found him at St. John's rectory in Bangor, Maine. He was a Monsignor now. Thomas spotted Sean as he walked from the church back to the rectory, and a boundless joy entered his heart that he thought he could not contain. Sean, his brother! He looked fine, solid on his feet, his small frame robed in black vestments. Thomas stayed back, watching carefully. How devoutly he wished to call out, but he understood now that such a shock, such a reappearance by one long thought dead or gone, would be an unfairness to inflict on his loved one. Kathleen had known the truth all along! Thinking this he saw Sean stop and turn, and for a second – the briefest instant – their eyes met. Thomas saw his brother's eyes soften then cloud, as if he could not quite believe the vision of his long lost brother on a white mule. Quickly Thomas spurred Willy into a trot, and he turned back to the island and to Kathleen.His heart was rent with sadness and exhilaration in equal measure! The past was gone! How simple, after all. He rode faster and faster, urging Willy to greater speed, and no gallop could have contained his desire to be back with his love. Willy seemed to understand, and he churned the earth under his feet, indefatigable, tireless, wild to be running. Thomas wanted to be back in Kathleen's arms, to hear the sound of her voice. So intent was he on his return to her, that he ignored at first the signs of his old illness returning. He felt it as a tremor in his spine, but the heave of Willy's body stirred it and brought it up through his system until his head began to grow light and nauseated. He stopped and purchased a rope from a man working in the fields, and he lashed himself to Willy as best he could with his trembling hands *Not now,* he thought. As Odysseus had been bound to the mast, now Thomas rode Willy. For two nights and two days he clung to Willy, fading in and out of consciousness, occasionally vomiting onto the road. He knew he must look like a scarecrow, a hideous dream rider out of a child's fantasy book. He kept his hands looped around Willy's neck and he whispered to his old friend that he must get home, that he must see Kathleen again. Nothing else mattered.

He arrived in a small seaside hamlet in late evening on the third day of his illness, his body convulsed with tremors, his mouth blistered and dry. The fever had affected his eyes, because he could not blink away the sandy grit that seemed to blind him. He had not gone far into the hamlet when a work party of men saw him and grabbed Willy's halter. They stood appalled at the sight of the shrunken man on the mule's back. Two of them felt it must surely be a religious observance, something to commemorate Christ's suffering, or his mother's ride to Bethlehem on a simple ass, but when they tried to unlash him from the animal's back the man slapped weakly at them out of what seemed like instinct. But they persisted. They had come to set stone for a bridge spanning a small stream; they were honest workmen and had given a full day's account of labor. The man on horseback offended their aesthetic, though they would not have called it that. He was a misplaced stone, a dip in an otherwise straight run of rock.

When they removed the last strand of rope they slid the rider off his mule and placed him carefully on the ground. Then something miraculous occurred, something they would talk about for years afterward, but only among themselves. They did not trust their senses at first, because the rider, weak as he was, had been at least a man of middle years when they slid him from his mount. But in the moments after he touched the earth, his age advanced as if it had been a storm outside the window, waiting to push into the room. His hair grew white and his skin bunched in tired folds and his eyes clouded. In the same instant a wind began singing from the sea and the mule — almost in pity they would say later — stepped close and hung his great head over the rider's body. The mule breathed heavily and everything around them, the late sunshine, the rustle of the trees, the glint of water flowing over stones, grew quiet and empty. Among themselves later they said the world seemed to listen for a voice it had always known, and then gradually the mule began to back away. It took several steps, slowly, reluctantly, and then it turned and bolted toward the sea. A young boy reached out and tried to grab its dangling halter, but he might as well have tried to arrest a train. The animal ran with its comical gait toward the sea, but when its hooves struck the tidal wash it transformed into a different sort of creature altogether. They stood and stared, amazed at what they saw because the mule began to fly apart, joining the water not by submerging, but by disintegrating. They saw the splash of its hooves going over the water, and that was impossible, that could not happen, and even into their dotage many of them refused to speak about it. But what they said at the time of the mule's disappearance was not that he had run into the sea, precisely, but that that the magnificent creature had turned to salt.

Weak and old, Thomas returned to his farmhouse when he regained some of his strength. He patched what he could. He shut off one room and let the rest of the buildings sink into the earth. He wrote a long letter to his brother, who received the communication with wonder and joy and they at last had their conversations on the porch of the house overlooking the sea. They talked of everything except Thomas's absence. He allowed his brother to believe he had gone away, lived overseas, had been a despairing man. What truth would satisfy his brother? Thomas did not speak of it.

But at night he would go often to the edge of the sea and he would look out and wait. On certain nights, under certain moons, he would see the island again. Perhaps it was a bank of fog, or nothing more than hope, and he read once that such islands can be seen only by those with a broken heart. In those moments he would whisper *I wait* and the wind carried off his words and his lips tasted of the salt that had consumed dear Willy.

The rest of the story is known only to Sean, who reported that on the night of his brother's death a wind arose like none he had ever known. The keening created by the wind passing through the old barn, past the pipes of the stall fence, seemed not without purpose. The wind circled and came closer and closer. In those last moments of his brother's life, he saw light return to his sibling's eyes, and Thomas reached upward from the bed, as if the sound had come for him, as if he had somewhere to go. The lamplight glowed silver with mist and the sound of hoof beats — yes, Sean swore it to be the truth — drummed under the wind like a sheet left on the line and shaken in a summer storm.

SEDNA

Wife

A LONG TIME AGO SEDNA WAS given to a man to marry. She was a beautiful young woman and the man she was given to was a fine hunter. The hunter promised Sedna's father that he would give her plenty to eat and wrap her in fine furs. So the father paddled away and did not return for many years. When finally the father did return, Sedna met him at the shoreline and begged her father to take her away. The man, she said, was a shaman, an evil witch-man, and he fed her raw fish guts and pissed on the igloo's ice. Wherever he pissed the snow began to smoke and crumble and the animals smelled it and could not be captured. She was starving; she had not eaten in years and had lived on stone and lichen. Furthermore, she could not bear children with the shaman — whose name was Oolocc – because his penis forked and was made of walrus ivory. Oolocc, she said, ran at night with the wolves and brought down caribou with his teeth. Other times, she said, he went onto the winter ice with bears and lay on the ice listening to the oysters and clams that held human wishes.

Her father – a short, cowardly man, who trembled at summer thunder and whose beard grew as white as a winter ptarmigan — did not want to make an enemy of a shaman, so he paddled away again, warning her to remain and be a good wife. This time, though, Sedna swam after her father and climbed onto his kayak. She clung to the kayak and pleaded with her father to let her enter the kayak and sleep at his feet. But her father shook his head and tried to hit her with the paddle, chanting as he went that he had no daughter, because no daughter would behave in such a way.

Oolocc watched these events from a high bluff, where he had been netting owlets. The owlets he trained to listen to the villagers, especially their secret bed talk at night, and he moved to the edge of the cliff and shouted that he would cause the sea to rise up and sink the kayak if Sedna's father failed to return the girl. But Sedna would not let go, and finally her father pulled out his savik and chopped off the girl's fingers. One by one he sliced them away, chanting and asking for forgiveness as he did so. Still, she did not cry out! But eventually, weakened by her loss of blood, distraught that she must return to Oolocc, Sedna fell off the kayak and sank to the bottom of the sea. She tumbled through the water like a leaf blown in circles against a tree trunk.

But that was not the end of Sedna! Her fingers became the fish and seals and walruses, all the animals of the sea, and even today, when hunting is poor, the shamans must take up the drum and dance into a trance. Then in dream-lands they go to the bottom of the sea and comb and braid Sedena's long hair, placing in its soft curls filigreed bones and fine, colored carvings. And if the dance is strong enough, the trance deep enough, Sedena releases the animals again. Food grows plentiful. Sometimes she rises up beside the shamans and returns them to land, but she watches, ever vigilant, for fear Oolocc will try to capture her. She is friend to all animals except the owls, who do Oolocc's business, and fly unnaturally at night.

Bird Rider

ONE SPRING SEDNA SHRANK HERSELF to the side of a robin and rode the birds. She swam from the bottom of the sea, and when the auks dove into the waves out beyond the retreating ice searching for capelin, she swung one leg over the bird's neck and straddled it. The bird, a great, thick billed auk named Jaiia, felt the legs around his neck like a band of light. He shot straight up from the water, abandoning his hunt, but Sedna held fast. Then they flew. It was spring and the water glistened and the ice hummed at its leaving. Jaiia made a loud cry, unhappy with this creature riding on its neck, but Sedna leaned forward to whisper in his ear. She whispered wind-talk and the bird listened, and finally they rode together comfortably. And when Jaiia dove again, Sedna called the capelin and the small fish came like dots of salt and surrounded Jaiia so that he could feed as he liked. Jaiia stored fish in his craw and ate his belly full, so that when it came time to rise from the water again he could barely fly.

Sedna rode with him and in heavy, deep wing-beats they flew back to land. Sedna felt the air in her hair and she turned her face to the sun, letting it enter her eyes and melt the spine of ice that held her in winter. They flew to the nesting grounds and Sedna dismounted on the scaled cliffs. Birds everywhere! She walked among them, climbing up and down on the cliffs, watching the blind infants stretch and screech for fish. Each infant had three or four inches of rock on which to live, and below, hundreds of feet below, the ice-water lapped and shook the shore line and the foxes gazed upward, their tongues thick with saliva and anticipation. Now and then an infant bird flapped away from the rock face and found its wings too weak to support it. The foxes chased the sailing infants like children chasing kites, and when the infant crashed, as it inevitably did, the foxes pulled its wings free of its body and ate them in quick sipping bites, the wings as hollowed as spoons. Then the foxes dug deeper into the birds and ate the infant's breast meat and livers, ate their webbed feet like saucers of flesh, and finally carried the mass of nutrient in their guts back to their kits, where they hunched their shoulders and vomited the dead bird into the waiting baby's mouth. Infant to infant, Sedna saw, and she did not interfere.

When at last summer came, Sedna went with the gannets – the bright, gray birds shaped like spears – and rode them as they dove into the water beneath the cliff. The birds slammed into the water in bright, white sleeves of bubbles, and the fish, cold and white, ran for their lives as the birds hammered the surface. The white belugas came and rolled their flesh on the sand, chafing it free of dead cells in an annual ritual, and Sedna called to them in their own voices, wishing them welcome and apologizing for making them white and conspicuous to all creatures.

On the deepest day of summer, Sedna climbed back onto Jaiia's neck and whispered that he should fly into the sun. Jaiia resisted. It was time to leave for the southlands, but Sedna insisted. And so they left the rock face and the cliffs of hatchlings and flew eastward toward the sun. As they flew Jaiia's wings grew in size and his heart beat white blood. Sedna lifted her arms and invited the sun to warm her one final time. They flew higher and higher and the heat increased until Jaiia refused to go on. But Sedna began to sing and around her all the animals of the world joined her. When Jaiia could travel no higher, Sedna rolled away from the bird and fell toward the earth. She became a cloud and then a mist and finally a flake of snow drifting on the wind. She returned to earth as the first flake of winter and she landed on the sea and dissolved. But her spine began once more to turn to ice and the sea collected around her, congealing and pulling to silence again. She returned to the bottom of the sea and her hair flowed in the waves and currents, and the seals dove in bright circles to salute her, and the great white bears pedaled their legs across the ocean, while the foxes turned their fur to white, and the snowy owls clutched dead lemmings in their beaks and dropped red dots of blood as they flew to their perches.

Caribou

ONE SUMMER SEDNA GREW TIRED of the ocean, and so she waited for a herd of caribou to approach the seaside and then slipped in among them. She changed herself into a caribou and travelled as they did. She remained inside the herd, careful to hide herself from Oolocc. Still, she took joy in the land! After a thousand years of water life, how good it felt to have the bones of the earth beneath her! She ate moss and grass and did not even mind the mosquitoes – entire swarms of them, deep, black swarms – that choked her breath and formed a second ear of insect legs inside her ear. She grew a stalk of antlers and her tongue licked salt.

She had been with the caribou a year when the wolves began tracking the herd. Wolves always track the herd, it's true, but these wolves – gray and thin as daggers – were really shamans. They thirsted for blood, not flesh, and sought to have their mouths on the caribous' throats, to feel the final tremble of their pulsing into the tundra. Oolocc was among them, she knew. He was the largest wolf, the alpha, who ran on the shoulder of the pack – not at the head, where one would expect to see him, but removed into the triangle of the followers. He was tireless and strong, and when he howled he placed his face to the moon and tried to catch its light on his tongue.

The wolves chased the caribou into winter, into the darkness, where the northern lights began to bend and twist the world. Green ropes and curtains of light flashed across the horizon and the great bears walked on the sea and grew white as snow. The wolves and caribou followed ancient trails, trails so old that their feet ran in grooves cut through millions of years into granite and basalt. Sedna kept the caribou strong. She found grass even in the deepest snow and she bent with them to lick moss from cold stones, the skin of her tongue pulling and ripping so that each mouthful tasted of blood and aged sunlight.

On the darkest night of the year, the wolves finally caught up to the caribou herd. The wolves breathed at the herd's heels, slathering the ground with their saliva, their lust for blood in full song. The caribou ran over the frozen land, their chests breaking against the snow, their antlers whistling in the bright black air. They ran to the top of the world! All the world stretched to the south! And as the wolves drew their teeth around the last caribou in the herd, the leg of the animal seized by the nipping jaws, the herd arrived at a cliff overlooking the sea. Without hesitating, Sedna threw herself off the cliff, bugling to the others that they must follow or perish. As she leaped into the air, the shimmering Aurora Borealis quivered and became a gleaming path of light.

And this the Cree saw! In the wavering light, the men and women of Kangiqsliniq heard the sound of breathing above them and they ran out of their shelters to witness the caribou flying! The momentum of the herd's running carried the caribou out to sea, and they ran with sparks crackling from their hooves, their nostrils breathing tendrils of light! What a sight! Along the ridge of the bluff the wolves halted, their tongues lolling, their paws scraping at the snow. They did not trust the light to support them. Instead, they turned their faces to the moon and howled, calling for the caribou to return. Their howls joined with the keen of the wind, and in time nothing separated the two notes. Wolf and wind. Caribou and light. And in between Sedna fell from the air and returned to the sea, cod and ling, capelin and haddock greeting her and swimming in the light of the darkest night, the stars dotting the fishes' backs and turning them into bars of gold and silver.

Seal

IN THE DEEPEST DAY OF winter Sedna swam with the seals. Her arms changed to fins and her skin grew sable fur. She chased haddock and herring, and nosed the deepest channels for the fish that swam like bright, silver beams. For many days she did not feel any difference between her body and the water that surrounded her. The world was black except for the ice. The sea was black and the night was black and the stars shined in a small circle when the seals went close to the air holes to breath. As the seals sipped air from the pockets underneath the ice, Sedna saw the bears walking above, the press of their paws the only thing to give them away. The bears shimmered white like the ice and they waited by the holes and fished with their quick paws. Sedna warned the seals when the bear was close, but the seals needed air and so could not listen. Twice Sedna saw young seals pulled through the ice, their rib cages crackling like pine kindling, and later she heard the snap of cartilage and the grunt of the bear swallowing. Sedna sang to the seal's spirit when this happened. She sang to the bear's blood.

Oolocc, still seeking revenge, turned himself into a bear to hunt for Sedna. Never did a larger bear prowl the ice. Oolocc stalked with the flashing green northern lights playing on his massive shoulders and gut. The other bears left him alone and when he walked the ice his nose smelled whatever breathed or walked or choked down food. His claws ticked into the ice like cleats and his bottom jaw opened to have air on his lips and tongue. In the great winds he did not bother to cover his nose and his eyes as the others bears did, but continued to hunt, ravenous, his lust for revenge against Sedna insatiable. Twice he entered villages and carried off children when they left their igloos to make water. Twice he carried the children into the deepest night and ate them from the ribs out, his heavy head dipping into the cavity of the body while his tongue ran over the sweet zippers of their spines. In the morning, or late at night, the parents would piece together what had occurred, and some dared to follow the tracks. But most understood what they would find and they told their friends and family members to leave the bear alone. What went unspoken was the possibility that the child had become a bear, or, worse, had learned to travel in dreams, and therefore could appear anywhere at anytime, the heat of its breath the last sensation anyone would know on earth or ice.

Underneath the ice, Sedna swam with the seals and sipped the air from the bubbles against the ice and she stayed away from the air holes, which looked like green curls of light in the aurora borealis. Twice she heard Oolocc pass. She smelled the children on his breath and listened to him moan in his anguish and loneliness. She swam farther out to sea, chasing the capelin and the herring, and she listened to the whales telling their stories. The whales sang old songs, songs of creation and death, and she sang back in the long nights and listened to the whales carry sounds around the world. When the songs finished, she knew, the ice would melt, but until then they hurried to move through the stories, retelling the legends that had been told to them. In time nothing separated her from the whales stories, or from the water and ice, and she became a pure form of motion and current, the songs passing through her and entering the wave of green curtains that pulsed like lichen attached to the sky.

One day as the sun moved just so that its aurora burned above the horizon for an instant, Oolocc captured Sedna. It happened like this:

A seal must see the sky from time to time, or how else can it navigate? A seal rises to breathe, but also to see the stars in their turning. In a glance a seal understands the compass points, and knows where the land is hidden under the snow and ice. Sedna, however, had become drunk on whale song. It had been bliss to glide under the ice, to cling to the frozen ceiling and feel the white clarity of air trapped for a season against the water below it. But now in her rapture she was lost, and the whales ceased singing. The hunger moon had risen.

On a certain night when Sedna swam too close to an airhole, Oolocc dipped one claw into the flesh on Sedna's throat and dragged her onto the ice. He knew at once he had her; he placed a paw on her sleek body and tilted his head to the northern lights in exaltation. Then he bent his head to her head and breathed the breath of all the animals that had passed down his throat. Sedna smelled the lesser auks and the caribou and the scent of children fleeing. She smelled wolves on his breath and the foxes who turned white in winter. She squirmed and tried to get away, but his grip was too strong.

—Will you return with me now and be my wife? Be careful how you answer, Oolocc said, forcing her harder into the ice. Be prideful and you will die on this spot.

—Of course I will return with you, Sedna answered. I have always been your wife.

—Then why have you hidden yourself all these years? Why run from your husband as you have?

—I was searching for you. Your disguises tricked me and I could not find you.

Oolocc was no fool and he did not believe her. He picked her up in his great jaws and carried her back toward land. Sedna did not struggle. She lay in his mouth and looked at the stars and the northern lights and she thought her days had finished. Even the slightest movement brought the gouge of his teeth into her body. She tried to think of a way to trick him, but he had won at last.

When he approached the land, however, she had an idea. She told him a story, one he knew well. She could not tell if he listened, but she deliberately left out parts of the story so that he would be compelled to speak and correct her. And that is what happened. When they came to a stretch of seawater she lied about the way an owl is born, and Oolocc could no longer stand it. He opened his mouth to correct her and immediately she slid out of his mouth and stabbed like an arrow into the water. His paw flashed after her but it was too late. She glided into the sea and slowly resumed her shape. Oolocc, in his rage, killed more animals than he could eat and left them for the crows. The bones of the dead animals became hollow and played like flutes whenever the wind passed over them.

Bee

FOR MANY YEARS SEDNA FLEW with the Arctic terns, taking to the air in autumn and flying the length of the globe until she landed in Antarctica. No animal flies farther; no other animal possesses such movement in its breast! The Arctic tern is urge, nothing more. It lives to fly and lives to move and for many years Sedna flew above the clouds, watching the earth spin below, saw mountains and rivers and tides, saw lesser flocks flying in carpet layers below, felt the universal winds, the perennial currents of air carrying her as a dust mote or a chaffing of grass. She abandoned herself to the wind! She dare not light for fear Oolocc might discover her, and so she lived in the currents of wind, her bones becoming hollow, her wing feathers fluttering like light through grass.

It was on one of these journeys that an idea formed, but she did not trust it for decades. But the idea grew and flourished in her mind and in the puddles of Antarctica, on the beaches and tuft grasses of Argentina, she turned the idea over in her mind. It took a century for her to trust the idea sufficiently, but eventually on her return to the north she stopped in the bogs of America and captured a bee. She held the bee between her upper and lower beak, and she flew with the northern winds, hurrying now for summer. The wind sang a song in her ears, the song of all creatures, the song of water, and she skimmed northward on her stiff wings, eventually alone. She saw the land lose trees and she saw the great sea water, and farther north, to the end of the world, she saw the white ghost of ice clinging to the earth like an old man eating a peach. She flew until she found Oolocc. She could not miss him. He had turned himself into a musk ox, his great horned head hanging like wood. He stood stolid in a pack of animals, their faces pointed out, and the snow collected in his fur. He might have blended in with the other animals, but his eyes, red and horrible, looked out from the deep brow of the ox, and his tongue, green and hungry, licked lichen in sweeps of drool from the rocks of the most northern land.

Sedna flew! She flew with the wind and let it carry her down, down toward the earth and in time she became nothing more than a drop of darkness in a land of white. The wind sometimes carried birds off the earth, lifted them to the moon, and this type of bird she pretended to be! In the last instant she ducked down, tucking her sharp wings against her side, and she became an arrow falling from heaven! At a thousand miles an hour, at the speed of sunlight, she ran in her sharp beak into Oolocc's ribcage!

Hear what a bee can do!

The bee found itself deep in Oolocc's flesh and with its last strength it turned and stung! The barbed stinger hooked into Oolocc's vein and the poison became a venomous knife flying toward the heart of Oolocc. The bee flew off, detaching its body, ripping its stinger free and condemning it to death. But Sedna rewarded the bee and sent it to heaven where it became a star and flicked with honey light for all to see.

And Sedna, who guessed correctly that Oolocc would not know bees, regained her human form. Oh, what she saw! She saw Oolocc's eyes go deep into his body and she watched as he understood at last what had happened. She had killed him! She had won! Sedna began to sing the oldest song she knew, and soon the animals of the world joined her. Fish and bird, insect and clever fox! The secrets of the world escaped the shelled creatures at the bottom of the sea and the bones of the dead rose up and danced like chimes.

—Why, wife, have you killed me? Oolocc asked Sedna. I am your husband and your mate. This venom you have placed in my blood, it cuts my heart from my body.

—It is a bee, Sedna answered.

And she no longer exulted in his death, but watched him with compassion. When Oolocc sank to his knees she sang a song for him, sending him to the bright rocks in small streams, where his body would remain forever scattered, where he would sing his song to the quiet woods.

POTATOES GROW FROM BONES

WHEN MY MOTHER BEGAN TO carry the cow's milk to neighbors, claiming it could cure their illnesses, my father did nothing to prevent her. This was in 1938 near Andover, Maine, close to the last log drive in that part of the country. My father had cut his foot badly in a logging accident in early autumn and his retirement to the chair beside the wood stove consisted of one winter-long splinter of wood and tinder. My mother was mad, of course, and trudged most of the winter through the deep copper cold, a vial of milk tied on a piece of rawhide between her breasts. She had not grown up in that part of the state exactly; she had been born in Aroostook Country, potato country, on the thumb of Maine close to the Canadian border. Even as an adult woman she could not bring herself to eat potatoes. Tubers of white, fleshy vegetable meat, she repeatedly scolded my father that she would one day choke and die on a potato. She said often, and perhaps believed it, that potatoes grew from bones. It was one of many things she said that tumbled from her mouth like saliva or poorly chewed food; hearing her make such statements, it was best to look away.

My father's accident impoverished us; a week after the men brought him in a chair to the house, his foot a red clot of flannel shirt and twine, mother announced we had no cash money left. He could not gather wood by himself and therefore ordered my younger brother, Ethan, and I deep into the forest to take from the logging camps. My father claimed it as his due for having been injured, though I knew the foremen did not see it the same way. Riding on the wooden pung with our large Percheron straining to pull us between pine and beech groves, I rehearsed the language father had given me if the foreman should object. Ethan, only six, was slow. He came as evidence of our need, and father tied him to the pung with ripped cloths, so that he rode beside me like a blank mummy, dead except for his busy eyes. At the logging camp I untied him and set him stacking wood. Piled properly, a pung could carry as many as ten cord of wood, but I was merely twelve myself, and we managed three cord. The foreman, a soot faced Cornish miner named Kylely, gave us the wood as you might give a dog food that had already dropped to the floor.

"Don't come back," he said. "Tell your father we're sorry about his accident, but he can't help himself to our wood."

I said nothing. My father had rehearsed me to say something about Ethan's condition, but instead I wrapped him in his cloth and tied him again to the pung. Back at our tiny cabin, my father opened his hand on my backside and on my face. His foot smelled of dying flesh. I feared his foot more than his punishments. It had begun to pulse like a red jewel, like a slow-blooded heart, in the core of our house.

Shortly after the accident, my mother declared our cow's milk could cure illness. It was a practical solution. Clara, our lone cow, produced little milk, certainly not enough for commercial value. By my mother's assertion that the milk had curative powers, she could prevail on our neighbors to buy small amounts for fees regular milk could not command. Her mind had adapted; she knew we could not survive long without money of some sort coming into the house. The fact that the milk failed to cure my father, or even Ethan, did not seem to enter her thoughts.

Each morning she took me into the pole shed to Clara's heated flank. She forced me to my knees and we prayed to Jesus and the Blood of the Cross. Then, carefully, she milked Clara's solemn teat, squeezing the white milk into the pewter pail. When she had the milk she needed for the day, she cut her hand and let a drizzle of blood drip slowly onto the creamy slick of the white froth. She closed her eyes at these moments; the old cuts on her hands, most barely scabbed, appeared like whip lashes on her palms. When she finished, she dipped the vial into the milk and filled it. She capped the vial with cork and slipped it between her breasts, whispering *Heart of Christ, Jesus purify this milk.*

Most days I stayed with Ethan, teaching him his chores. I kept him on a stiff leash made from the cob of a buggy whip. In the pole barn I locked him in a spare stall while I dragged hay to the Percheron, threw grain to the chickens, then knelt and finished milking the cow. Ethan watched me from the stall, his eyes running up and down the horizontal slats. Sometimes I forgot about him. Other times I squatted outside the stall and put my eyes in front of his, trying to get him to stop and stare at me. But he could not be still. His eyes moved as if feeding on something. I remembered stories my father had told me about loup garoux, the French-Canadian wolf boys who had devoured children and maidens and had built towers with their bones. They had eyes like Ethan; if you saw them in the forest, my father said, you were to urinate in a circle around yourself and refuse to move no matter what occurred next.

In the afternoon, Ethan studied the large picture books donated by a Bible group. As winter grew hard, Ethan concentrated on the books, running his finger up and down the pictures as though he could discern a track or the picture's origin. He liked to sit outside with them, avoiding the sharp whittle of the wood stove corner where my father carved deer antlers. My father turned them into coat hooks and knife handles and sold them, by mail, to the Collie General Store in Bath, Maine. Each evening we swept the scrapings from the floor and chair around him, bone matter thin as grass, and carried them outdoors. We let the pale clippings fall like dice, cutting half moons or arrows into the newest snowfall. Ethan often moaned after casting the bones. His voice rose and fell according to nothing any of us understood. At times his moaning matched the wind; at other times it fell in cadence with his rocking. My father was obliged to open his hand on Ethan if the moaning went on too long.

Then one day in January my mother did not return from her milk rounds. A cold snap flowed in on an Alberta Clipper, whispering down the valleys and choking everything with silence. The Rapid River a mile from our cabin bent and warped with ice. A maple exploded with frost, the sap in its bowels so expanded the wood could no longer contain it.

Men came and searched the hills around our house. They

retraced what they knew of her movements from neighbor to neighbor. Snow had turned a thousand lumps and gulleys into the shape of a body. The men carried birch sticks to jab into snow banks, hoping to strike her frozen corpse, but the search remained fruitless. In time common wisdom held she had wandered onto the ice of the Rapid River and had fallen through. Water had carried her away, people said, and she was held beneath the ice like oatmeal rising and striking against a pot lid.

In March a hurricane struck our house and the forest around it, turning the pines into a game of jackstraws. Summoned by the governor, an official from Washington arrived in a black Packard to assess the damage. My father, who had begun returning to the logging camp for work that spring, informed us that there was to be a log drive. The official from the Timber Salvage Administration warned that worms, the white puss slugs that clung like tubercular tumors to the brown pine, were set to invade the wood if the logs were not soon submerged and driven down to Lake Umbagog. The government guaranteed a price.

My father worked at the Wangan at Pond-in-the-River, a temporary camp where he set logs in booms before they were floated down the last stretch to Umbagog. He walked across the floating mass of wood, his fin foot false and stuffed with a cube of birch to round out his boot. He relied on his cant dog, prying the wood into better positions, his stabs at the logs as resonant as a man hammering two by fours half a mountain away. Ethan could not watch him. When he saw his father out on the water he began to moan and shake and nothing could relieve him except to be led away. Mr. Kylely speculated that the sight of our father in the middle of the lake, his weight sufficient to push him down so that his thighs appeared level with the water, seemed always to be sinking. Ethan did not comprehend the buoyancy of wood.

We lived beneath a piece of tarp behind the men's wangan. The tarp ran between two oak trees and each night my father tied Ethan's foot to a sapling; he did not want him to wander with water nearby. At night my father drank with the other men.

We watched him next to the fires, his skin becoming redder, his hands reaching to his face as if striking flint against his lips. While the men drank and told stories, we cleaned and greased their boots. The boots, clotted and wet as jaws, became rigid with frost each night. I rubbed them with oil made from cows' hooves, massaging the boots until they became supple again. Ethan licked the boots; we could not prevent him from doing this. He did not lick every boot, or do it in a consistent pattern, but the men saw it as an omen of good fortune and tipped him an extra penny or two if he licked their boots. Then we brushed the cleats free of mud and pulp and I carried the boots to the cook stove where they warmed for the morning.

We had been at the wangan three weeks or more when we returned one afternoon to find a logger had gone missing. It was a man named Deveraux, an experienced logger who had slipped between the logs. No one had seen him fall, or roll down among the logs like paper spooled into a typewriter.

"Hard to know," Mr. Kylely said. "Be only luck to bring him up."

Elemsme , a Swedish cook, took us to the edge of the water and cast bread up on it. He was an enormous man, white as paper, who piled his white-gray hair beneath a tall, gray cap. He handed us each a stick and told us to inscribe a Crucifix in the wet sand and speak our mother's name beside the name of Deveraux. Ethan drew six crosses; he seemed to mistake the purpose of the exercise and began dotting the tops of each cross, thinking them to be j's or i's. Elemsme did not interfere with Ethan. We stayed beside the water until mallards came and ate the bread.

I began to imagine Deveraux walking on the logs, riding one down through current after current until he splashed into Umbagog, the cleats of his boots glinting talons fixed permanently to the whaleback of a gigantic fir. Sometimes, in my imagination, he rode beneath the log, hugging it, his arms calipers, his cheek turned to the bark so that he might watch the water ahead, the green murk of what was to come.

We did not find my mother until April. I went with my father as he paddled through the last reluctant snow, a slow, lazy walk up Corter's Mountain. Zeke Monroe had come across her and had not disturbed the body. Peculiar it was, Zeke said. She had frozen while lying on a rock, her body arched over it, and her hand, cast away from her chest, dipped into a stream. She had been drinking, or she had pulled herself onto the rock in hopes of getting to her feet. Either way her hand had been chained through the winter by the pale skin of ice collected in the drinking pool. When we came on her the milk vial rested between her breasts like a wink of white. My father threw it into the woods and we listened for it to break. We stood looking at her body; her hair still moved in the wind.

Twice the children's welfare agency came for us and both times we escaped to the woods. The third time Mr. Kylely came with three men, none of them familiar to us, and pitched us on the Percheron and led us to Middle Dam. A black car waited. A woman with a nurse's cap examined us for lice. Then she shined a light into both of our eyes and clucked when she caught no light returning from Ethan's eyes. She walked a few paces off with Mr. Kylely. They spoke. Mr. Kyley's three assistants watched us and smoked.

The nurse woman nodded at Ethan when she returned and asked, "Can you control him?"

I nodded. I asked about my father.

"It's better like this," she said.

Then two of the men climbed in with us. They kept Ethan and I pressed against their thick thighs. A third man drove us. The nurse rode in the passenger side. She knitted gray wool into something as wide as a sheep's back. She spread the material on her knee again and again. The driver smoked. Smoke seeped as gray as the wool from his cigarette.

We were delivered to a children's farm twenty miles north and west of Portland, an orphanage sponsored by Moravians. The farm revolved around a five story chicken barn that smelled high and quick when we arrived. Gustav Zkelehli, a Czech, put us to bed in a basement beside a fieldstone wall. Other boys had slept in those beds; the walls beside our tick mattresses were jammed with bits of paper. Ethan spent his first hours in our new quarters examining the scraps of letters, calendars, and pictures from catalogues that boys had stored there over the years. Perhaps he identified a pattern in the chinks and holes. He could hardly bring himself to rest in bed. When I crossed two sheets over him and secured them to the bedposts, his hand still reached behind him to worry the papers.

Zkelehli was a kind man in everything but his hands. Blunt and dark, his teeth a mountain range of neglect, he smiled in his eyes while his hands carried out countless cruelties. Every six weeks he received twenty thousand Leghorn pullets from the incubators in Portland. In turn, he fed the chickens for six weeks, then crated the juveniles and sent them off to a local bean company that boiled them into stock. He had little time for careful husbandry; his spatulate fingers twisted the heads off lame chickens. With a hot knife blade, he debeaked chickens that tended to cannibalism. A spot of blue comb brought his hands to a chicken's neck, and he tossed the limp body away as another man might return a sock to a drawer.

We helped him. We gathered the dead chickens and delivered them to Mary, the cook and housekeeper. She was a pointed woman, fair as a lion, built too tall for her own tables and chairs. We delivered eggs to her, the few that appeared spontaneously in the pens, and bouquets of dead chickens cinched by their feet with twine. In the afternoons I shoveled the chicken droppings into a bucket and emptied it down a system of planks that leaned against the barn boards. A potato farmer named Mr. Tallus removed the manure twice a month, shoveling it into the back of a horse wagon. Nothing pushed potatoes like chicken manure, he said. We learned to eat raw potatoes, turning them like apples against our teeth. I carefully chewed the potatoes, mindful of my mother's warning that potatoes grew from bones.

Then one day Ethan could not move. When I woke at dawn he had managed to free himself from his bed restraints. He had been at the papers and catalog photos. They lay around the base of the wall, scattered as if he had searched for something but could not find it. He rested on his back, his eyes up, his hands soft at his side. *Wake up*, I said. *Come on, get up.* The papers had paralyzed him. I put my ear against his chest to hear him breathe. His air came in pants; his heart beat as quickly as a chicken's.

When I reported Ethan's condition, Zkelehli bent Ethan's penis into a medicine bottle and capped the urine with a cork. Then he placed a needle through the cork, saying aloud that he asked in the name of Jesus for the boy to be cured. Together we buried the bottle of urine beneath a flat stone in the heat of the fireplace. Zkelehi told me the heat would remove whatever curse had been cast on Ethan. He cut Ethan's hair and nails and burned them as well, reciting something in Czech as he ladled the particles into the flame. We waited to see the result. Mary visited Ethan and knelt a long time beside him and talked quietly into his head. When she finished, she collected the papers at the bottom of the wall and put them in the pocket of her apron. Ethan remained like a pale note himself, tucked into the gray pocket of his bed. He did not close his eyes night or day.

I brought him milk and cut my hand for the blood it required. I didn't know what else to do. Crouched beside the black and white flank of Zkelehi's Holstein, I yanked milk into a red bottle, then pierced my hand against a leather awl. Before sleep I tilted Ethan's chin against his chest and poured the milk into his mouth. He hardly swallowed. But the blood and milk seemed to enliven his cheeks. In the mornings I fed him oatmeal, packing it like mortar between the red brick of his lips.

"In my country, we would send for a doctor," Mary said, "but this is an uncivilized land. It is expensive. And the doctors know nothing."

Yet I understood that whatever payment they received for our care was placed in jeopardy by Ethan's illness. Three days into his paralysis, a team of four men arrived to help with the loading and unloading of the chickens. The men were loggers. I asked if they had heard of the drive down the Rapid River to Umbagog and they said they had. I asked if they had heard of my father, and they said no. Then the chickens demanded our time and we had no room for talk. We crated the juveniles and loaded them onto a line of trucks throughout one long day. The second day we cleaned the pens. Near midnight on the third day a final convoy of trucks arrived with twenty thousand pullets. The chickens flashed under our hands. By dawn of the last day, the chickens no longer possessed individual identity. Dead chickens, ones pressed by packing against the wooden rails of the crates, sometimes remained standing in mockery.

Before the loggers left one of them lashed me to Ethan. His name was Robert, a French Canadian, who explained he had seen the Cree Indians along St. James Bay work such a cure. He rolled Ethan onto his stomach, then made me lie on top of my brother. Using strips of cloth, he tied our ankles together, our wrists, even our necks. Then he wound a large bandage around our stomachs, flattening it so that I felt Ethan's breathing as my own. When he was satisfied with his work, he rolled me onto my feet and helped me stand.

"There," Robert said, "now walk. These types, they forget how to do anything. They have lost their spark. They will draw it from you. "

Mary did not like the treatment, but Zkelehli saw no harm in it. Each evening I walked with Ethan tied to me. At first it was difficult. I could not lift my hand without lifting his as well. The weight of his legs, his sagging torso, threw me off balance repeatedly. But in time my movements compensated for the extra weight and resistance Ethan's body represented. I walked him up and down the basement floor. Twice I took him outside and forced him to look at the stars. His head aligned with mine, we stared up until I felt dizzy. Crickets flung themselves ahead of us in the grass on our return inside.

Zkelehli dug up the bottled urine and discovered that all trace of liquid had seeped out. Maybe the cork had failed; maybe the pin through the cork had somehow wicked the urine away. He repeated the collection and this time made doubly sure the cork was properly stopped. The pin through the top, he explained, would remove any curses. Cobblers sometimes broke off their awls in the heel of a boot when repairing the shoes of a known witch. Witches could not abide metal pins.

The weather turned hot and the chickens began to suffer. We kept the doors and windows wide despite visits from foxes and fishers. We doubled the water rationing; twice daily I carried buckets to the pens. The chickens panted through their orange beaks. Crows came and landed in the shade of the large barn. The weathervane did not move or register wind. The odor of the chickens rose like talc; one could not breath without sensing birds or tasting their collective breath on one's tongue.

In the evening heat I walked with Ethan, his body limp and moist. He felt thinner. His leg bones clicked against mine as we stumbled along. Occasionally Zkelehi walked in front of us, a lit candle pressed close to Ethan's eyes. We looked for any sign that Ethan felt our presence. Once Zkelehi held the candle flame against Ethan's palm. He kept the flame against my brother's flesh until my own body flickered and twitched. After that experiment, Zkelehi did not believe in our remedies.

"God has whispered to that boy," Zkelehi pronounced, "and the boy has been silenced to listen for more."

Then one day Ethan's life returned. Rain hung against the barn. After we put out barrels to catch the rainwater spilling from the roof, we retired to the edge of the barn and watched the water fall. The heat lifted and the chickens spread their wings as if to gather air against their chests. An old beagle bitch named Chessy lolled beside us. She had given birth not long before. Zkelehi had drowned the pups he couldn't give away, but he was fond of Chessy and rubbed her with his foot. Flies rolled like cinders in and out of the building. Thinking the rain might be a tonic to Ethan, I went and lashed myself to him. By this time I could do the job myself. Rolling onto my feet, I walked him stiffly to the edge of the barn and held my hand out. For a time the water flattened against it. Then I felt his hand flex.

It might have been my imagination. I moved him back and away from the water, then returned with him again. I held out my hand beneath his. His fingers curled as if taking root in the water.

"A miracle," Mary said when we put Ethan in bed that night. "That's what it is."

"He's no better, though," Zkelehi said. "If God is going to bother to touch the boy, He might as well cure him altogether."

"Don't blaspheme," Mary said. "God knows His own heart."

Late that night I asked Ethan where he had been. He moaned but he couldn't say.

When I turned sixteen I took Ethan and walked back to the Rapid River. It took us a month and a half, mostly because I could not say where I had been raised. Neither Zkelehi nor Mary could help me. Their contact had been with the child welfare agency. I had arrived in a car; that was all they knew. They had seven children living with them now. They did not attempt to stop me.

Using what memory I had, and the few details of what I knew, I struck the upper dam on the Rapid River in August. I stopped at a fishing camp on Richardson Lake and asked if anyone could direct me to my mother's house. I am sure our appearance after all these years astonished the owners of the camp. A tall, bearded man who wore a dimpled guide's hat called to a woman in the kitchen. The woman appeared from a wave of heat, wiping her hands on her apron as she approached. Gretta was her name and she was a wide, bosomy woman as dense and as fertile as compost. Yes, she remembered my family. She couldn't say if the cabin still stood. Some hard winters, she said. An ice storm had brought trees down along the river. It took a team of horses and a worker from the county a full summer just to clear the access path to the dams. She always wondered what had become of us. Terribly sad about our mother. She remembered the story well.

She fed us apple pancakes and let us sleep in the wood shed. We left before breakfast the next morning. The lake turned into a river just by pushing against the early light. Then it became the sound I remembered and I loosed my lead on Ethan. He walked easily, happy, I guessed, to be near water.

What was left of the cabin was not difficult to find. The pole barn where Clara, our cow, had lived had long ago caved in; the roof of the cabin shone green with lichen. The porch, too, had gone soft and flexible. Mushrooms pushed up through the boards. The cook stove remained in what had been the pantry, but rust had climbed it. A stack of kindling, dry as crackers, rested beside it. The remainder of the furnishings had been stolen. Even the glass windows had been removed and carried off. No shards of splintered glass remained inside or outside the windowsill.

I tied together birch rushes and put Ethan to sweeping. I found a bucket underneath the collapsed pole barn and went and drew water from the river. We had bread and cheese for dinner. I started the fire in the stove and it burned correctly, though pits of oxidation had made the stovepipe porous. In the darkness where we slept the stovepipe resembled the constellations, yellow pricks in a black night. Owls called in the beeches. The sound of the river was like thought, or like memory, and I could empty myself into it, spill down the dark riverbanks and float until I felt nothing.

Gretta and her man, William, visited four days after our arrival. In the wagon parked on the access road, they brought a bow saw, a sack of flour, metal plates and cups, an ax with a half-broken handle, spoons and knives, three live Rhode Island Reds, a vat of peanut butter, sugar, a fly swatter, a fold of blankets, and a dozen boots of various sizes, a cast iron skillet. They had it to spare, they said. It was morning when they arrived and William looked at the stovepipe and promised to bring a replacement next time he visited. Gretta did her best to arrange the panty. She kept Ethan beside her while William took me down to the river and showed me how to catch trout with a string, a hook and a grasshopper. Corn would work for bait, too, William said. We caught ten fish in less than an hour. God's pantry, William called the river. Summer and winter, he said, we could have trout. Salmon, too, made their way up from Umbagog. I would have fish, he said, as long as I never killed a blue heron. Blue herons carried the fish inside them, he said. When they put their heads into the water they did not catch fish, as most people thought, but regurgitated them and distributed fish to all corners of the watershed. Then he winked and led me back to the cabin.

In the afternoon he helped me build camp beds from spruce boughs. Gretta promised to bring sack ticking for mattresses next time she visited. Then they left. Ethan ate three trout for dinner, then helped himself to two spoonfuls of peanut butter. After dinner we sat outside and watched the moon. The air smelled of pine and rock. When the owl began calling again, Ethan answered with his moans. Both sounds fell away to the water. I listened and tried to hear where the water sound ended, where the limit of my hearing became indistinguishable from the sound of my own mind, but that proved impossible. I told Ethan that the river was a fiddle bow and the trees the sounding board.

The next day I took Ethan and walked to the wangan. Mr. Kylely had been replaced by Mr. Courmier, a red-headed French Canadian who had hacked off three toes with a saw and now used an ax handle as a cane. His boot was as square as a miter joint. Courmier put me to work as a limber for the Portland Pulp and Paper Company. I worked with Jewel and Hank, a two-man saw team, who logged the boles that I had cleaned. Ethan pulled the limbs away after I cut them, although his slowness irritated Jewel. We ate our evening meal at the wangan. On Sundays we returned to our cabin and worked to repair it. With my first pay we bought flour, sugar, and coffee from the wangan commissary. We put in bacon from a local pig farmer named Selmer. I bought Ethan a root beer sucker that he licked for three days, wrapping it carefully away each time he finished, preserving it in a twist of newspaper.

When the snow arrived we had provisions to make it through the winter. Work slowed at the wangan; other men, permanent workers, were given our jobs. We stopped making the trip. Each morning we went to the river and hauled water. We watched ice move down from the lake, burning the boulders with white spray, though the water never halted by half. Ethan became attentive to the tracks we found around the cabin. Sometimes I hid from him in the woods and made him find me by tracking. He moaned happily when he struck my hiding place. Then I ran and hid again. Afterward we collected tinder and carried it back to the cabin. We filled every spare corner of the cabin with wood.

At the turn of the year I came down with a fever and when it finally broke I could no longer hear. At first I thought that the river had taken all sound from me. I watched Ethan's mouth move in a moan, or saw a bird open its beak, and I imagined the sound being scraped from my ears by the white hurry of the water. When I turned my head from side to side the sound, or what I believed was sound, changed. For days I remained unsure if I could trust my senses. I deliberately pounded the iron skillet with a spoon; I bucked a hammer against the slanted eave of the cabin, my head turned to give my ear full value. And still I could not be sure. The river poured relentlessly past us and our actions became a silent pantomime. Not until Gretta and William came in early spring, their wagon again loaded with supplies, did I understand my hearing had been all but lost. Leaning close, I could hear them imperfectly. Several times they tapped me on the shoulder to alert me to their movement nearby. Otherwise they disappeared as soon as my attention drifted from them.

"Rheumatic fever," Gretta shouted to me, "you're lucky to be alive."

"Did the boy get it?" William asked.

I said no, he hadn't.

I went back to work for the Portland Pulp and Paper company in May. I had worked there two weeks as a limber when Audrey Courmier arrived, granddaughter to the foreman, Mr. Courmier. I married her that autumn and brought her back to the cabin when we returned for winter. She was a sturdy girl, bright in the eyes, with hair the color of fire after it has given its best heat. She spoke French and English equally well, though her hands moved more when she spoke French. Her grandfather made us a present of a cow, a draught horse named Saul, and three two-man cross cut saws. Gretta and William contributed a real foam mattress and a ream of cloth.

We moved Ethan into a shed we built beside the pole barn. It took two weeks to carry a spare stove from the wangan to our cabin. We put the stove in the shed and made Ethan comfortable. I watched him closely to see if he took to the move. For cordwood I brought him out with me and taught him to bend over the two-man saw. He did not comprehend it at first. He rocked back and forth like the curved runner of a chair, hardly putting any force into the draw. But I explained he did not have to push, only pull, and in time he understood the movement in his arms. We cut a year's supply of wood, twenty or thirty cord, in half the time it had taken with an ax and bow saw. Ethan stacked when I split. We made the wood climb between two trees, a blank white wall of cord wood drying.

Ethan did not take to the shed, or at least he did not see it as his proper place. He began returning to the cabin at night, or at odd intervals, that made Audrey uncomfortable at first. Sometimes she woke in darkness and found him studying his books at the table. Maybe he had done this for years and my near deafness had deadened me to it. He read by a single candle. She said the sound the pages turning made her think of wind.

For seven dollars I bought a canoe from one of the loggers, Jerod Combs, and Ethan and I rode it down river to our cabin one Sunday. Afterward, when we pulled the canoe to high ground, Ethan took me by the hand and showed me an illustration of a flat-bottomed barge in one of his Bible books. The picture showed Egyptian men and women floating down the Nile. He ran his finger from the barge to the water, motioning for the barge to continue. Audrey liked the canoe, too, and sometimes we went out and fished together in the water below Middle Dam. Ethan sat in the bow, his hands solid on the gunwales. He did not turn to watch the fish we caught come aboard. His eyes remained on the water.

The following spring Mr. Courmier put together a log drive. It was nowhere near as large as the one that my father had worked. I piloted the Alligator Boat, a flat, steel hulled vessel that tugged a boom behind it. We looped the logs into black pods and set them in slack water, ready to drift when we canted the flash boards to add water over First Dam. The pine bobbed in the water and smelled as sweet as gum. Mr. Courmier declared it was time to put Ethan to work and he paid him fifty cents a day to clean dishes and help tidy up around camp. The loggers nicknamed him Quoin, after the metal spikes driven into granite to cleave it. They said he was as persistent as a Quoin wedging its way into stone. I took that to mean he was an annoyance to them, but they treated him well and did not mock him overmuch. I called him Ethan, and so did Audrey, but he was Quoin to everyone else.

We rode the logs downstream on the flood of snow melt at the beginning of June. Ethan and Audrey followed in the canoe. They fished behind us but did not have good luck. The logs stirred the water too much. When the logs legged into Umbagog a reporter from a paper in Conway snapped a photograph. Someone said it was the last log drive anyone would see on the Rapid River, given the weakened state of the dams. To keep running wood, the dams needed to be rebuilt and there were no funds for such a thing. The photographer took a photo of Ethan and Audrey, too. They sat in the canoe. Ethan wore a red plaid mackinaw.

With his salary Ethan bought a mink. He built a cage for it beside his shed and doted on the animal. The mink curled like muscle whenever anyone other than Ethan approached it. Ethan fed it fish heads and trained it to sit up and beg for its supper. Gretta, on a visit, stated that minks could be sent to listen for gossip. They carried a witch's ear to corners of buildings and they could eat the ear if apprehended. Ethan did not name his mink. I am not sure he understood he could give it a name.

On a cold January morning he followed the mink in the pines and froze to death. I put the story together later. At first light I had gone out to bring in more wood and discovered his tracks leading away from our cabin. I did not think much of it. He was free to go where he wanted by this time and he knew to stay away from the river. Had I noticed the empty cage, I would have taken steps to find him. Only later, by mid-morning, did I see the ribbon of mink tracks laced with his larger steps. The mink had chewed through its cage at last and Ethan, coming to feed it breakfast, had followed the drip of its ribboned body through the snow. I trailed the tracks for three miles at least, always heading uphill. Then the tracks began to circle; he had become confused or disoriented, the mink slipping away like water. He had not dressed properly for such weather. He had stepped outside to deliver food. Seeing the mink gone, he had thought nothing of following.

We could not bury him until late March. A French Canadian

priest named Clevete came in the spring and spoke over him. I marked his grave with stone, but Audrey insisted on a crucifix. My mother was buried near him, though I could not remember where precisely. I searched for several days, harvesting fiddleheads as I went, and came away with nothing. The stone that had once covered her remains had pressed the hillock flat. I suppose in the end it did not matter.

Our first child arrived a year later and we talked about naming him Ethan but decided against it. We named him Samuel instead. Though my hearing failed me in other regards, I was able to hear my son. At times I believed I heard Ethan, too, but of course it was merely habit and the force of water over stone.

THE BOAR HUNTER

(A NOVELLA)

THE BOAR REMAINED AT BAY in a small clump of beech and hazelnut near the bottom of the hill. Standing beneath the wood in a position to drive the animal up toward the waiting hunters, I saw several saplings shake as the boar quartered in different directions. The boar was confused and exhausted. We had chased him for more than six kilometers—his occasional breaks from the undergrowth wild and maddening to the hunters—and now he had made a last stand in a place well suited to him.

Beyond the trees, on the crest of the hill, I watched the horses breathing. Their noses were covered with frost and their lungs worked hard to take in air. The land we had traveled was wooded and almost entirely uphill, and the horses were as fatigued as the boar. Only my father, who everyone called the Colonel, kept his horse in complete control, his legs tight, his right hand indifferent on the rein. He held a rifle across his lap while the other hunters, all visitors from Vienna, all uniformly dressed in new loden huntsman clothing, fought to steady the heavy lances with which we had armed them earlier in the afternoon.

Despite the rifle, which he carried in case of an accident or failing of nerve on the part of one of the guests, my father was more involved in the chase than the others. He gave commands. He sometimes reached out and held the bit of a horse that had become too fractious. It was he I watched for the signal to begin the drive once more.

He spoke to the men sternly, but did not prohibit them from taking a drink from the flask one of them passed around. He refused a drink himself, not because he did not resort to alcohol often, but because he was in charge of the party and did not want to blur his judgement. Even as the men drank his eyes repeatedly moved from the party to the stand of wood where the boar waited; I could tell he was eager to carry out the kill.

At last he succeeded in stationing the men at various intervals across the hillside. The men appeared reluctant to be separated — a symptom I had often witnessed in visiting parties — but my father continued to instruct them until they could not ignore his suggestions.

"Have your lances ready," he shouted, and the men lifted the unwieldy metal poles. Two of the mounts shied at the lances, and I watched one man cuff his horse with his open left hand. The horse shied again, but eventually settled, and it was at this moment that my father waved me forward.

I had three dogs on leash. I had gathered them after the last run at the boar and all were now eager to resume the hunt. Each was a combination of Doberman and hound, unlike any other breed I had seen, yet perfectly suited for boar hunting. Their pelts were black, their muzzles squared and intimidating. My father bred them himself and insisted I regard them as working animals rather than pets. They were less attentive to me than they were to him, but I knew their temperaments and worked well with them. Asta and Sasha were reckless and dumb, while Issa, their mother, could be counted on — through intellect, and a lethal persistence — finally to chase the boar from hiding.

The dogs strained against their leads; the resulting tension made it difficult to set them free. I released them in the order prescribed by my father: first Issa, who was intelligent enough to wait for the others, then Sasha, the coward, and finally Asta, the idiot.

As soon as they were free, the dogs began to howl. It was a powerful sound. The bell of their cries went down the hillside, rolling out into the October evening, then echoed and finally disappeared. In an instant they were inside the wood, the crashing of bushes as they rushed forward returned and bettered by the frenzied boar. The howls continued and gradually twined into a tight whine—Sasha's—and I heard my father call to the other men.

"They're on him. Stand ready now!"

It was impossible to penetrate the heavy underbrush, so I climbed a low-limbed beech in order to watch in safety. Five meters up I caught a glimpse of the dogs, but I could not see the boar until I climbed somewhat higher.

In this position, my arm around the trunk of the tree, I watched Asta rush at a dark object standing beneath the autumn branches of a chestnut. It was the boar, of course, but it wheeled so rapidly that I could not at first distinguish its tail from its head. Asta made a pass, leaving the flank open for Sasha, who in turn made a half-hearted run at the boar before veering off. The boar chased him to the edge of the clearing and hit its shoulder on a stout sapling. The shock of the contact knocked a rain of chestnuts to the ground.

The rush by the boar had raised dust, which lifted and swirled around him. Long strings of saliva dangled from his mouth. He was clearly too exhausted to guard effectively his rear. His head hung low to the ground. He nosed at a nut, perhaps trying to lure one of the dogs forward, but it was a desperate maneuver, much like a man pushing his last schillings forward on the roulette table.

Issa chose that moment to dash at him.

She charged without sound. She appeared, remarkably, to account for the leaves under her paws and compensated by taking long, controlled bounds. She was almost on the boar before he sensed her approach. She struck with her whole weight, leaving the air entirely as her teeth found the boar's side, then clung with her forelegs while the boar began to spin.

The boar screamed, more from rage than pain, but its spin lacked the tenacity it had held in previous skirmishes. Asta rushed in just as Issa jumped clear and he raked the boar with his paw. Sasha came in on a poorly timed rush and received a quick smack from the boar's cheek, but Issa had returned and now had her teeth on the boar's ear. Immediately she settled her weight back, so that any movement by the boar would only intensify its pain. Her legs remained poised, prepared at any moment to relinquish her hold and dart clear.

The boar stumbled and fell, but came up quickly and lunged at

Issa. Asta blundered in from behind, his growls more menacing than his teeth, but the boar perceived the new weight on his flanks and began to run in desperation.

"Here, over here!" my father cried as soon as the boar crashed into the open field.

From all sides I heard hoof beats. A tree in front of me partially obstructed my view, but I saw one of the guests gallop forward, his lance held awkwardly beside his horse. I did not see the lance touch the swine, but the rider shouted and whooped while the boar gave off another squeal, this time in agony. The man continued galloping past the boar, his lance reddened by blood, his expression one of exultation and relief at having carried out his attack without shame.

"Cut him off! Cut him off! Don't let him back into the wood!"

My father shouted this command even as he kicked his horse into a run. I could not see the boar, but I could guess my father followed his own order and steered the boar back into the open meadow. Another guest rushed forward, bending low over his saddle, and this time I saw the lance strike the boar's shoulders, running up through the flesh and eventually jarring free of the man's grasp.

"We've got him!" the guest yelled. "He's bleeding!"

My father was busy whistling off the dogs — the job I was to do, and would later be scolded for not performing — as the three remaining guests swarmed around the boar. Dust followed the boar everywhere, penetrated only by the wind created by galloping horses. The riders staggered their charges at the boar, tagging him with lances whenever they passed. The boar, surrounded, turned viscously at each assault, but was too bewildered to defend himself.

I saw the final blow clearly. The boar broke free and ran uphill, away from the pack of men. A lance embedded in its hide clanged behind it, hitting and bouncing on the tufts of grass. A single horseman galloped beside it. The boar, if it had been fresh, would have taken a new direction or turned to confront its enemy, but fatigue had turned it into a coward and it ran stiffly in a straight line, red spurts of blood dripping down the shaft of the lance.

The rider galloped beside the boar and lifted his lance like a pike. He stabbed straight down, shattering the boar's spine in a single stroke. The thrust of the lance was hideous. It travelled down through the boar, impaling it. The sharp barb came through the animal's stomach and glinted red from its intestines. In the next instant the barb hit against a high hummock of grass and the boar let out one final cry before falling. Its back legs continued to kick, but the length of the protruding barb prevented it from regaining its feet. If not for the violence of its ending, it might have reminded me of a carousel animal tipped to one side, its sustaining pole useless on the ground.

I climbed down from the tree and hurried around the wood. My father cut me off. He handed me a second leash with the dogs safely fettered, looked at me once with disapproval, then turned back to the men.

"Nicely done," he said, cantering toward them.

The dogs strained at the leash. I allowed them to pull me up the hill. The guests were down off their horses, passing the flask around more quickly. One lit a cigarette. Another reached his boot forward and kicked gently at the boar. He did not press too firmly, probably fearing the boar still contained some life, but this, I could have told him, was impossible.

My father jumped off his horse and pulled the lance free, running it forward, completely through the center of the boar. I turned my head, but the dogs began whining and my father told me to let them have some of the intestines. I leaned back, just giving enough lead to let them near the carcass without any possibility of destroying it. They nipped at the intestines and tried to pull the entrails backwards toward them.

"My god, they're fine dogs," one of the guests said. He was an ugly man with a wide scar across his forehead. "They're animals a man would be proud to own. I don't suppose you sell any, do you Colonel?"

"Not the thing for the house," my father replied.

"Probably not...you're right, but, my Lord, I admire them. Look! They like that taste, don't they?"

I yanked back on the leash to keep Asta from pulling too fiercely at the intestines. Already they had dragged the boar a meter over the cold grass. My father finally kicked them away.

"How big would this one go, Colonel?" one of the guests asked. He was a stout man, the poorest rider in the group.

"We'll know when we dress him. Do you want Herr Meuller to mount it?"

"Of course," the stout man answered. "But we'll have a steak from it at least, won't we?"

"As much as you like. We'll see to that."

The men stood around drinking and smoking. Evening passed down over the hillside. It was colder now. I wanted them to leave so that I could wait alone for Herr Mueller to come with the wagon. The men, however, seemed intent on prolonging the excitement of the hunt, and they went over the events several times before they seemed to realize it was dark.

At last my father suggested they head back. The men agreed readily, taking a last round from the bottle before they mounted. My father told me to wait; he said I could let the dogs go. They would follow him back to the inn.

"Don't let the wolves get you," one of the guests said to me, then laughed.

They trotted off in a loose group while I unleashed the dogs. Asta began sniffing at the boar immediately, but I picked up a clod of dirt and hurled it at him. The clod hit his side and he lifted his head, suddenly realizing the other dogs were running up the hill behind the horses. He started after them in a full sprint and caught up with them before they were out of sight.

I waited an hour before Herr Meuller returned with the wagon. He came up a dirt road at the top of the hill and spent a few minutes looking for a place to enter the field. I shouted to him, but he simply waved and continued inspecting the ground at the side of the road. Finally, finding a spot to his liking, he twitched the rein on old Kase, and coaxed him onto the uneven meadow.

Herr Mueller brought the wagon as near as he could to the boar. He did not look closely at the animal, nor did he say much to me. When he was satisfied that our lift would be as short as possible—he had a bad back, and something he referred to as his hernia—he climbed down out of the wagon.

"So, what did we kill this time?" he asked.

He came around the wagon and examined the boar. He was a portly man, with gray hair and white eyebrows. He was, in many ways, a perfect caricature of an Austrian, though I did not have the perspective to realize it then. He was fond of schnapps and beer and good sausage. He was a devout Catholic who went to matins two or three times a week.

He had worn his butcher's apron over his normal clothes, and now, as he knelt before the boar, he first wiped his hands on the vest of the garment. He rolled the boar so that its legs pointed downhill, then leaned from side to side, inspecting it.

"Oh, he's had a good life," he said, feeling the body with his hands. "You see, William, except for the dogs here ... and here... not a mark on him. Not bad to live to maturity in perfect health, then die quickly. His old age was cut off, that's all."

"He broke from them three times," I said, kneeling next to him on the cold ground.

"Those men couldn't kill a rabbit ... they're sportsmen, not hunters. Did they say how they wanted it mounted?"

"No."

"Well, we'll do what we like then. Here, take the knife and truss it."

I did as I was told. I cut into the fetlocks and separated the stringy muscle from the bone beneath. Then, taking the heavy twine from Herr Mueller, I slipped the twine between the muscle and bone and gradually pulled the legs together.

"A bouquet," Herr Mueller told me when I had the legs pulled together, each hoof like a black rose. He helped me with the final knots, then pushed a thin steel pole between the legs. With the pole in position, it was a simple matter to hoist the boar onto the back of the wagon.

"There we go," he said when the boar was secured in back. "You're getting the knack, all right. You'll be a better hunter than your father after all is said."

I was seventeen and attentive to such statements. I climbed in the wagon beside him. He flicked his rein against Kase's flank and we bumped over the meadow and onto the road. Kase knew the way from there, and Herr Mueller handed me the reins while he lit a pipe. He brought up a small bottle of schnapps and took a drink, then passed the bottle to me.

"You remember what I told you," he said, smoking and leaning back against the wagon seat. "You let these gentlemen get a few drinks in them, then you stay close, you understand? It won't break them to give you a little something for your troubles. Don't be shy about it...you have the right. They expect it. If you miss them tonight, then be around their car in the morning when they start packing.'

"I will, sir."

He looked at me. He knew very well that I was shy and never pressed for the tips that were rightfully mine. He was also protecting me from my father, who would certainly expect me to get something from the men. Whatever tips I received would of course go back into the family coffers, but the important thing was to extract as much money from the men as possible. To do less was simply bad business.

When we arrived back at the inn, I saw a small horse cart parked near the front entrance. The cart looked like a child's cart, only slightly larger. The cart was attached to a very thin horse, which had obviously been driven hard on few feedings. The horse was unsteady in the stays; it shifted feet as we approached. Each time it moved a string of bells tangled solemnly.

"Whose cart is that?" I asked as we passed.

"A strange couple who just arrived as I was called out. When we get this boar inside, you come back up and stable the horse.'

"Where are they from?"

"Hungary. The man is as big as an oak. I thought he was a giant when I first saw him. He's the servant of a woman named Madame Lacome—old aristocracy, from the looks of her. She came in and demanded the best room—the one at the top of the stairs—then had me running to fix a fire for her. The giant has been bringing in baggage. He carried in three, four, suitcases without a thought. You wouldn't think a cart could hold so much."

I turned to look again at the cart. The cart was covered with signs of the zodiac. The hub of the wheel closest to me was elongated into a spike. It was a cart unlike any I had ever seen.

I strained to see the giant, hoping he would appear at the door, but by this time we had turned the corner of the inn and went down the small road that led to Herr Mueller's shop.

I ate a bowl of soup in the kitchen. My mother was busy preparing dinner, and she gave me the soup to get me out of the way. I sat at the small kitchen table to one side of the large fieldstone fireplace. The heat of the flames was welcome after the cold work of butchering the boar. I bent over the soup and began eating it quickly. Without turning to look at me, my mother told me not to slurp.

I ate more delicately, watching my mother work in front of the stove. She was red from the heat; her hair had slipped free of the bun she habitually wore at the back of her skull. Her forearms tensed with surprising muscle whenever she lifted a pot onto a different burner. I watched her move from side to side, as she stirred and tasted the different sauces.

She was an unhappy woman. Her figure and looks had been eroded by hard labor as a cook and laundress. She had, she often said, been born to a better life. Marrying my father had been a drop in station—one, I vaguely sensed, tied to my own birth and an impending scandal. As a girl she had been a guest in inns similar to the one we ran for the Czekeli family, but now she was mistress of the inn without any claim to ownership. She resented this enormously. As a result, her work around the hotel —folding sheets, cooking three meals a day for guests, tending a garden at the back of the grounds — filled with sharp angles. Often I watched her hands strike a fold in a tablecloth with movements far surpassing efficiency. She hated the Czekeli family and was cross for weeks before and after their annual visit.

On this night she was particularly short-tempered. When Herr Mueller climbed up the back stairs from his shop with a trough of meat cut from the boar, she shook her head and waved with one hand for him to put it on the counter.

"They want steaks, I suppose," she said, turning her attention to a pot she stirred. The violence of her stirring caused a splash of gravy to leak out on the stove.

"I wouldn't know, Frau Loebus," Herr Mueller answered politely. "It's might be wise to ask your husband."

"Now this," she said, but apparently could think of nothing to say which would adequately convey her frustration.

Herr Mueller hung in the center of the kitchen, not sure if he was required to make another statement. His hands went to his pockets, checking for his pipe, and I knew from this that he wanted to have a smoke beside the fire. Finding the climate somewhat cold, however, he must have thought better of it.

"Did you stable the horse?" he asked me as my mother turned to the fresh meat and began picking through it.

"Yes, sir," I said.

"What do you make of that cart?"

"The right wheel is loose. I thought it would fall off before I got it inside."

"I wonder," my mother said, taking a rib section of the boar and slicing it into strips, "if anyone has thought to ask our guests how they intend to pay? Naturally my husband would not risk his own embarrassment by asking them for an advance."

"The new guests?" Herr Mueller asked.

"Of course the new guests. The woman has already ordered tea twice within the first hour of her stay. I had to send Eva up with it...then she complained the service was slow. The woman is a gypsy and now you hear her cart is about to fall to pieces."

"Have you seen the giant yet?" Herr Mueller asked me, backing to the fire. He warmed his backside and flexed his folded hands behind his pant's tops.

"Not yet," I said.

"The men inside want to put up a wager that he can't knock out a cow with a single punch. They tried to draw him into the conversation, but he wouldn't answer them. Maybe he doesn't speak German."

"Whose cow?" my mother asked, turning to look at us both.

"Any cow," Herr Mueller answered, uncomfortable with the question.

"No, you mean our cow. So the bet will be won or lost, and we'll wind up with a cow that doesn't give milk. I won't hear of it."

"The giant won't go for it anyway."

My father walked in at this point. His face was red from drink; his boots, unchanged, were still splattered with mud. His bearing, as always, was stiff and upright. He carried his rifle in his right hand. He nodded to us and went to the gun cabinet near the back door and placed his rifle in it.

"Do they want steaks?" my mother asked.

"Yes, naturally."

"I've cooked three other courses. You might have told me."

My father looked at her. He was never wrong. Never did he admit that he may have overlooked another's feelings or obligations. He prided himself on logic—no matter how obscure and one-sided—and now stared at my mother with the equation folding out before him: the men were guests, they had killed a boar, why did he have to tell her they would like to taste the meat they had won?

He said nothing else. My mother turned to the stove. Herr Mueller patted his pocket once more. I bent over my soup, hoping to escape him.

"William, Sigfried was favoring his right leg. He needs some looking over . . check on him later," he said to me, referring to one of the mounts. He closed the gun cabinet and locked it.

I continued to eat my soup.

"Did you hear me?" he asked.

"Yes."

"Look at a man when you speak to him.'

I looked up and nodded, then went back to my soup. Herr Mueller coughed and pretended interest in the fire.

"Serve the new guests the meal you prepared. The others will have steaks," he told my mother, then departed.

Eva entered the kitchen a few minutes later. She was a distant relative of mine, though the connection had never been adequately explained. A cousin of a sister—a female line. Eva was a good-spirited girl, probably twenty-two at the time. She was well built, if a little homely; her sexuality seemed forged in barns and country lanes. I knew she sometimes let herself be kissed by the guests; she was pinched and cornered in upstairs hallways. She told me, in her serious moments, that she was looking for a match—not with a dumb country boy, but with one of the rich guests who came for the hunting.

My mother put her immediately to work cutting up the steaks. Eva did as she was told. She was excited by the arrival of the new guests and began to describe the things she had seen unpacked when she carried tea to their room.

"The woman is a fortune teller . . . she told me so herself. She already had that huge man drag the gate-leg table to the window, and she covered it with a tablecloth that had the strangest designs . . . stars and half-moons. She smokes cigarettes, too."

"Did you tell her she must return all the furniture to its original position?" my mother asked.

"Oh, yes, but she said not to worry. She intends to stay for at least a month."

"Did you talk to the man? The giant?" Herr Mueller asked. He had at last drawn out his pipe and filled it. He did not pull a chair to the fire, perhaps realizing my mother would pounce on him if he did. She did not like idleness while she worked.

"I didn't talk to him. He's quiet as wood. I'd be afraid to meet him on a dark night as gloomy as he looks. But he's polite, I'll give him that. He seemed worried about the woman. He wanted to make her comfortable and nothing else seemed to matter. I appreciate that in a man."

I finished my soup. Herr Mueller gave me a look to indicate it was now time I went into the dining room to tend the men and wait for tips. It was useless to pretend I didn't understand him. He even nodded his head in the direction of the dining room when I passed carrying my bowl to the sink.

I looked for a reason to delay, but, having eaten, I knew my mother would not permit me to linger in the kitchen.

I went into the large common room, which served as the inn's restaurant and lounge. The ceiling was low; the walls and roof beams were covered with racks of antlers and a few mounted heads. The men sat before a birch log fire, listening to my father. The men's faces were red; they were still dressed in their hunting clothes. Chips of dirt surrounded each man, knocked off and dried by the heat of the flames. The odor of wool slowly drying against skin filled the room.

My father looked up quickly at my entrance, but continued reciting a story I had heard any number of times. A guest down and being gored by a boar; a dog rushes in; a well placed rifle shot; the guest sewed together by the village tailor. The men listened intently, just as hundreds of guests before them had listened. I crossed the room and sat somewhat behind the group, so that I could watch their glasses without inhibiting their conversation.

I was there only a few minutes when the giant appeared. He was not at all a giant—his features were well shaped and had none of the grotesque squareness a true giant's face might have held—but he was exceedingly large. He moved with surprising grace, as if unable, from experience, to trust floors and chairs to accommodate his huge weight. Indeed, despite his size, he was far more elegant than the men sitting near the fire. His clothes fit him well; his bearing and demeanor did everything within their power to deflect the attention he necessarily received. He possessed the careful manners of a man born to a high station, or, more likely, one born with an unassailable opinion of himself.

He ducked beneath a beam as he stepped into the room, then straightened his coat as he stood to his full height. The other men, chattering a moment before, turned without pretense to study him. My father stood and offered his chair, but the giant—for that is how I still thought of him at that time—politely shook his head.

"Herr Schliemer," my father said most cordially, "won't you join us? We're having a drink in celebration of our hunt. Are you a hunter by any chance?"

Herr Schliemer, the giant, smiled. His silence seemed to mock—though I cannot say exactly how—the conventions of the hunt and the seriousness with which the men perceived themselves. That I was not alone in this interpretation I sensed in the discomfort among the men. They turned more fully in their chairs to watch Herr Schliemer, annoyed, it seemed, to have their authority undermined.

Herr Schliemer smiled again, then said in a remarkable baritone, "I do not hunt, Colonel. My schedule won't permit it, I'm afraid."

"You're a busy man then, are you, Herr Schliemer?" one of the guests—the portly gentleman—asked.

"Probably idle by your standards," the giant answered in formal German. "But please, don't let me disturb you. Madame Lacome has asked me to give each of you her card."

He stepped around the room dispensing ivory colored cards from a leather case. The cards were incongruous in his massive hands. Each man, as he received the card, glanced at it quickly, then returned his eyes to Herr Schliemer.

"Madame Lacome is a fortune teller?" my father asked, studying Herr Schliemer, then reading from the card. "Tarot, the crystal ball, divination . . ."

Herr Schliemer ignored him.

"Madame Lacome will be in to visitors after dinner. Please speak to me if you desire her services."

He left with a small bow. The room was silent as we listened to his weight creaking up the stairs. It was not easy to enter a room and upstage my father, and I liked the giant for doing so. It was not merely by his size that he did this, but also by his dismissal of the men's attempts to include him. My father's authority stemmed from his pure maleness and the regard he won from his visitors by his accomplishments during the hunt, yet suddenly here was a man not only more formidable in his person, but who also seemed to view my father's occupation as childish.

No one said anything until the giant's steps were safely upstairs. Then the short, portly man laughed out of nervousness.

"A fortune teller, Colonel! You have a strange guest list," he said. "Will there be tumblers as well?"

My father did not answer. He was distracted by Eva who appeared with a tray full of dishes. The men saw her and sat up, causing a mild blush to pass over her cheeks. My father looked at me, and I silently filled the men's glasses with more schnapps.

I carried the bones from dinner — carefully collected by my father from the guests' plates — down the back stairway to Herr Mueller's shop. The staircase was old, the center boards springy with each step. Herr Mueller stood at a long workbench, which was scattered with pieces of a hundred different animals. A few successfully mounted animals waited for stands; more were lined against the wall, ready to be crated and sent. Each of the completed animals was tagged with a brown piece of cardboard stating the time and date of the kill, the names of the hunting party, status of payment, and appropriate address. The tags would eventually be transcribed to a small brass plaque at the foot of the mounted animal.

The shop was heated by a tile stove stoked with coal. The room was never allowed to become too warm, and I did not have to ask this night to know that Herr Mueller had severely banked the fire. The smell of his pipe was very strong on everything inside the room, the odor undermined only by the scent of skins and hair and hooves.

Herr Mueller was busy filling the right socket of a recently killed stag with a brownish amber eye. He imported the eyes from Italy at great cost. He took all possible pains, he often said, because the eyes restored, the animal's life. As a result, he spent a great deal of time setting the eyes, the work making him short and ill-tempered if he could not get them right.

"Set it down," he told me without turning from his bench. "Did you get everything?"

"Yes, it's all here."

He could fashion artificial bones well enough, but he preferred to have his specimens whole. He glanced at the trough of bones and meat, then threw a tool onto his workbench and put down the eye he held in his hand.

"It won't go in the way it should," he said. "It's too big. Makes him look scared for his life."

"Can you press it in farther?"

"I'll think of something. I had it in solidly, but it was off balance with the left. You must have the correct symmetry, otherwise the whole thing is a waste of time...especially with the eyes. The eyes tell the tale."

He rubbed his hands on his apron, put his pipe on the worktable, then examined the trough of meat more closely. His lips moved silently as he added up the bones: ribs, femurs, thighs, and joints. He counted the joints with particular attention, since they were more difficult than anything else to replicate artificially.

When he satisfied himself that we had a complete carcass, he began stripping the bones of their remaining meat. He made a pile of fat and gristle to give to the dogs later. As he worked, he reached to a large radio and adjusted the dial to a broadcast of Die Zauberflute coming from the Vienna Stadt Opera. The signal was weak. It faded in and out as it wandered through the mountains from Vienna, but Herr Mueller didn't seem to mind. He hummed with the music, occasionally forgetting the work before him during the more magnificent arias. At times he stopped altogether and remained motionless, a rough bone in one hand, his knife in the other.

"You should see the opera, William. I'd take you myself if we could arrange it," he said to me with surprising longing as he returned to strop the meat from the bone. "You can't imagine the splendor. The singing is only a small part of it. Do you know in one production of Carmen they brought ten horses onto the stage? Ten full grown horses! They must have pasted pads onto their hooves, because I didn't even hear them enter. I had my eyes closed, and then, pffff, suddenly they were there. It's magic, you know."

"Was this in Vienna?" I asked, though I knew the answer. He had lived in Vienna for ten years, working as a butcher.

"Yes, in Vienna. I went to a hundred nights of opera—maybe more. Such bosoms! The women out-do each other trying to show off their bosoms, and I was glad enough to watch, I promise you. They spend more on a dress than I make in a year. I'll tell you a story. I saw a girl sitting across from me once . . . a very rich girl. I was better looking in those days, and at intermission I followed her to the refreshment stand. She had champagne. I couldn't afford anything, of course, and I was poorly dressed by comparison. But she saw me watching her, and her eyes stayed on me over her glass. When she finished her drink she said something to her mother, then walked toward me. I was in the middle of the crowd, so she might have been walking toward anyone there, but I knew she was approaching me. When she came within a meter of me I saw there was no way for her to pass. I pushed back against a fat man behind me, but he wouldn't yield. The girl saw all this and didn't stop. She turned sideways, face to face with me, and slowly moved past me. She deliberately pressed herself into me—her bosom, her silky dress, even her hair. Her breath smelled of champagne and her perfume—well, I can't describe her perfume. She kept her eyes directly on my eyes . . . she knew what she was doing, you understand? It was a strange mixture of things. She was attracted to me, but she was also interested in showing me that I had no right to look at her with such longing. I would never have a woman like her, never, and she wanted me to know that, just as she wanted me to know how easily she could seduce me if she cared to."

"What happened afterwards?"

"I couldn't go back inside. I was too embarrassed. I'm afraid I was young enough to believe a new suit of clothes might change things, so I saved half of my salary for two months and bought an expensive outfit before I returned to the opera. Naturally she wasn't there. I went out at intermission and bought a glass of champagne—the first of my life—and looked through the crowd for her. While I searched a man burned the hem of my jacket with his cigarette . . . just an accident for which he offered to pay . . . but I became very rude and told the man he was a clod. It was a terrible night. He began to berate me in return and he was far more gifted in that sort of thing. The rich have language on their side...remember that, William. I did the only thing I could and pushed him backwards. We scuffled and I was removed by three ushers. My jacket lapel was torn. Suddenly I was outside, looking up at the opera house with the music just faintly audible. I went to the Kris Kindle mart and ate sausage and beer and finally got in a good fight. My clothes were ruined, but I knew where I was by the end of it."

"Did you ever see the girl again?"

"No, only in fairy tales does that sort of thing happen. But I went back to the opera. That was a little victory for me."

He had worked through the pile of bones as he told me this story. Finished, he shoved two fists under his apron front and pushed it out.

"Bosoms!" he laughed.

Afterward he carried the stripped bones to a large cabinet made of pine. The cabinet was situated near the back door where the rotting meat might benefit by some ventilation. I went to his side and opened the cabinet door.

Inside the cabinet he kept a colony of dermestid beetles. They were perfectly ordinary looking beetles, the kinds one might see clutching to carrion on a forest floor. The beetles were an effective means of cleaning a skeleton; they were additionally valuable because they shunned the cartilage between the joints unless deprived of food for too long. Herr Mueller, therefore, was able to keep the articulated joints in tact, while gaining from the beetles a perfectly cleaned frame on which to remount the animal's hide.

He set the bones out in a rough outline of the boar's skeleton. The beetles remained huddled in the corners of the cabinet until we closed the door sufficiently to darken the interior. At last the beetles surged forward and covered the bones.

'They're in good appetite. I would have given them something tonight no matter what," Herr Mueller said, closing the door. "It's quicker to use acid, but this way is better. You don't weaken the bones."

He went back to the stag and picked up the amber eye, then began measuring the deer's head with a pair of calipers. He told me to take the meat out to the dogs.

I climbed the back steps with the meat under my arm and pushed out into the garden. The air was very cold; leaves from a large oak frosted into the soil beside the cart path. The iron rims of the wagon wheels shone bright with mist just turning to ice.

The dogs were waiting by the fence when I reached them. Asta and Sasha stood with their paws on the top rung while I fed them scaps. Issa sat patiently behind them. Whenever I flipped a morsel to her, she ran off with it and devoured it in private.

I was nearly finished with the feeding when I realized I was not alone. At first I thought it was merely my imagination—the dogs had given no warning of another's presence after all—but when I squinted I saw the giant standing across the pen from me. It was sufficiently dark to make me question my senses for an instant, but then he cleared his throat and started around the pen toward me. The dogs ran to him, even Issa, and jumped against the fence. They seemed very excited and ignored me even though I still had meat to give them.

"You are William?" he asked.

His voice was deep, but very soft. His size was intimidating—more massive than I could have believed if I had never stood near him. Without question he was the largest man I had ever seen.

"Yes, sir," I replied.

"The bitch . . . she is the smartest, isn't she?"

"Yes. Her name is Issa."

"Issa? Does it mean anything? The name?"

"Not that I know of. You should ask my father."

"I will when I have a moment," he said. His German was imperfect, and I understood this phrase as something he relied upon to avoid lengthy explanations. He leaned against the fence and watched as I continued feeding the dogs.

I should have felt uncomfortable with him so near — my shyness often made me feel ill at ease with stranger — but his size seemed to preclude such emotions. It does not quite fit to say he absorbed my typical uneasiness, yet it is close to the truth. I had the impression that whatever one felt near him would be accepted; he made no judgements. I glanced frequently at him as I finished the last of the feeding. With my attention divided, I made the mistake of throwing two or three scaps at a time. The dogs quarreled over some of the pieces. I shook the brown paper above them to dislodge the last morsels.

"Are they always penned?" Herr Schliemer asked me.

"Except when they're hunting."

"Of course. But otherwise?"

"We keep them here. They would kill livestock if we let them run free.'

"I imagine they would. Do you know the young male . . . that one . . . is bleeding from the hip? The boar must have gored him."

I looked closely at Sasha, but it was a difficult business in the darkness to see red blood against black fur. I held the brown paper above the fence and made Sasha put his paws up high to seize it. Leaning down to inspect his side, I saw the wound. I couldn't tell if the wound was deep, but, at the very least, his leg would be stiff for several days. My father, I knew, would be angry that I had not checked the dogs thoroughly after the hunt. We expected a new hunting party in less than a week.

"Don't worry, it isn't serious,' Herr Schliemer said.

"Are you sure?"

"Run and get some tape. We'll patch it up."

I did as I was told, partly to escape a confrontation with my father, but also because the giant instilled me with trust. I hurried to the basement, begged a roll of tape from Herr Mueller, then ran back up the stairs.

The giant stood inside the pen when I returned. The dogs remained remarkably docile. Even Issa, who was exceedingly wary of strangers, appeared to accept the giant's presence among them. The giant rubbed their backs and rolled them over—something not even my father would attempt. He scratched their bellies and called them by name.

"It's probably too cold to find cobwebs," Herr Schliemer told me as I stepped into the pen, "but a good cobweb would be just the thing. You set it under the bandage and it helps the wound to scab."

"I could look in the barn."

"Don't bother. It isn't deep. Sasha here told me he hardly feels it."

It was a curious phrase to employ, but I attributed it to the giant's poor command of German. He took the tape from me, wadded a handful of mud into a compress, then called Sasha to him. Sasha, to my surprise, did not hesitate. He walked with his head down and stood directly in front of Herr Schliemer.

The process must have been painful to the dog, but he did not budge. He stood quietly and let Herr Schliemer bind the wound. The mud worked well; the trickle of blood ceased immediately. I had seen my father do the same thing, but never with such cooperation from the dog. Indeed, Sasha seemed aware that this was all in his best interest.

"He'll be better soon. Check him in the morning to make sure he doesn't bite at the bandage. If he does, we'll put a fan collar on him to keep him from getting to his hind quarters."

"Have you worked with animals before?" I asked, taking the tape back from him.

"Now and then. You pick up some things if you travel."

"And you have travelled? Are you from Hungary?"

"I was once. Now I am from here, in your town. Madame Lacome would say we are all from chance . . . or destiny, as you like. Have you met her?"

"No, sir."

"She is quite approachable. Don't be frightened to go up to her room. Don't form any opinions of her from listening to others. She is different than you might suppose. In fact, she said she would like to meet you when you have the time."

I was intrigued by this. I wanted to ask more—were they married, was she really a fortune teller, what was the meaning of the symbols on the cart—but Herr Schliemer touched my shoulder and led me out of the pen.

He closed the gate gently. We watched the other dogs come to sniff at Sasha's bandage. Sasha endured it for a moment before he growled at them both. Herr Schliemer laughed.

"They are drawn to his weakness. It's very human, isn't it? Would you say we are drawn to one another's weaknesses or strengths?"

"I never thought about it."

"What have you been thinking about then? That's something Madame Lacome will ask, so be prepared. Now, I should be getting back inside."

He touched my shoulder again, then left me. I turned to watch him. As he approached the door to the kitchen, his form almost obscured the light.

The next morning I was awake early to carry the guests' bags down to the car that would take them to the railroad station in Salzburg. The guest had drunk a great deal and they moved around their rooms cautiously. They were short with me; they said hardly a word except to tell me to keep a bag straight or to be careful of the contents of a valise.

In my trips up and down the stairs I did not see the giant or Madame Lacome, but I heard talk of them both. Madame Lacome had read the men's fortunes after dinner, and the men made frequent reference to her predictions. They made inside jokes—be careful of strangers, your aunt is ill, take heed of something in the post—which were obviously bred from the fortunes described by her. They exhibited no sign of taking her words seriously, nor did they worry about her overhearing them.

When I was nearly finished transporting the baggage, my father came to the foot of the stairs to see the men off. He enjoyed moment's of departure, I suspected, because he found in it a sense of triumph. He was a man of the woods and the hunt, while his guests remained city dwellers who could not leave without granting that my father lived a life of greater personal danger. Perhaps, it might be said, his life was more fully masculine. In these departures he wrestled from them a subtle admission which his station in life could not win otherwise. Combined in this was his pardon of them for living lives of boring wealth—for being overfed and necessarily timid in the hunt—and in this forgiveness he gained his greatest power, and maybe a place in the visitors' mind that made them return to him.

Because it was not a hunting day, he had laced his coffee with brandy. Brandy made him garrulous with guests, but stern with his family and staff. Watching me go up and down the stairs the last few trips, he ordered me to hurry, to watch where I was going. On my last descent he called me to stand beside him and began whispering further instructions.

"Don't disappear. Stay beside the men. Damn your shyness," he said in quick bursts. We could hear the men making their final preparations at the head of the stairs.

"Yes, sir."

"Their pockets are full enough to drown a man. Look lively and pay close attention to their wants. I won't have you turning the blushing bride on me, will I?"

"No, sir."

As the men started marching down the stairs, he slipped his

arm around my shoulders. He turned and called to the kitchen. A moment later my mother and Eva appeared, both wearing fresh aprons. It was a tradition of the inn to say a formal farewell to our guests—though my mother dreaded it—and they took their positions in line without a word.

One by one the men came down and shook our hands. My father positioned himself to receive the last hand shake, as if saying goodbye to him would mark their true departure from the inn. To his credit, the men seemed to have the same perception. Each man stopped and passed a word with him; each cuffed him on the shoulder and remarked on the fine hunting and brandy. The same man who commented earlier on the dogs, asked again if the Colonel was positive the dogs were not for sale.

"They would terrorize the Volksgarten, Colonel," the man said. "They would dig up the roses . . . what a fine mess they would make."

His question needed no reply. The dogs were bred—just as my father was—for a rougher life. This was all understood. The man did, however, slip a wad of bills to my father, which I knew from experience constituted a sizeable tip for him.

I held the doors for the men, balancing a last bag against my hip. My father walked them out. Herr Mueller was already in the touring car behind the wheel. I ran forward and opened the car doors, trying to be of service in any way possible. I deliberately lingered before closing the doors, hoping that one of the men would call me to him and press money in my hand. But I could not stall too long without appearing rude, and so, after asking to make sure their legs were in, their coats pulled around their legs, I shut the doors. Herr Mueller started the engine. They pulled off slowly, waving through the windows until they had left the grounds.

I had received no tip; or, perhaps, my tip had been included with the money given my father. It hardly mattered because I knew my father would chastise me for the former and never believe the latter. He could not conceive that a tip was meant for anyone but himself; he kept this money apart from our household funds and used it for his own entertainment.

He waited in the sitting room. I tried to walk past him, but he told me to stop. My mother had already returned to the kitchen and we were alone. I squared my shoulders and raised my eyes, knowing full well that this was my only hope of escape. My father stepped toward me and pinched my cheek, squeezing the flesh and twisting until tears came to my eyes.

"Nothing, right? I don't blame them. Honestly, I don't blame them," he said, still twisting the flesh of my cheek. "Guests don't tip girls in a hunting lodge. I've told you that before."

His hand stopped pinching, but he began to pat my cheek softly, as if trying to flatten the swollen skin. I dared not move. I could not, however, keep my eyes from becoming full with moisture, though I knew this would only provoke him. His hand became heavier on my cheek—not a slap exactly, but a constant tweak of derision. At any moment he might have pulled his hand back to deliver a solid blow, yet he seemed more intent on embarrassing me.

"Where did you come from really, William? You should ask your mother . . . I'm telling you something now. Ask your mother whose child you might be. These men were generous. Very generous. They found something in me to reward, I promise you, what do you think you are lacking?"

I knew I had to reply. It would be better to give the answer he expected, but I couldn't think clearly.

"I don't know what I lack."

"No, you probably don't. Ask the girls in town what you lack . . . they'll tell you readily enough," he said and pulled his hand back. I flinched inadvertently and he laughed aloud.

"Oh, you're a fine one. So manly. I think your mother was right to keep you in dresses. I told her so. She's done her work well. She dreams you'll make us all rich, but men make money in this world. . . not little girls. Not girls like you, in any case."

He reached his hand to pat my cheek once more, this time bringing it sharply against my jaw. He patted me twice, increasing the strength of each blow, until it was all I could do to keep from ducking. He would have hit me full force, I'm sure, if the stairs had not creaked at that moment. We both turned to look. The giant stood halfway down the staircase, watching us.

"Good morning, Herr Schliemer," my father said nervously. He instantly pulled his hand away from me.

"Good morning. Good morning, William," the giant said deliberately.

My father did not move, though he tried to regain his composure. It was a strict rule in our household that we never discussed family matters before the guests. Now standing in the sunny sitting room, we had obviously transgressed. My father coughed, took a step back, and pretended to search his pockets for a cigarette.

The giant came down the remaining stairs. He ducked under the beam at the end of the staircase. His face appeared freshly washed.

"Colonel, I once owned a pony who would not do as he was told," the giant began.

My father interrupted, "Really, Herr Schliemer . . ."

"No, it is an interesting story. I used to goad the pony with my whip, and no matter what I did, no matter how hard I hit its flanks, it would not follow my lead. After hitting it for a month or two, I learned a lesson. Do you want to hear what the lesson was?"

"I regret, Herr Schliemer . . ."

"No, the lesson I learned was quite simple. I learned the animal was a pony. You're smiling, but it is more profound that you might at first realize. Why was I beating it for being a pony? Did I expect it to be a race horse? Once I understood its nature, I stopped beating it altogether. We got along much better afterwards. We came to an understanding. It was an interesting lesson for me."

"I'm sure it was," my father answered.

"Since then I don't allow ponies to be beaten in my presence . . . not because I worry too much about a dumb animal, but because I am pained by how stupid a man looks trying to whip a pony into a race horse."

Never before had anything like this occurred in the lodge! Never had I seen my father bested in such a manner. Herr Schliemer was shrewd; he was a guest and could not be contradicted. His size, also, prevented any thought of retaliation.

My father pulled the hem of his tunic and bowed, then turned and left the room. Herr Schliemer returned the bow, but it was lost on my father's back.

"I hope I haven't caused you more trouble," Herr Schliemer said when my father has passed into the kitchen. "These things don't go away, I suppose."

"I doesn't matter. Thank you, Herr Schliemer."

He smiled. I felt very warmly toward him in that moment. The sun hit him squarely in the face and he squinted at the light. He seemed amused, not at my expense, but at life in general and the silliness of what he saw around him. For the first time I envied him his size. It seemed to place him higher above life than any one I had encountered.

"Now, perhaps, you can do me a favor, William," he said. "Madam Lacome is waiting for her breakfast. Would you ask your mother to send up a tray? Maybe you could bring a tray to her yourself. I'm sure she'd appreciate that."

"Certainly, Herr Schliemer."

"I'm going for a walk. Afterwards, shall we check Sasha?"

I nodded and went to the kitchen. Fortunately my father had already gone outside. From the vacuum of silence he left, he apparently departed in an angry state. Eva and my mother busily washed sheets from the departed guests' beds. When I told them Madame Lacome desired a breakfast tray, my mother threw her sheet down and wiped her hands on her apron.

"Breakfast was an hour ago. I don't have time to make special meals for every guest in the lodge. Oh, what's the use? Eva, put together a tray. You'll find some rolls left over... in there, right there. Give her some coffee and that's all. She'll have to be satisfied with that."

I waited for the tray and pretended to be doing Eva a favor by offering to carry it upstairs. Despite her annoyance, my mother supervised the preparation of the tray, scolding Eva when she did not fold the napkin properly.

When the tray was ready, I carried it carefully through the sitting room. I looked for my father, afraid he would see me doing women's work, but then realized he had received a large tip just that morning and was doubtless in town with his companions, probably treating them to drinks. He would not return until late. It was a relief to have him gone.

Madame Lacome was still in bed when I knocked and entered with her tray. The curtains were pulled back and the room was bright and sunny. Herr Schliemer must have readied the bedside table before he came downstairs, because she motioned for me to put the tray beside her within easy reach.

She was, to my surprise, a normal sized woman—perhaps even slightly smaller than an average woman. Because of her association with Herr Schliemer, I had expected her to be large, but she was small-boned and delicate, with sharp, slightly rodent-like features. Her front teeth were too prominent; her eyes set too narrowly. Her skin was dark, baked, it seemed, not from sun, but from an inner heat.

Her manner, however, was light and airy, almost festive in the first few minutes of our meeting. I was convinced she remained in bed not out of laziness, but from an appreciation of the sunlight and warm quilts. Life would not run away with her; she would take it in proportions, and in a tempo, appropriate for her.

"You must be William,' she said as I crossed the room with the tray. Her voice was tinged by an accent, which I assumed was French. "Right there is fine ... not too close, dear, I don't like the smell of things so early in the morning. You are the Colonel's son?"

"Yes, Madam."

"Herr Schliemer has already met you, but I haven't had the pleasure. You're better looking than your father. Much better looking."

I placed the tray on the table without making any reply. I might have been embarrassed that she was still in bed, but somehow her manner made such feelings impossible. Besides, her shoulders were covered by a sort of bed jacket, which effectively obscured the outline of her breasts. And clearly, she saw no cause for embarrassment herself.

She took her cup of coffee immediately. She held it between her palms and warmed herself with it. She closed her eyes when she sipped it, then lowered the cup carefully.

"Be very careful about the first thing you take in the morning. Your entire day will be built around it. Or is that too silly for you?" she asked, watching me intently.

"I hadn't thought about it."

"Well, then, what have you been thinking about?"

I had fallen prey to the question Herr Schliemer had warned me about. Yet it wasn't a trap at all—she appeared genuinely interested. When I stumbled over the answer, she placed the coffee cup beside the rolls on the tray and asked for my hand.

"Oh, you're very shy, aren't you, William?" she said when I hesitated. "Shyness is much under-valued . . . very much. Shyness simply means you are able to view the consequences of your actions. The most disastrous consequences, true, but at least it suggests you are willing to make a leap ahead and consider the feelings of others. It speaks of imagination, and imagination is the beginning of compassion."

She reached for my left hand and brought it to her lap. I was too intrigued to consider not giving her what she requested. She held my hand between hers—much as she did the coffee cup—then gently massaged the bones and muscles along my palm. She did not look at my hand; in fact, she did not look at any place in particular, but stared ahead, her breathing becoming slower.

Had Eva burst in, or worse, my mother, I would have been mortified. I must have looked a fool standing beside the bed, my hand in Madame Lacome's lap. But the warmth of the room, the gentle push and pull of her fingers, made me very peaceful. Indeed, I felt drowsy; my knees felt weak and I wondered if I would be capable of standing much longer beside the bed.

"Do you see this X in the center of your palm? That is the mark of Christ . . . his hands were pierced by nails, as you know. I've met only one other man who possessed such a mark. He was a doctor in Budapest . . . his name isn't important. He died ten years ago, maybe more. He was the most successful doctor in eastern Europe . . . royalty vied for his attention, but he was only one man and insisted that his patients, when possible, wait their turn. He never knew he possessed the gift. He believed his medical knowledge was the cause of his success. But his mark was not as deeply cut as your own. . . .what a doctor you could be!"

"Are you sure?"

"Sure? Don't be stupid, William."

Madame Lacome dropped my hand and took a roll from the tray. Her features became more pinched as she thought and chewed. Her table manners were not good. She chewed with her mouth open and covered the bread with large swipes of butter. She drank coffee to help her swallow, something my mother found abhorrent in anyone.

"I am thinking of a way to tell you this so that you will understand. All right, here then," she said, waving her knife. "Do you know how to play chess?"

"A little."

"But you know the relative value of the pieces? Sit down for a moment."

I sat across the room from her, but she laughed and told me to bring the chair closer. I nearly told her about my mother's orders not to move the furniture, but decided against it. As I moved closer, she filled her cup once more with coffee.

"At any time," she began, "the world is filled with black and white pieces. Each color has approximately the same number. The pawns are mostly money men—bankers and the like—who realize they have a certain power, but only respond to a world created by others. Nevertheless, a pawn is a great deal more powerful than the average man or woman. You will run into one or two in a lifetime, and you'll know them by the effortless way money comes to them.

"There are other pieces, like yourself, who occupy the second tier. Rooks, bishops, even the queen and king . . . the actual rank means little. Say there are eight—if we stick to chess—for each color in each generation."

"And I am a white piece?" I asked.

"Yes, of course."

'Where are the other white pieces?"

"Who knows? Maybe in Asia. Maybe India. This is just one corner of the world, remember."

I smiled. The entire idea seemed silly to me. I smiled because

I enjoyed listening to her, and because she talked to me as an equal. I was cynical about her ability to tell fortunes—mine in particular—yet I found it very shrewd that she had granted me a gift. I possessed no such thing, but it was intriguing to feel her manipulating me. I smiled again. My smile was the smirk of one who discovers how a trick is done after all. One is entertained, but it is the unraveling of the trick, rather than the trick itself, which is enthralling.

She smiled back, but it was a smile unlike any I had ever seen. It was superior; it suggested that I did not know what was in store for me. The smile frightened me and I found my own cheeks becoming tight.

"We'll talk about this again, William," she said. "Now leave me so that I can dress."

I removed her tray. I thought to rearrange the chair, but my hands were already full and Madame Lacome said Herr Schliemer would attend to it.

In the kitchen my mother took the tray without a word, scraped off the plates, then ran everything under water. She had already begun lunch—a soup made from the leftovers the night before. Through the windows I watched my father removing the last grapes from the vines of our vineyard. The grapes, sweetened now by frost and a full season, would be used for eiswien. It surprised me that he had not yet disappeared into town.

"Don't you have chores to do? We have guests coming tomorrow," my mother said.

"I'll get to them."

"Stay clear of your father. He was in quite a mood. Did you cross him?"

"No, not really."

"I sent Eva to the market. Herr Mueller will pick her up when he returns. Don't disappear . . . we'll need your help."

I went out the back door and hurried to the barn. I did not want my father to see me, but I could not risk ignoring my chores. Fortunately my father was talking to Marcus Leitle, our neighbor, whose vineyard abutted our own. I saw Marcus bring a bottle to his lips, then pass the drink to my father.

I caught a quick glimpse of the dogs and was satisfied to see

Sasha's bandage still in place. The dogs ran to the fence at the sight of me. I told them to be quiet, then ducked into the dim barn. I closed the door behind me, pleased to be alone. Herr Schliemer was nowhere in sight.

The barn was large as country barns go. Old harness and tack hung from the walls, most of it in poor repair. An ancient anvil stood in the center of the barn, but it was used only when the blacksmith came to shoe the horses or to sharpen the lances. Except for the front portion where we kept the car parked when it was not in service, the barn was taken up by our horses. We stabled eight. My father's horse, King Arthur, was the pride of the lot. The rest were reserved for guests. They were poor mounts, bought from the army after hard use, and they frequently did not last more than two seasons before they died and were replaced by similar hacks. Kase, our dray horse, was kept in a stall by himself. He was a tired, comfortable old horse, who was seldom called on to work except on hunt days.

I skirted Herr Schliemer's trap and went about my chores. I raked out all the pens and carried the soiled hay around to the manure pile at the back of the barn. I pumped fresh water into the drinking trough, and spent a few minutes cleaning the drain so that the water would remain clear. Afterward, I curried the horses, giving special attention to Herr Schliemer's mare. She had not been thoroughly combed in some time, and her tail was matted with manure and loose bits of hay.

When I finished, I climbed to the loft and used a pitchfork to toss down fresh hay. The horses became skitterish at the sound of the hay falling, but their appetites soon won out over the apprehension. They began to eat in long, soft crunches, which were somehow matched by the grate of the fork's prongs against the dry rafters of the loft. I was careful to sprinkle the hay so that it would not fall on their backs and undo the work I had just completed.

I was still up in the loft when Herr Mueller returned with the car. Eva held the barn door open for him while he backed the car inside, his head out to spy any misplaced farm equipment. His cheeks were red; I suspected he had stopped several times on the way back from Salzburg.

I descended from the loft as they came to a stop. Eva, climbing from the car, wore her finest clothing. She was evidently worried the barn mud would stain the hem of her dress. She bunched her skirt in one hand and did not move without first inspecting the ground in front of her. She took large steps toward the barn door and only halted when she was free of the mud. She resembled a woman relieved to have gained the far shore of a stream.

"There's shit in the city too, Eva, and you won't be able to step around it, I assure you," Herr Mueller said as he climbed out of the car. "She was talking with that banker, Miklas, when I drove up, William. Did you know Eva had such an interest in financial matters?"

"Herr Mueller, you're not a gentleman," she answered, enjoying his linking her with the banker, a man we all knew to be single. She let her skirt drop after looking in a circle around her.

"Was the banker telling you how to invest? Or was he interested in making a deposit of his own?"

"You're horrible," she said, laughing.

"I've been through it all, Eva, and come out the other side. He has eyes for you. Play your cards right and you'll have him. I don't know why you'd want him when you have William and me around, but some people prefer a chicken when there's steak on the table."

Herr Mueller opened the trunk and told me to begin unloading. I handed some of the lighter packages to Eva, who seemed reluctant to fill her hands while the question of her skirt remained open. When I gave her a last package, she clamped it to her chest and walked to the back door.

In the meantime Herr Mueller lit his pipe. Smoking was not allowed in the barn, but because he stood near the doorway, leaning on the fender, he wasn't worried. I smelled alcohol as I passed him.

"William, you would not believe what I saw in Salzburg," he said, looking out at the hillside. "The Nazi are everywhere. You can't have a coffee in a cafe without watching three grown men click their heels at one another, shouting, 'Heil Hitler' to impress the ladies. You wonder that they don't see how ridiculous they look. But who am I? I was ready enough to go in the first World War. As long as men can wear uniforms, there will always be fighting."

"Were they everywhere?" I asked, interested because the idea of being a soldier appealed to me.

"Ach, everywhere! You turn around and suddenly you realize the man in a uniform was a barber the day before. Now, pffft, he is a sergeant. The next one, a baker, is in charge of twenty men. It's a masquerade ball, that's what it is."

I had no real opinion on this; I was too young and far too rural. I had listened to a few of Hitler's speeches on the radio, and a number of my schoolmates where already members of the Hitler youth, but we were relatively untouched by the Anschluss that had taken place in March. Austria was now called a "province of the German Reich" which caused some grumbling in parts of our town, rejoicing in others, yet these machinations seemed distant affairs to a boy living in a hunting lodge well up in the mountains.

Herr Mueller, however, wasn't quite finished.

"Don't go to sleep, William. Things are moving around you, things that will pull you in if you're not careful. Man is a wonderful creature, but men...collectively, William, men have no minds. Now is the time when a man has to separate himself and take everything into consideration. A nation can't return your life once it's gone."

"Will they come into our village?"

"Everywhere. Don't delude yourself. The Germans want war. The munitions manufacturers will get rich, the poor will die, and then, if you survive, you'll be sent back to this village. But you won't bring all of yourself back . . . no one does, William. That's the lie."

I had never heard Herr Mueller speak on such topics before. He rarely spoke about his own participation in the first World War, though he had clearly taken a stand against warfare and arms in the years since. My father, on the other hand, was intrigued by the Nazi and on the few occasions carloads of German officers stopped for lunch or an early dinner, he played up to them, bringing them bottles of wine in an effort to be included in their fellowship.

I finished loading a wheelbarrow with groceries and pushed it past Herr Mueller into the sunshine. I glanced up the hillside and was pleased to see my father had departed. I was free until the evening meal. Herr Mueller followed me out and, at my request, took a quick look at Sasha. Afterward he disappeared to his shop for a nap. I pushed the wheelbarrow to the kitchen door and carried the groceries inside.

"How rich is this Frau Halder?"

"Very rich, I suppose. I don't know exactly."

"I will give you a handbill to bring to her later. Herr Schliemer usually takes care of our advertising, but I've found it's better if someone from the village itself delivers the information . . . . a neighbor is more easily trusted. Besides, Herr Schliemer has the unfortunate talent of making people uneasy. He's aware of it, so don't think I am speaking behind his back."

"I understand."

"Her husband died? How long ago was this?"

"Six or seven years. I could ask around town and find out."

"Yes, do that, William. Find out how he died as well. Find out everything you can, but please don't be obvious."

We sat in the dining room. Madame Lacome was enjoying a late afternoon tea beside the fire. She had a large appetite for such a small woman, but her eating seemed as much a product of nervousness as true hunger. Eating gave her something to do with her energy.

I had spent nearly an hour with her and was entirely enchanted. I was aware that her purpose in talking with me was not pure; she had guided me slowly through local history, asking after family trees, finding out who had died and from what cause, where there was bad blood between relatives, and so on. Her memory was remarkable. Not once did she confuse names or familial associations. Indeed, she corrected me on several matters, remembering accurately that this or that woman, already mentioned, had a sister who lived in this or that town.

She made no notes, but even while eating I saw her filing information away, doubtless storing the past against a time she would be called on to tell the future.

The afternoon had grown dark before Herr Schliemer returned. He came in through the front door, ducking into the sitting room while he arranged his clothes around him. He bowed slightly to us both.

"Where have you been?" Madame Lacome asked him as he came closer. "Did you have a good walk?"

"Yes, the hills are quite lovely. I didn't go far. . . just up to the crest of the nearest mountain, near the monastery. It began to turn cold . . . there seems to be some weather coming in."

"Herr Schliemer never feels settled in a place until he knows the back roads," Madame Lacome said to me. 'He is like a rabbit in that regard. He likes to know there is a way to escape even if the main hole is blocked."

"A habit . . . ." Herr Schliemer said, sitting carefully on a chair beside the table.

"A useful one. William, take it as a lesson. Only fools believe they can go out the same way they entered. Now listen, Herr Schliemer, William has been telling me all about the people of this town. We shall try to wring some schillings out of Frau Halder. She's rich and doesn't need half the money she possesses. I think a seance, don't you? She is attached to the memory of her husband."

I was shocked that Madame Lacome could scheme so calmly in front of me. She saw the look of disdain on my face and laughed. Herr Schliemer smiled. They glanced at one another, then both leaned closer, as if they could not wait to hear my objection. This will be rich, they seemed to say, and I found myself rearranging my words before they left my mouth.

"I didn't tell you all this so that you could use it against people," I said, though I knew this was not entirely true. "Even Frau Halder . . . yes, she's rich, but she doesn't deserve to be taken in."

"Do you think she became rich by giving her money away to the poor, William?" Madame Lacome asked. "I didn't know the man personally, but I'm sure from what you told me that her husband sucked the blood from a hundred men to harvest his lumber. When we call that business the name makes it honorable, is that it?"

"He paid the men wages. They had a choice."

"And so will she! It is commerce, nothing more. We will offer her certain opportunities, and she will either accept or decline our services. We will sell her a few ideas, that's all. We could not take everything from her even if we wanted to. People have a limit to what they will believe."

"I won't take part in it."

"You already have. Now, you are thinking perhaps you should tell someone, but part of you is ready to admit that Frau Halder is a useless woman who doesn't deserve to hold onto such wealth. If it helps you to think of it this way, consider it a form of natural selection. You hunt, so the concept is not foreign to you. Only a child thinks it's cruel when the lion pulls down the lamb."

"How will you do it?" I asked, intrigued despite myself.

"There are a hundred ways to take money from a person who hasn't earned it. The poor are a different matter. They have earned their money, but seldom believe they deserve it. It shouldn't surprise you that many of the poor are happy to be quit of it. But let me ask you a question since you are indignant about our plans. Are you positive we will not offer Frau Halder an opportunity to converse with her late husband?"

"He's been dead seven years!" I said, feeling a tightness in my voice and the echo of my own inexperience in debate.

"I might argue that the illusion is everything, but what if it isn't an illusion? Suppose we can find a way to let her talk with her husband?"

"You see," Herr Schliemer said calmly, "Madame Lacome is a medium as well as a fortune teller. She is quite famous. She has written books on the subject. I assure you she is not a table-knocker . . . . nothing as tawdry as that. She is an artist, if you will. The effects of her séance are genuine."

I smiled—probably from nerves—because I could not accept this. Madame Lacome smiled in return, but once again it was a superior smile, one which indicated her knowledge of the subject was greater than mine. For his part, Herr Schliemer sniffed and rubbed his nose. He seemed indifferent; I could believe what he said or dismiss it, but he would argue no further. Nevertheless, even in his short sniff there was a note of derision that I should be so firmly fixed to my beliefs.

I tried to collect myself. For some time we sat in silence and watched the room grow darker. No one had ever demanded that I examine my beliefs before, and my attempts at doing so were extremely tentative. Each time I approached their way of thinking, I was distracted by the seediness of their dress. I had not noticed before how badly worn was Madame Lacome's dress; neither had I noticed how hastily coifed was her hair. Similarly, Herr Schliemer's suit was badly stained. Raw stitches held together the material over his right knee, and his cloak was tattered near the edges. Their appearance, collectively, made me suspect them. I wondered if I was being tested to see if I would make a reliable informant; I wondered if they had not carried out the exact same conversation before, preying on the gullibility of country boys like myself to aid them in their tricks.

We were at an impasse. I wanted badly to be let in on their secret, especially whether or not they themselves believed Madame Lacome might raise Frau Halder's husband, but it was not the moment. Madame Lacome arranged for me to carry the handbills around town after dinner. Herr Schliemer went upstairs and returned with a packet. He handed it to me and asked that I retrieve as many as possible. Printing was expensive, he said. I told him I would do as he asked, but at that moment I was not sure if I intended to deliver the bills at all. I knew I could not bring them to my father or allow my mother to see them; if they discovered I was going about town dropping off advertisements for our guests, they would blame me while maintaining a polite distance with Madame Lacome.

I tucked the packet under my sweater, said goodbye to them both, then went into the kitchen. I felt nervous, yet oddly exhilarated. Fortunately Eva was alone in the kitchen; I am not sure what I would have done if my mother had been present. Eva was busy preparing trays of table settings for the evening meal. She arranged the silverware silently on the trays, and from this I knew my mother had gone off for her afternoon nap.

"Have you been talking to them all this time?" Eva asked in whisper, nodding at the sitting room. "They're a strange pair. Are they man and wife?"

"I don't think so."

"Don't tell your mother, for God's sake. She would kick them out tonight if she knew. What are they doing here, anyway? That man looks like a huge steer...and the woman, the woman is a nasty little thing, isn't she?"

"Madame Lacome is a fortune teller."

"I know that," Eva said, exasperated at my slowness. "But why here? It's not as if there's money to be made in a town as poor as this one. We all know our fortune if we stay here. We'll work, drink too much, and die. You too, William, if you're not careful."

"If you hate it so much, why do you stay?"

"Where else do I have to go? You're not a woman, so you can't understand. Men can pick up and go. Women, well, it's different for a woman, although I won't say I'm not tempted. You won't see me sell myself short though. I have one chance at making my life comfortable, and you can bet I won't squander it."

"You mean your banker?'

She shrugged and continued setting out the silverware. I stood by the fire and watched her. She knew I was attracted to her—as most men were—but she was charitable enough to permit me to look without reprimand. She was like a school teacher in this regard; I might look and dream, but, for her part, it was merely a lesson

"You still haven't told me why they're here," she said, leaving the table and going to the stove. "Are they in hiding?"

"I think they're travelers."

"Travelers at the toe of a boot. Mark my word, there will be trouble before everything's finished. Some people carry it with them. Do you know the woman, your Madame Lacome, ordered a whole new set of clothing at the tailor's? No word of how she might pay for it, of course. And not a cheap dress. . . Helmut must order the material from Salzburg, and the cloth must come from the center of the bundle, not where the sun had bleached it a weaker color."

Hearing Eva recount this made me more uneasy than I had been before. The packet beneath my sweater seemed an enormous burden. I wanted to turn around and put the handbills in the fire. It would have been easy to do. I could have lied later and told them I had delivered them all. By the time they discovered my deception, they would be on poor terms with my father, and, if Eva was to be believed, with the town in general. Or perhaps they would never discover the deception at all, and simply believe their services held no interest for the townspeople. Either way I would be free of the obligation.

But then I remembered Herr Schliemer coming down the stairs that morning, his careful words to my father, and I thought better of them both. It would be easier to trick my father and mother; both would be occupied with the new guests. If I delivered the bills as I promised, and neither of my parents visited the town in the next few days, the matter of who delivered the bills would pass from memory.

I calculated all this quickly. At any moment I expected Eva to spy the lump beneath my sweater, but she was occupied with the pots on top of the stove.

I needed to hide the handbills regardless of what I decided to do. I said goodbye to Eva and went downstairs to Herr Mueller's workshop. He was polishing the hooves of the stag he had finally finished; the eyes, at last, were set properly. He buffed the hooves with a soiled cloth. He flicked the cloth back and forth, only occasionally stopping to apply more wax. In the moments of silence between his buffing, I heard coal ticking in the tile stove and the light scattered running of the beetles inside the wooden cabinet.

"It's you," he said, looking up and then bending closer over the hooves. "If I can get this finished and crated, I'll need your help lifting it into the car. Maybe I should crate it outside... Yes, I'll do that. I don't want to fight the box up that narrow stairway."

As casually as I could manage, I asked, "Herr Mueller, may I leave something down here with you? It isn't large."

"I don't see why not."

"I wouldn't want my father to find it."

He looked up. I was being too dramatic, but now that I had said it in such a manner, I saw no way to retreat. He did not move his eyes away from me. I sensed that he was judging whether this was a boyish request or something more important.

"Everything considered, that's probably a wise decision," he said. "Do you want to tell me what it is?"

"I'd rather not."

"Put it in that drawer in the first bench," he said, pointing to a drawer where he kept his tools.

"He won't go in there. If I have to go in it, I won't look ....you have my word."

I opened the drawer. Herr Mueller watched me draw the packet from beneath my sweater but said nothing. I wedged a few tools on top of the envelope, which would at least make it difficult for anyone to open it. Finally I closed the drawer.

Herr Mueller resumed buffing the hooves.

'I'll take it out this evening,' I said.

"Suit yourself. I'll guard it with my life."

"It's not as important as that," I said, smiling.

"Turn on the radio while you're here, William. It's almost time for my opera."

I did as I was told, then sat on the corner of his bench and watched him work. The stag standing above him looked quite real. He worked with his head near the animal's mouth, as if listening to the beast's breathing.

After dinner I retrieved the packet and began my walk into town. I took a path through the vineyard, which was the most direct means of entering the village. The trail was hilly; fog already covered the fields and it made the rocks and grass slippery under my feet.

The vines were picked clean; straw was scattered around the base of each plant. Here and there I found a strip of white cloth attached to the wires supporting the plants. The cloths fluttered close to the vines to keep the crows from ruining the crops, but I knew it was a poor trick. A few of the larger vineyards routinely set off explosions to make the birds nervous, yet even this only made the crows swoop up for a moment and descend again like a net of ash.

It was a full kilometer into town. I walked carefully, afraid of encountering my father. He had not yet returned to the inn. He would be drunk by now, I realized, and he was a man to avoid when he had been drinking. But I heard nothing. Had it not been for my mission, which I was still reluctant to undertake, I might have enjoyed the walk. The moon was bright, though not quite full, and the land smelled of frost.

I became more cautious as I entered the final vineyard bordering Reitlinger's heuriger. The back of the heuriger was empty; benches and tables, set at an angle to shed the winter rains, were abandoned haphazardly around the garden. The path continued straight through the garden, passing close to the frosted windows behind which the guests were now drinking, and then onto Krotenbachstrasse on the other side. I could not chance the light, so I crept close to the wall at the far side of the garden and made my way into the village center.

Once arriving there I felt paralyzed. Did I simply go door to door with the handbills? Was I to slip them under each door and then dash to the next? Or—more likely—did Madame Lacome expect me to knock, hand the bill to the resident, vouchsafe an endorsement, then move on? I knew without question that I could not approach Reitlinger's dining room, because my father undoubtedly would be there, holding court by the large fireplace.

In the end I fashioned a plan of compromise. I would slip a handbill under each door, knock, then flee before I was required to answer any questions.

This was not easily accomplished. At the first house, owned by Herr Sammler, I was nearly nabbed before I made good my escape. At the next a dog was whistled up and pounded to the door at almost the exact instant I slid the bill over the sill.

Nevertheless, I made my way down Krotenbachstrasse without serious incident. I knew the street as only a boy raised in a place can know a street, and it was a fairly simple matter to pause in a hedge, or duck under a low tree for cover. Gossling an der Ybbs was not a large town, and it took only a half hour to canvass both sides of the street. I gave some thought to nailing up one or two handbills in well-traveled places, but Herr Schliemer's injunction to bring back as many bills as possible stuck in my mind. Besides, if people did not read a bill delivered to their own home, what would it matter if it hung from a pole beside the street?

Out of conscience I skipped Frau Halder's residence. I circled back to it when I was almost finished, but I could not bring myself to run to the door. Though I knew she would find out soon enough—gossip leaking as it does through small towns—at least I did not deliver the bill myself. It was a shallow victory, but it preserved a line of moral behavior that I was not then prepared to cross.

The remaining handbills fit easily under my sweater. I tucked one edge of them into the belt of my pants and with this done found I could walk more naturally. I was no longer frightened of encountering anyone—except my father—and I decided to pass by the residence of Herr Oster, the schoolmaster, who kept a library of books which he permitted townspeople to borrow.

It was a short trip. His house was one of the few wooden structures in the village, but it had the advantage of being centrally located. Herr Oster was a bachelor; he was also a scholar, though not one of any repute. He was singular in the village for his devotion to learning and literature, and had achieved the nickname of "Bookmark" from students and parents alike. Talk followed him that he was engaged in writing a serious epic, much like Mann's "Magic Mountain", and he did nothing to discourage the rumor.

To arrive at the library, one had to walk through a small lane of hedges at the side of his house, ring a bell to let him know he had a visitor, then step into a glass porch where the books were stacked on raw wooden shelves. The volumes were badly affected by the weather, but Herr Oster often said books had a life of their own and it was up to them to survive. He attempted to keep track of the books, yet he made no demands that books be returned. You could keep a favorite novel for a week or a year and it mattered to him not at all.

On this night the light was on in the porch. Herr Oster appeared as soon as I rang the bell. He was dressed in an ugly smoking jacket that was several sizes too large for him. His hair was long; his complexion poor. Seeing me, he frowned. I suspected he hoped for female company, or at least an adult with whom he might pass a few words. Instead he was confronted by an old student, and an indifferent one at that.

"William, you're turning into quite a reader," he said, trying to cover the disappointment in his voice. "It's a pity your appetite didn't sharpen somewhat earlier."

"I suppose so, Professor."

"There's nothing new," he said, waving at the books. "Frau Feiling donated her son's primers. He's gone off to join the Nazi. You are a little old for primers, but we must have something here for you. Did you read the myths I lent you last time?"

"Most of them."

"Begin at the beginning, that's my advice. How did you find the myths?"

"I liked them very much, Herr Professor."

"Well, onto the next stage. Did you have anything in mind?"

"Not really. I was just passing by and I thought I'd see what was available."

He nodded and turned to the books. It struck me then, as it had before, that the books were his companions. He ran his fingers over the bindings of the books, as if touching them might bring forth a volunteer. If he had a system in his arrangement of the books, I could not perceive it.

"You must be careful to read a book at the proper age. Reading is like wine in that regard—though even that is too simple an analogy. The best books one can read four or five times at different periods in one's life and each time it is new . . . only of course, it isn't the book at all, but your own circumstances that are changed. For instance, I would be doing you a great disservice if I recommended, say, Balzac to you now. The taste of Balzac would be ruined for you. Let me think a moment. You might be ready for Dickens, yet even there we would be risking something. Certainly not Spenser, none of that. I might consider a Russian . . . but which one? The taste might be too rich."

While he roamed the small room inspecting each shelf of books, I noticed the handbill protruding from the pocket of his jacket. I should not have been surprised to see it, but it filled me with guilt nevertheless. I would have liked Herr Oster's opinion of the handbill—by our standards he was a man of the world and might have shed some light on the matter—yet there was no easy way to bring up the subject.

He eventually selected "The Last of the Mohicans." I was familiar with the title, if not the content, because some of the advanced students had read it for a discussion group. Bookmark told me to read it as an adventure story, nothing more.

"It will enchant you, William. It is . . . some say the greatest expression of Rousseau's philosophy, and I am leery on that count. Put it down at once, if you find it too much a labor, though I daresay you won't. It will reward you if you finish it, that goes without question."

I accepted the book and thanked him. He remained in the room, reluctant to leave, and tightened his jacket around him. It was cold enough to see our breath. I took a chance and mentioned what was on my mind.

"That handbill is all over town," I said, pointing to the crumpled paper in his pocket. "The woman is staying at our inn."

"This?' he asked, removing it. "Let me see. A fortune teller, is that it? Everyone wants to know the future. . .it's the final purpose of religion, William. Religion not only tells the future, it promises it. Very seductive all of this. Are you her agent in town?"

I nodded.

"Do you believe it's possible to tell the future?" I asked.

"No, not at all," he said, studying the handbill. "What I believe is that a woman like this . . . this Madame Lacome. . .is she French?"

"I think so."

He examined the handbill thoroughly, then spoke.

"She's a chimney, William. She enters a town and the smoke that lingers about will pass through her. An old woman will go to her to confess her sins, and a young woman will ask to find if this or that man is right for her. Maybe a man will want to know about his crops ... it's all very innocent, really. Of course, they'll come to hate her eventually because she'll collect too many secrets. But then she'll move on, won't she? It isn't a bad bargain."

"Then you find nothing objectionable in it?'

"Are you as sensitive as that, William? Really, I never took you as one for such delicate judgements. She won't wrestle any money away from people who are not willing to believe along with her. Belief at any price . . . well, it will be cheap at her prices, I'm sure. Don't worry yourself, William. You aren't responsible."

I nodded again, thanked him once more for the book, then left. He remained on the porch, the handbill still unfolded in his hand. I kept to the shadows and worked my way back to the vineyards. The night was growing cold.

The handbills had already pulled business to the inn by the time I returned from distributing them. It is a measure of how tedious a small town can be that the response was so immediate.

I learned of this as soon as I entered the kitchen. My mother sat beside the fireplace, a cup of tea in her lap. She dozed, but woke at once when I came through the door. She was in a generous mood, which was unusual for her on a night before new guests arrived; but her duties were finished for the day, the fire was warm, and she seemed happy to have some moments of peace before going to bed.

"Madame Lacome has been asking for you," she said without her normal venom. "She has guests. See what she needs, and make sure you keep track of what she orders. She is writing quite a bill."

I entered the sitting room eager to see who had nibbled at the bait. Two women sat in soft chairs beside the fireplace, talking to Madame Lacome. I knew the women, of course, though they were not women I would have suspected of harboring an interest in the occult. The women were sisters, the Brockdorf sisters by name, who lived in a sturdy house at the edge of Gossling. The elder sister, Anna, had disappeared on the arm of a man when she reached maturity, but she returned within a year with no husband and sordid rumors of a miscarriage. Sylvia, the younger, had never found a man; instead she was said to have flirted with the convent. Herr Brockdorf, the girls' father, had intervened by dumping a pail of water on a visiting priest, so that the priest might, like a dampened bird, be seen for what he was. Whether any of this was true was in many ways beside the point. The sisters were the type of women destined to remain together, and the appearance of a husband or even a calling to God, was only a temporary break in a life dedicated to each other.

Madame Lacome sat beside them drinking sherry. The sisters, obviously nervous, perched on the edge of their chairs listening intently. They started as I walked through the door. Sylvia smoothed her skirt; Anna tucked two strands of hair away behind her ears. Both appeared surprised to find themselves in such an intimate conversation with a stranger.

"There you are, William," Madame Lacome said, looking up and waving me closer. "This young man has been invaluable . . . you know him, naturally?"

The ladies nodded. I bowed slightly.

"William, would you be a dear and run upstairs to my room? I need my cards and my ball. Both things will be on the table ... you know the one. Go right up. Herr Schliemer is in town."

I went upstairs and opened the door to Madame Lacome's room. The room was in a poor state; it smelled musty and close; clothes had been left hanging over the backs of chairs. A few chocolate wrappers lay crumpled on the bedside stand. Again I was dismayed by Madame Lacome's slovenliness, for these were certainly her clothes and refuse. Herr Schliemer's belongings, in contrast, appeared carefully arranged in a small armoire on the other side of the room.

The cards and ball, however, were exactly where she promised them to be. I picked both up and returned downstairs, where Madame Lacome had moved to a table beside the window—the same table she had occupied earlier in the afternoon. The ladies had followed, though their uneasiness, if possible, seemed even greater than it had a moment before. They laughed with false gaiety at the smallest comment from Madame Lacome, doubtless to imply that they took none of this too seriously.

"Now we can begin," announced Madame Lacome when I

began across the room. “Bring everything here, William. You have the cards?”

“Yes, Madame Lacome.”

“Since you are my first customers in this town, I will use both methods . . . . the ball and the cards. You are probably wondering what are the advantages of each, but in fact there is little difference. Think of it as a man mowing a swatch of hay with a tractor. When he turns the mower, it’s necessary to overlap by a fraction in order to ensure he gets the second row started properly and to make sure he misses nothing. I accomplish the same thing by using both methods.”

She explained all this as she spread the cards on the table before her. Then, growing quiet, she rolled the crystal ball from its sack of silk. Watching her, I was ready to penetrate any tricks that might escape the Brockdorf sisters, but the crystal ball was more stunning than I had anticipated. It’s weight and solidness I already knew from carrying it down the stairs, but its ability to hold and, at the same time, shed light, was remarkable.

Using the silk sack, Madame Lacome made a nest for the ball directly in front of her. The firelight caught the crystal at once; more haunting was the gleam of moonlight—or at least an unexplainable light from outdoors—which turned the glass milky and silver. Incredibly, the ball seemed to take in its surroundings. Had such things been conceivable, I might have believed it altered its composition according to the room and light and people nearby.

“Beautiful, isn’t it?” Madame Lacome asked us, removing a fleck of dust from the crystal. “It has four sisters. Two were destroyed, but two remain. This is the youngest, though it is quite ancient in its own right. It was cut from a moonstone, and the story goes that it was buried in a box on a bed of human hearts. Gruesome, yes I know, but nothing is accomplished without sacrifice. Shall we begin?”

Sylvia Brockdorf looked uncomfortably at me. Had I not been so avid to watch, politeness would have demanded that I excuse myself at once. But I had no intention of volunteering to leave the room. Madame Lacome caught this immediately.

“I’m afraid,” she said, reaching across the table to pat Sylvia

Brockdorf's hand, "that he must stay. I understand your desire for privacy, but the crystal can not be used with an odd number of people. The cards, certainly. If you want to interview the crystal one at a time . . . then we can dispense with William."

It was shrewdly done. She had read their desire to be present together, while simultaneously rewarding my curiosity. Although I remained skeptical that she could tell the future, I had new respect for her ability to see through people. The Brockdorf sisters were badly overmatched. Madame Lacome gathered the cards and shuffled them, apparently indifferent to their response. She did this with all innocence, the weight of her stalling working only to confuse the sisters more than before.

The Brockdorf sisters conferred. Bending to whisper to one another—though how they expected to keep secrets from a fortune teller I hardly knew—they debated the propriety of allowing me to remain in the room. Price seemed a consideration, for Anna hissed several times: "Two readings, that's why." This statement wrung a nervous nod from Sylvia each time it was spoken.

In the end, however unhappy with my presence, they agreed to let me remain. Anna was not entirely satisfied; she smelled a hoax, or at least realized the terms of their reading had not been discussed, and proceeded to bombard Madame Lacome with questions.

Would Madame Lacome read from both the cards and ball for both of them? Were there additional fees, costs? Could they ask an unlimited number of questions? What guarantee of satisfaction did they have? The devil did not partake in these revelations . . . wasn't that so?

These questions were rattled quickly at Madame Lacome, with little attempt on Anna's part at civility. I knew, from growing up in Gossling, that this was a precaution against what fellow townspeople called "buying a pig twice." It carried with it no deliberate insult, but signified that they were reluctant to conclude a purchase before setting all the terms. Otherwise, it might be necessary to buy the pig twice—a circumstance that would satisfy no one.

Madame Lacome answered each question patiently, and even

reached across the table to pat Anna's hand now and then. I expected Madame Lacome to grow annoyed, but watching her from a slight distance, and with the benefit of our conversation earlier in the afternoon, I discovered that she was even now at work. What was a hand pat other than a chance for her to rub Anna's hand, checking for calluses? And indeed, each time Madame Lacome touched Anna's hand, I saw her fingers lightly brush against Anna's palm. It was done masterfully, with no possibility of getting caught, and it made me marvel that she had probably already subjected the women to a hundred similar tests. Rings, shoes, an earring, a charm bracelet—certainly there were clues surrounding each woman. The women would not be aware of them, no more than they would be aware of their noses, but not a thing was lost on Madame Lacome.

Anna finally exhausted herself of questions; she passed a look to Sylvia, who nodded shyly. Madame Lacome asked me to dim the lights. I complied quickly, though not without some cynical thoughts about how she might have doctored the table earlier in the day. I vowed to keep my eyes on her. I would not be distracted, regardless of what took place in the next half hour.

Madame Lacome began speaking before I returned to the table. In the dimness I was guided back to the table by firelight.

"I will use the Celtic method with the cards. . .the crystal needs no format. The cards, and even the ball for that matter, only provide a focus for our concentration. Think of them as tuning forks, forks which you can cause to vibrate by the power of your thoughts. There, sit now, William . . . your thoughts are needed as well."

Madame Lacome leaned forward and cleared her throat. She sighed deeply, then imparted the following message as if reluctant to speak of such a topic.

"I caution you both that there is no death in these cards ... spiritual death, perhaps, or a chance at rebirth, but do not be alarmed if the card of death appears. I may find death in your reading, but you will not discover it on your own. Do not interpret the cards yourself and do not jump to conclusions. Remember that your destiny is unraveling even as we speak, and that these cards are only signposts."

If her speech was somewhat melodramatic, it was also quite powerful. Her tone was modulated; it grew slower and more serious as she reached for the cards. I felt myself becoming apprehensive for the first time. The Brockdorf sisters, I saw, grasped each other's hand beneath the table.

I confess to feeling superior to the Brockdorf sisters, which was a sensation new to me. I was in on the trick, or at least I believed myself to be, and they were not. For the first time in my life I saw the nature of my village—the ignorance and unworldliness, the gullibility and desire to pierce the world's mysteries without individual effort—and knew that I might rise above it. This was not a simple emotion, nor did it come all at once, but it had its birth in that moment and did not leave me afterward.

Madame Lacome began to lay out the cards. I watched her, my eyes flitting to her hands, then to her lap which was pressed against the table. I granted none of her movements innocence. If there was a trick to anything she did, I promised myself that I would see it.

She began to speak. Her voice was careful, though not tentative. It reminded me—as I'm sure she intended—of a door slowly opening. She was drifting away from us, or at least peering into corners we could not see for ourselves.

"Anna, you are very tired . . . poor health, yes . . . you have been engaged in a labor, a very arduous labor, that has sapped your strength. You must give it up, or at least moderate your efforts. You are trusting your stamina, and it is not what it once was . . . do not refuse help when it is offered. Is that clear?"

Anna nodded. I almost laughed, the advice was so general. But Sylva leaned close to Anna and touched her sister's shoulder with such tenderness that I felt my laugh sink back inside me. A log snapped and I twitched at the noise.

"Oh, Sylvia, how dark your thoughts are. . .you worry, you worry constantly, and it is to no avail. Ask yourself next time why it is that you worry. . .what was ever gained or altered by worry? You carry a wound from your father . . . be careful of your money. You are tight on funds just now, and there are some bills, some outstanding bills that have begun to fret you inordinately. But money will come. . .do not be afraid to sell something . . . the sentimental value you attach to it is misplaced."

This went on. Only once did I see Anna's face appear puzzled by Madame Lacome's comments. The remainder of the time one or the other of the sisters responded with a short nod, indicating the message was clear and perfectly received. In fact, as Madame Lacome continued, a change occurred in the sisters' posture. Relief and calm touched their features; they leaned forward, not nervously, but comfortably, opening themselves to Madame Lacome's probing. She, in turn, became more confident. She began to guide them through a series of questions, never demanding answers but accepting those she received as stepping stones by which she moved to the next line of inquiry.

Madame Lacome's reading was impressive, but in no way was it extraordinary. She had won the sisters' trust, which in itself was an accomplishment, yet her comments remained decidedly general. Objectively, I saw that she had hit some nerves, but who could not surmise with some accuracy what the lives of the Brockdorf sisters might contain? They were village women with typical complaints; their lives were of sufficient dullness to make them wide to interpretation. It did not take a fortune teller to determine they were worried about funds, or weary from overwork.

It was at this moment, however, that Madame Lacome abandoned the cards and pulled the crystal ball closer to her. The air about us tightened immediately. Try as I might, I could not now watch for tricks or sleight of hand. The crystal captured my attention, and I found myself falling into the center of the ball. If that sounds peculiar, it was no less peculiar to me at the time. The weight of my thoughts, my consciousness, was drawn into the ball and imprisoned there. Perhaps it was a form of hypnotism; perhaps it was only my own suggestibility and my willingness to glimpse what the others glimpsed.

The Brockdorf sisters were likewise transfixed. I heard their breathing, though I did not look up at them. Yet—if this is possible—I was aware of their thoughts existing in the crystal beside mine. I had no clear understanding of where Madame Lacome might be, but I felt infinite trust in her combined with a profound embarrassment that my mind was open to her.

"You have come to me with a question and I will answer it," Madame Lacome said softly. "You wonder if you had a sister, the youngest of you . . . killed in infancy. This is a question that has remained hidden because you have been afraid to ask it. Are you sure you truly wish to know the answer?"

The Brockdorf sisters nodded. At their nod I felt an enormous weight touch my heart. The crystal's hold over me was broken, and I looked up in time to see Sylvia begin to cry. Madame Lacome stared at her.

"You had no other sister," Madame Lacome said to them both. "It was your mother's delusion."

Sylvia began to weep. Anna placed her arm around Sylvia's shoulders. I was not certain what had transpired. What sister? How could a child be a mother's delusion? But Madame Lacome interrupted my thoughts by sliding the crystal toward me, as much to wake me and bring me back to my senses and to get the ball away from her.

"Turn on the lights, William," she said. 'We've had enough for now."

It had ended too quickly. It was difficult to recover. I looked about the room as if seeing it for the first time. In contrast to the strength of my own feelings, Madame Lacome appeared quite clinical. She scooped the cards up, shuffled them quickly, then set them in a neat pile beside her. The crystal she allowed to remain uncovered on the table, but it now seemed an ordinary object.

I went about turning on the lights, though I looked frequently at the table. The Brockdorf sisters were overcome with emotion—an emotion which was, I realized, primarily relief. Sylvia was more distraught than her sister; she cried until she developed, ridiculously, a wave of hiccoughs.

Anna did what she could to comfort her sister. She kept her arm around Sylvia and gave her doses of water whenever Sylvia's erratic breathing permitted. Madame Lacome made no soothing comments, nor did she resort to reaching across the table to pat Sylvia's hand. Like a surgeon comfortable that her knife work was satisfactorily concluded, she left the healing to the sisters.

By the time I returned to the table, Anna was already reaching in her purse to make payment. She did this gladly, as though unable to believe her good fortune had been purchased as such a small price. Madame Lacome accepted her fee with disinterest, saying only that she hoped the ladies would recommend her to their friends.

Then it was over. The Brockdorf sisters stood, thanked Madame Lacome profusely, and left. I walked them to the door. Anna found a moment to make me promise that I would reveal nothing of what I had heard. I assured them I could keep a secret, then opened the door and let them out. Sylvia still hiccoughed on her way to the street.

"So now you have seen my profession," Madame Lacome said when I returned. "What do you think of it? Is it as sinister as you thought?"

"How did you know about their sister?' I asked with as much authority as I could summon.

"How do bees make honey?" she countered, reaching to collect the money for the first time. She handled the money expertly, with none of the awkwardness of those unaccustomed to bills and currency. When she saw I was unhappy with her response, she put the money before her and looked at me.

"Don't think the world is all gray and dull, William. You are too serious. You are worried about being tricked. The world is more magical than you admit. If you examined it, you would see that your belief in logic is the true absurdity. Besides, they paid happily enough . . . you saw that. Indeed they should have paid. Their mother wasn't deluded in the least. A child was born, but circumstances . . . poverty, really, and an unstable man, put an end to its life."

"Then you lied?"

"I selected a truth. There is a difference, which perhaps you will discover in time. I lied when I said they came with a question. They came to me with a burden and I relieved them of it. Don't you think that is worth the fee?"

"But they have a right to know the truth . . . and not one you selected."

"Oh, you're more childish than I realized. My gift, William, is to read the fortunes of people. But my greater gift is to distinguish between what is wanted and what is needed. One has nothing to do with the other in most cases. In an instant Sylvia has forgiven her father of a sin that haunted her for years. Yes, he killed the child, but now he himself is dead. The mother is gone. I selected an adequate truth for those sisters, just as we select truths for ourselves. You would do better, William, to look to yourself and cease worrying about your abstract notions of honesty and rightness."

Remarkably, Madame Lacome yawned as she concluded. Her fatigue and apparent boredom were so opposite to my own feelings that I couldn't speak. My tree had been given a good shake and I could think of no rejoinder. How blase she was about doing it! How immature she made me feel!

Unfortunately I compounded my feeling of immaturity by being peevish as she said goodnight. I hated myself for behaving in such a manner, but I couldn't help it. I sat silently while she collected her things, slipped the money in the bosom of her dress, then drained the last drops of sherry from her glass. When she began to the steps she reached to touch my shoulder, and, in an infantile gesture, I pulled away.

"Sleep on it," she told me. "You are one of the white pieces, and the game is already in progress."

She yawned again, waved softly, and climbed the steps.My mind was too filled for sleep. I lay in bed forming answers to Madame Lacome's statements, reconstructing the conversation until it came out in my favor. What advantage I sought I could hardly have said, but it was clear to me that I had been bested. Madame Lacome, while yawning, had provided me with more riddles that I could comfortably entertain, to say nothing of the puzzle created by her actual reading of the Brockdorf sisters. How was that to be explained? How had she known of the dead sister? Certainly nothing of that nature could have been detected by rubbing Anna's hand, or examining the ladies' shoes.

I lay in bed until the inn was quiet, but my room, near the attic as it was—with an angled ceiling and close, confining walls—fairly smothered me. My eiderdown quilt would not stay in place. Now a knee was exposed, then an ankle. I wrestled with the cover until I could no longer stand it.

Finally frustrated and increasingly restless, I sat up and began dressing. I would not have dared to take this step if I hadn't heard my father return an hour before. No singing or merriment marked his drunkenness; instead I could tell the extent of his drinking from the long pauses he made in climbing the steps, the slow jingling of his belt and coins as he undressed. He was very drunk, from my estimate, and the long watery rake of his breath that I now heard down the hallway confirmed the opinion.

I finished dressing and went quietly down the hallway. The rasp of my father's breathing was louder as I approached his door, but I moved beyond it on the tide of his great intake of breath, so that his sound drowned out any noise I might have made.

I kept my eyes on the doorknobs of each room. When I was a boy Herr Mueller warned me that a doorknob becomes an eye at night—doubtless a cautionary tale fabricated to keep me in bed—and it was an image I had never discarded. Even now, as I passed on tip-toe down the hall, I could not entirely ignore the notion that the doorknobs watched.

I knew the stairs well, which one squeaked, where one might step to be silent, and I was able to move quickly down them. Gaining the sitting room, I went at once to the desk where Madame Lacome had read for the Brockdorf sisters. I wanted to examine the desk without her nearby. If she had somehow employed a gimmick, I was certain I could find it. I did not intend to expose her—except to myself—yet I felt that there must be something in the configuration of the chairs, the angles of light, which had worked to her advantage. Doubtless she had chosen the table with care. Sitting in front of it, she had gained the history of our town from me; in the same position, she had seen through the Brockdorf sisters.

I pulled her chair out by lifting it clear of the floor and setting it down a comfortable distance from the table. I sat tentatively, worried that the chair would bray. But it was silent; indeed, the entire inn was almost completely silent. No noise came from upstairs. The fire, gone to ashes, sometimes snapped in the darkness, but these infrequent sounds only served to measure the stillness.

My nerves felt extraordinarily alive, as if I was in the process of doing something dangerous. I smelled the stale odor of the fire, but sensed also that it was cut by the sharp chill emanating from the sealed windows. The animal heads looked down from the wall, their furs darkened from years of smoke and dust. I was conscious, as I had never been before, of the expression on each animal's face. Here was a stag whose eyes were touched by terror; here a boar, defiant yet pleading, its last breath swelling the shape of its nostrils. Such expressions were not solely the result of Herr Mueller's art. I marveled that the animals had saved something of themselves throughout these many years.

After sitting quietly for a moment, I placed my hands on the desk before me and examined its lines. It was an elegant piece of furniture, a writing desk with a single drawer in the center. The drawer was kept stocked with stationary carrying the Czekeli coat of arms, but, as we were a hunting lodge, the stationary was seldom used. On this night, however, the drawer was empty. I peered into its deepest corners and found nothing at all, save a letter opener fashioned from a World War I bayonet. Letter openers of such a design were a common curio in Austria at that time, though I did not know this one.

I sat for ten minutes in the chair, my hands slowly taking in the dimensions of the table. I am not sure what I expected to find. Surely I must have realized no mechanical trick could give Madame Lacome the key to the Brockdorf sister's secret. And yet, as I remained in the chair, I felt a strange ability to concentrate. It might well have been my imagination, but I was conscious of the lives around me: my father with his bull's heaves and drunken murmuring; my mother's softer snores; and, beneath me, Herr Mueller sleeping peacefully on his cot in the basement. I was conscious of the house, its inhabitants, and that we were in some manner connected.

I was woken from this sensation—for it was very much like a

doze—by a sound in the kitchen. I stood carefully and looked around me. The room was dark; the kitchen door seemed a black rectangle. I squinted to see the furniture, then moved carefully across the sitting room. The hair on my neck came up; I held my hands in front of me, ready to attack or defend myself.

I was almost to the kitchen door, parallel to the fireplace, when I saw Eva and her banker friend, Sigried Miklas. I knew at once that I had blundered onto something I was not to witness. They sat at the kitchen table with only a corner of the surface separating them. Had they not chosen those particular seats, I would not have seen them at all until I entered the kitchen. But their positioning exposed them; they were, in fact, framed by the doorway communicating to the sitting room.

What I saw, naturally, was a late night exchange of sex. "Exchange" is the word that came to mind, because it was clear to me that Eva allowed herself to be fondled in order to gain an advantage over Miklas. She had reclined against the chairback, the buttons of her blouse loosened sufficiently to gap and uncover her breasts. They were ample breasts, and quite beautiful. The sight of them under Miklas's hand stopped me.

Miklas's other hand was equally busy under Eva's skirt. He leaned forward dangerously on his chair, apparently trying to accommodate the awkward angle he asked of his wrist. For an instant I almost burst out laughing, because he appeared a ludicrous accordion player, trying desperately to shuffle his hands in harmony.

I'm not sure how long I stood there before my presence alerted them. I made no attempt to hide, nor did I have the wit about me to retreat. It was Eva who saw me, but before her eyes took me in, I saw on her face an expression of complete resignation. It was a look she could not control; it was bored and empty, one that was given to the dark room from which I entered. Had Miklas seen it he would have been compelled to stop immediately in order to preserve his dignity. He seemed a clawing, absurd figure perched stupidly on his chair. But he was not meant to see the look. As it was, her expression, bland as meat, only began to sharpen when her eyes discerned my shape.

A mad scramble followed. She pushed down her petticoats and grabbed at her blouse. Miklas, wrenched from his pleasure, actually jumped to his feet and awkwardly lurched against the table. He brought his free hand toward her, as if ready to apologize, but she had already darted away, back to the darker recesses of the kitchen where she doubtless arranged her clothing.

Miklas saw me a moment later.

"I thought you were the Colonel, for Jesus' sake," he hissed nervously once he recognized me, at the same time combing back his hair. He was a good looking man, but unfortunately knew it. His reputation as a dandy—or as close to a dandy as our village could produce—was well deserved. He finally collected himself sufficiently to take the offensive. "What are you doing sneaking up on people? How long were you there, you little ant?"

"Not long," I answered.

"It's a disgusting thing to do, spying on people . . . get out of here."

"Bring him in," Eva said with surprising force. "I want a word with him."

Miklas patted down his clothing, then told me to enter. I hesitated. Eva, still buttoning her blouse, appeared around the corner and shook her head. Strangely, I saw that she wasn't angry. She did not even appear to be embarrassed, which was a remarkable thing in my experience. Her hands slowed on her buttons. She smiled at me.

"Come here and be sensible," she said quietly.

I stepped into the kitchen. Eva lit two candles and carried them to the table. Miklas continued to arrange himself and deliberately stayed away from the light.

"I thought it was the Colonel ... I swore he had a gun-in his hand," he continued to bubble.

"My virtue isn't the Colonel's business. It isn't yours either, William. Sit down. Miklas, stop being a jack-ass and sit. I warned you this was not the place for that sort of thing. If it had been the old lady, we'd have been in plenty of trouble."

I was aware, as I sat, of Eva's careful manipulation of Miklas.

I was aware, furthermore, that she had complete confidence in me. She knew I would not betray her, and she was correct. But Miklas knew nothing of the kind, and, oddly, I felt she was aligning herself with me. I understood what she was after with Miklas, and it was only this understanding that made her cautious with me.

"Now, I think this can all be forgotten quickly enough, don't you, William? Miklas, sit . . . . quit pretending you're the injured party. It's the woman who suffers in these instances. William, you wouldn't tell your parents what you saw here tonight, would you?"

"No, I don't think so."

"Think so . . . you little bastard," Miklas said, sitting finally. "I'll break your neck if you start any damn whispers."

"It isn't his fault you're such an animal, Miklas," Eva said coolly.

She sat down near me. I felt a blush begin that soon swelled into a hot band across my forehead. It was not entirely unpleasant. She reached one hand to Miklas and made a motion with her fingers to indicate she wanted something from him.

"Give me your wallet, Miklas," she said, her eyes on mine.

"I'm not paying that little ant a schilling. He can shout it at Mass for all I care."

"But I care," Eva said with such authority that I knew her command over him was unquestionable. "Are you going to employ me if I lose this position? William would be quiet even if we didn't pay him, but a favor deserves a favor. Now give me your wallet and quit being such an idiot."

He grumbled and protested a little longer, but the matter was settled. He made a mistake in not paying me himself, since Eva dug through his wallet with great relish. She paid me fifty schillings—an astonishing amount—and would have laid out more if Miklas hadn't grabbed the wallet back from her.

Afterward she asked me why I had come downstairs. I didn't know what else to say, so I told her I was hungry. She cooed over me, much to my pleasure and Miklas's discomfort, and insisted I eat something. She found a few pastries, then made an elaborate show of seating me comfortably and letting me eat while Miklas looked on with disgust. She was in a good mood; she had calculated, I'm sure, that her hold over Miklas was complete. He might have easily departed, effectively removing her leverage, but he remained and watched, only once demonstrating his impatience by glancing at a vest pocket watch.

She kissed me when she finished—something she had never done before—then told me to go up to bed. Miklas informed me once more that he would break my neck if he ever heard a single rumor of the night's events, but the wind was out of him.

I went upstairs and tried to sleep. Thoughts of the day would not stop. I tried to recollect how I had felt sitting at the desk, and how it was that I had sensed the others in the hotel around me. I tried to picture Madame Lacome exactly, but her face wouldn't come into focus.

Eva appeared an hour later in my room, flushed and heated. She knew I was awake; I did not try to pretend otherwise. She knelt by my bed and whispered, her breath and smell exciting.

"Half, don't you think, William? He'll propose soon enough, and when he does I'll pay you back . . . . but I need the money now to keep looking as he likes me. Where is the money?"

"Under my pillow," I said, reaching under it. I had no power to resist, even if I had wanted to.

She took half the bills, then slid the rest under my pillow. She paused, her face close to mine. She kissed me squarely on the lips. It was a good kiss, not rushed, not doled out to a young man. She flicked her tongue against my teeth and gums just enough to let me know this was a language at which she was a master. While she did it, she reached down on top of the blanket and stroked my penis. I flinched away, pushing down into the mattress, but she calmly kept her hand between my legs and waited for me to raise into her palm.

"You're on my side, aren't you, William?" she said pulling back from my lips but continuing to pet me. It wasn't a question. She ran her hand over me again, then once more, and finally pushed up to her feet. She said nothing else, but I listened to her steps until they disappeared into the kitchen.

After feeding the dogs early the next morning, I helped Herr Mueller carry up the stag he had readied for crating. The stag represented one of Herr Mueller's better efforts. The eyes glistened perfectly; a single vein across the muzzle worked backward to the jaw. He had captured the animal's quivering nature through a slight flex in the front legs, and it was impossible to look at the creature without imagining it bounding off.

It took some time to wrestle the stag up the small stairway leading from Herr Mueller's workroom to the plot of ground separating the barn and inn. The antlers proved to be wide and cumbersome; the wooden base, complete now with a plague indicating the animal's origin and the victorious hunting party's names, threw the animal off balance. Herr Mueller lit a pipe while he sent me around the barn to collect the wood needed for the crate. He was particular about the wood, and the crates in general, because, he claimed, they colored the client's perception of the final mounting. A poor crate could conceivably undo the work he had put into bringing the animal to life, and this he intended to avoid.

For this same reason, I was sent to bring fresh hay from the loft in order to pack the deer properly. While I carried three loads down the precarious ladder, Herr Mueller planed a piece of raw pine to get a bed of shavings. The shavings were unnecessary for packing purposes, but they left the animal with an excellent scent, and again reinforced the client's perception that he was receiving a work of quality.

None of this was discussed; I knew, from past experience, what Herr Mueller sought. Moreover, I was happy for the work, because it took my mind away from the provocative sensations of the night before. It was good to be outside on a warm fall day with solid labor in hand.

We worked together well. Herr Mueller required me to do most of the packing, since he felt, perhaps not mistakenly, that I was something of an apprentice to him. He knew, as I did, that my father would only reluctantly make room for me to work as a guide beside him, and taxidermy did not seem a bad alternative. My options in such a small town were limited, and Herr Mueller took a justifiable pride in teaching me a trade.

We built the base first, lined it with the pine shavings, then carefully constructed the crate around the upper portions of the body. I cut boards to Herr Mueller's specifications, then held them steady while he hammered each one into place. As each successive tier was completed, he supervised the final packing, testing the straw with his red hands to make sure the stag was supported without being crushed. Satisfied, he would have another go at his pipe while I prepared the needed lumber.

It required an hour to finish the crate. Herr Mueller left me while I hammered home the last nails. He returned five minutes later with a heated stencil he had fashioned some years earlier. He pressed the stencil against the wood and branded the name of the inn on the top and sides. Then, using black paint, we added their proper address, and marked that postage should be demanded on delivery.

My father came outside as we concluded these last steps. His face was red, his eyes close-lidded against the sunlight. He carried a shopping list from my mother, and one, not as extensive, for himself. He coughed and spit to one side as he came to a stop in front of us. He rubbed the back of his hand across his mouth.

"These are the things we will need from Salzburg," he said in the way of greeting. "The guests will arrive on the one-thirty train from Munich . . . four of them—two couples according to the reservation. Make sure you're not late."

"Of course not, Colonel."

"You have the stag ready? For Dr. Kapp's party?"

"Yes, the one you got up on the ridge just at sunset," Herr Mueller said, flattering my father slightly.

"Damn animal almost slipped away from us. It cost us a full day's hunt and we nearly came up empty. I thought the horses would collapse underneath us."

"It wouldn't be a hunt if the animals didn't try to escape," Herr Mueller said.

My father grunted. He moved slightly closer and I smelled alcohol still clinging to him from the previous night. He handed Herr Mueller the two lists and began paying out a stack of schilling notes. He was not comfortable handling money; he rubbed each bill between his fingers to check that he was not inadvertently giving Herr Mueller two bills instead of one. He stopped several times to add something new to the list, or to remove something he now considered superfluous, but it was obvious the true reason for his halting was his discomfort at parting with money.

"Try to get me three boxes of cartridges . . . .you know the ones. We should all say a prayer the army doesn't rely on shotguns," he said as he finished. He pushed the last bill into Herr Mueller's hand strongly enough to make Herr Mueller's arm nod almost to his waist. It was a way of declaring the worth of the stack of bills so that he and Herr Mueller would not argue about the change when Herr Mueller returned.

"Anything else?" Herr Mueller asked, tucking the bills in his pocket.

"It's all written down there. Make sure the car has oil. Try to get back at a decent hour."

He left a little while later, after passing a few more comments about the crate and the stag that had made the mistake of running for its life. He checked on the dogs, who met him with whines and barks, then went into the kitchen.

Herr Mueller and I were left to heave the stag into the truck of the automobile. We accomplished this with much backing and edging the car closer to the crate until the rear bumper scraped the wood. Herr Mueller made me place old burlap around the trunk of the car to protect it. I did as he ordered, then counted with him until we hit three, and lifted.

The crate went in unevenly, and there followed a few minutes of straining and cursing until we had it right. Herr Mueller spun against the car when we finished, breathing in short bursts as he leaned on the back panel. He rubbed his testicles openly and shook his head.

"The rattle's gone out of the castanets," he said and laughed.

"Are you all right, Herr Mueller?"

"You wouldn't believe it, but there was a time when I could have hoisted that crate into the car with you riding it. But these old castanets have sand in them. No more pebbles for me."

After rubbing himself a little longer, Herr Mueller went to the house to clean himself for the trip to Salzburg. He had been gone only a moment when Eva appeared at the back door, a shawl gathered around her shoulders. She stood for an instant to make sure the way was clear, then ran across the yard, pinching the ends of the shawl together with her left hand as she went. Her breasts bobbed up and down, a fact she was doubtless aware of, because she laughed as she came to a stop beside me and chucked me under the chin with the curled knuckle of her index finger.

"Good morning, William," she said, smiling broadly. She obviously felt we shared a secret. "Oh, you poor lamb, you don't look as if you rested at all. You look like you were awake all night."

"It's you who were awake," I said feeling surprisingly defensive.

"But it was worth it, wasn't it? Do you know that Miklas was so sorry for me that he gave me more money? I cried and carried on after you had gone—I know it isn't fair to do, but a woman's weapons. . . . Well, in a word, he is ready to marry me, I think. I am going to ask your Madame Lacome if the match would be wise. Do you really believe she can tell the future?"

"I don't know. No, of course not," I said, uneasy at suddenly finding myself Eva's confidant.

"Well, the Brockdorf sisters are going around town telling everyone who will listen that this Madame Lacome is the genuine article. They won't let on what she said to them, but they swear that her ability was uncanny. Miklas told me last night that the sisters were so unnerved by it and they went to see the priest to make sure this couldn't be sorcery. But you were there, weren't you? She's your great friend, isn't she?"

"She's not my friend. I hardly know her."

Eva looked at me strangely. I had trampled on her friendly nature without understanding why I did so. Nor did I know what made me denounce Madame Lacome so vehemently; I hated myself for betraying the strange woman. I pretended to push the crated stag into a better position in the trunk, while Eva stepped to one side and waited for Herr Mueller. She had money in her fist beneath the shawl and a small list for him. She moved into the corner of the barn to be out of the wind.

Herr Mueller returned shortly afterward. He wore a suit of city clothing topped by a small felt hat with a feather curling up from the hatband. He was in an excellent mood. He took the list from Eva and examined it. While he read she leaned closer and sniffed at him. Even from where I stood I could smell his cologne. It was powerful enough to cover the odors of the barn.

"What on earth do you have on?" Eva asked, still sniffing at him. "Did you empty the bottle on yourself?"

"Don't be smart, young lady. It's called *Midnight Waltz.* Why, don't you like it? It wasn't cheap."

His eyes were still fixed on the list. Eva leaned near him again and made a show of sniffing at him.

"I might like it if you stood upwind from me. You must be going to see your lady friend, in Salzburg. What's her name — Frau Schact, isn't it? Tell me, Herr Mueller, do you promise to be as gentle with the woman's heart as possible? It isn't fair—a man of your looks—to lead a woman on. Think how easily you could shatter the woman's health. And think of the difficulty she would have catching her breath with so much cologne about."

She finished by gently knocking her shoulder into his. Herr Mueller smiled and shook his head, continuing to pretend interest in the list. Despite my ill-temper I found myself smiling as well. Eva looked in my direction and quickly stuck out her tongue at me. She did this so happily, however, that I couldn't help smiling even more in return.

While I lashed down the trunk to secure the crate, she went over the list again with Herr Mueller. There was a question of ribbon; a second question of a scarf and they talked for a time about the proper color. Herr Mueller kept inching toward the car, nodding his head as he went, saying that he understood but that the stores would be closed if she did not let him depart. Finally Eva let him go. Herr Mueller backed the car out and waved at us. I smelled his cologne lingering in the air for a moment even after he had gained the dirt road. We were still standing together watching him when I heard someone knocking loudly on a windowpane. I expected to see my father calling me inside; or, at the very least my mother signaling for Eva to return. Instead, far up in the house, I saw Madame Lacome rapping her knuckle repeatedly against the windowpane of her dormer. Eva, turning to look, pointed to her own breast to ask if she was needed. Madame Lacome shook her head no, then, almost in the same motion, pointed to me.

"Your girlfriend," Eva whispered as Madame Lacome crooked her finger, telling me I was wanted immediately.

Madame Lacome's room was being transformed. Herr Schliemer stood in front of the largest window attempting to pin up a dark woolen blanket while Madame Lacome directed him from the center of the room. He made for a strange handyman. He could reach the highest portion of the window frame merely by going onto his toes, yet his tremendous size seemed too lavish for such a domestic chore. The hammer he held looked small in his hand and his lips, pursed as they were around a packet of nails seemed almost infantile.

If Herr Schliemer looked out of character, however, Madame Lacome appeared entirely in her element. Already she had rearranged the furniture. She had pushed the huge bed against the wall and dragged the armoire in front of it, effectively creating a small sleeping chamber sealed off from the rest of the room. The gateleg table was placed squarely in the center of the room, and was covered by a strange tablecloth of black and gold. The tablecloth's border was intricately designed with stars and signs of the zodiac, as well as one or two figures from mythology. I recognized a swan with a man's head, and a woman slowly being transmuted into a laurel tree.

"There you are, William," Madame Lacome said when I had been in the room for a moment or two. She had seen me before, and had even called for me to enter, but only now chose to acknowledge my presence. She possessed the air of a theater director, a woman willing to listen and converse, but only if it did not remove her attention entirely from the work on stage.

"Your Frau Halder has sent a message to say she would like an interview with us. We are invited to stop by immediately—the sooner the better, her note said. She merely wants to talk with me, but of course, once they talk, they bite."

"Frau Halder might be more difficult to persuade than that. She's tight with a schilling," I said, unwilling to have Madame Lacome so sure of her success.

"But, you see, she has already bought. She wishes to believe and I certainly won't do anything to dull that impulse. Why else would she send for me? Think, William. People give signs constantly to tell you what they will do. It's as accurate as a telegraph if you'll only listen. Now look, I've lost my concentration talking with you. Herr Schliemer, do you need William's help up there?"

"No, I have it," Herr Schliemer said, pinning the last of the blanket around the window. The room grew dim. Herr Schliemer took the tacks from his mouth and bowed to me.

I returned his bow.

"We'd like you to show us the way — and introduce us, if you would," Madame Lacome went on. "Perhaps I can arrange it so that you can watch. A seance isn't to be missed . . . . certainly not one given by an expert like myself."

"If you are going to Frau Halder's, why are you altering this room?" I asked.

"We're preparing it for others," Herr Schliemer said, his baritone calming. "Once the news of the seance spreads... well, you can imagine the appeal and the ensuing demand. Word will leak out that Frau Halder has engaged us. She's the most prominent woman in the town, isn't she? It's been our experience that it is best to have a room available. It's more private than the sitting room. People don't want their secrets known to every guest who stops here for the night."

I nodded, but I did not agree. I saw for the first time how badly they had misjudged our village. They were correct in thinking there would be some appeal, but it would not be large. A few old woman would call; perhaps, as Bookmark had suggested, a farmer would visit to ask about his crops. And yet as I watched them continue fussing around the room, I realized they prepared for a village some time in their past, for better days when the demand was greater for such services. They were like two once prominent actors preparing to put on a well known play on a small schoolhouse stage. They could not consciously admit the house was smaller; they could not acknowledge that the ticket sales were exceedingly slow and that perhaps their talents had been left behind. In just such a manner, it was necessary for them both to continue preparing the room in hopes of a sharp demand.

Finally Madame Lacome stopped.

"We should go. We'll walk slowly . . . through the vineyard, isn't it? I don't want Frau Halder to think she can simply summon me. It would leave the wrong taste," Madame Lacome said.

She plucked her long cape off a chair near the wall and swung it over her shoulders. Herr Schliemer, caught off guard by Madame Lacome's sudden decision to depart, put down his tacks and hammer and pulled on his long greatcoat as quickly as he could. In a moment we were out the door. Madame Lacome carried a knitting bag which she handed to me. It contained, I was sure, her crystal ball and tarot cards.

We went through the vineyard. It was not a pleasant day. The sky was gray; clouds covered the hillsides and seemed to spread their dullness to the trees. The weather proved oppressive to Madame Lacome. She was impatient with the walk. She did not realize it was this far, she said. Once we reached the village proper . . . was it far from there? Had she known there was so much mud, she informed us, she assuredly would have selected a different pair of shoes.

Her comments wore on me, but Herr Schliemer greeted them with solicitude. Was the pitch of the path too steep? He offered her an arm. Mud? He actually placed his foot on the edge of the muck so that she could use his instep for a stepping stone. She was, in every manner possible, a prima donna. I had never met anyone like her. I despised her, and yet felt it an honor to accompany her. No rational reason suggested why I should care what she thought of me, but I did.

We arrived at Frau Halder's large back door almost exactly at noon. The house was gloomy; the bushes and hedges in the yard poorly kept and overgrown. A few lights shone in the interior of the house, but these were hardly inviting. Frau Halder was notoriously parsimonious. Her miserliness radiated from her until it dimmed the household lights and allowed the paint on the facade's trimming to chip. For all of this, or perhaps because of it, she was the wealthiest person in our hamlet.

Herr Schliemer, at a glance from Madame Lacome, knocked loudly. The door was answered by Vicki, Frau Halder's lady companion. Vicki was fifty, gray, and quite severe. She wore a dark dress with a shawl knotted around her shoulders. Her mouth pursed instantly after she greeted us, as if she did not like our taste but was forced to swallow nonetheless.

"Frau Halder sent for us," I said as Madame Lacome's squeezed her fingers on my elbow.

"Come this way," Vicki said, giving Madame Lacome a long look of appraisal. She hardly looked at Herr Schliemer, although ignoring him could only be the most deliberate of acts.

For her part, Madame Lacome had grown silent. Her vitality seemed sapped by the cold walk down through the vineyard. I could not help wishing that Madame Lacome had made a better impression in that instant. She looked harried and ugly; she had made too great an effort over her vanity table and her make-up had turned her into something cheap. All of this was captured in Vicki's pointed glance.

We went down a long passage. Portraits covered the wall on either side of the hall; at the far end stood two country trunks for boots and jackets. The air was cold, and somehow unused. I noted that Madame Lacome, though not obvious by any means, paid special attention to the photographs she located on the walls. I had mistaken the nature of her silence; she was not depressed or sullen, but rather acutely engaged.

Vicki left us to wait in an ornate sitting room. I had been to the room once before to help my father deliver wood, though my memory of it was dim. The room smelled of smoke and cotton bottle-stops from the various medicines set out on a table beside the fireplace. In contrast to the hallway, this room was overheated and dense, the furniture ponderous and neglected. An old-fashioned globe stood in the center of the room, several cobwebs anchoring the surface of the planet to the brass stand.

I stood beside a large easy chair and waited. A clock chimed high up in the house; a chair slid across a wooden floor as someone cleared his throat. I attempted to read the book titles on a shelf behind me, but the room was too dark to see clearly and I was hesitant to move about while we risked a sudden entrance from Frau Halder.

Herr Schliemer likewise seemed willing to stand quietly and wait for Frau Halder's appearance. Madame Lacome, however, whirled about the room examining whatever came to hand. In other circumstances it might have been comical, but her attention was so concentrated, her appetite for detail so clearly insatiable, that it became almost gluttonous. Her hands were particularly greedy. She touched everything. Her fingers trailed the heavy curtains at the window, ruffled a basket of dried grasses, spread wide on the peeling floral wallpaper. A chair, a glass, an andiron, an ivory paperknife—and of course the pill bottles received her attention. She was not self-conscious about examining another's home while the owner was absent. Indeed, she even lifted things to her nose in order to have the house's scent.

At last I heard a shuffling sound from the hallway. Madame Lacome heard it as well and stopped her perusal immediately. Herr Scliemer straightened to his great height and stood quite still. A moment later Frau Halder entered the room, her weight divided between a knobby cane and Vicki's arm. Vicki motioned for me to make way. Frau Halder glanced at us both, but then quickly surrendered her attention to the navigation of the room.

I had the opportunity to observe her as she slowly crossed to her chair by the fire. She was old and hunched. Her head was covered by a sleeping cap, which had the affect of making her seem to have no ears. Indeed, the grayness of the cap blended with her frail skin and made her appear entirely bald. Her passage by me left the air coated with a weary fragrance—medicine, old cloth, worry.

She sat with a great deal of backing and nervous encouragement from Vicki. Her fall into the chair was surprisingly sudden. She slapped her hands onto the arms of the chair and leaned her head back against the headrest. For a moment she closed her eyes, then slowly extended her feet to the fire. Vicki snatched up a footstool and placed it beneath Frau Halder's heels.

"Are you comfortable?" asked Vicki. "Do you need anything else?"

Before Frau Halder could reply, Madame Lacome jumped forward and curtsied. She did so not as a proper woman of society, but as a gypsy instead. She swept her hand nearly to the floor and flashed a glimpse of petticoat at her ankle. It was unquestionably a ploy on her part to play a woman of hot blood and Mediterranean spirit for Vicki and Frau Halder. She had gauged them accurately; they did not desire one of their own kind to read their future. With precise psychological intuition, Madame Lacome had rendered herself an exotic menial. Only by adopting such a posture might she become genuine in their eyes.

"I am Madame Lacome," she said a little too grandly as she finally stood before Frau Halder. "I am pleased to be of service."

"We will determine whether you are of service somewhat later, won't we? Who is this boy with you? And this large man?" Frau Halder asked, squinting in my direction.

"It is the Colonel's son . . . the innkeeper," Vicki explained. "The man is her attendant."

"He's a conceited man, your father . . . but you must know that already," Frau Halder said, again straining to see me more clearly. "He has nothing to be proud of, and so he's inordinately proud of himself. He's a woodcutter. My husband employed a thousand of his kind."

I said nothing, despite the fact that my father no longer cut wood for his livelihood. Herr Schliemer put his hand softly on my shoulder. Frau Halder touched the medicine bottles on the table beside her, then seemed to think better of taking anything at the moment. She dropped her hand in her lap and leaned back again. She closed her eyes once more and did not open them when she spoke the next time. Notwithstanding, I felt she was more interested than she let on. Her voice betrayed her. Her eyes were shut simply because she wished to pretend indifference and perhaps arrange a better price.

"You claim to be able to summon the departed. I am thinking of my husband. Does your handbill represent you correctly?"

she asked Madame Lacome with feigned weariness.

"Yes, I can contact the dead. It is one of my gifts."

"Is it an elaborate process? I tire easily . . . my husband has been dead for nearly eight years. I have always wondered — it's something I've always wanted to ask a person of your calling... where is he right now? The dead, I mean. If you can summon him you must know that much.

"He hasn't left this house. He is in the wood of that door. He's in the creases of that bookcase," Madame Lacome said at once, waving her hand slowly around the room. She responded with such assurance, and in such an unlikely fashion, that Frau Halder lost her composure. She glanced at Vicki as if to ask how Vicki had permitted such an imposture to enter her house. And yet Madame Lacome did not retract her statement. In the ensuing silence she simply stared at Frau Halder, setting the ground for a test of wills.

"Do you mean to say he is actually in the wood?" Frau Halder asked after another moment or two. "Not in heaven, not in hell, but in that old door?"

"He is in the wood. You're looking at me with amazement, and yet I tell you it's true. Human spirits are often imprisoned in inanimate objects. Your husband is not a free soul in death. He is suffering."

This, I felt, was too much. I did not particularly care if it pained Frau Halder to hear such foolishness, but I fully expected her to send Madame Lacome packing. Apparently sharing my thoughts, Vicki clicked her tongue and rustled her skirts impatiently. The whole notion of a soul residing in a door or a bookcase was preposterous. Vicki was eager to show her satisfaction at Madame Lacome's inability to come up with even a reasonably interesting philosophy. Indeed, I had expected better from Madame Lacome myself; her lack of accomplishment disappointed me.

Remarkably, however, Frau Halder appeared more intrigued than ever. She nodded; she pressed her hand nervously across her skirt. Something in Madame Lacome's statement had rung a note of familiarity, though what that might have been was inconceivable to me. Nevertheless, it was evident they understood one another.

"We'll have the seance you advertised," was all that Frau Halder offered.

Madame Lacome demonstrated no relief or surprise at this declaration, despite the fact that it meant a good wage to her. She nodded and quickly took the bag I had carried down through the vineyard from my hand. As I had suspected, it contained the crystal ball. She asked Vicki to open a card table for her and told Herr Schliemer to assist; she requested a personal item from Herr Halder's wardrobe and this a second servant, a timid girl named Katrina, fetched immediately. She also demanded the presence of at least two more participants, impressing on us all the importance of having an odd number at the seance table so that the spirit of Herr Halder might unify us in an even number. Vicki, after a close conference and much whispering to Frau Halder, agreed to allow me to stay rather than Katrina. Our party was to consist of Madame Lacome, Herr Schliemer, Frau Halder, Vicki, and I. The spirit of Herr Halder would unite us by being the sixth.

The preparations took only minutes. Madame Lacome, after directing Vicki back and forth, tucking at the table cloth hastily spread across the card table, setting up the crystal ball in the center of our circle atop a coil of braces from Herr Halder's wardrobe, suddenly withdrew into one corner and stood motionless. It was a masterful ploy. Without saying a word or demanding our attention, she had won our slightest glances. She was, it appeared to all of us, beginning her communication with the spirit world. She crossed her arms over her chest and stared at the bookcase. Watching her and settling into our assigned places around the table, we became absolutely silent.

Sitting with Vicki to my right, Madame Lacome's empty chair to my left, I was likewise entirely absorbed. Madame Lacome's stance by the bookcase had seasoned the room with remarkable expectation. Cynic or not, one watched. Was she receiving vibrations? Words from the departed? Was she conversing with a corpse or merely the phantom image of Herr Halder? Anything seemed possible. Madame Lacome did not seem as rigidly anchored to this life as the rest of us.

At last she turned from the corner and inspected the table. She said nothing. I waited to see her share some glance of conspiracy with Herr Schliemer, but she appeared too far away for such worldly concerns. Her movement seemed retarded, as if the weight of several specters clung to her arms and legs. She approached the table cautiously. Vickie lowered the lights at a word from Frau Halder, only to have Madame Lacome countermand her in a voice clearly not her own.

"Leave the light on!" Madame Lacome said.

The voice chilled me. It was a man's voice. It did not come from her throat and mouth, but instead from deeper in her diaphragm. It came forth in an eruption as if it had strained through muscle and sinew in order to reach open air. Indeed, it was a gasping, greedy sound; I could readily believe the spirit who sent the voice wrenching through Madame Lacome had been buried for years. The impression it made was that of a bottle being opened after years of quiet storage, or better still, a crypt. It was beyond human capacity to reproduce the voice; the realization that this could not be a trick on Madame Lacome's part seemed to strike us all simultaneously. Vicki pushed back her chair and spoke a short prayer. Frau Halder leaned forward to bring herself closer to the source of the voice.

"Jacob, is that you?" asked Frau Halder. "Jacob? Jacob, I'm here."

Frau Halder's voice was sadly pleading. Her hands shook. Instead of answering, the voice manifested itself in physical contractions that made Madame Lacome's limbs move as if guided by marionette strings. Her cheek spasmed; her right leg leaped forward as if trying to take a step only to find some hitch in the musculature rendering it impossible. As a result the leg continued to paw the ground unsteadily; Madame Lacome's light shoe sole scraped the braided carpet beneath her as if seeking a proper footing. Then, a tremor moving up her body, Madame Lacome's head suddenly bent to one side. Her neck muscles flickered and became unbearably taut. In the same instant the lights, without explanation, dimmed. I looked quickly to Vicki, then to Herr Schliemer. In a manner I did not fully understand, I could not see any expression, any human warmth, in their eyes.

Vicki seemed possessed by whatever forces now occupied the room. I heard her begin to giggle, and it was the laugh of someone on the border of insanity. This all happened far too quickly, and I felt, in addition to my very genuine fear, a moment's anger at Madame Lacome for being so reckless. She was no longer in control of the situation. Vicki's giggles continued to build until she was very nearly cackling. The sound, remarkably, seemed to dislocate itself entirely from her body until it echoed in the fieldstone chimney above us.

In the next instant the room turned bitterly cold. A page from a book or a loose letter flapped softly. A wicked draught slipped through the room, but before I could turn to locate its source Madame Lacome began to speak.

"I have come from the wood. . . .this lumber was cut with a saw bathed in blood. The lamb is dead and the spring will come no more. Here the winter wind blowing in the eaves of this house, the woods of the forest have weeped. . . ."

It was gibberish. Not only did the pronouncements lack content of any kind I could discern, they bordered on the ridiculous. Only the timbre of the voice held any power; the rest, the words and attempts at oracular precision, were lost in hocus-pocus and bombast. I felt myself begin to grin. The others, surely, would give up the joke now. I attempted to turn to see the expression on the others' faces, particularly Herr Schliemer's, but my cheek bumped against something. I tried to turn in the other direction; against my cheek collided with something soft. A count of three passed before I realized Madame Lacome had somehow gained a position directly behind me. I hadn't seen her move, yet she was there nevertheless. She stood with her arms bracketing my head, the crystal ball held gently against my throat. The voice, it seemed, had passed through me.

We sat around a wide table in the kitchen, sipping tea and eating buttered scones. No one had wanted to remain at the seance table, not even Frau Halder. It was a tribute to Madame Lacome's ability to handle people that she had, in essence, invited Frau Halder to tea at her own table. She did this with such cozy familiarity, and with such earnest solicitude for her new employer, that the discrepancy in social class seemed meaningless. We had all survived an uncanny experience, Madame Lacome seemed to say, and we were now united in a conspiracy of understanding and trust. So shrewd was Madame Lacome in her assessment of people, that she dismissed Herr Schliemer, because, unquestionably, his presence was too large and too firmly rooted to the corporal world. He would remind us of human flesh; as women grouped together, the discussion could be less inhibited. Besides, she explained to Frau Halder, Herr Schliemer had arranged a full docket of readings and consultations at our inn. It was necessary he leave to tell the clients she would be delayed.

I remained, however. I volunteered to go with Herr Schliemer, thinking the women would prefer to be alone, but Madame Lacome wouldn't hear of it. She insisted I sit beside her in case of relapse. It was not an idle precaution. I felt empty and hollow. I still could not understand what had happened. I sat quietly at Madame Lacome's side, watching Katrina, the servant girl, bring scones and tea to table. Katrina was not happy that a seance had been held in her place of employment. Once, as she served Frau Halder, she whispered that it was against her religion to invite the devil into her home and she did not like these "unholy doings" as she called them. Frau Halder did not bother to respond. Employment, any employment, was dear in our village. Frau Halder did not intend to let a serving girl dictate policy in her home.

Besides, Katrina was as curious as the rest of us to discover what had actually transpired. Certainly I was intensely curious about my own participation. Had I been speaking for some time while Herr Halder's voice passed through me? Why couldn't I recall the spirit's presence? And, most important, why had the spirit of Herr Halder selected me as a medium?

The entire episode had been exquisitely troubling, and I had the sense, mistaken or otherwise, that Madame Lacome had taken on more than she had anticipated. I had many questions I wanted to put to her, but I realized she was now at Frau Halder's leisure and that to interrupt would be to over step my position. In addition, Madame Lacome was intent on setting the hook deeper while devouring an excellent meal. My role, I understood, was to be silent and remain grateful that I was able to witness such a conversation.

"There is more than one spirit in this house," Madame Lacome started by way of clarification between hasty bites of buttered scones and regular sips of tea. "I should have guessed, but I wasn't thinking along those lines. A woman died here . . . an angry woman, I should say. Frau Halder, you'll have to look into the history of this house to discover who it might be. How long have you lived here?"

"Thirty years," Frau Halder answered, pushing at the scone on her own plate. She had lost all pretense of superiority. She was a convert to Madame Lacome's mysticism. In fact she appeared revived.

"And no one has died in the house beside your husband?"

"No. . .," Frau Halder looked to Vicki, who shook her head. Vicki sat close to Frau Halder, prepared to butter or cut a scone as her employer required. Although Vicki seemed doubtful the seance was not a matter of trickery, she was intelligent enough to know that Frau Halder believed in it and therefore it became true for her servants. She would not contradict the mistress of the house, though she reserved her judgment so that she might have a position to fall back to if the seances proved inauthentic. She was a mirror to Frau Halder and at the moment understood the desired reflection.

"Well, I hesitate to say it," Madame Lacome said, showing no hesitancy whatsoever, "but something wicked occurred here—a murder or a suicide. Suicides are the great tragedy. I have talked to several people who were at the gates of death, actually finished their last breath in this life and then were suddenly pulled back. All of them report that suicides are invariably the most angry and unsettled spirits in the entire afterworld. I don't mean to scare you, but it might be better to rid the house of this particular spirit's presence. Have you sensed a heaviness in the house? Worrisome odors? Anything of that nature?"

The three women—Frau Halder, Vicki, and Katrina—looked at one another. It was obvious by their hesitation that there had at least been a discussion of some odd occurrences. Perhaps they had never conferred about them, but each seemed to have a portion of a shared understanding. Frau Halder spoke first.

"There have been times...Vicki won't agree, but times when I was positive a malevolent spirit resided here. I've said as much. Every house has its creaks and quirks, but this house has more than its share," Frau Halder said.

Then, looking directly at Katrina, she said, "Tell them what you've seen."

"It was nothing," answered Katrina.

Frau Halder raised an eyebrow, which was sufficient to make Katrina cave in. She was nervous about speaking; in addition, she was obviously embarrassed to be included in a conversation as an equal with Frau Halder. She stood with a cloth in her hand, nervously knotting the corners. Under different circumstances, it might have been humorous to see her called on the carpet in such a manner. Now, however, she seemed genuinely afraid. A twitch tugged at the crow's feet on her left eye.

"I really don't think . . . it might have been my imagination," she began.

"Tell us what you've seen," Madame Lacome said, rolling her hand to encourage Katrina's story. Crumbs fell from Madame Lacome's lips. A dab of butter clung to her knuckle.

"It was a corpse I saw. A corpse in the basement. I'm not the only one who has seen it!" she said defensively before anyone could question her. "Ulie, the man who delivers coal . . . he once began shoveling coal from one pile into the furnace and he uncovered her face. One big shovelful and there she was . . . he screamed so you could hear him on the top floor of the house."

"What she says is true," Frau Halder said. "This man, Ulie, claimed to see it. I wouldn't have believed him except that he described the woman's corpse in the same way that Katrina has. There was no reason for him to make up his story."

"And where do you see this woman?" Madame Lacome asked Katrina.

"In the mirrors. Occasionally when I'm looking at myself suddenly there will be another set of eyes looking over my shoulder. It's horrifying. I seldom see the woman's entire face...

just her forehead and eyes. It's very fleeting. She's there, I begin to draw in my breath to scream, and then she's gone."

"How do you know she's gone?" Vicki asked.

"Well, I know, that's all. You can feel it when someone comes near you, can't you?"

"Oh, she's not telling you everything," Frau Halder said with a sigh, yet still far more animated than she had been when we met her. "This spirit is also able to carry objects around the house. A poltergeist. We have found candles lighted in the middle of the night; once a small table was locked in the sewing room without any noise at all. The door was locked from the inside, and the sewing room is just a small alcove on the attic level. There was no possible means for anyone to climb through a window. Besides, who would bother to do such a thing?"

"The woman is sometimes on the steps," Katrina said, now warmed to the stories, the dish cloth still strangled in her hands. "I'll see her there, waiting, looking directly at me. It's horrid."

It seemed something remained unsaid, but I suspected it would not be quickly revealed. I felt very tired; Vicki, her stern features betrayed by fatigue, yawned loudly in an embarrassed snap. After extracting a promise from Madame Lacome that she would aid them, Frau Halder dug in a skirt pocket and paid Madame Lacome. As she had with the Brockdorf sisters, Madame Lacome made the payment seem the most natural thing in the world. She took the money and slipped it in the bag containing the crystal ball. That finished, she slid out from behind the table and waited for me to follow.

"We should rid the house of this spirit as soon as possible. Now that it has been recognized and pulled out of hiding. . .well, it becomes somewhat more dangerous," she announced as she arranged her shawl around her shoulders.

This caused a stir. When could she be ready? Was the next night appropriate? Yes, that might be arranged, Madame Lacome said, although it would mean breaking another appointment. I was fairly certain no other appointment existed, and so I listened with interest as Madame Lacome made her possible visit that much more prized.

Nothing was made final. Vicki would visit; Madame Lacome

would check her appointment calendar. Perhaps she could rearrange her schedule for such a perilous situation. At the end Madame Lacome bowed once more, then backed to the door with a great flourish. The gesture was over done by a large margin, and yet she carried it off. She attempted to leave a room diminished by her absence, and despite the transparent bow to carnival life, it worked astonishingly well.

She waited until we were well into the vineyard before she put her arm around my shoulders and shook me gayly.

"Oh, William, you have a talent. . . .an unexpected talent! You're as sensitive as a radio tube to the spirit world! You're a natural medium."

"Did Herr Halder's spirit actually speak through me?" I asked, not sure whether to be cross or proud.

"Of course!"

"And what did he say?"

"You didn't hear it yourself?" Madame Lacome asked, genuinely curious.

"No, I didn't."

"It's a shame. . .you only transmit then. Some people hear themselves as well. Herr Schliemer, of course, makes everything up yet it is just as persuasive. He has no natural talent. Not for your line of work, anyway."

"You're not telling me what I said on behalf of Herr Halder."

"Puwfff, nothing at all. The usual drivel. It's cold here, now it's hot. Water the plants. . .who cares? But this other spirit, this angry woman, now there's something of interest. She won't be chased away like a mouse, I promise you that much. That was a stroke of luck finding her lurking about. We can soak your Frau Halder for a good deal on that count."

"But is the spirit real?" I asked, trying to fix things in my mind. "Is there a poltergeist haunting them?"

"Don't be foolish . . . light, light, everything is light. Spirits are formed of our own wishes. No, the real spectra is Katrina herself. She's a perfect madwoman. You find it often enough in these small villages. A little giggle at the wrong moment will give it away every time. No wonder she finds a woman spying over her shoulder when she fixes her face. You didn't see old Vicki falling for it, though, did you? We're both after Frau Halder's money, this Vicki and I. . . it's an interesting arrangement, actually. We're both determined to tell Frau Halder what she wants to hear. The spiritual versus the practical," said Madame Lacome, slowing to pick her way around the end of a vine.

We were now well into the vineyard. The temperature had dropped. Fortunately there was sufficient moonlight to see small obstacles in the path and we were able to increase our speed. We walked steadily, both of us with a mind to arrive at the warmth of our beds. Nonetheless, I couldn't dismiss the topic so easily. Madame Lacome's logic seemed inconsistent; or rather, she seemed to have no logic at all. On one hand she praised me for receiving impulses from the spirit world, and on the other she said it was all a question of light.

"I don't understand you," I said, surprised to find myself impatient when I finally spoke. "You said a moment ago that I was a perfect sensor for the spirit world."

"And you are. The spirits will come through you like, well, like a brook."

"But there are no spirits. You said yourself that Katrina is a madwoman. You can't have it both ways."

"And why not?"

"It doesn't make any sense that way. Answer me, I need to know."

"You need to know, do you?" Madame Lacome asked, stopping and squeezing my forearm in her right hand. "I've devoted a lifetime to this search and you want me to give you an answer the first time you ask. Isn't that so? You'd like things to be tidy because you've grown up in a little square house in a little tidy village. I told you it is a matter of light, and that's true. I can't say what these women have seen about their house. Or the coal man either. . . .if he saw a face beneath his shovel, I believe him. What does it matter if it was there or not as long as he believes it was? A thousand things are possible."

"But when you spoke in a man's voice it was an obvious fake."

"I never spoke in a man's voice," Madame Lacome said, releasing my arm. She said this so sincerely it was difficult to dispute her. I felt my arguments crumbling.

"Yes you did. You told Viki to keep the lamps turned up. I could hear your voice through the man's voice," I said.

"Then you heard my voice through a voice coming into your own head."

"You're confusing me."

"Confusion is healthy. Why should you know all the answers at your age? That's what wouldn't make sense. But for your peace of mind, let me tell you that there are spirits and that I contact them frequently. There are also mad creatures about like our Katrina who are able to tighten the air in a room. Don't ask me how they do it. Haven't you ever passed someone who sent a chill up your spine?"

"Yes, of course."

"What is that then? If they haven't touched you physically, then surely it must be a spirit has influenced you. Why should all the dead be floating above us or buried below us?"

As we began to walk once more, I realized Madame Lacome's thoughts were impenetrable. It came as a mild shock. She was surpassingly clever, but no form or logic cemented her arguments together. She was like a handful of seed thrown at raked soil—she broadcast statements and wild conjectures in the hope that one might take root in the listener's heart. For my part I could not account for my behavior at the seance, but that was a mechanical manifestation. I gave up looking for the supporting thoughts and fully understood, for the first time, that Madame Lacome was a masterful illusionist.

I left her at the front door of the Black Pine. I could not risk my father, or even my mother, observing me escorting Madame Lacome into town and back. Besides, I was eager to be alone with my own thoughts. I desired to speak with Bookmark, imagining him able to put the occurrences at Frau Halder's into an understandable light, though I doubted his experience, however extensive, might have included an encounter with one such as Madame Lacome.

It was late; I hurried to finish my chores. I checked the dogs and fed the horses. I examined the hunting equipment to ensure it was ready for the next day's outing. By the time I finished, sufficient cold air had slipped into the barn to turn the horses' muzzles into ghostly masks of weariness combined with expectation. I imagined the horses eating mist and ice all the night long, their bodies gathering shimmering chinks of frost deep into their blood.

A nearly full moon had risen by the time I stepped back into the barnyard. I entered the kitchen, expecting to find my mother cross and ill-tempered at the arrival of new guests. Instead only Eva was in the kitchen. She stood at the table near the fire place, fixing a tray with warm tea and light meats. She looked up as soon as I pushed open the door. She appeared harried.

"There you are, William," she said, her hands instantly returning to their work on the tray. "Your father has been asking for you . . . . your mother too. You better look to it."

"I will," I said, though I walked to the fire and turned to warm my backside. I felt oddly independent. Eva hardly had to tell me my father wanted me to serve the guests. That was routine. I decided to ignore her.

"Listen," she said when she saw I didn't go immediately into the sitting room. "Herr Mueller had car trouble on the return trip. The guests have only just arrived. Dinner was ruined. Your mother is angry as a seedy cat . . . . she's upstairs seeing to their rooms. This isn't the time to drag your heels."

I nodded. I didn't answer. Eva shook her head, then moved to the sink where she prepared a cheese for the men. I turned to expose my front to the fire. Below me, in the basement, I heard Herr Meuller hammering at something. He, too, would be in a terrible state as a result of the car letting him down. That was how he viewed the failure of anything mechanical. The car did not misfunction, but, instead, betrayed him.

Eva shook her head again, doubtless anxious on my behalf.

"You should go," she said, her voice more insistent. "If your father or mother comes in to find you standing about . . . ."

"I'll go," I said, still not moving.

Eva nodded absently. She was flushed with the new guests. She began to speak again, although it was directed as much at herself as it was to me.

"They're important guests . . . . wealthy soldiers, wealthier than we anticipated. The older one is titled, and the younger one, he is a hero already. He has a reputation, a military reputation. We should all do well. At least that's what your father whispered to me."

"He should know."

"Now, now, William," she said, returning to the tray and folding napkins for it. "Go ahead and assume your position. This isn't the moment for you to rebel."

I had no clear intention of rebelling, but Eva's point was well taken. I pushed away from the fire. My hands and feet were still cold. As I entered the sitting room, my father merely glanced at me. Luckily I was safe; he was engaged by the men. He was always particularly cordial with guests in the first hours of their arrival, but the fact that these men were soldiers made him even more attentive than usual. Visits by military personnel gave him occasion to remind us all that he had been a Colonel in better days; it afforded him an opportunity to speak in military parlance without seeming ludicrous in our small town. Combined with this was his appreciation that these men might compete with him on the hunt, or at least keep the kill something trim and essential. After all, these were not overfed industrialists from Vienna, but German soldiers keen to draw blood. He looked to them for confirmation of their common fellowship, a fellowship he could not share with Herr Mueller or myself.

His hospitality, therefore, was somewhat boisterous. It was also, at times, acutely painful to watch—a fact the more astute guests realized in short order. Always he was intent on showing them that he, too, was a man of spirit, not a back-country hunting guide gone soft in retirement. They were welcome at the Black Pine; they were met by a man who shared their tastes and interests. Had the men known him as I did, they might have discerned his desire to show them he was, in matters of arms and hunting, their superior. In order to be their superior, however, it was necessary to first be their equal, and that was why, when military guests visited, he was especially quick to issue orders to the rest of us. Commands set him apart from us. He was not precisely in the soldiers' employ; we, on the other hand, were their servants. All of this was implied in the first evening of their arrival; it was communicated in his glance at me when I entered the sitting room.

Fortunately the men were too satisfied with their own conversation to care if I joined them. I was a servant, nothing more. My father was spared the obligation of introducing me. I walked quietly into their circle and picked up the bottle. I replenished each man's drink—the senior guest first, then the more junior guest, then finally my father. Afterward I stepped out of the circle and settled on my customary bench. The men continued talking. They discussed a military manner, something that had occurred in Munich, and the subject obviously had them heated.

". . . .don't you think?" one said, his profile to me.

"Yes, I quite agree, but in other regards, this situation, this solution as it's being called, well, it's hardly worthy of the Fatherland."

My father nodded. I listened for a few moments, but the conversation was beyond me. I stared at the fire and felt sleepy. I was roused only when the more senior of the guests removed a flask from the pocket of his sport coat. It was a different sort of brandy, one he had discovered in the Wauchau. He wanted the others to try it. As he passed the flask to his fellow guest, I had an opportunity to study him. He was a dignified looking man, perhaps fifty years old, with a small moustache held tightly against his upper lip. The moustache was cut so cleanly, however, that I could not help noticing the white flesh where the rest of his moustache would have formed had bristles been allowed to grow there. He was a man who, though handsome in his way, possessed a skin that was more deeply pored than others. He was obviously the titled guest, though I listened for some time without hearing him referred to except by military rank.

The second officer, a younger man of thirty, drank from the flask when it was offered. He was blond and somewhat effeminate. His brows were light; his uniform too finely cut. His habit—which became apparent as soon as one met him—was to touch the edge of his lips with the pinky of his right hand.

One side to the other, he brushed his lips as if determining by tactile sensations whether they were composed in a smile or frown.

My father received the flask in turn. I looked to see if they required glasses, but my father did not acknowledge me. This was not a formal drink; it was the establishment of a fraternity. He drank. At the same moment I heard someone on the stair behind me. I turned to see my mother descending, her hand lightly gliding on the banister. She did not raise her eyes, nor did she look to see the guests. She turned at the newel post and disappeared down a back hallway toward the kitchen.

She was followed a moment later by Herr Schliemer. He descended the stairs quietly, though it was impossible, as a result of his size, to ignore his approach. One sensed him before he arrived. I observed my father's face darken and understood his expression. The guests were too recently arrived to permit Herr Schliemer to pass among them with Madame Lacome's calling cards. It might place the Black Pine, and thus my father, in a poor light. These were not men of commerce, as the earlier guests has been; such intrusions as Herr Schliemer was about to make were unwelcome and unquestionably distasteful.

Yet how could he be stopped? The soldiers turned. Herr Schliemer bowed before formally entering the sitting room. His size, in the firelight, was foreboding. The men turned in their chairs, intrigued at his remarkable bulk. The blond soldier, the younger of the pair, brushed his lip with his finger. My father straightened in his chair.

"Yes, Herr Schliemer?" asked my father, trying futilely to forestall him, or at least to let the other men see that Herr Schliemer independently pressed himself on them.

"Good evening, Colonel," Herr Schliemer replied, then bowed again slightly to the soldiers. "Gentlemen, my pleasure."

The men nodded. They were obviously unsure how to take Herr Scliemer's presence. He, on the other hand, appeared not at all disconcerted by the possibility that his visit was ill timed. In his lack of comprehension, or his choice to ignore it, was the bare-kneed greediness that I had come to despise in both he and Madame Lacome.

He dug in his pocket. My father crossed his legs. Herr Schliemer produced the calling cards. He handed them to the guests, then announced Madame Lacome would be in this evening if the men required her services.

"Divination?" the older soldier said, reading the card, then tossing it on the table. "This is the type of thing we were discussing, isn't it, Colonel?"

"Exactly," my father answered.

As if to illustrate a point, the titled soldier swivelled farther in his chair so that he might inspect Herr Schliemer more fully.

"May I ask where you are from, sir?" he asked.

"From destiny," Herr Schliemer answered.

The older soldier smiled. The younger one, the blonde, ran his finger over his lips. Right to left; left to right. He smiled and nodded.

"From destiny? Is that a joke?" the blonde soldier asked. "Are you being deliberately impertinent?"

"Not at all."

"You're eastern European, aren't you? East of the Danube, at any rate. Poland or Hungary I should guess," the older soldier interjected. "I ask because I'd like to have your views on current events. We we're just discussing your situation."

"I'm afraid that would be impossible," Herr Schliemer answered.

"And why not?" the blonde asked.

"I am not a political man."

"No such thing," the other soldier said. "No such thing, not in today's world. You must have your views, surely. On Germany, all the rest. . . .important questions, wouldn't you say?"

"No doubt they are exactly as you say, but I am not equipped to answer them. Now, if you'll excuse me."

Herr Schliemer bowed. It was not a satisfactory conclusion. Herr Schliemer appeared to be in retreat. He had avoided something, though what it was I couldn't begin to guess. My father snatched up the cards as soon as Herr Schliemer was gone and tossed them in the fire. As he turned back and motioned for me to see to the quests' drinks, the blonde soldier spoke.

"Jewish scum," was all he said.

The older man, the titled officer, grunted slightly as he stretched forward for his brandy.

Vicki came at noon the following day. It was a cold damp morning, and the afternoon held no promise of sun. Vicki arrived wearing a large wrap against the falling temperature. Perhaps it was merely the dreary day, but she appeared grayer and more colorless than usual. Her wrap provided a hood, which she wore up and knotted close to her throat, but unfortunately the hood was too deep and succeeded only in making one search for Vicki's face in the texture of the wool. She resembled, in that first instant as she entered the foyer of the inn, a weary turtle whose skull and cheekbones were diminished by a tedious age. I understood, from conversation with Madame Lacome, that I was to welcome Vicki, invite her in, then explain that Madame Lacome was currently occupied with another spiritual matter and would accommodate her as soon as possible. Meantime, my instructions were to escort Vicki into the sitting room and place her at the small table used by the Brockdorf sisters a day or two before. Madame Lacome was explicit about seating Vicki at the table. If necessary, I was to insist on it.

"How long do you think she will be?" Vicki asked nervously as I walked her to the sitting room. For once I was not worried about encountering my father or the hunters. They had gone out for an early ride to get the lay of the land. My father had arranged with one of the game wardens for a late afternoon interview. A boar would be selected from a specific region; an initial fee would be paid by the two officers; on the following morning the hunt could begin in earnest. Until then, the inn was comparatively quiet.

"She's quite busy," I answered according to the script prepared for me by Madame Lacome, at the same time hurrying forward to pull out a chair at the black lacquered table. "She told me to invite you to tea, if you like."

"Here?" Vicki asked. "Or in her chambers?"

"Here," I said. "I meant I could get you something from the kitchen while you wait. Madame Lacome asked me to look after you."

"I see," she said, taking a seat at the small table and removing a pair of calf skin gloves. "Tea would be fine, I suppose. I hadn't really planned on stopping long. But it's such a raw day outside. . . yes, tea, if I must see this through."

"I'll get it straight away. My mother is marketing, so if you don't mind, I'll see to the tea things myself."

I left her and entered the kitchen. The kettle was already on the boil, the tray set out. I arranged things quickly and carried the tray back out to her. She did not seem at all comfortable to be seated in the Black Pine. Or rather, she seemed nervous at being sent to arrange a meeting with Madame Lacome. As soon as I put the tea before her, she poured it out, added milk and sugar, then sipped loudly. That done, she placed the cup back on the tray and pretended interest in the animal heads. I was uncertain whether I should stay or go. In compromise, I remained standing, a servant as long as she would keep me one.

Vicki did not look at me for some time. Her gaze alternated between the weather she could glimpse through the window near the table, and the animal heads along the walls. In the dimness of the early afternoon, the animals' eyes were conspiring and clever, almost as though they waited to hear what might occur next. In Vicki's mood, I'm sure they appeared malevolent. She regarded them only for a moment, then deliberately cast her eyes elsewhere. Nevertheless her vision was drawn back to the heads over and over, and the animals' eyes flickered with the questions of firelight and drying wool.

"Who is up there with her, anyway?" Vicki asked at length.

"A local woman, I think. I wasn't here when she arrived."

Vicki whispered something about 'foolishness' and 'folly' just loud enough to let me hear. Then she sat quietly and looked down at her lap for a time, but it was merely a stall. Inevitably she turned her head to me and started to speak, then rearranged whatever it was she was going to say, and finally spoke softly.

"Your lady has made quite an impression on Frau Halder. Perhaps you saw that yourself. My mistress is convinced your Madame Lacome has spiritual powers."

"And what do you think?" I asked, sensing she had volumes to say on the subject.

"I admit I was taken in at first. Anyone can be deluded given the right circumstances, the proper tone, a skilled necromancer. And your Madame Lacome is good; I grant her that. But in the end, I think she hypnotized us all," Vicki said, turning to observe how these words hit me. Obviously this is what she wanted to tell me from the outset. "Do you know what 'hypnotized' means?"

"Not really," I answered, wanting to have her interpretation.

"Hypnotism is a cheap carnival trick," Vicki said, carefully picking up her cup and sipping from it. She seemed to relax now that she could parade her expertise. "Father Garlitz explained it clearly enough. You should visit him. He's a worldly man and can place things in their proper light. He says we have yet to understand the human mind, the brain actually, though our science is the best in the world. He says hypnotism is a type of satanic rapture. He also said it is additionally dangerous because it trifles with that portion of the brain we have not yet charted. But you saw the symptoms, didn't you? You were the most affected of us all. Tell me, when you woke did you have any sense of what you had said?"

"No, not completely."

"There, you see?" she asked triumphantly, as though we had both reached the same conclusion at the same instant.

"I'm not sure. . . ."

"If you had not been hypnotized. . .if you had been awake throughout, conscious throughout, then you would have recalled exactly what was said. Don't you see? You were under her suggestion, your Madame Lacome's suggestion, and she merely persuaded you to say those ridiculous things. They made no sense by the way. Father Garlitz went over the statements one by one and shredded them. Even Frau Halder had to concede she could not make much of them when you examined them in plain daylight."

"How could Madame Lacome have persuaded me?"

"That's what I asked Father Garlitz. The very same thing, actually. He said it was likely she hypnotized you earlier, without your knowing it, then triggered the proper response when the time was ripe. Do you see how easy it is to explain when you approach it rationally? Father Garlitz insisted he wanted to be at the next seance, but Herr Halder wouldn't hear of it. She's angry with him. She says he is trying to undermine the only enjoyment she's had in years. So you see. I'm here, but against my will."

"Father Garlitz might be wrong, you know. He wasn't there, after all."

"He didn't have to be. He explained it to me as though he had been there. He has seen this woman's tricks before. Tricks of her kind, anyway. I don't travel much, as you know, I prefer a quiet life. . . .so she was able to pull her tricks on me. And as for Frau Halder, well, bless her, but she is getting on in years. She misses her husband and then along comes this woman. . . .you can see how ripe she would be to listen to anything that might bring him back. But, as I was saying, Father Garlitz has travelled. He has seen the way of the world, you might say, and this isn't the first time he has encountered such a one as Madame Lacome. He even suggested your cooperation might have been purchased. I'm sorry, but that's what he said. He's certain, at any rate, that the giant is involved in the illusion."

"I didn't deliberately cooperate, I promise you."

"I'll take your word for it," Vicki said, drawing her chin in as if she had never intended the insult. "I told Father Garlitz he was wrong on that count."

"If this is all a case of simple hypnotism, why did you claim to see the ghostly woman who stalks your house?"

"It wasn't I! It was Katrina. Think on it. Remember things clearly. You see, that is Madame Lacome's great gift. She makes you doubt and then imagine things differently than the way they transpired. As for Katrina, she sees an omen under every dust cloth. You can't take her word seriously. And Ulie? The coal man? He's a drunken old man . . . well you know him, don't you? He has the visions whenever he begins to dry. You can't take his word for anything."

Suddenly Vicki's eyes caught something over my shoulder. She turned from me, cutting off our conversation, and picked up her tea cup. She had been animated an instant before. Now, catching sight of something, her face resumed its more typical rigidity. I turned to follow her glance and saw Madame Lacome entering from the stairs. She wore a purple gown that appeared better suited for the opera than an afternoon in a country inn. Nevertheless, she carried it off.

"Ah, so you've arrived at last! No time to wait, is there? How is *ma cher* Frau Halder? You know, I had dreams last night concerning her. . . .dark dreams, I don't need to tell you. She was in a large forest, a pine forest, and everywhere around her there were wolves. Wolves and wolves and wolves and they were all coated with frost and you saw only their hungry eyes and their tongues. Oh, it was horrid, simply horrid, but then she was able to open a door in one of the trees and simply step inside. A trap door! I suppose that is her husband's spirit looking after her. He was in the lumber business, after all. He is mixed up with wood and resin. . . .pulp, I should say. Yes, it was a vivid dream, but we'll put all of that behind us, won't we?"

I had never seen Madame Lacome appear more vibrant. I knew very well that she had rested in bed until noon, consuming an enormous breakfast from the wicker tray my mother prepared before leaving to market. Madame Lacome had entertained no visitors and certainly had not been telling fortunes for hours. It was a pretense to make Vicki wait and to "whet Vicki's peasant appetite, because peasants value nothing that comes easily" according to Madame Lacome. I was aware, furthermore, that her entrance had been timed and carefully choreographed. She presented herself in a favorable light and deliberately employed the stairs as a flattering backdrop. I did not doubt that she had waited on those same stairs, intentionally eavesdropping on our conversation.

In short, all advantages were hers. She swooped in on Vicki and offered her hand. Vicki, startled, held out her own hand and had it gobbled up by Madame Lacome's fingers. In the same instant Madame Lacome sat across the table from her, not releasing Vicki's hand for a moment. To accommodate the awkward angle, Vicki was forced to lean across the table, her shoulder flexed to an uncomfortable degree. Madame Lacome simply smiled.

"So you've come to arrange an exorcism, isn't that so?

Frau Halder has wisely decided to rid herself of that gloomy presence," Madame Lacome said. "I'll say it out front: it will cost her. My services are not cheap. Is she prepared to begin at once?"

"Yes, she thought this afternoon might be suitable," Vicki said, finally succeeding in extracting her hand. She pulled back across from the table. "If you are available, that is."

"It will rain this afternoon," Madame Lacome said, looking out the window, apparently in touch with thoughts extremely rare and meaningful to our purpose. "We will require lantern light by three o'clock. Snow isn't impossible. Is it likely to snow at this season, William?"

"Perhaps a little," I answered. "Probably a covering if we get anything. We call it a deer snow, because it makes tracking easier."

"Mood is everything. For the spiritual world as well as our own. A rainy day, a gloomy day. . . . well, it is more conducive to our enterprise. A mad woman doesn't leave a house easily on a sunny day. Where would she go?"

"Then you will visit? Shall I say at three?"

"Three is fine," Madame Lacome agreed. "Tell me, before you go, is Frau Halder's health. . .?"

"She's not well," Vicki finished for her.

"And is her heart sound? Would you say a sudden shock. . . ?"

"A sudden shock? Oh, yes, I see what you mean," Vicki said. "The doctors are not certain about her condition. She receives medication twice a day. Shortly before three she will take one of her pills. She is most active at that hour, which is why she hoped you could come promptly at three."

"Tell her I am at her service. I will bring William, of course, and my man, Herr Schliemer. I will also bring the ball and my cards. Is there something more personal we might use of Herr Halder's? His shaving razor, for example. Or his nightshirt? I don't mean to venture into his personal effects, but you understand the need I'm sure. Anything which was in personal contact with his skin . . . his hair clippers, for instance, would be exactly right. I'm afraid the braces we used last time were not sufficiently powerful."

"I'll look into it," Vicki said in a dry tone, beginning to pull on her gloves. "Now, if you'll excuse me, I should be going. Frau Halder asked if you would write down your fee on this piece of paper. I will stop by the bank on the way back to her house. I should tell you that she trusts me to negotiate in matters of business. The price must suit us both."

Madame Lacome accepted the paper handed to her by Vicki. She opened the drawer near her stomach and found a pen. She demonstrated no hesitation. She wrote quickly, though at greater length than I would have thought necessary to scribble a fee. I leaned to one side, trying to spot the figure, but it was no use.

Vicki read it, smiled, then pushed the paper back at Madame Lacome and said, "You haven't written a number. Is this a joke?"

"It's a piece of folk wisdom. A saying from Hungary. Frau Halder will understand. She and I will determine my price. Tell her I trust to her generosity."

"She is not a generous woman," Vicki said, tucking the note into the wrist of her glove. "Not with money at any rate. You can ask William about that. But suit yourself."

Vicki stood. Madame Lacome remained seated. It was evident that Vicki felt Madame Lacome behaved foolishly not to name her price in advance. I believed so as well, given the famous miserliness of Frau Halder. Madame Lacome, however, simply smiled her goodbye and then motioned with her left hand that I should escort Vicki to the door.

I did as she wished. Vicki went to the door and turned her back to allow me to help her on with her wrap. She tucked the hood up over her head, then stood directly in front of the door as she knotted the hood close to her throat. She was, I realized, the type of woman who would not venture into the elements without every imaginable space on her body carefully buttressed against wind and weather. The attention she paid to the knot at her throat was almost childlike in its innocence and single-mindedness.

Vicki said nothing else as I held the door for her. She seemed guilty now that she had once taken me into her confidence. She nodded her goodbye, her bony head a clapper inside the soft bell of her hood. I closed the door on her as soon as she was gone. It was a relief to see her depart.

I returned to the table only to find Madame Lacome consuming what remained of Vicki's tea. She had not bothered to clean out Vicki's cup. She drank the tea in large swallows, her face turned to the view out the window. I wanted to ask her why she had insisted that Vicki be served at this small table, but she did not appear in a mood to answer questions. That is not to say, however, that she appeared glum. On the contrary, she was immensely pleased with herself. She patted the table across from her to indicate I should sit. I did as she suggested, although not without my mind passing to recollect Vicki's words. Perhaps now, in preparation for the seance, Madame Lacome would attempt to hypnotize me.

"So, the die is cast, the game is afoot, the fox is out of the hedgerow. Isn't that right, William?" Madame Lacome asked, her hands busy pouring the remainder of the tea into her cup. "Are you getting a sense of how things are done? Delay, then reward, then delay, another delay, and finally more reward. That is why gambling is so addictive, you know? Men lose their entire fortunes waiting for that reward. They lose sight of the losses and become fixated on the reward. I've seen in happen, believe me. I stood next to a man in Baden-Baden, at the casino, and watched as he lost ten thousand shillings. An exquisite moment, I assure you. He was almost divine in his suffering. But the rewards! The rewards were quite fabulous as well. You will see. We will give Herr Halder a reward she will savor."

"Vicki spoke with Father Garlitz," I said, wanting, for some reason, to see some wind removed from her sails.

"Did she? The local crow? Yes, all black and wearing their death gowns . . . . so tell me, what did he say?"

"He said you perform hypnotisms."

"I would like to ask him what he calls his Masses, but that's another matter. And what do you think? Do you think I have hypnotized you?"

"I don't know. I don't think so."

"And what if I did? Would that be so terrible?"

"Vicki said Father Garlitz thinks it's the devil's rapture," I said, aware I was not recalling the words precisely. "He said you were trifling with an unused portion of our brains."

"My goodness, the man is denser than I imagined. How do I accomplish this mass hypnotism? Did he explain that? Wait, before you answer, do me a favor and get a few biscuits from the kitchen. Be a good lad. We have two hours before our work begins and I have missed lunch entirely. Go on. And while you're there, think carefully about what you want to say. Don't forget butter either."

It was remarkable she possessed an appetite after her enormous breakfast. I realized, as I pushed through the door, that she wanted more to eat at this moment in part because we were alone at the inn. She could eat without the meal appearing on her bill. Her smallness over such matters proved more remarkable when contrasted to the largess she exhibited by writing a silly folk saying on the bill for Frau Halder.

I brought her three breakfast snails—a cinnamon swirl pastry my mother made at least once a week—and a large vat of butter. Immediately she buttered one, then ate it from her fingers, ripping the chunks of cinnamon pastry as a dog might dismember a soft carcass. She sloshed it down with warm tea and then smiled at me to go on. I had forgotten where we were in the discussion. Madame Lacome rolled her knife at me and said I was going to tell her how she performed this mass hypnotism.

"I don't know," I said, slightly annoyed to be bullied once again by her. "Father Garlitz did not explain it to me."

"But he explained it to Mistress Vicki. Oh, I would have given good money to have heard that," she said, devouring the remainder of the first roll. "Well, why concern ourselves with small town superstition? That's what religion is in the end, William. It's superstition, with a gilded edge. But I'm curious about you. Why are you so ready to believe everyone except me?"

"I didn't say I believed Vicki."

"But you made certain to tell me about Father Garlitz. Were you simply warning me? Is that it? If so, then I should thank you."

Her assertion made me uncomfortable, because of course I wasn't warning her. I was trying, in an obscure way, to discredit her. She saw that at once.

"I don't know what you might be doing," I said, feeling my indignation suddenly blossom. "You have me confused. I don't know how a voice came from inside me when I wasn't even conscious of speaking. You haven't explained it to me so why shouldn't I look to other people for an explanation? You're using me even though you pretend we are friends. It isn't fair. You're not being fair."

"But I have explained it to you!" she countered, at the same time pushing away the plate of rolls. "You refuse to listen, that's all!"

"How? How have you explained it?"

"I explained you are a white piece. Didn't I tell you that at our first meeting? Don't blame me if you refuse to accept you own destiny, William."

"But saying I am a white piece...... I said, groping for words in my sudden anger. "Don't you see, it's just so many words? It doesn't mean anything. You've told me nothing. You want me to go with you to steal money from Frau Halder, but then you make a joke of it afterwards."

"Steal money? A joke? Oh, William, I misjudged you. It's true. Never mind then. Leave me alone. Go along. We'll part as friends, but we can no longer work together. Shall we shake hands? Would that restore you self-respect? A clean break . . . that's what you want. Do you know the expression, it's Russian I think. It says 'To a man carrying a hammer, all the world resembles a nail.' Do you know it? You should if you don't. Your father is like that. So are the soldiers, but you, well, I had hoped for better."

She held out her hand. Even in this, however, she played with me. She was not the sort to shake hands in any event. She extended her hand to mock me. I deliberately ignored it. I stood and arranged the dishes along my arm, then carried them into the kitchen. I placed them in the sink and washed each one carefully, happy to have something to do in order to occupy my mind. It was only after I turned the water off and had brought in wood for the kitchen hearth, that I heard Madame Lacome go upstairs. She walked in a solemn rhythm, her steps finally lost behind her bedroom door.

I went to the barn and spent a nervous half-hour feeding the horses, the soft hay raining on their backs like wind made solid. I worked with a distracted, worried heart. When I was nearly finished, Herr Mueller entered the barn beneath me and began working a pine board, deliberately collecting the shavings for another shipment. He had finished mounting a small red squirrel, a frightened, tremulous creature that he had been at pains to make merry. The squirrel was a gift for a child, the spoiled ten year old belonging to a friend of the Czekeli family. Herr Mueller had not been happy with the job, primarily because the Czekelis had commanded him to restore life to the squirrel in hopes of placating the mewing child. The taxidermy had been used as a trick to soften the child's exposure to death. The squirrel – besides being difficult to mount because of a desiccated pelt, and the tender, waving paws of such a small creature – had proved to be particularly troublesome. Its eyes, two amber stones Her Mueller had been saving for a badger killed on a winter hunt, had widened the squirrel's stare until the animal seemed terrified to be brought so unwillingly back to life. To soften the effect, Herr Mueller had affixed an oak branch beneath the squirrel's feet, a trick to give the stuffed creature an appearance of movement, but the squirrel preferred death to life. That was obvious. As I watched Herr Mueller continue to plane the board, his annoyance translated into sharp, particular movement.

I moved on the mow so as to dislodge hay and alert him to my presence. He looked up, spotted me, then continued shaving the board. I climbed down the ladder and went to sweep up the shavings. He did not acknowledge me one way or the other until I had the shavings safely knotted in a burlap bag. He hung the plane on a peg by a stall door and dusted himself. I carried the bag of shavings to the barn door, where he stopped to have a pipe. Beyond us rain dripped softly from the eaves. The sound of water striking the ground matched the husky munching of the horses in the barn.

"It's finished," he said, understanding I would catch his reference.

"How did it come out?"

"You've seen yourself," he said. "Raised from the dead. Some things are better left alone. We can't always have our way.

"Do you think you will get paid?" I asked, though I knew it was a sore subject with him. He suspected, as did I, that the Czekelis would view his work on the squirrel as part of his responsibilities. It was a gift they wished to make to their friends, therefore they saw Herr Mueller's labor as a gift as well.

"It would be payment enough if the squirrel kept the boy awake nights, scared to death," he said and lit his pipe. "What's the use? Well, a day's work is its own payment, as my father said. Work is what we have. And you? Are you working with this Madame Lacome now?"

"Is that what she said?"

Herr Mueller regarded me over his pipe. He held a match to the bowl of tobacco and for an instant I saw his eyes grow glad.

"Oh, she has you in a flux," he said. "That's as it should be. Tell me, do you think she is evil?"

"Do you?" I asked. "It's something I've wondered…whether she is evil or not."

He finished lighting his pipe, then cocked his head. He smiled. I knew he found my position humorous, but I couldn't say why. He shook out the match.

"Evil? To talk about such a thing suggests we believe in it. Evil? No, I wouldn't say so. I doubt she is anymore evil than a horse with a habit of kicking. Tell me, is it true what people are saying? That she intends to perform a séance at Frau Halder's?"

I nodded.

"And she wants you along?"

"Yes."

"Well, keep your wits about you. Water has a way of getting deep faster than we expect."

"She seems to know what I am thinking before I do myself."

"She's a smart woman. Why shouldn't she be a step ahead of you? She's older and has seen more. Whatever you do, keep it to yourself. Your mother and father will not approve. They have little patience for this sort of thing. But as she is a guest, you may be on safe ground for a little while."

We watched the rain for a time. The gray morning had turned into a gray afternoon. The soil about the barn could not absorb the moisture rapidly enough and water lay in sodden puddles that reflected the gray sky. Herr Mueller's tobacco smoke floated slowly above us, then, when the wind found it, it tucked in a flat wall and disappeared into drops of rain.

We remained that way until Herr Schliemer appeared. He stepped across the barnyard, his feet too large to escape the puddles. His size appeared to increase as he approached. He bowed to Herr Mueller even while he remained beyond the cast of the eaves. Herr Mueller returned his bow. Then Herr Schliemer removed a black leather satchel from under his greatcoat — the crystal ball, I knew, and doubtless other necessities for the séance. He held the satchel out to me.

"Will you take these, William?" he asked. "Place them in the driver's boot, if you would be so kind. And if it would not be too much trouble, please ready the cart. We must go out for the afternoon."

"An errand?" Herr Mueller asked, though he knew perfectly well where they intended to travel.

"Of a kind," Herr Shliemer said. "I'd see to the cart myself, but I must help Madame Lacome prepare. We will be down in thirty minutes. We intended to walk, but with the rain, Madame Lacome thought it better to ride. She does not suffer the cold well."

"A cold day for a walk," Herr Mueller said.

"Our thinking exactly. And if you would be so kind, Herr Mueller, we must soon prepare the cart for departure altogether. If you might look it over? See that the wheels are greased, the harness in good repair? Our time at your lovely inn is almost at an end."

Herr Mueller simply nodded. Herr Schliemer bowed again and returned to the inn. We watched him go. The dogs, I noticed, kept pace with his as he crossed the barnyard.

"Well, you'll be rid of them soon enough," Herr Mueller said to me. "If that's what you wanted, that's what you'll have."

"I'm not sure what I want," I answered.

"Come along and help me. We'll take a look at their cart. You can lend a hand and get the horse into its traces. "

Together we pulled the cart into the center bay of the barn. Its wheels creaked comfortably as we maneuvered it into place. Away from the shaggy stalls and left to stand in the dull quiet of a rainy afternoon, the cart appeared exceedingly fragile. At one time, surely, the trap had been quite lovely. Its black sides, now replete with zodiacal signs, held the ghostly imprimatur of a crest of arms. It had escaped my attention before. The cart, however, had been overburdened, doubtless for many years. The undercarriage had grown swayed with its cargo; the wheels, thicker than the cart should have employed, more suitably belonged to a small dairy cart.

Herr Mueller did as he had been asked. He circled the cart several times, greasing the axles and checking the wheel spokes. The harness, when he examined it, needed only brief repair. Using a leather awl, he attached a new section of leather to a cheek strap. When he finished, he stepped back and shook his head. He did not like the conformation of the wagon, the riddled age of the tack.

We had no time to comment. As we finished returning the tools to the barn's workbench, Madame Lacome appeared. One glance was sufficient to determine that she was keen to be at her business. She walked with a quick, natural step, not in the least bothered by the sloppy mud or the dusty floor of the barn. She had wrapped her head in a wide purple cloth to create a turban, and her coat, lined by black fur, swirled about her skirts as she approached.

"Don't forget the bells, si vous plait," she said as soon as she neared the cart. "Have you ever noticed that horse sleighs are always accompanied by bells? A jolly sound, true, but it's also true the devil cannot abide bells. Every cathedral has its bell and a deacon to ring it. I wouldn't think of going out on such a dreary afternoon without bells."

"Find the bells, William," Herr Mueller told me. "They're hanging beside the stall door."

"Yes, do, William," Madame Lacome said, her tone indicating that she felt in good spirits. "We must keep our adventures bright."

"You're off to tell the widow's fortune, then," Herr Mueller said, crossing the barn floor to get their horse. "The whole town speaks of it."

"What else should a town such as this have to talk about? A dull, backward place, by any account, wouldn't you say, sir? I take you for a man who has traveled in his day."

"I suppose one place is as good as the next, if you'll pardon me for saying so. I've always thought a place may draw a person as easily as a person finds a place. But then, what do I know? I'm an old huntsman, that's all."

"I doubt that very much. You're a philosopher. Isn't he a philosopher, William?" Madame Lacome asked me. "What a queer little village and a queer little inn. But yes, Frau Halder had commissioned me to rid her house of spirits. As for her fortune, well, who has difficulty telling an old woman's fortune? She'll grow dry as a bed ruffle."

Herr Mueller walked their horse into position. The horse had gained weight since arriving, yet it still appeared too thin and overworked to be dependable. It grew fractious as Herr Mueller attempted to back it to its traces. Its front hooves grew nervous on the barn floor and it flicked its head twice to indicate its displeasure. Herr Mueller, who knew horses, had none of it. He spoke sternly to the horse and tried to catch the animal's eye. Finally the horse settled and accepted its station. Madame Lacome rubbed the horse's cheek as Herr Muller and I harnessed the creature. Together we draped the bells around the horse's neck. Instantly the wagon took on a merry air, the barn busy with the sound of jingling.

"William, you must oblige me by escorting me to Frau Halder's residence," Madame Lacome said when all was prepared. "Don't look so startled. I won't ask you to participate, though it would be an education for you. No, Herr Schliemer has gone ahead to ready the house. He's a great walker, you know. Unfortunately you are charged with driving me to my appointment. Don't worry, I have already cleared it with your mother, so there is no misgivings on that count. Now come along. You've driven a trap before, I suppose."

"My mother gave her permission?"

"Certainly, William. Women are not quite as ridiculous as men. A woman will not reject an appeal from another woman if it is done directly and without foolishness. So enough of that. We're on our way. Herr Mueller, if you please."

She held out her hand. Herr Mueller, taking his cue, helped her into the wagon. Watching her, I could not help feeling she was as spry as a lizard and might have sprung into the wagon in one bound had she been so inclined. I climbed in beside her, uncomfortable to be shoulder to shoulder with her. She reached down to the footboards and searched for the leather satchel containing the crystal ball. Finding it, she sat back and stared straight ahead. I clicked softly to the old horse and felt it shrug against the harness. Then it finally balanced the weight of the wagon and began slowly walking from the barn. Madame Lacome did not raise her hand to wave to Herr Mueller, nor did she acknowledge me beside her. We – Herr Mueller and I — had returned to being servants.

The bells, merry as they were, did little to penetrate the dark, sullen weather. A dreary, miserable day altogether, I thought. The usual click of a horse's hooves had turned to a wallowy slurp as the horse trudged wearily along. Rain misted through the trees and lay on the white rows of grapes. Certainly the weather was atmospheric for a séance. I nearly mentioned the fact to Madame Lacome, but she seemed in no mood for idle chatter. She sat staunchly beside me, her face forward. She did not protest the rain, nor did she wear herself out trying to bundle against every drop. Unquestionably she was accustomed to hard travel. We sat for a long time in silence. The world became reduced to the rhythmic tilt of the horse's hips undulating beneath its coat, the shimmering drops of rain that ran down the sloped reins toward the horse's flanks, the syrup hum of wheels passing through mud and loose earth.

"Do you believe that a man has several fates, William?"

Madame Lacome asked me in the dreary splash of the cart. "Do you believe you might become anything at all if you devote yourself to the idea?"

"I suppose."

"Free will?"

"I'm not sure what you mean by that."

"Oh, we always complicate things to make them sound more important," Madame Lacome said. "It is the entire purpose of teachers and universities. What I am asking is whether you believe you are free to refuse service at Frau Halder's house? That right now, driving to this small spot of business, you are making up your own mind?"

"My mind is already made up," I said, flicking the reins on the horse's back. The wagon swayed and burbled in the mud. I wondered, feeling the horse strain at times to keep the cart moving down the winding path, how we would negotiate the return to the inn.

"And yet you will participate," Madame Lacome said, her face still flat into the rain. "I know you will attempt to be obstinant, but it's pointless to pretend you are not curious. Curiosity has its own demands. Imagine what it will be like, months from now, if you fail to lend yourself to our enterprise. Won't you wonder what might have occurred?"

"I suppose we will all hear about it. It's all the town talks about."

"Second or third hand," Madame Lacome snorted. "Unsatisfying, at best. Cowardly, one might say, if one didn't know you better. I could have Frau Halder request your presence. I could say it is necessary. Would you like that? Then you would not be responsible in any later accusations."

I refused further conversation, though it wouldn't have mattered in any case. Herr Schliemer suddenly appeared from beside the road, his greatcoat as black and damp as the trunks of the apple trees bordering our way. He bowed slightly to Madame Lacome, acknowledged me with a glance, then took the horse's bit by hand and encouraged the animal forward. I could not help sensing that he had transacted business somewhere, had arranged something to their advantage, and his meeting us had been prearranged. Frau Halder, as guarded and frugal as she might be, could not hope to withstand their combined forces. My stomach rattled with uneasiness and I fought against the blame, earned or not, that gnawed at me when I realized I had abetted them in their pursuit of Frau Halder's money.

We made better time with the giant leading the horse and soon I spotted the dim lights of Frau Halder's manse. Two large oaks clogged the front views, their wet brown leaves glued to the fieldstone walk that guided visitors to a large portico. Herr Schliemer led the horse to the front of the yard and secured it to the black iron fence that circled the house. He returned to the cart and lifted Madame Lacome to the ground. She drifted in his arms as lightly as a hay bale.

"Come along then, William," Madame Lacome said. "You are wanted inside, I can guarantee. The spirits have a use for you."

My former resolve, my sense of participating in something unseemly and immoral, held no sway against the allure of the séance. I wanted to satisfy my curiosity after all. Sitting in the cart, the rain digging at the collar of my coat, I saw how futile my protest had been. Call it fate, or mere convenience, but I saw no point in resisting. I did not like to cave in to Madame Lacome, but she did nothing to make me feel embarrassed. In fact, Madame Lacome, seeing me move, looked about her and quickly bent to pick something up. She poked around on the ground like a black, furtive crow. Then she stood and extended her hand and poured three acorns into my lap.

"Luck for you," she said. "Carry an acorn with you always, William. Now come. I am happy you have decided to be reasonable. We will not ask more of you than you are prepared to give. Herr Schliemer will tell you that."

At her prompting, Herr Schliemer nodded. Without waiting for me, or even for him to add a word, she hooked her arm on Herr Schliemer's forearm and walked through the iron gate. I stared down at the acorns as if they had been bright coals left to burn in my lap. I brushed them off my legs and stood to have them clear of me. The horse stepped twice sideways at my sudden motion, then calmed and began pulling at the perennials that poked through the iron rails. I climbed down from the cart and hurried after the odd, mismatched pair. Rain continued to smolder and boil the ground as I followed them to Frau Halder's front door.

Vicki answered at our second knock. Without more than a cursory greeting, she escorted us into the large sitting room where the first séance had taken place. Someone had laid a dedicated fire against the rain; the sweet scent of oak branches filled the room. Vicki wore a black dress that made her all but disappear in the dimness of the afternoon. She seemed to be resolved to the séance, though she in no way appeared eager to begin. She asked us to help ourselves to tea. Obviously the hospitality did not originate with her; she simply carried out orders from Frau Halder.

Naturally Madame Lacome went instantly to the table and helped herself. She puttied a brown biscuit with butter, then walked around the room, eating and talking at once. Her eye pecked as sharply as chicken's at the furnishings and paintings.

"A perfect evening for it," she said to no one and to whomever might listen. She ate her biscuit in full, greedy chomps, the back of her hand serving as a napkin. "Water draws the spirits from the walls. Did you know? They are not so magical as people assume, these spirits. They can not abide the dampness, and so they wander about to be dry. We should have good luck moving this spirit along."

She stopped suddenly and asked if I had brought the bag inside. Herr Schliemer withdrew the bag from one of his large pockets and laid it on the séance table. Madame Lacome nodded.

"Spirits are air, after all," she continued. "They are molecules of light, a physicist might say. Yes, molecules, but they possess a will. Lightning, too, can have its effect, but only in violent instances. It's not prudent to nudge the spirits when lightning is about."

Vicki made a slightly dismissive sound with her tongue. Madame Lacome ignored it.

A moment later, Frau Halder appeared. She had not

prospered in the space between our visits. She appeared more wan than before; her cap, gray as an egg, fit about her face like the white paper cup of a pastry. She walked with difficulty, leaning heavily on her cane. Katrina, the foolish serving girl, attended her. Katrina did not lift her eyes, but instead kept them rooted on Frau Halder's shaky steps. Finally, after backing and bracing, Katrina lowered the old woman into her chair. Two pill bottles rattled on the stand beside her. Then for a moment nothing happened.

I recalled that Madame Lacome had swept forward on our last visit, but now she played diffident, nervous servant. She held back against the wall, only a wide lump in her cheek revealing that she had stuffed the last of the biscuit into her mouth. Perhaps, I thought, she was only refraining from speech because she could not talk around the biscuit. It made me smile to watch her. But then Frau Halder brought us up short by speaking. Again, age had not impaired her voice.

"My girl here is not happy with us," Frau Halder said, referring to Katrina. "She thinks we're about the devil's work. Our priest, Father Garlitz, holds the same opinion. I confess, given the interval between your last visit and this one, my skepticism has returned."

Madame Lacome did not reply; neither did Herr Schliemer. I wouldn't have spoken for the world. Vicki, behind Frau Halder, cleared her throat but said nothing.

"Well?" Frau Halder asked. "Someone say something. At least give me the satisfaction of pretending to allay my reservations. You should be able to out duel a country priest, for heaven's sake."

"I would not presume," Madame Lacome said finally, curtseying near the bookcase. "But I can tell you the devil has nothing to grasp in my work. Like vampires, the devil must be invited into a home, Frau Halder. He cannot enter of his own accord. Unless someone else summons the devil, you have no fear of my presence here."

"Then by what force do you summon these spirits?" Frau Halder asked.

"By the force of their lives, Frau Halder. Please, let me show you. If you take your hand and hold it in front of your face. Yes, just so, as if you were pushing away something distasteful. Would you oblige me? Now move it very quickly to one side or the other. There. Perhaps you see. The hand moves, but behind it lingers the trace of another hand, behind that one another, and another, and so on. You see? Which hand is the genuine hand? Are you seeing a hand that is in the past or present? That is the force – the force of the hands behind the present hand—that speaks to us."

Frau Halder moved her hand several times in front of her face. I did so myself. A clever trick, certainly. Herr Schliemer did not bother to work out the trick, nor did Vicki. But Katrina did. Eventually Frau Halder lowered her hand.

"I see what you want me to see," Frau Halder said slowly. "It's a parlor trick, but not a bad one. Naturally you have had experience explaining such things, but don't flatter yourself that I believe completely. I have returned to my senses at least that much. You caught me at a particularly worrisome time at your last visit. In short, I missed my husband. But I don't find it reassuring to believe he sleeps in the wood of the door over there. Or in any wood whatsoever. So I want you to expel whatever spirits surround us in this house. Expel Katrina's house spirit, if you will, and my husband's departed soul. A spring cleaning, if you will. Then we will finish with these matters and you may move along."

Madame Lacome nodded and gathered herself.

Yet before Madame Lacome could commence, Frau Halder reached in her sleeve and extracted a folded piece of paper. She took her time spreading it out, then coughed at Katrina, who quickly handed the old woman a pair of pince-nez glasses from the table beside the chair. I recognized the stationary as belonging to the Black Pine Inn; this was Madame Lacome's bill for the séance. Shaking, Frau Halder read whatever Madame Lacome had inscribed. Then she folded the paper in half and slid it between the armrest and her thigh.

"You're very shrewd, Madame Lacome," Frau Halder said. "In not naming a price, you have placed the responsibility on me. I would have balked if you had asked for an extravagant sum. You must have realized that. Instead you give me a line of folk wisdom. *The eggs do not teach the hen,* you say. By that I trust you mean you would not presume to ask a price?"

"Exactly, Frau Halder," Madame Lacome said with as fine a show of humility as I had ever seen from her.

"Then I choose to pay afterward," Frau Halder said. "When I have seen this business to its conclusion. I will know if my husband has been contacted. You may count on that."

Madame Lacome gave no sign of worry. She nodded and set about directing us. As we set up the card table for the séance once again, I marveled at Madame Lacome's intelligence. She had rightly twigged Frau Halder. A thrifty person sets his own value on things, as we all knew. Madame Lacome would have gained nothing by scribbling out a bill. This way, she established a claim on Frau Halder. Frau Halder understood it, too.

The old woman softened somewhat as we scooted the table over to her legs. Despite her protests, clearly she enjoyed the prospect of a diversion. The day hung decidedly heavy on the house; winter was not far removed. What else could an old woman spend her money on, I thought. The notion consoled me. As I lifted chairs from the sides of the room and placed them around the table, I no longer felt ill as ease. In fact, I found myself again greatly enjoying the complicity of the seance. Knowing afterward that Madame Lacome would mock these people, that she would find humor in their boorish country skepticism, that she would give them only what they anticipated, pleased me immensely. As before, I was in on the joke, and I may have moved more gladly than was absolutely necessary, so much so that Herr Schliemer placed his huge hand on my shoulder to still me.

Madame Lacome established the same configuration around the table. She took the head, directly to the left hand of Frau Halder. Then came Katrina, next Vicki, then Herr Schliemer, then me. Madame Lacome placed the crystal ball in the center of the table, though she minimized its importance by saying she doubted it would be needed. She fiddled for a moment with the chairs, making sure no wood might touch wood. Then as she lowered the lights, she requested that Katrina place the fire screen hard against the bricks of the hearth. Fire, she informed us, might react violently to the spirits. Spirits might draw the heat, she said, and we should be prepared.

A clever ploy. It forced Katrina, the most susceptible of our company, to cross the large sitting room by herself in comparative darkness. Furthermore, because she must stare into the fire to get the screen in position, she would be temporarily blinded when she turned to face the darkened room. I watched Madame Lacome closely, expecting at any moment to see her launch something at Katrina. To my surprise, Madame Lacome did nothing at all until Katrina had rejoined us.

"There," Madame Lacome said. "We are assembled."

"Begin," Frau Halder said and crossed herself.

Katrina and Vicki also crossed themselves. I noted that Herr Schliemer did not. For my part, my hand stalled on my lap. Before I could give it more thought, Madame Lacome began.

"We must first invite the spirits," Madame Lacome said, her hands restless on the tabletop. "They have lodged in this house for too long. Spirits! Come out. Come to the light of the orb, to the circle, to the life you have left. Come now, I call you."

She spoke in Hungarian. I recognized a few words, though the language resembled German spoken at a much rapider rate. Then the language began to swallow Madame Lacome; it entered her chest and vibrated there, so that the motion of her mouth, the heave of her chest, did not seem connected to the syllables spilling from her. I felt my hands squeezed on either side. I tried to turn my head to observe Frau Halder, but it was impossible to remove my eyes from Madame Lacome. I concentrated on the language and sound of her voice, checking repeatedly that the voice did not emanate from me. As far as I could determine, the language had remained with her, tumbling backward down her throat in great gulps. She seemed to gorge on the words, like dogs swallowing bones and meat whole, until the words, incredibly, slid forward and took residence with Katrina.

I watched but failed to comprehend. Yet a transference occurred, the language and train of words snapping like a tendon from one woman to the next. Spiritual possession, perhaps. Katrina spasmed, then became painfully rigid. Her body twisted and bent, as if a great hand jerked her back and forth. I recalled Madame Lacome's observation about Katrina that the girl was suggestible, but nothing had prepared me for this. The girl groaned in anguish.

"You are here?" Madame Lacome asked finally. "Tell us your name."

"Gwendolyn," Katrina answered straight away. Her voice bent and scraped against her teeth.

"Did you die here?" asked Madame Lacome. "Why do you haunt this place?"

"The basement," Katrina replied.

Katrina's body jerked and stiffened. Her tongue pushed between her lips not outward, as humans might be expected to do, but inward, as if her tongue hid from us.

"What about the basement?" Madame Lacome asked. "Tell us."

"Raped," Katrina said. "Then strangled."

"Who strangled you?" Frau Halder said. Her voice came as a bend in a saw.

"Who?" Madame Lacome asked.

Suddenly the table lifted. It danced for a moment back and forth, teetering as if trying to find its balance. I lifted my knees to see if it was possible to maneuver the table that way, but my knees did not even touch the bottom board. Herr Schliemer, I thought instantly, but when I looked to see him he had pushed away from the table, his face clouded. He seemed to be protecting Madame Lacome with his body, though why or how I could not begin to guess.

The table slammed to the ground. It rammed against Frau Halder who let out a shriek. Vicki stood up and shouted that that was enough, enough, we had to stop immediately. She had her Crucifix in her hand, holding it before her as a shield. Frau Halder continued to shriek, her voice climbing in pitch as Katrina continued to sway back and forth. The two women – Frau Halder and Katrina – had connected in some manner impossible to understand. Frau Halder shared thought; Katrina constituted the body of the spirit moving around us. Before I could adequately form these theories, Katrina slammed back against her chair and told us to dig, dig beneath the flagstones of the basement, dig deep.

"Buried there! Buried there! Buried there!" she screamed three times.

As she screamed, she began to float.

I watched and understood that it could not be. She could not float. But just as the table had lifted, so now did Katrina lift from the chair. Her face resumed its former expression suddenly and she appeared petrified with fear. Her arms clamped to her chest, covering her breasts. Her face looked from one to the other of us. She opened her mouth to speak, but she was beyond such level-headedness. She did not go high or drift around the room. She simply seemed to be above us, floating in the confines of her chair, her gray dress merging with the tablecloth so that we could not see where the table left off and she began.

"No!" Madame Lacome screamed. "You may not have her!"

Herr Schliemer barked. He barked as realistically as a human can bark. Then he growled. The growl sounded more menacing than anything I had heard in my brief life as a hunter. I looked quickly to him and saw that he now stood beside Madame Lacome. His great weight pressed down on the center of the table.

A cold wind blew through the room. The fire flashed and licked at the screen. Katrina fell into her chair and collapsed, insensible, obviously drained. The curtains at the window flapped and then stilled. The ancient globe spun on its brass stand, the creaking sound a lid being opened. Far away, near the bottom of the great house, we heard steps running down the stairs, running until all the steps in all the houses of the village could not have remained untouched.

"Raped by Herr Halder, is what I make of it," Madame Lacome said. "Raped in the basement. And maybe raped by the coal man as well. Such a tuning fork! We could not have invented a superior woman. I'm tempted to invite her along with us. Katrina rings at both noon and midnight, I promise you. The poor unfortunate."

Madame Lacome said this over a plate of lamb. She also drank from a bottle of red wine, exultant with her success. Though she refused to tell me how much she had been paid by Frau Halder, she had obviously fared well. She had ordered the food as soon as she returned to the inn, then sent me scuttling from my mother to Herr Mueller for more cord wood. She liked a warm fire, she said, on such a cold evening. Before long she had things arranged to her liking. Even my mother could not supress her curiosity. She lingered after serving the meal and added more wood herself to the fire. Madame Lacome ignored her at first, but then told her the barest outline, pleading fatigue. "These events tire one so," she said. Then she informed my mother that something had been buried in the basement of Frau Halder's house, something that had better be exhumed, and left my mother gasping for more. When it became impolite for my mother to linger any longer, she abandoned me in the Madame Lacome's sitting room, doubtless hoping I would secure more details. Madame Lacome played my mother as she had played everyone along the way.

I watched her eat. Her hair still shimmered with the raindrops, though she had toweled it dry as much as possible. She now sat at her ease, expansive, happy, her slippered feet outstretched to the fire. She ate the mutton off the fork as if trying to draw a tune off the tines. She followed these bites with quick gulps of wine, her hands restless. She appeared happy. Several times she smiled at me for no apparent reason. When she had eaten enough to quiet her hunger, she turned to me as if ready to indulge another appetite.

"So what do you think occurred, William?" she asked. "You haven't said much. Was any of it authentic? Or what this more of my trickery?"

"That's what I'd like to ask you."

"Of course you would. You have a peasant's mind about these matters. Yes or no, real or unreal. The Blood of Christ, is that real?"

"I suppose it is," I said. "The priests say it is."

"But they don't mean the wine in the chalice is actually blood, do they? Do you think they are ghouls, standing up before the congregation and drinking blood? We should have a different opinion of priests if that were the case."

I shrugged. Madame Lacome asked me to put more wood on the fire. I did so. I recognized the oak branches as ones I had cut up beyond the vineyard. She told me to put on more. I followed her order reluctantly, knowing my father's caution about chimney fires. But I did not want to displease at that moment.

"Sit, sit, William," she said, lifting her wine. "I owe you nothing at all, you know? You are thinking that you have a right to understand, but you don't. I want that clear between us. Now, when you have seen something you can't explain, now you are interested in what I have to say. Floating women, eh? A clever trick, wasn't it? And how did we manage the boom of the stairway? Simple illusion, is that what you think? Tell me, William. I'm curious to hear your reaction."

"I don't know. It frightened me."

"Well, naturally. What if I told you we paid this Katrina enough to put her on our side? Would that make you feel better or worse?"

"Worse. I wouldn't like to know you had a conspiracy."

"A conspiracy?" Madame Lacome laughed. "Yes, a conspiracy, William. We have tricked everyone in this village by actually listening to them. People don't expect to be heard, you know. Most people will tell you everything you need to know about them in the first five minutes of your acquaintance, but no one listens. It's true. You look at me as if I've grown a second thumb, but it's true. And even if someone does succeed in listening, she doesn't believe what she hears. It's human nature; that's our conspiracy."

"But did Katrina float? And don't turn it back on me, Madame Lacome. Tell me yes or no."

"Perhaps she raised up, half standing, and the table cloth obscured her legs. Isn't that what you thought?"

"Yes or no?" I repeated.

"Yes," she said, and drank off the last of her wine glass.

"She floated?"

"Yes, of course. The spirits held her. Or perhaps she raised into the air on her own. Who knows? She was a remarkable woman. Insane, of course, this Katrina. But give me a woman of madness anytime over a dry peach pit like Vicki. Truth is, Vicki is the mad woman in that household. She will torture Katrina until the young girl is quite beside herself. Then Vicki will be able to discount everything that has occurred and return to her former beliefs. You see how it goes? Katrina could lift them all up if they would only listen to her. But when a person holds a hand out from the edge of a lake, is she pulling drowning people out or asking to be pulled in herself?"

Before I could ask more questions, someone knocked at the door. Madame Lacome nodded at me. I opened the door to find Eva nervously fingering the hem of her apron. She appeared flushed and worried. I raised my eyebrows, but Eva ignored me.

"M'am," she said over my shoulder, addressing Madame Lacome, "you better come straightaway. The gentleman is in the barn and it's bad. William's mother told me to fetch you."

"What gentleman?" Madame Lacome asked, though she had already begun to push up from her chair.

"Your gentleman," Eva said. "Herr Schliemer. The large man."

Madame Lacome pushed the table away, upsetting the wine glass in the process. Red wine dripped off the table and crept into the mortar creases of the stone fireplace. Madame Lacome moved with great agility: shoes, coat, gloves. She did not pause or check her room a second time. Watching her, I could not rid myself of the feeling that she was accustomed to speedy departures.

Eva stepped to one side to let Madame Lacome pass.

"Some men from the village and your father," Eva said at my back as we hurried down the steps after Madame Lacome. "They are in a ugly mood. The men are saying Madame Lacome is in league with the devil. They wanted to burn the cart and run them out of town, but the giant stepped out and stopped them. Something terrible is going to happen, William."

"Tell Herr Mueller," I said. "Get him."

"He's gone into town. The two German soldiers are with your

father. They put him up to it. They told him he shouldn't harbor such people at the inn."

We heard the voices as soon as we stepped outside. Madame Lacome flashed in front of us. By the time we reached the barn, she had burst into the midst of the men. I recognized a few roughs from the heurigers in town, but they merely formed a background for the main drama. The titled soldier, the older gentleman, stood to one side of the group. Clearly he had been drinking; his face beamed red, like the wet flank of a sorrel horse. My father stood close to him, drunk also, happy to gain the approbation of a soldier of superior rank. I hated seeing his superciliousness. Though I couldn't know for certain, I suspected he had ingratiated himself by allowing this confrontation to occur. I imagined the idle boasts, the escalating venom of his assertions.

The blonde soldier, however, held center stage. In the dim lantern light, he stood in the center of the half moon of men, his sidearm loosed from its holster. His hair, fastidious in the time he had spent with us, had become disheveled. His stance, while arrogant, showed signs of drunkenness also.

He had been pushed to this spot, no doubt, but he enjoyed riding the wave of his companions' lust. He reminded me of a pigeon turned sideways to court. Now and then his free hand lifted and he ran his ring finger over his slender lips. I knew he had stalled. He was not sure how to go forward or what exactly he hoped to gain from this bracing.

"Stop!" Madame Lacome commanded as she made her way to the center of the barn. "You vile men! Stop this immediately! You sad, sad cowards!"

The men laughed. They laughed in the way drunken men laugh – all stomach and no eyes. My father joined them, his heavy note a bass for them all. Hearing them, Madame Lacome raised her hand and pointed her index finger and pinkie at the men, in what we could not fail to recognize as the evil eye. The men grew silent. It was an extraordinary moment. She circled slowly, as if holding them at gun point. Her skirt dragged through the hay of the barn floor. Her black hair appeared to absorb the jaundiced glimmer of the lanterns. She could not reach any of their eyes.

"You will be cursed beyond your children if you touch this man or our possessions," she said quietly. "Leave this barn immediately. You have no quarrel with us."

Then she spoke in Hungarian or another language I could not understand. Her voice became a murmur and it seemed to me that she had receded somewhere, gone into a trance. She continued turning slowly, pointing at each man so that there could be no mistaking that he had been sighted. The men sank back slightly when her hand passed over them. I felt the chill of her hand myself. The men's skepticism grew more blank as she continued to speak her warm flow of imprecations.

"Such a dark Jew," the blonde soldier said, his voice a pale soprano. "A Jew has nothing to say to us. She's a dirty gypsy, that's all. I am shocked, Colonel, that you would permit her to remain here."

"If you leave now, you will wake tomorrow and be no different from today," Madame Lacome said quietly, this time directly to the blonde soldier. "If you do not, you will wonder what has changed, won't you? And at the first shift in your health, you will wonder if it is not my curse that has touched you. I will grow in your mind until you cannot be sure of yourselves. I promise you, I will burn in your consciousness like a coal in a thick rug."

The blonde soldier lifted his sidearm and shot Madame Lacome.

For an instant, nothing else occurred. Before the solider could so much as lower his gun, the giant leapt forward and snatched him from the ground. No one, I think, could believe the giant could move so quickly. The giant lifted the solider and shook him, knocking the gun from his hand. Then in a short, violent stroke, the giant lifted his knee and cracked the man in two across it. The blonde soldier's body broke as easily as icicle snapped from a porch on a warm winter day. His legs went limp and jangled for an instant before the giant cast him away. The body skidded against a stall door, the head and shoulders turned in an unnatural way from the legs and feet. Then the giant turned to the other men.

They had no heart for it. The older soldier backed quickly away, his eyes moving from the body of the blonde solider to the giant, then back again, his mouth open in a wide circle of a surprise. Madame Lacome groaned on the floor. The giant moved toward the next man in line, a wide, ugly fellow named Linklon, who turned and ran like a goat. His companions moved after him, though they attempted to leave without running. My father began to move away, too, though I knew he would return with a rifle.

The giant caught him up with two great strides and hit him so viciously I was certain my father would die. His body slumped. The giant struck him again, this time using the momentum of his blow to lower my father's body to the ground. I knew that the giant had not killed my father out of deference to me.

"Get our things, William," the giant said to me. "Hurry about it. We leave tonight."

He turned and slipped to one knee beside Madame Lacome. His great hand pressed the blood at her breast. Without turning, he repeated his instructions to me. Quickly, and without hesitation, I followed his orders.

HIGH SCHOOL

ON AN AUGUST NIGHT YOU go with your best girl friend to a pasture you know about. A stream runs through it at the foot of a long slope of timothy grass. You have been here hunting woodchucks, wading for frogs. You turn your lights out and park in the dead center of the meadow, no one around, no dogs barking, nothing but crickets and cicadas and the stutter of stars. You kiss a while. You kiss a lot, falling into her, because you love her, love her like nothing you've ever felt before. And you reach behind and pull out a blanket. You have done this before, some of it, so the blanket is no shock. You roll it on the sweet grass, lay down with her. She wears a pair of shorts and a man's shirt. She has paint on her hands, because she does landscapes, paints in a small room above her dad's automobile. Her studio, she likes to say. She has big books she gazes at for hours at a time, but not tonight. Tonight she slowly unbuttons her white shirt, a man's shirt, and shows you her white bra. You unhook it and lay down with her and you kiss, kiss a thousand times, kiss until it's time to take off her pants. Immediately you enter her, her panties pushed to one side, the crickets louder this low to the ground. A few mosquitoes, but not many, because you are moving, moving constantly, the kissing like a great anchor that holds you both. Then you have to have everything off, every speck of clothing, and she surprises you by standing and stripping in front of you. And when you thought she would come back to you, she surprises you again by running away. She is so quick and beautiful that she is gone, presto, hidden in the darkness. You hunt for her and eventually spot her shadow form, the black image of her, and you catch her in three or four great leaps and tumble her to the ground. Fuck her. She fucks you. It's nutty and wild and sweaty. Grass everywhere and you roll over, roll again, fuck and dig and throw yourself into her. Then you let her up and you repeat it. She hides and you chase her, again, again, fucking just for five minutes whenever you catch her. Once you fuck her in the small, tadpole pool you remember. You lie down, belly up, and let her straddle you. Mud and water. You put your head back and let the stream cover your ears until you listen to nothing, to water and nothing but water, even she is gone. But she fucks you hard, up and down, and you chase her again. This time you spread her legs as wide as you can and fuck her until you come. Hard, you can't help it. A little later you lay in the blanket, close, both of you huddled in the scratchy wool. You kiss and look at the stars. You kiss more and you can't have enough from this woman, this girl, you love her You kiss and eventually fuck again, this time not fucking, this time smooth and gentle as dice in a dry hand. You tell her you love her. You tell her over and over, the truth of it so undeniable, so powerful, and she answers that she loves you too. An owl calls somewhere and that's a sign of death, can be, but that isn't what you're thinking about. You hold her afterward and the wind keeps the mosquitoes off. When you drive her home, she puts her head on your shoulder. You love her even more now than before. You walk her to her door and kiss her good night, chastely, and you wait until you see her light come on in her room. You go down the stairs and then out on the walk. You smell an autumn smell, something like candle fire in pumpkins. In the car, you keep the windows cracked and drive slowly. You think about her. You cannot remember anythıng but her.

And you kiss her one night outside the library. You are both supposed to be studying but you have come out for a break to sit in your car, at least that's what you say, and she leans against your car door and talks. Then she stops talking and you kiss, you pull her neck toward you, too hard, you apologize, but then it is all covered with her kissing, her lips, both of you pushing books to the floor, swimming toward each other over World Geo 1, U.S. Hist 2, Intro To Literary Themes, brown paving stones of dullness. The books land and slide and she goes up onto her knees and pours into you, your arms wrapped and tied and solid. And you cannot take your mouth from hers, not for a moment, you kiss, and you dust your hands over her breasts, her ass, her thighs, cup her pussy once for an instant, but the kiss is it, that's all, and you have strange images of her as your sweetheart, your one and true sweetheart, and you want to go steady, want to rake leaves with her, want to give her a letter sweater, these 1950's dreams, want to take her to a hop, want to kiss her and reach up her wide poodle skirt, want to see her legs go up the stairs while her white panties ring like a clapper in the bell of her skirt, want it to be Christmas and lights and a fireplace and cocoa and her wearing angora. That's what you want and you keep kissing her, the heat finally slowing, until she pushes back, says, *whew*, and fluffs her hair in the mirror on the backside of the passenger visor. She says she has to study, and she does, but you reach your hand over and put it on her thigh, flat, calm, and then you move it a little toward her pussy, just a bit, and the tension in your hand is enough to explode her, she jumps back and you kiss harder, fiercely, her bracelet clanging off the steering wheel, her hands running over you as though she could mend bones with them, until she pulls back and says, stop, stop, we should stop, but turns and lays across your lap and stays there, and you take long kisses, calm kisses that rush up just to the edge, just like water going over a curb, and then you rest your hand on her breast. I love you, you say and mean it and she says it back and you kiss, and it's a middle ground, this kiss, somewhere that is deeper and calmer and more important, something that has to do with libraries on a Tuesday night.

— My parents are going away for the weekend, she says on the phone one night.

—When?

—This weekend, she says.

In your locker you find: *I Love You.* It is written on a note of pink paper, scented by something, and you hold it to your nose, carry it with you until you find her by her locker and wait patiently while she opens her locker door, the note in your hand, and you lean forward and kiss her behind the door, shielded, and the kiss blooms like a Ouija planchette skidding out of control, until she has to close the door and iron her hands down her sweater and skirt, while a faculty member you've never seen coughs and walks past.

You stand knee deep in the Cold River and cast toward a wolf maple. The maple has been hanging over this pool for thirty years, a hundred years, since it was water itself. The trick is to let the fly bump off the bark of the tree, stall, then drop into the pool as though chance had thrown it there. You have on a Muddler Minnow, a wet fly that can be mistaken by a trout for a grasshopper, a sculpin minnow, a dace. But it's autumn so terrestrials are a good choice and you decide the grasshopper is a grasshopper, spent for the summer, its last ride a swirling down the currents while trout shark underneath. As the Muddler falls into the water you hear Gary, your buddy, shout that he has one. He is fishing the pool upstream, to the north, and you glance up and see him in the early fall sunlight, and he stands with insects whirring around him, spinners, and a row of birches behind him. The birches are white and you stare at Gary and in pulses he disappears and you keep looking until you have nothing in your head except the pull of the stream on your shins and the thought that in two days, on Saturday, you will sleep beside her.

Her father is checking the oil on the Jeep when you pull in and park to the side of the driveway. The floodlight is on and he moves back and forth to remove his shadow from the engine so he can see what he is doing. He holds a paper towel to the dipstick as though it had a nosebleed.

—Hey, he says, there's the guy.

You lift the two trout out of the front seat. You have them wrapped in mint in your creel.

—Whoa, he says, holding the dipstick to one side as you present the trout. I may eat those for breakfast. Where'd you get them?

—Cold River.

—That pool by the tree?

—And Gary caught three up above.

He puts the tip of the dipstick back in the engine and stabs it down.

—Ms. Rembrandt is painting, he says. You take those into Mrs. C and then you can run up and see her.

Mrs. C is working a crossword, a cola colored drink in front of her. She looks up when you walk in and pushes her chin at the sink. You slide the trout out of the creel. For a second a reflection flashes off Mrs. C's glasses. Mrs. C asks if they are cleaned and gutted and you say yes. You put them on a white plate and then slide them into the refrigerator. When you close the door, you imagine the trout believing themselves to be back in the dark cold of the stream.

—Not too long, she says, meaning you can go up and see your girlfriend, but not for long.

—I have to get home anyway, you say.

You could follow the smell of paint to her studio. The studio is uninsulated and chilly, a garage storage area. She is working on a landscape. The easel is propped up beside the one window, but the light outside is gone. She does not turn when you come in and you like that about her. You sit down, knowing better than to disturb her when she is painting. She has music playing, Japanese music, strings plucked at odd intervals. For a time you sit and watch her paint. Her shoulder blades move under the skin of her back, under the fabric of her blue oxford. The slant of the roof does something with perspective, so you can imagine her farther away, then closer, then away again. She does something with her brush in the painting sky. Trees. Birds. A green smear.

She turns and smiles. Moths hit against the window.

Driving home a deer stands next to the road but doesn't cross.

You slow and lift your hand. It still doesn't move and for a moment you wonder if the deer is there at all. Then you tap your hand on the roof of your car, just to see the deer go, and it does. It bounds in half-moons toward the Kramer's orchard, its hooves mashing dropped apples, you guess, as it goes.

On Friday you pack your dad's old pick up. It is September and beginning to be cold. You pack a Eureka tent, a fly rod, a sleeping bag, oatmeal, water, cookies. You pack a sleeping pad, a box of strike anywhere matches, a copy of *A Separate Peace*. You kiss your mom, tell her you will be home Sunday, drive to Gary's. He throws his stuff on top of yours, shows you a joint in the palm of his hand, wiggles his eyebrows. You drive to the Cold River and camp where you always do, on a bright spit of stone and sand that sits in the elbow of the river. You spend the first half hour collecting firewood and setting up camp, then you fish until you can no longer see.

—A big mother up in that hole, Gary says when he returns.

—You catch him?

—Not hardly.

You cook oatmeal and eat a peanut butter and jelly sandwich while the oatmeal warms. Gary feeds wood into the fire, poking it slowly. He lights the joint and you both smoke for a while. A little later a raccoon shows up at the smell of cooking. It waddles in the dim light of the fire, keeping its distance. Gary pegs a stone in its direction and it looks up, cat burglar, masked.

You sleep with your head pointing east. The river runs beside you and you can hear it in the stones, in the sand, and it could be running beneath you for all you know. The sound fills the tent and fills everything in your earshot. You think of her and for a while she floats in the river, or rides above it, you can't tell. You get hard thinking of her, and you picture her turning to you in her studio and lifting her skirt, her jean skirt, and reaching down with her green brush to paint a heart on her white panties. On her pussy. Your eyes stay on hers as she paints.

Then it is morning and you wake to the sound of crows picking over your fire. You slip out and build the fire up, yellow flames in the gray fog of the river bend. Tonight, you tell yourself, you will sleep next to her. You read for a while with your back propped up against a log. Finally Gary pushes out of the tent and keeps coming on his hands and knees to the fire.

—You put on tea water? He asks.

—Not yet.

—Asshole, he says.

He fusses with the teakettle while you lean back against the log. Out in the river, close to the far bank, a trout rises. It tilts its fins and accepts the push of the water until it is a jet, a confirmation of the law of physics, the insect down its gullet before it is fully in the water again.

You come up through the meadow in back. You arrive on foot because it would be crazy to park your car in the driveway all night. She has promised to leave the back porch light off if it is clear, on if something has come up. But the light is off. Her house sits in the pale evening, the black metal roof pulling into the darkness above. The living room light is on. The den light is on. You walk through the meadow and feel the dew coat your jeans. Coppy, their black cat, sits on the split rail fence close to the house. Coppy's eyes move past you for birds and bats and mice.

She answers at the first tap in jeans, bare feet, a button up sweater. Her hair is clean. She smells of soap. She pulls back and lets you into the kitchen, shy. You feel shy, too, suddenly, and she fixes you iced tea and tells you about how hard it was for her parents to leave, how you have to be careful because Mrs. Phillipone may call or swing by to check on things, how you have to be up early, no kidding, really early, before light, and get out of there. Then she kisses you against the kitchen island and tells you you smell grungy but not bad, and she kisses you some more and leans against you and the whole thing has started. You reach and cup her ass in your hands, pull her into you.

The rocker is big enough for her knees to fit on either side of your legs so that she can sit on your cock, her pussy juiced with your first come, her body quiet and beautiful in the light from the porch. You kiss her neck. She lifts and moves so you can kiss all of her neck, her breasts close to your face, her clothes gone, her hair wet at the ends from sweat. It is silent in the house. No music playing in case she had to hear Mrs. Phillipone pull into the driveway, she said, so you put your head back after you have finished with her neck for a time and you hear crickets and toad trills and wind. You rock slowly, in an out, her pussy covering you, and you believe there might be no end to either one of you, that you might go somewhere, into each other's bloodstream. Then such thoughts are emptied because her body is there, and here, and there, and you kiss her, building a little. She fucks you hard for three thrusts, getting at something she feels, then she soothes you again. She kisses you, lips, teeth, tongue. Then she puts her head against your neck, tucks her arms close to her body, fucks you slowly until the phone rings.

She kisses you as the phone rings again, pulls away, covers your mouth with her hand.

—Hello? she says.

Then: —No, just getting ready to go to bed. Yes, I locked everything. Sure. Okay. No, he's fishing this weekend with his friend Gary. The Cold River. Yes. Yes, he likes to fish. Yes, he is a good guy. They should be home tomorrow. Yes. Okay. That's would be great.

You arch and push your cock hard into her pussy.

—Okay, well thanks. Yes, I have your number. No, really, everything is fine. Yes, I'm a big girl. Well, thanks. Okay. Thanks, thank you for checking in. Goodnight.

She hangs up and kisses you hard. Over and over, she kisses you until her tongue is in your mouth and you cannot breathe without breathing her.

Shoulder to shoulder, you cook eggs, onions, toast, cheese. A black skillet on the stove. She wears a terry cloth robe, white, her hair wet from the shower. You have showered together, water and soap, your hands gentle on each other, a tide of sex washing away with water. You are starved. You sprinkle salt, pepper, watch the eggs grow yellow. The onions are already brown. When it is ready, she serves it on one plate, two forks, both of you in the dark. She does not want the lights to be conspicuous in case anyone drives by, so you eat at the breakfast bar, a low set of Joni Mitchell on the player, light from the stereo the only illumination. You sit with your legs around hers, knotted, both of you eating without talking much. You wear your shorts, a t shirt, your green flannel shirt. It is 2:30 in the morning. She holds up ketchup, raises her eyebrows, you nod. A squirt. Then back to eating. Without thinking, you hold hands. Left hands, so your right hands can move.

In her studio, next to the slant of the roof, you hear the rain begin. Maybe it is light. At first you can't tell. Then your eyes move gradually open and it is early, four thirty, five o'clock, an autumn morning. For an instant you are not sure where you are. Then you feel her next to you, naked, her left leg over yours. You roll closer and she turns and pushes her ass toward you, spoons, you hold her for a long time and fall back asleep. Ten minutes, a half hour, you linger. You move forward until the length of your stomach rests against the length of her back. Rain slides and pulls against the roof. The sun is slow. You feel yourself getting hard, then you are inside her, that easy. You mount her, shoving your cock in her hard, pushing her into the bed. She arches. You lean over her, kiss her neck, push her again and again into the bed. She gets your motion and starts jamming into your force, rises onto her knees, fucks. She puts her hands on the headboard and lets you look at her, morning light, her hips perfect. Then you roll her over, or she rolls, and you enter her that way. The heat climbs you. It is no longer in your groins but in your hearts. You kiss. Wind comes in through the window and the smell of rain on the grasses and you kiss and hold her. She holds you, too, and her legs come around you and you put your arms around her as far as they will go and you fuck slowly, gently, in and out, cock and cunt and lips. You kiss her and kiss her and feel near to crying somehow, you don't know why. You kiss until you empty into her, everything, deeper and stronger until something in your spine begins to shiver. You keep kissing her and for a while you don't move. The rain hits the roof hard and you doze, or she dozes, and finally she laughs because you have to go out in the rain. Go, she says. You have to go. I love you, you say, and she says she knows, she loves you too, and neither of you has moved. Then you push away and stand next to the bed and dress. And she falls back asleep. You like that. You like that she will sleep and you will go and the rain is harder on the roof. Downstairs, quietly. The china cabinet shakes a little when you reach the ground floor. You go onto the balls of your feet. You think about leaving a note, saying something, but someone might arrive and see it. Parents, Mrs. Phillipone. You cross the kitchen, see the black skillet in the sink. Coppy, the black cat, comes in through the door as soon as you open it. His tail is up. He whets himself against your leg, purrs. You step out on the back porch. The meadow grass is white with rain.

A MAN'S GUIDE TO DIVORCE

HER LAST LOVER CALLED HIMSELF Sir Fuckalot.

She tells you this as you stand at the stove, stirring spaghetti sauce, impressing her with your sensitive side. You stop and smile down at the sauce, because you're older, wiser, been around, and you aren't easily intimidated.

"Was his name apt?" you ask.

"He was crazy," she says as she twists a little on the white wine stool, her fine, angled ass perching perfectly.

She crosses her legs and you see, down at the ankle, a small glimmer. A bracelet, an anklet, whatever the hell it is, but it charms you. She has blonde hair, a silk blouse, black pants. She has dressed for you, you understand, although you can't help feeling you are both wearing stage costumes. You in a flannel shirt, jeans, a Dodge Dakota pick-up out in the yard. You playing wounded, gut shot divorced man, no son, no daughter, little serious income, but an excellent fire place, decent brandy, and a love of poetry. *Outdoor Magazine*. A kayak tucked in the rafters of the garage, the splash skirt still damp.

First night, blind dates, all that. You want to be her Sir Fuckalot, you want to fuck every man out of her memory, every damn one except maybe Daddy. Daddy can stay, but the rest have to go, and you intend, like stone, to whet her against your body until she remembers only you.

Tonight, getting the yard straightened for her arrival, you pulled in the hose and found it stiff and heavy with the first clots of winter. The grass beneath the hose was yellow.

Winding the hose at the back of the garage, you looped it carefully, a kinetic still life, the season creeping up the rubber tubing and remaining there until spring.

Pottery Barn checked napkins, Pottery Barn pasta bowls. You serve the dinner, and a third glass of Chardonay, beside the fire on a small table you bought at a yard sale in Ashland. The table has an aged blue design across the front and down the legs.

"Varicose veins," Pete, a kayak friend, your only real local friend, said when you loaded the table into the Dodge Dakota.

Women like the table, though. The table looks comely beside the fire.

You folded the napkins yourself, pressed them too, though you took care not to make the table fussed over. New York asters in a jelly glass, the petals just weary enough to flake and dust the table. One stem holds a black conga line of infinitesimal insects. The chairs on either side are mismatched.

Holding just the edge of her chair to seat her, polite but not overbearing, you remember the chairs your wife carried away in the settlement. Large, elegant chairs, with manly arms and lions' paws. Chairs that sprang forward at table. These chairs, here beside the fire, are more rickety than your wife's chairs. Less certain. They rock slightly as your guest sits.

"Oh, everything looks lovely," she says. You say you wanted your first dinner to be nice. She repeats that things look lovely and you joke that she hasn't tasted anything yet.

Hold your horses, you say, which is a phrase outdated by about one hundred and seventy five years. You also realize, standing beside her chair, that you have had too much wine. You had a beer, no, make it two beers, before she arrived, deliberately anesthetizing your nerves. You're not ashamed to admit a drink can calm you and that you depend on scotch on the rocks existing in the world.

You place your hand on the chair back again to steady yourself. Then you duck around her, around her chair, and throw two hunks of birch in the fire. You know these particular hunks of wood because you cut them yourself, borrowing Pete's chain saw to clear out the land around the back of the property. The birches came down so quickly, you cut them with something like regret. The timber at the base of the trees had oxidized and turned to rust. The saw going through them seemed to churn through time.

Standing from the fire, you look sideways down her blouse and see her left breast. Her bra is green, the color of dragonflies.

"So are you from this area?" you ask.

"No, actually I was raised in New Joisey," she says, turning Jersey into "Joisey" in a voice you recognize as Curley's from The Three Stooges.

"Joisey, eh?"

"Exit 135," she says.

"Really."

"Really. I have a theory that everyone, at some point in her or his life, comes from New Jersey. It's like a sacrament of modern living. Or like the stations of the cross. That and New York. You have to live in each place once in your life."

"Really," you say, your tongue a bit redundant with wine.

"Why do you keep asking really? Do you think I'm making this up? By the way, the pasta is excellent. Really."

She laughs and spears more spaghetti.

The fire is hot. You scooch your chair away from the heat a little. You notice, not for the first time, the bingle of her earring against her neck. The flash, delightful, reminds you of a spoon to attract trout.

You smile and behind your smile you are there, locked away, gazing out. Do you like me? you want to ask. Am I what you thought I was when you thought I was worth knowing?

You want to take her hand and lead her to bed and sleep, that's all, under your comforter. Sleep and sleep and sleep the windows open and frost rolling in like the mists of Dracula through the screens. You have a notion that she might say yes, she would do that, although you also wonder if more is expected.

Sir Fuckalot.

You pour more wine, wondering, as you do, if you aren't making her passage home impossible. She can't drive home with too much booze on board. At the same time you think, out of no reason you can pinpoint, that you should get a dog. A puppy around the place. A cat, actually, would be the thing. Let it roam the forest in back, stealing from the woodpiles, snakes, chipmunks, squirrels, all of them running into her fury.

Mice are a problem in your house, so a cat would answer,

yet a cat, scraping its claws on your couch, ruining what few good things you have, is not a good idea. Your thoughts are becoming blocky and you resolve to cut off your wine for at least a half hour.

Watching her, seeing the red heft of spaghetti travel to her mouth, you remember music. You've forgotten it completely. You pop up, head to the small office at the rear of the house, and say, "God, I haven't played any music for you."

"I was afraid to ask," she said. "I thought maybe you were into some sort of spiritual silence. You know."

"No, no, nothing as profound as that, believe me," you call in a movie voice, a voice you always associate with Katherine Hepburn and Carey Grant flinging words to each other in "The Philadelphia Story."

"Any requests?" you ask.

"No, you play what you like. I can make all sorts of judgements about you from what you select."

"Fair enough."

Van Morrison? Frank Sinatra? Or the safe bet, the Chopin Mazurkas. You put on the Mazurkas, listen to two measures of their dark, venomous sounds, and know they don't cover the mood. "Sorry," you say, "I just had a moment of taking life seriously."

"That's okay," she calls back. "Who was it? I didn't recognize it."

"Chopin, the mazurkas."

"Moody son of a bitch, aren't you?"

"Yes I am," you say in the stilted, wooden inflection of the recent tv commercial.

In the commercial an imposter steals a ride in a stretch limo by affirming that he is, indeed, Dr. Krakowskowitz. Or something like that.

You put on John Lee Hooker, a blues man, which is maybe too sexual and night club for what you have going. But you like John Lee Hooker, and besides, no one can criticize you for liking a black blues man. It's safe, yet demonstrates a breath of knowledge.

You turn it low and go back to the table, pick your napkin off the seat of your chair.

"John Lee Hooker?" she asks.

"You're good."

"I like the blues."

"But do you really like my spaghetti sauce?"

"Yes I do," she says, using the same tv commercial inflection you used a moment ago. "You like to cook?"

"Sometimes."

"I'm the same way. I hate cooking for myself, but that's a given, I suppose. I mean, I went through this stage where I told myself, ok, Carol, you're on your own, so you're going to have to make things nice. You probably did the same thing, right? So you cook these elaborate meals, telling yourself it's okay, until you eventually find yourself cleaning all these dishes. And for what? Life in the nineties, huh?"

"Absolutely."

"What's the most ridiculous meal you ever cooked for yourself? Wait, I'll go first. I only asked the question because I wanted to tell you that I once cooked an entire Thanksgiving dinner for myself. I told myself that I wouldn't feel sad or absurd eating it by myself. It was a low point, believe me."

"I think Sunday brunches are a little tough. When I first got divorced I tried to make a big deal out of hanging around Sunday mornings. The New York Times, bagels, expensive coffees. The whole works. Now I eat a bowl of cereal and get on with it."

"On with what though? That's the question."

"On with kayaking, mostly. Or something outdoors. I spend a lot of time outdoors doing the Boy Scout thing."

"How about doing Girl Scouts?" she says, and you can't tell if it's the wine or a sudden surge of sexuality.

"It's politically incorrect to do Girl Scouts, isn't it?"

She shrugs. Her earring flickers again. Her earring reminds you of a goldfinch at your bird feeder. Goldfinches, you thought the other day, are like yellow tennis balls with wings.

After the last bite, the plates pushed forward, the phone rings and you don't answer it. You don't have to explain because she is single too. It might be out of politeness, your desire not to compromise your time with her, or it might be your desire not to talk to another woman while this one is here. The machine picks up and is serious for three full minutes. Carol, in front of you, crosses her legs and smiles, sardonically, yes, you believe it is a sardonic smile, at the fire.

"So, tell me about kayaking," she says.

She is back on the stool, a cup of coffee smoking on her knee.

You are at the sink. You are also aware that you should be careful not to say too much. Men talk too much about themselves, you understand, and you generally find it more interesting to hear what women have to say anyway.

"It's good," you say. "I like it. It gets me away for the weekends. We've got a group that sort of goes. It's like a party, loose, and of course it takes us to pretty places. I'm not very good at it."

"Do you think it's important to put your life on the line from time to time?"

You turn. You think this is one of the better questions you've been asked in a while.

"Maybe," you say. "I hadn't thought of it exactly that way, but maybe."

"That was the first thing that popped into my head when I heard you were a kayaker."

"Really?"

"Sure."

"How about you?" you ask, your fingers in the drain. Spaghetti is curled in the drainer. "Do you think it's important to put your life on the line from time to time?"

"Well, I could say we risk our lives constantly. Driving, walking around cities. Going on blind dates, that's putting your life on the line," she says and laughs. "But I don't do it much. Not like that. For me it's more a question of quiet desperation. You know."

"Quiet desperation? Really?"

"That's melodramatic, I guess. I just think living as a single person, you're closer to death. You think about falling down in your bathtub and hitting your head and no one finding you for a week or two. That kind of thing. So I guess I feel like I put my life on the line now and then."

"I see what you're saying," you say, although you don't, quite.

At the same time you wonder if it isn't time for a kiss. For an embrace, at any rate. You wonder how you're supposed to cross the kitchen floor and bend slightly and kiss her.

So much is understood in the first kiss, though it has to be casual and light. Suave.

Calculating, you carry dead pasta in a plastic grocery bag, single man bags, she has called them, and you deliberately fill the other hand with a head of lettuce. At the refrigerator you ask her to pull open the door.

Then you turn, hands full, and say, "Is this a good time to have a first kiss?"

"Maybe," she says and goes up on her toes.

You kiss. Handless, just lips. You dance in the middle of the living room. Dancing is a cliché, at least it was for the first minute and a half, but now it works. You hold her close, arm around waist around waist around fingers around fingers. Passing the fire, slowly, your groins growing knowledgeable, heat colors your shins.

Van Morrison, finally. When you should be thinking of her, Carol, you think instead of Ruth, your first lover after your divorce, who told you once that she deliberately sent heat to you through her stomach. That she tried to bake you, turn your flesh to glazed pottery, capturing your heart inside like a frog in a watering can.

You think, too, of a bend on the Deerfield River, where two fishermen looked up, startled at your sudden appearance in their waters. The kayak turned tail back, and you realized you drifted toward them like a cowboy, his horse stepping back end right. Then the river carried you past, down white cliffs of foam, and the last you heard from the fishermen was the whistling of their fly lines silenced by the water.

You think all this as you smell Carol's neck, smell it again, pull her closer. She pulls back, slowly, hardly discernable, two flowers moving toward sunlight. You kiss her again, her temple, her ear, and she tucks in, making herself small against you. Your cock stiffens and you do nothing to move it away from her groin. Let her know how she affects you. Let her know what's happening between you.

Your hands, you notice, smell of Ivory dish soap.

If you could fuck any woman you like, or have a million dollars, which would you choose? Pete asked last week. You didn't answer.

"I know it sounds silly," Carol says in the near darkness, the fireplace dying and making movies on her skin, "but could we not go all the way?"

"Of course. Whatever you say."

She covers her face and rolls a little out from under you. Her shirt is open. So is yours. She laughs.

"Christ, did I actually say that?" she says. "Did I actually say `go all the way'?"

"Yes, you did," you say, using the tv commercial inflection again.

"I mean, it's just....."

She shakes her head. You kiss her, and kiss her some more, and some more, and eventually her hands drop. She pulls you back squarely on top of her and kisses you passionately. *Lordy, lordy, make my backbone slip*, you think, a song lyric out of somewhere in the fifties.

This passion is a treat she's giving you, a promise of things to come, a message that she finds you just fine. You go along with it, ride it, give her one or two extra volts in return, but deliberately hold back. Sex with Carol will be good, but you wonder if it will be as good as she seems to think it will be.

Sir Fuckalot. You wonder, holding her against your shoulder a little later, if he fucked her frequently from behind, if she liked him to come in her mouth, if she let him put it up her ass. Your cock gets hard at the thought, at the mental picture, and you squeeze her close, letting her interpret your ardor anyway she likes.

It's a hug that melts into sleep and you wake at 3:17 in the morning, the fire popping loudly, consuming a last vein of birch sap. You slip out of bed, move the fire screen more snugly against the brick hearth, tip toe into the kitchen and drink a glass of water.

You drink two. You think for an instant about your wife, her new lover, her life out on the west coast. You wonder if she drinks the milky coffee she loved so much in Venice. *Latti makadi.* Prego, *lattie makiaddi*, you learned to say, both of you, murdering the word at every stop in Italy. And how she loved Rome, the Coliseum, the cafe beside the ancient chariot course, and a plate of calamari she had at the Gladiator Restaurant very close to Christmas. How she looked, shining, happy, her love of travel so fresh on her that you held her hand almost all afternoon.

You think about her hand, and it is transformed to a lion's paw, reminding you again of your lost dining room chairs. Then you think of your own chairs, still standing at the sink, and you suspect dinner went well. Went better than well, Carol liked it, liked you, and the fact that your ex-wife is maybe climbing on some guy's horn out in Portland, Oregon shouldn't bother you.

Stomach fluttery, you step outside and pee off the back porch, arching a strong geyser into the chilly evening. The moon is impaled on a pine in the western sky. A shiver runs up and down your spine, shaking you hard, extremely hard. *Lord love a duck*, you whisper, then shiver again, your stream of urine creating the sound a sprinkler makes when it hits asphalt.

Three days from now you will kayak on the upper reaches of the Baker, then journey over to the Pemigewasset. A weekend of fun, but the rivers are nothing special, and you worry sometimes that you are an absurd little boy, a man-boy of forty paddling away weekends in a bright, yellow boat.

The hell with it, you think. You decide you will eat bacon for breakfast both days camping, because to hell with it all, to hell with cholesterol and fat and any goddamned other thing the FDA wants to throw at you.

You shake off your penis, tip toe back in, slide under the comforter. Carol is warm and facing away. You tuck closer, remembering the pleasure of sleeping with a woman in winter, and to your delight Carol lifts her rump and pushes it against you.

Maybe you are Sir Fuckalot, maybe she is dreaming, but you put one hand across her and hold her breast. She makes a sleepy sound and nudges her rump at you again, so you rub her vagina, her genie, and slowly slide down the pair of boxers she's borrowed. It's dark and groping, that's all, but you enter from behind, first time, and she arcs back and kisses you, still sleepy.

You hold her, hoping she isn't somewhere in a dream, somewhere in the arms of Sir Fuckalot, but then you're straining together, pulling, because it's October and the sky is not far from snow.

SECONDARY VIRGINITY

JULIE GOES UP THE CLIMBING wall like a monkey, like a spider, all tight arms and spandex. The muscles in her back flex and give a shadow to her movement. She looks beautiful going up the wall, her black pony tail bobbing left and right as she swings from side to side for secure grips.

"Sweet Jesus," I say and wait for the instructor, Tom-Tom, to wrap the harness around me.

"Now Julie," Tom-Tom says, "is a fucking climber."

"Yeah," I say.

"No, I mean it. She has the gift."

"And I don't."

"We'll see if you do," Tom-Tom says. "Julie definitely does."

"Belay, right?" I say. "Is that what I'm supposed to say?"

"Not yet," Tom-Tom says. "You'll know when.

I look at him. He's straight out of Outdoor Magazine, bushy hair, blue eyes, innocent skin. He wears sunglasses on a cord around his neck. He drives a Jeep Wrangler with a rack that fits skis, bikes, kayaks. Tom-Tom used to date Julie, but now that's over, it's done, both have gone on to other things. Julie has gone on to me, a lawyer, and Tom-Tom has no hard feelings. That's the deal. This is our third date. This is New Hampshire in April just before Daylight Savings Time.

"Climb," Tom-Tom says to me. "You're doing okay. Climb to your right."

Julie is still above me. I look up and see a drop of sweat flick off her and fall to the floor beneath us. Julie, it seems, never looks down.

"How are you doing, Jule?" I call to her.

"Not bad, Bobby," she says to me. "You?"

"Okay," I say.

"Quit talking you two," Tom-Tom calls to us both. "Quit talking and climb."

I grab the square hunk of wood, about the size of a box turtle's carapace, that Tom-Tom has hammered into the wall of his barn. I grab it with my right hand, shift my weight to the left, then hoist myself higher. For a moment I am suspended, weightless, a spider casting himself away from the wall. But I find another block with my right foot, my climbing shoes, ballet slippers, hooking their resin-ed bottom to the wood. I lean forward and press my cheek against the barn slats.

"You think you get traction by leaning in," Tom-Tom says calmly below me. "But you don't. It's a lesson in life. You only get traction by leaning away."

"Fuck you," Julie shouts to him. "When did you become the fucking Zen master?"

"Grasshopper, take the pebble from my palm," Tom-Tom says.

"I hate this," I say. "I'm not built for this."

"You're doing fine," Tom-Tom says.

"Not really," I say. "I'm a ground feeder."

"Bobby, you're doing great," Julie says. "Tom-Tom, isn't he good?"

"What kind of freaking name is Tom-Tom?" I yell, feeling giddy suddenly.

"Belay. Belay belay belay. I always wanted to call that. How's that, Tom-Tom?"

"Don't say it unless you mean it," Tom-Tom calls up the wall. "Don't do that."

"Or what?"

"Or I'll hoist you."

"Boys," Julie shouts, "I'm climbing here."

In the Catamount Bar, later, Julie says she is practicing secondary virginity.

"Excuse me?" I ask, reaching for a bowl of gold fish. It is a dark, dingy bar, the kind she likes. A climbers' bar. Her keys on the table are held together by a carabiner.

"Secondary virginity. I know, I know. You think it's weird. But it's something I have to do."

"I'm trying to understand it," I say. "It's kind of a new concept, isn't it?"

The bartender arrives and replaces our beers. Julie drinks Sam Adams. I drink Rolling Rocks. My arms ache from wall climbing. My finger, the right index especially, is raw from clinging to Tom-Tom's wooden blocks. I lean closer. Julie smells of resin and lilac soap. She smells a little bit of sweat.

"It's just I'm sick of it," she says. "The sex and all. I'm not frigid, so don't even think about that. It's just I'm tired of sex being the damn tail that wags the dog."

"Isn't it kind of an oxymoron?"

"What?"

"Secondary virginity?"

"Not necessarily."

"Sounds a little like it might be."

"It's just," she says and drinks from her Sam Adams in a big gulp. "Just a stand, sort of. I don't know. We can't be virgins again, obviously, so it's called secondary virginity."

"Who calls it that?"

"Whoever makes this stuff up. I don't know for sure. It could be the Christian right."

"Why not call it abstinence? I mean, as a term? Wouldn't that be more accurate?"

"You think it's funny."

"No I don't. I don't know what I think of it."

"But you don't want to keep seeing me?"

"This is new wrinkle. Give me a second."

"But that's what you're saying," she says.

"Julie, take it easy. I'm not saying anything. I'm thinking."

Julie drinks, says, "It's a matter of discipline. That's the point. It's like climbing."

"Not everything is like climbing."

"Almost everything."

"I'm a lawyer," I say. "I guess I look at things differently."

"Not everything is a contract either."

"I agree."

"So," she says. "You think I'm kidding about this secondary virginity?"

"Are you?"

She smiles. She drinks her beer.

I say, "I guess it's something I should probably know about. I guess sex is something that generally comes up between a man and a woman."

"So I've heard," she says.

"So are you?"

"Am I what?"

"A virgin again?" I ask.

"Yes," she says, "I've declared myself a virgin again."

"That's great," I say. "I always wanted to date a virgin."

On Saturday she picks me up in a purple Volvo station wagon, the back crammed with climbing gear. She hands me a Dunkin Donuts coffee, large and creamy, like I like, and a cinnamon coffee roll. Then she kisses me.

"It's a great climbing day," she says. "Perfect, really."

"I'm psyched."

"You really don't mind going with a group?"

"Because I'm the rookie, you mean? The beginner? And because my male ego is going to suffer? Not at all."

"And Tom-Tom will be there. He's really good on a mountain."

I toast my coffee to her.

"I shouldn't have said that," she says. "About Tom-Tom.God, I never think before I say anything."

"None of us do."

"You do," she says. "You do, Bobby. That's what I like about you. You think before you speak."

"Tell me one thing," I say, taking a bite of the cinnamon roll.

"Okay."

"Were you practicing secondary virginity when you dated Tom-Tom?"

"No, I guess I wasn't."

"Okay," I say.

"It's not okay. You don't think it's okay right now. But what men never understand is that it really, really isn't about sex."

"It is to men."

"My point exactly," she says. "He was a jerk, if it makes any difference."

"Tom-Tom?" I ask.

"Yes, he was. All he cared about was climbing. So you can do what you want with all that."

"Was he good in bed?"

She looks at me. Then she shifts the car into first and pulls away. Inside my paper cup, the coffee leans toward me, then away as we gain speed.

We are going to boulder first. Julie, standing behind the Volvo, strips to spandex tights, a spandex halter top, climbing shoes. She resembles a ballet dancer, a Martha Graham of rock, except for the small, circular pouch, like a billiard pocket turned inside out, that dangles behind her. The pocket is filled with chalk. When she is finished dressing, she reaches behind her and washes her hands in chalk. Her black spandex turns dusty white when she brushes her hand against her ribs. When she moves, a faint aurora follows her.

"We're going to warm up with some bouldering," she says, although she's told me this before. "It's good practice. Try bouldering your way around without falling off."

"Okay," I say, looking at the huge boulder propped beside the road. "Where's everyone else?"

"You'll see," she says. "Tom-Tom is late. He makes everyone late."

"The tide waits for no man."

"Yeah, but he always drives. He's got all the equipment so everyone let's him drive, then he gets to pick the time. You know what I mean. He's a control freak."

"What's the opposite of a control freak?" I ask, staring at the boulder, the red flank rising up to two stories, the weight sufficient to surprise the land around it, as if the boulder fell as a meteor might.

"Is this a knock knock joke or something?"

"No, just a thought."

"You're a funny guy."

"You think so?"

"I think I need to climb," she says. "That's what I think."

She approaches the boulder with something like reverence, dusting her hands. I walk behind her, but reach over her shoulder and put my hand flat on the rock. The rock is cold. For a moment we stand together, my hand over her shoulder, the rock cold beneath my fingers, her right leg lifted so she can rub the bottom of one sole against the calf of her left leg.

Five feet up on the rock, my climbing slippers digging for a purchase, I stick to the stone, look for hand holds. Julie is perfectly opposite me, her voice occasionally reaching me over and around the cold boulder.

"Sweet, sweet, sweet," she mutters once, apparently pleased with a maneuver. I fall off the rock, get back up, fall off again. My back is sweaty. The April air is chilly, but clean. I press my cheek to the rock and try to hear her through the stone.

"Here they come," Julie says.

She hops off the boulder. I hop off, too. I am aware of my rookie status, my baggy sweat shirt and regular jeans. Tom-Tom drives a Toyota pick-up, which is no more surprising than the sun coming up. He pulls past us, then backs slowly toward the boulder, inching into place. The rear of the pick-up has a bumper sticker that says: Rock Climbers Do It Hard. Another says: You All Look Like Ants, only the last word, ants, is scripted in tiny letters, making the point.

"The lady and the lawyer," Tom-Tom says as he steps out, nubbly fleece zipped up around his throat. "How you doing, Bobby?"

"Okay," I say, hating him more than I remembered.

"Jules," he says to Julie, "you remember Margo, don't you?"

"Sure," Julie says and nods.

Margo is blonde. She wears a fleece the color of mashed peas. Her sunglasses dangle from a coyote weave croakie and she carries a cup of tea in her hand. I smell the tea as she comes around the truck. She puts her arm around Tom-Tom's waist and smiles an orthodontic smile. Braces. I like her. We're the outsiders and both know it.

"Where's Harry and the others?" Julie asks.

"Can't make it," Tom-Tom says.

"Why not?"

Tom-Tom shrugs.

"I'm going to get a new set of friends," Julie says. "I really have to. I'm tired of this irresponsible shit."

"It's time for Julie Knows Best, ladies and gentlemen. Have you seen this one yet, Bobby?" he asks me.

"No, can't say that I have."

"Julie stars in it. In the show she proves that once again she is Julie and knows everything, how everyone should behave. It's a fascinating show, really."

"Fuck off," Julie says. "Let's get climbing."

"Okay," Tom-Tom says, "Margo is pretty much a beginner, too, so I thought she and Bobby could boulder a while. I thought maybe we could do one face, then we'll go slow up one together as a group."

"I'm climbing with Bobby," Julie says. "I'm not climbing with you."

"It's okay," I say. "I feel more comfortable bouldering. I'm not sure how much I'm into this anyway. How about you, Margo?"

"Whatever," Margo says and throws the remainder of the tea on the ground.

"Let's just warm up here," Tom-Tom says, "then we'll decide. Who knows? Maybe Harry will show up."

"Fucking Harry won't show," Julie says. "Don't even run that bull shit on me. Harry won't show."

"Julie knows best," Tom-Tom says.

Then he proves that he is good on rock. It takes him five minutes to change, but when he finally approaches the boulder he seems not to leave the ground, but decide to walk in a different way. His hands go to holds I hadn't seen. And his fingers stay tucked in right angles to the stone, cobra heads snapping forward and finding purchases.

"I'm going to pee," Julie tells me and heads off into the bushes. Margo stands beside me. She still hasn't thrown away her tea cup, although she dumped the liquid inside it. She stares at the boulder.

"They fucked the other night," Margo says. "Just thought you should know."

"Who did?"

"Julie and Tom-Tom. That's what they're like."

"They fucked?"

She shrugs.

"You sure?" I ask.

She shrugs again.

"You don't care?" I ask, then turn to see Tom-Tom. He is off at an angle, safely out of earshot. His foot has slipped on the boulder and for a moment he appears awkward, dangling as he does from one hand and a foot hold.

"People do what they're going to do," Margo says. "I gave up expecting a long time ago. I'm happier not expecting anything."

"But you're willing to go out with Tom-Tom? Knowing that he still has a thing for Julie?"

"I'm using him," she says. "I wanted to learn to climb."

Julie comes back. Her hands are white against the green buds of spring.

"Margo said you slept with Tom-Tom the other night," I say. "Is that true?"

Julie smiles, shakes her head, looks at Margo as if Margo should know better than to reveal such things.

"I did," she says. "I surely did."

"You want to say anything else about it?" I ask.

"I slept with him so I wouldn't sleep with you. I wanted us to be right, that's why."

"That's a very strange approach," I say. "That's one for the record books."

"But it's true," she says. "Whether you believe it or not, it's true."

"Am I supposed to be flattered?"

"Not flattered," she says and turns to Margo. "Margo, you're a bitch, you know."

"I know," Margo says.

"Climbing makes it all go away," Tom-Tom says as he sets out sandwiches and coffee and beer on the tailgate of his Toyota pick-up. It's five and getting dark. Margo has more tea, poured from her own thermos. She has told me, during the course of the day, that she is a vegan. No animal products of any type. She wrinkles her nose when Tom-Tom says there is turkey, roast beef and peanut butter and jelly.

"Bobby," Tom-Tom says, "help yourself."

"I'm not that hungry," I say, although I'm ravenous.

"I think we're going to go," Julie says. "We've had enough for one day."

"I fixed these sandwiches," Tom-Tom says. "Can't let them go to waste."

"We're going to go," Julie says.

"Then at least take some sandwiches."

Tom-Tom smiles. He's slept with the two women, I realize, we all realize, and for a second no one speaks. Spring peepers call from the Baker River. A biologist friend once told me that the mating call of the spring peepers is one of the most aerobically demanding performances on earth. I can't listen to them now without picturing them in a box, a scientist leaning over them to gauge the oxygen consumption. It's a fact that kills something about my appreciation of their sound.

"Are you going to fuck him again?" I ask in the Volvo.

Tom-Tom has succeeded in foisting two sandwiches on us, two Coors Lights. Julie eats and drives, the Saran Wrap from the sandwich spread on her lap. Our beers sit side by side in he drink holder in front of me.

"I don't think so," Julie says.

"But you can't say?"

"No, I'm not going to fuck him anymore. Are you going to keep seeing me?"

"I'm not going to climb anymore."

"That wasn't what I asked, was it?"

"But it's what I answered," I say.

LUNCH

ALMOST NINE YEARS TO THE day since your divorce came through, you run into your ex-wife, Kendra, on Ogunquit Beach, Maine. It's July, eighty-three degrees and hazy with heat. She sits on a blanket, a wide straw hat throwing shade over her shoulders, a red Coleman cooler beside her. You see a man's Tevas beside hers, a second dent in the blanket, a T-shirt balled as a pillow. But he's temporarily missing, gone, maybe in swimming. For a long time you stand wondering if that could really be her, despite knowing, almost from the first instant you spotted her, it can be no one else. You know her in some way you can't even describe for yourself, some way that is down in her movements, the way she might be seated with a book in her lap. It reminds you, for just a second, of how together you once owned a cat named Gray Man and how the cat, whirling around your legs, became a motion that attached itself to your own, how, looking down while doing dishes, you knew the Gray Man was nearby, playing with his cat punching bag, or sitting and watching you. And when you divorced you looked for Gray Man for years, until one day you received a postcard from this same ex telling you Gray Man had died, killed by a car while staying at your former mother-in-law's house, a friend's presence lost. And still, at unpredictable moments, you feel the Gray Man nearby, a slink around your bare feet when you walk to the bathroom at night.

You feel the sun on your shoulders, the rise to your stomach, an odd shortness of breath. You are slightly behind her, off to the right, catty-cornered. You look at the ocean as she is looking at the ocean, and you try to see her new man, her husband. You picture him coming back, wet, sprinkling a few drops on her for fun and to tease, then dropping, Burt Lancaster in *From Here to Eternity*, flesh, shoulders, knees, his hand reaching out and collecting her white legs in his arm. You imagine her hand reaching down in response, tickling his hair, perhaps telling him something interesting she had read. At the same time, you page through your own life, rehearsing things you thought you'd say if you ever did this very thing, ran into her. What should you say? How to sound confident, happy, glad you separated all those years ago, without bragging or sounding pitiful?

Then you realize you are standing with your beach chair half unfolded, a sandal free, one foot dug into the sand. You drop, from under your clamped arm, a Robert Parker mystery and a copy of the New York Times. Together they thud on the sand. Nearby someone switches channels on a radio and you hear Bruce Springsteen's "Thunder Road." A mom says, *Wait a while until you've digested, I don't know, a half hour, I don't know, take a nap, I said so that's why.*

And the heat climbs you from your foot, reaching up your leg and heating you, making you lean part of your weight on the folding chair to catch your balance.

He's a big bastard. That's what you realize as soon as you see him. He's tall, wide shoulders, handsome. He has dark hair, though it's gone to gray some. But he is handsome, no question. He stops at the foot of the blanket, reaches down, pulls up a towel. You think you will learn something by the way he dries himself and you do. He's thorough. Where you would let the sun do most of the drying, he uses the edge of the towel and dries every inch, scrubbing hard at his hair to get it dry. Then he tosses the towel down, uses ten fingers to fluff his hair.

Something, something, something, hungry, he says, you discerning only the last word. She looks up, says she is ready to eat in a voice that carries you through time, through everything, her hand reaching out to close her book and plop it in a tote bag. She is still beautiful, but older, gray where before there were only auburn highlights. She runs two fingers under the rear of her suit and settles it evenly on her buttocks. Her legs are scratchy and rubbed by the blanket. She wipes at the tops of her thighs, then turns quickly to pack things.

You bend over the folding chair, deliberately hiding, another tourist on a beach in Maine. You realize, as you do it, that you are invisible to him, the new husband, because you have never met him. You are a spy in your wife's camp, your ex-wife's camp, you remind yourself, and you feel pleased and full of blood, your mouth open to take in steady breaths. A moment later you hear her voice again, saying, *I've got everything, Tom, don't bother with all that. Let's get something to eat. I'm thirsty.*

You kneel and watch them walk away, and you consider packing, getting everything together and going to another part of the beach. But you can't help yourself, you would never miss this, not this, so you let everything fall in a pile and follow. You slip on your Teva as you walk, a comedy bridegroom asked to answer the door before he can consummate his pleasure. The sun is directly overhead, making your shadow a thing that walks upside down in the earth, its soles touching yours with heat.

For a second, out of caution not to be seen, you almost lose them. But you spot her a moment later, spot her movement in a way that draws her from all the other people on the crowded walkway. You hear Canadian French, one man saying he is tired and wants to lie down. Another man, his companion, says he is burning, has received a burn, and they need more zinc oxide. You follow your ex and her new husband, trying to view them objectively. A handsome couple, really. You wonder at the body language. They don't hold hands. They don't touch. And you hate yourself for taking some joy in that, hoping, you admit, that things are not all happiness and light between them. Seeing your ex's flanks, her walk, you think about the last time you made love, the last time she wanted you, and you wonder how all this is transferred to her new husband. You know how, you aren't a kid, but you wonder still, you wonder how she is with this man on top of her, a competent man, you don't doubt, and whether what they kindle from each other is exactly what you kindled with your ex.

They park at a white plastic table on a crowded deck at a restaurant called Pete's. The restaurant is judiciously casual, with beach grass and flowers in old fashioned milk bottles on each table. A waiter — probably gay, because Ogunquit is famous for its gay population, and also because he wears a button that says, "Queer for Years" — seats them, then steps back to take their order. You wait outside pretending interest in bulletins stapled to the curve of a telephone pole. A whiff of Coppertone hits you and you move back, careful to keep the pole between you and them. Really, you think, you should go over, sit down, say hello. Have a chat. But where to begin? What to say? How can it be anything but awkward? There's no point to it, you realize, none whatsoever. No, it's better this way. This is a story you're living, something you can tell at a bar someday, at a dinner party of divorced people, saying, *You know, one day I was in Ogunquit and I saw my ex and her new husband at the beach but they didn't see me.* You'll get sympathetic laughs, that odd, complicit smile divorced people give one another. They will wait to hear the end of the story, because life has become a tragedy and a comedy and there is no longer any division between the two.

By luck, her new husband, Tom, excuses himself. A trip to the men's room, no doubt. He passes the waiter, walks carefully around, then pads off, soundless on the rough boardwalk of the restaurant. It doesn't require an instant take off after him. Why not? Suddenly you find yourself enjoying this, pleased at your advantage, however transitory. Carefully you pass near the darkened bar, the stools lined with people in bathing suits. Jimmy Buffett is singing "Margaritaville." You glance quickly at Kendra and see her looking out to sea, a graceful, middle-aged woman occupying herself until her escort returns. You stop, for the hell of it, and lean over the bar. The bartender, a handsome young man with a tan as deep as pie crust, asks what you want.

"Can you send that woman a drink?" you say, poking your chin at your shoulder. "Please don't look, though."

"I have to look, sailor," he says, "to know who you want me to send it to.

"Do you see her? The woman with the straight carriage, sitting in the middle of the patio? Looks like Katherine Hepburn's mean older sister?"

"I think so."

"That's my ex-wife who happens to be having lunch with her new husband. Can you mix a drink and put a note on it that says you are still beautiful?"

"Want to say she was great last night, too?" he asks and smiles, trying to be a little funnier than he needs to be.

"I guess not. I haven't seen her in over nine years. I want to keep it that way."

"What would you like to send her?"

"A bottle of Bud."

"Big spender."

"I'm kidding," you say. "You pick."

"How about a Sex on the Beach?"

"That sounds good. Wait until her husband gets back, will you?"

You dig in the pocket of your shorts and throw a ten dollar bill at him. He smiles again, shakes his head. You walk to the bathroom, listening to Jimmy Buffett talk about stepping on a pop top. The divorced man's anthem. But you feel good now, real good, and you duck through the door of the men's room, the sun gone, the coolness surprisingly refreshing. Tom is standing at the urinal, finishing. You walk over to the sink and bend down to splash some water on your face. When he moves over to wash his hands, you note that he has three inches on you. A good looking guy, really, and seeing him you realize you had always been too short for Kendra.

"Hey," you say, catching his eye in the mirror, "how you doing?"

"Okay," he says, "great day, isn't it?"

"Every day is a great day," you say feeling your lips twitching, the joy you're taking in this sharp and precise. You could be anything to this guy, a Jesus freak, an insurance salesman. You smile with what you imagine to be a Jack Nicholson madness beaming from your expression. He smiles back.

"Great beach day anyway," he says.

"You from around here?"

"No, visiting from Oregon," he says and then bends to look under the towel machine. Then he dries his hands with the same thoroughness he used to dry himself on the beach.

He balls the paper carefully and tosses it in the waste bin.

"See you," he says.

"Okay," you say and smile him out the door.

Van Morrison is singing about the big-time operators in the New York business scene when you return to the bar again. It's a good song, one you listen to often late at night when you're cleaning house. The bartender sees you and winks. You wink back, although it doesn't seem as funny as it did a few moments ago. You look over at the table and see they are holding hands now, both peering out to sea. A gull slips by sideways in the air, a boomerang of a bird never spinning but endlessly floating. Your eyes follow it until you see a kite out on the horizon, a red speck that is attached to a group of three people staring up. A child has the string, but you can tell the adults around the child are anxious and willing to take over at the first sign of trouble, their hands raised as if their coordination could be transferred to the child.

What you would like, really, is something dramatic to happen. What you would like is a significant moment, a poignant symbolism that would suggest to Kendra, and to her husband Tom, that you are there, benign, not vengeful, a good man, a man who gives his blessing to them, a man who may stand above the crowd, letting life's petty sadness wash away from him in the wake of his ongoing vessel. Instead, you realize, you are a forty-something guy who is inordinately proud of his flat belly, whose life is no joy ride, whose existence is as confused and odd as anyone else's. The drink, you understand now, was all wrong. You look to the bartender, hoping to catch him before he sends it off, but he is already in conference with the waiter, and the waiter looks quickly to you and nods with satisfaction. You shake your head, but the waiter seems to perceive the motion as a funny guy's waggish bonhomie, and he tucks the drink tray up above his shoulder and weaves through the tables. Suddenly you feel panic, the need to flee, and you head through the bar, moving quickly, arriving at the telephone pole in time to hide yourself. Next to you a woman says, *It's too hot to leave the dog in the car.* A man answers that the dog will be all right, and you have to control yourself not to assault the man, a wide, chubby fellow gnawing at an ice cream cone. If you had a gun, you might put it to the man's head and make him march back to the car, release the dog, and then promise never again to eat anything in public.

You take to the beach, not caring now, wanting to get your things. You reach the lawn chair and the book and newspaper and tuck them up under your arms, an idiotic suburban dad of some sort, carrying too much to the beach. You begin moving away from the lunch area, away from Kendra and her new husband. *It's no day at the beach*, you think, and nearly start to laugh. It becomes a refrain, *no day at the beach, no day at the beach, no day at the beach*, and you walk faster and faster. Sand fills the spaces between your toes with heat, slides in between the soles of your feet and the sandals. You hold everything closer to your body, sure that something is going to slip away. When you reach the short boardwalk near your parking spot, you look back.

Kendra is there, standing at the railing to the restaurant, scanning the beach. She's figured it out, you imagine, figured out who sent the drink. Now she's searching and you feel a hunk of tenderness close your throat, your Kendra, your wife, the woman you slept beside for ten years. She turns and faces in your direction, and you stop and lift your hand to wave. And she lifts her hand, too, although whether it is a wave, or just a hand to block the sun, you will never know.

LICHEN

I SAW THEM STANDING AT THE check-in desk and knew they were my party. The man wore neoprene waders and a fly jacket and the woman wore an expensive camera around her neck. She had a light meter around her neck, too, and the meter sometimes hit against the camera, making the sound of casters on a desk chair knocking against a file cabinet. They had money. That was obvious. You could tell, too, that the man wanted something out of the trip that the woman wasn't understanding. Twice, while I watched him, he made short, impatient gestures to her. They were small things, hardly noticeable, but they demonstrated his reluctance to let her lead at all.

I'd seen it before. The couple got the idea to go to Alaska together, but the man, deep down, wanted to test something, or see something about himself that he figured only Alaska could show him. Strange, really, but I had seen it enough so that I no longer questioned it. The woman, on the other hand, tried to step back, tried to give him full access, which was, conversely, exactly the wrong thing to do. He felt he had to make sure she was having a good time. It made the men edgy and the women pissed off.

Marty called me over.

"This is Keith, your guide," Marty said, introducing us. "Keith has been with us five years. He knows the area you'll be visiting today. If you have any questions about equipment, he's the guy to ask."

"I had a question about fishing equipment," the man said.

"He's Bill, and I'm Lois," the woman said.

She held out her hand. I shook it. Then I shook Bill's hand.

Bill said, "I bought some red and purple streamers for the coho. Is that what you would recommend?"

"Sure," I said. "That will do fine."

"Where are you from?" Lois asked and Bill continued looking at me, his cheeks flushing just a touch so that I had to look hard to know he was annoyed.

"Seattle," I said. "How about you folks?"

"Pennsylvania," Lois said, "outside of Philadelphia."

Bill saw our conversation as superfluous — not the kind of conversation men needed to have on their way to fishing in the bush of Alaska. If you put a gun to his head he wouldn't have known what kind of conversation he wanted to have, but it wasn't this one. He turned and looked at the wall. We had a large map that took up one side of the waiting room, all the destinations marked with red arrows. Bill walked over, his shoulders half-cocked so I understood he wanted me to follow. I did. He took out his fly box and showed me his streamers, which were exactly the kind of streamers everyone used. He had picked red and purple, the cheaper kinds made in Korea. He could have done better, but I didn't want to tell him so. He wasn't the kind of guy to tell that sort of thing.

We spent the next five minutes going over the destination while Lois excused herself to go to the ladies' room. Bill wanted to know details that would never be of use to him — water temperature, insect life in the river, feeder streams, and so on. I had held that conversation plenty of times before and told him what I knew, but even then I could see it wasn't enough. He had it bad. I used to think these kinds of guys wanted reassurance that they would catch something, but it wasn't that exactly. They wanted to know that what they were embarking on was real, not canned, that their success depended on their ability as fly fishermen. It was all about a certain kind of language they wanted to let me know they spoke. So I spoke it with Bill until Lois returned.

"What about bears?" she said after listening for a little.

"Oh, we'll probably see bears," I said. "There have been a couple hanging around."

"Browns?" Bill asked.

I nodded.

"Will we get close enough to take some good pictures?" Lois

asked. “I’d love to get some good slides.”

“We’ll be plenty close,” I said.

Then Marty called our flight.

It was a half hour to the drop off point. Lenny, our pilot, answered most of Bill’s questions. Bill sat up front, naturally. I learned that he was a manager for Thompson McKinnon, a financial securities firm, and that he travelled most of Pennsylvania and Ohio supervising sales. Lois worked as a freelance photographer, mostly doing weddings, although she hoped to open her own business out of their barn one of these days. They had two children. They didn’t tell me their ages, but I put them in their late forties. Bill fished a lot, he said, a sentiment to which Lois rolled her eyes and said he fished constantly and tied flies almost every night.

Lenny brought us across the Cook Inlet, in over the Chugach Mountains and put us down on the middle of the Tikakilla River, right where it widens enough to have a deep bottom. Lenny showed off a little by dropping us quickly, hardly any approach angle, and then pushed it hard right into the shore. Lenny the bush pilot. Lois put her hand over her heart and widened her eyes at me, playing. She didn’t like to fly, she said.

Bill climbed out first. He insisted on helping load the rowboat we needed to get to the headwaters, even though he was paying me to do that sort of thing. I didn’t fight it. It was dank and windy, the kind of weather that could turn easily. Lois pulled a baseball hat out of the front of her anorak and put it on, then zipped her jacket closed. Bill said he was okay, though I made sure we took my extra clothing bag from the plane, the bag I keep so that we would be warm even in an emergency. I put it in the middle of the boat, as much out of the water and weather as possible. Lenny said he would be back for us at four o’clock.

“Same bat time, same bat channel,” he said, as he always said, and climbed back in the plane. Usually the clients liked to watch Lenny take off, but not Bill. He pulled the boat into the water and held it steady while Lois climbed aboard. Then I held it while Bill climbed in front. By the time I was in back and rowing, Lenny had already skimmed off the water and had wagged his wings, saying good-bye.

The coho were showing off by the time we reached the headwaters. They cleared the surface, jumping and swarming, their bright silver bodies shimmering for a second before they tucked back into the water. With polarized glasses, you could see thousands of fish moving around the bottom. They always looked like the iron filings in an etch-o-sketch to me, moving back and forth for no discernible reason.

A small waterfall fed into one end of the river, but this was the end of the trail for most of the salmon. This was where they spawned.

"Oh, aren't they beautiful?" Lois said as we pulled into the middle of the fish.

No one answered her. Bill had been assembling his fly rod and he told me I could leave him off on the bank. He could get to the fish from anywhere, so I let him call the shots. I brought the boat in and put out an oar to steady us. Lois said if I didn't mind I might row her around a little so that she could take some photographs. That idea seemed to please Bill, but not before we had a quick conversation about the fishing. He had on a sink tip line and one of the purple streamers. I said that sounded good to me. I told him he was likely to foul hook a lot of fish, which wasn't legal, but was almost unavoidable given the number of fish he was going to work over. It seemed to surprise him. He had a bunch of eastern Pennsylvania brook trout streams in mind, I guess, which is something a lot of them come with. He thought he was going to put a mayfly on their noses, the more delicate the presentation the better, and watch them gobble it up.

"It's more like meat fishing," I told him before we pushed off, which was perverse of me to tell him, because it was just what he didn't want to hear.

Lois sat with her back to me, her camera on her lap. She was already cold, I guessed. I asked her if she wanted more clothes, a hat, anything, but she said maybe later. The weather was turning darker. I rowed her along the south east shore while she asked me all the usual questions: how many moose were around, bear, wolves, and so on. She also asked how long I had been up here, what did I think of Alaska's future, did I think I'd ever return to the 48? The whole time she asked, she took pictures. She took pictures of waterfalls and trees, all the usual, but she impressed me when she asked me to pull over so she could photograph an interesting growth of lichen that covered a particularly large boulder.

"My real interest," she said as she held the camera upside down over the rock, "is microscopic photography. It's expensive as hell, the equipment I mean, but that's what I like. I like seeing the smaller world."

I told her I thought that was interesting.

She shrugged as soon as she took the picture and said, "And that's one of the many differences between Bill and me. He likes the big picture."

"Most people do," I said, not quite sure what we were talking about any more.

"Bill prides himself on seeing the big picture," she said. "Half of life is light, I think."

I didn't say anything. She climbed back in and we rowed along the shore line toward Bill. Maybe an hour had passed. Watching him from a distance, I ranked him as a C+ fisherman. His cast was smooth, but he didn't much care how the fly landed, which is the real thing that distinguishes a fair fisherman from a good one. In this case, though, it didn't matter. He fished over a thousand fish, all of them swirling and crazy, all of them dying.

Lois and I set up lunch back on the bank. Bill hadn't hooked anything. He was still fishing for their mouths. What I couldn't tell him was what he needed to know. He needed to drag the heavy streamer through a school of fish and be satisfied if it hooked the fish above the gills. He wanted the fish to take like eastern brookies, which was a mistaken notion. But I couldn't say it because, legally, he still had to catch the fish on a fair hook.

"Can't imagine they can't see it," Bill said when he took a break and came over for a sandwich. "I dragged it right across their noses."

I nodded, then unscrewed the thermos cap and gave them each a cup of chicken noodle soup. Mary, the camp cook, made it from scratch every two days. Everyone liked Mary's chicken noodle. Lois curled into herself a little and held the cup between her hands. It was cold. We had been out for three hours or so.

"Bring it through fast," I said, trying to tell him without telling him. "They might go after something."

"Now, are they actually feeding? I mean, are they just here to spawn, or are they actually feeding?"

"I guess to spawn."

"Because king salmon," Bill said, "are just spawning. We fished down in Ship Creek, the one that runs right through Anchorage, and you know, it was really something. But most of the fisherman were getting them on marshmallows and really heavy spinners."

"I've seen it," I said.

"It's so funny to see those kinds of fish come out of a river that runs right through the downtown," Lois said. "I mean, they are enormous."

"Because I'm wondering if these fish," Bill said over Lois's remark, "I'm wondering if they're interested in my fly. They don't seem to be."

"Run it by them fast," I said. "That might be my advice."

"Okay," Bill said. "I'll give it a try."

The wind blew hard enough to make the light meter around Lois's neck bobble a little against her jacket. She tucked in closer to the cup of soup while Bill went back to fishing. I cleaned up a little, putting away wrappers. I offered Lois more clothing and this time she took a watch cap. She pulled it down hard on her head. The zipper thermometer I wore said it was forty seven degrees, but it was a wet forty seven.

Bill caught a fish almost immediately.

"Fish on," he yelled and for a minute we all scrambled. Lois stepped back and took a bunch of pictures while I grabbed the large net and waded in behind Bill. He played the fish well. It ran out into the mouth of the river, then circled back. He correctly tipped the rod forward when the fish jumped, reducing the tension and not permitting it to shake free. Bill didn't exclaim at the jump, although to our side Lois whooped. Bill wanted to give me information instead. *He's heavy*, he told me. *He's tiring.*

I agreed with whatever he said. When he brought the fish to within ten feet, I walked out and scooped it up. It was a good sized coho, about twenty seven inches long, maybe fourteen pounds.

Damn," Bill said.

"Stand next to him," Lois said. "Stand next to the fish."

Bill ignored her and said to me, "You were right. You bring it through fast. How was he hooked?"

"Good enough," I said.

We could keep three, so I cleaned the fish on the bank. Lois watched and took pictures. Bill went back to fishing and caught another, though it broke free. He had to re-tie his gear. I cut the fish into fillets and put them in aplastic bag. My hands shook from cold when I finished with the fish. Lois asked if I could row her out so she could take some pictures of Bill from the boat. A different angle. I held the boat steady while she climbed in, then pulled her out twenty or thirty yards. Bill had a spot he liked to the right of the small beach where we had eaten. He thought he had it figured now. Each cast was tied to his brain now. He was like a gambler who forgets it's mostly luck.

Maybe because he was so involved in what he was doing, and because Lois was busy with the camera, I saw the bear before either of them did. It was a mid-sized brown, an adolescent male, that came down along the waterfall, picking its way hesitantly. It was common to see bears near the coho run, although I didn't recognize this one as a regular. He had smelled the fish or maybe he was simply making rounds. He wanted to come down, either way.

"Bill," I said, "we've got a bear behind you"

"Oh, Jesus, look at him," Lois said moving the camera away from her eye.

"Right there, Bill, right over your shoulder. Up on the waterfall."

Bill turned his head.

"Am I okay?" he asked me.

"I'm going to come over and pick you up."

"What about the bag? Honey, you have camera equipment in the bag?"

"Leave it, Bill."

But Bill was already moving. The river bottom was muddy and he peg holed with every step. The bear stopped to watch him. They were separated by about thirty yards, which wasn't much when you thought about how fast a bear can run. I didn't like that it was an adolescent. They could be unpredictable. And I didn't like that Bill was stepping between the fish and the bear.

"You're going to have to leave the bag," I said to Bill in a level voice. "He's not going to stop."

"I got it," Bill said.

It wasn't about the bag any longer. Maybe Bill knew that and maybe he didn't. A smarter man would have understood and acted accordingly. But Bill kept moving closer, his hand out as if he was telling the bear to hold on a second, he'd get to it and be on his way.

"Bill," Lois said, nervous, her voice fencing him.

"Shut up, Lois," he said.

"You don't want to make him think this is about dominance," I said, level-voiced but trying to hurry the boat to shore. "Just back off if he moves for it."

"Bill," Lois said again. Her voice went up. Bill — llllll.

He grabbed the bag. The bear stood ten yards away, its head down and swaying side to side. The posture wasn't a good sign. Then the bear began moving to the side, picking up the scent of the fish offal. Bill moved in the other direction, his fly rod quivering, his other hand tangled int he pack straps. He kept his eyes on the bear and only turned to us when it was clear the bear was going to eat the scraps and forget about us. Bill smiled. He didn't care any longer about the boat.

"Damn," he said. "That was really something."

"Why don't you hop in?" I said. "I don't recognize this bear."

"Come on, Bill," Lois said. "Come on, this is crazy."

"It's exciting," Bill said. "Damn, it was really exciting."

Bill climbed in, first handing me his rod and the bag. Then

he pushed us off and sat in the bow, his back to us both, while I pulled away from shore. We sat for a while and watched the bear eat. It yanked at the entrails, snapping them with its paws and teeth. Lois fired photographs until the rain picked up and made her stop and cover the lenses. Bill didn't say anything, but after a while he cut the streamer off his tippet and cranked in the line. Then he pulled apart the fly rod and tucked it back along the row boat.

"We should start back to the pick up spot," I said. "If you're both ready. There's more soup there if you're cold."

"Maybe on the plane," Lois said.

"How about you, Bill?"

He raised his hand, showing us his knuckles, a sign that he needed nothing. He was like that the whole way back to the pick up spot, quiet and still. When I pulled the boat up among the bushes, then tied it down, he didn't offer to help. Lois pretended to be busy with her camera, but we all knew something had changed. We went about our work — me securing the boat, Lois working on her camera bag, and Bill sliding his fly rod into the aluminum case — and hardly talked until the plane dipped out of the sky and landed hard on the choppy water.

"A bear came right up to the bag, the camera bag, we left on the shore," Lois said to Lenny in the plane on the way back. We had just lifted off the water. Lenny waggled his wings, a good luck omen, as we climbed out of the valley.

He pushed his headset off his right ear and said, "Really?"

"It was an adolescent male," I said. "Good sized. Maybe a two year old."

"Trickiest kind," Lenny said, his eyes still on the rim of mountains sinking below us.

"And Bill went right up to it and chased it away from the bag," Lois said. "Saved my camera equipment."

Lenny looked at Bill, who sat next to him. Bill shook his head a little and stared out the window.

"You must really like that camera," Lenny said to Bill.

"It was my camera," Lois said. "He was being gallant."

She pronounced it, gallant, to rhyme with *gal wants*.

"Could you just shut up about the bear?" Bill said, turning suddenly to look at Lois. "Just shut up about it."

"All right, Bill," she said. "You don't have to get testy."

"I don't know why you have to talk about everything," he said, his face flushed. "Everything's just a story to you."

"Well, excuse me," she said. "Excuse me being along."

"Oh, the hell with it," he said and turned back to the window.

"So what was it? Man against beast? Is that what it was? Because maybe as a poor little female I can't understand what you big men are up to. Maybe that's it."

"Oh, just shut up," Bill said, not even looking at her anymore.

Lenny pulled his headset over his ears and got busy flying the plane. I put my head against the window and pretended to sleep the rest of the way. Bill didn't say anything else and Lois fussed with her camera equipment, snapping pictures of Cook Inlet as we covered it again. When we landed in Anchorage, Bill had to climb out first, then me, then Lois. She didn't get out right away. I moved away from the plane. I caught Lenny's eye as he tied the plane down to the dock and he raised his eyebrows. I raised my own at him. Bill unloaded a few things, then he put the top half of his body in the plane and talked to Lois. I couldn't hear what they said, but Bill pulled out of the plane once, angry. Then he ducked back in, his legs nearly lifting as he leaned closer to her.

Finally he left to go change out of his waders. Lois climbed out slowly, settling on the dock as if she couldn't quite trust her footing. She swung her camera bag up over her shoulder. She took off my watch cap and shook out her hair.

"Well, this has been interesting," she said to me. "I'm sorry about our exchange right then. It wasn't very polite."

"I'm glad it was interesting," I said. "Don't worry about the rest."

She handed me the watch cap and said, "My dad had a dog in Pennsylvania that was a good dog until one day it began to run deer. It was never the same dog after that. You couldn't keep it near the house. Billy thinks he can run deer now, but he can't. That's what's happening right now."

"He'll get over it."

"Maybe, but he'll still be thinking about the deer, won't he?"

"Hard to say."

She smiled. She reached in her pocket and gave me two hundred dollar bills that had obviously been put there for my tip. I didn't pretend to refuse. She smiled again and then walked over to the door. Before she got there, Bill came out, his jeans discolored from dampness, the waders' legs dangling over his shoulders like parachute straps. He raised his hand and waved to me. Then he held the door for Lois, his hand touching her back as she passed beside him.

THE FRENCH RULE

THE FRENCH SAY THE IDEAL women for any man should be half his age, plus seven. I was forty-one when I met Chrissy, which means, following the French rule, she should have been about twenty eight. She was twenty-three and fresh out of Bennington College, Vermont.

I'm going out to Montana, flying fishing, I told her. You want to come?

She did.

It was sexy, I admit. The whole thing. We got the truck ready, a Dodge Dakota pick-up, by putting a futon in the back and stacking our bags around the futon, then covering the bed with a raised, fiberglass cap. At night, or during the hottest part of the day, we carried the bags around to the cab, locked them in, then laid in back and had the kind of sex that is part guilt and part abandonment. I wanted her a lot. She wanted me, too, which suggested something Freudian about her dad and various uncles. We didn't like thinking about that too much.

We had as our destination the Sun River, Montana. I knew the Sun. It's an out of the way river, not the Madison or the Big Horn, or any of the blue ribbon streams that attract fat, beer bellied heart attack guys standing around in their Neoprenes who make me want to vomit. The Sun is a friendly, wide river, with even pools dipping slowly down as far as you can see. You can wade it in sneakers and shorts or in water sandals. Chrissy wore a bathing suit every day, a halter type that was cut high on her hip. I fell in love with her on that damn stream, which is something that happens often to forty one year old men when they ignore the French rule.

After the Sun River, we went down to Jackson Hole. I hate

the place, but she hadn't seen it and it was something she felt she wanted to see. It was her trip too, I kept telling her, and she took me up on it.

You know what Jackson Hole is going to be before you get there, but you have to go anyway. I'd been there three or four times, mostly on fishing trips to the Whiskey Mountains. Driving down from Montana, I told Chrissy about rafting the Snake River, and about hiking up into the Whiskey Mountains to tease some cutthroat with a friend of mine named Dale Pretty-on-Top, a full blooded Crow. It used to be the kind of stuff that impressed her. It was right then, though, driving down the highway with the Grand Tetons coming into view on our right, that I realized I had finally bored her. The age difference had been too much after all, but I hadn't expected I would be the one to bore her. But I did. I saw it enter her eyes. She made a remark about me being obsessed with fishing.

"Well, I guess you're right," I said. "I probably do it too much. Talk about it too much, too, right?"

"Darn tooting," she said, which was an expression that bored me.

"So what are your obsessions?" I asked. "At least I have one."

"You think having an obsession is important?" she asked.

She pouted out her bottom lip as though she had never considered such a thing before.

"Well of course you would, I guess. Right? I mean, you have one, therefore you think it's important to have one. That only makes sense."

She never looked better. Sitting in the passenger's seat of the old Dodge, wind tugging her hair, she looked free and wonderful. I wanted to grab the rear view mirror and turn it to her, tell her she didn't know how lucky she was to be young. I wanted to say, *you, sitting there, you're something like poetry,* but I had run out of that kind of collateral. She was tired of hearing it from me. Still, I might have handed her a knife and let her stab me in the heart if she had asked right then. That's how bad I had it.

We stayed in a crappy camp ground on the outskirts of town. It was filled with Winnebago's and some bikers, too, and the bikers, one after another, gave me a look when they saw Chrissy. Some of them nodded and I nodded back. I wanted to tell them, though, that she was in control. I hated that look of conspiracy and tried to bounce it back at them, but most of them were too thick to get it. Chrissy didn't help by arranging our bags wearing nothing but short shorts and a halter top. Then she put a towel over her neck and went to take a shower.

I opened a beer and sat on the tail gate of the truck, seeing things in a new way — seeing it her way. All the equipment — the camp stove, the lanterns, the fly gear —looked fuddy-duddy when you saw it from her point of view. It wasn't romantic. It didn't really look like it promised adventure. It was just old camping equipment stuck in a truck by a guy who liked to fish too much and work too little. Chrissy had stolen my conception of myself as a romantic figure. She had done that just by being young.

When she came back, her hair clean, her body smelling of Love's Baby Soft, she told me she had called home.

"Really?" I asked. "Talk to your mom?"

"No, to Millie," she said, naming one of the countless friends I was supposed to keep track of. Her friends were always running off to grad school, or getting a new job, or breaking up with someone.

"And how's Millie?"

"She wants me to come back. She needs a roommate and she just broke up with Johnny."

"Why did she break up with Johnny?"

"Too much coke."

"Johnny did?" I asked. "Or Millie?"

"Johnny, for God's sake. Johnny was a hop head. Millie is a vegan, remember?"

"And vegans don't snort coke?"

"No way," she said. "Their bodies count for something."

"Everybody's body counts for something," I said, which must have sounded like something her father might say.

She raised her hand and held the middle three fingers at me. The fingers formed a W. The W stood for *whatever*, the signal for her indifference, or her exasperation at my thick headedness.

I hated that symbol more than anything else about her.

We went to the Million Dollar Cowboy Bar. It was doomed from the start. She wore a pair of very high heels, black skirt, black top. She made me buy a pair of steer horns at an overpriced tourist trap on the main square. Standing next to the famous elk horn arches, she attached them to the front of the Dakota so that we would look like Texas Long Horn fans, or bloated oil millionaires, wherever we went. She thought it was hysterical.

"It just is," she said when I asked her to explain why it was funny. "It's campy. Don't you get it?"

"It sounds like a bunch of Bennington arty crap," I said mostly for effect. "Condescending bull shit about you taking peoples' art and laughing at it while you are too fucking constrained to make decent art yourself. At least they're trying to make the world prettier. Bennington assholes just teach themselves to laugh at everything else."

"Fuck you," she said. "You don't know dick about Bennington."

As soon as we hit the bar, she started drinking hard. The bar had saddles lined up on both sides, so you can sit like a cowpoke and drink beer. I knew Chrissy thought that was funny, but she wasn't about to say it. We drank a lot. Somewhere in our tenth beer or so I asked her if she knew that it was over and she nodded. She said her friend Millie had offered to send a ticket to the Jackson Hole Airport. That's what the call was about. She said she would call back and tell Millie it was probably best to do that. Millie had plastic from her parents and the funds were essentially unlimited.

"I'm sorry," I said. "I think maybe we're just going in different directions."

"I liked the Sun River," she said. "I liked that a lot."

"Thank you," I said. "It's one of my favorite places."

They started the music at nine. The band consisted of five guys wearing western shirts. Chrissy and I were drunk by then. Naturally we were friends again now that we could see our way to the end of it. We whooped and yelled as the band played its first few numbers. She looked beautiful. We danced two line dances with a bunch of women who wore swirl skirts and white cowboy boots. The women knew the steps and performed them with as much dedication as show horses. Chrissy liked that. The bar was new to her, and slightly tacky, which was the kind of thing she liked best. If I took a step back, as I did once or twice, I saw she lit up the bar. Again I wanted to take a picture of her, to show it to her and say she would want to remember this someday. I wanted to tell her that somewhere someone had a picture of me like this, a vision of me, young these last twenty years, curly haired, red cheeked, lithe. I wanted to tell Chrissy I would hold that memory for her and that I would give it back to her if she ever needed it down the line. But she wouldn't know what the hell I was talking about.

It was around then, after the music started, that Bo Bob showed up. His real name wasn't Bo Bob, but he looked western, with a hat and boots and the whole deal, so Chrissy called him Bo Bob. He was a good looking son of a bitch, with a wide belt buckle and a jaw muscles that flexed whenever he chewed or drank. His skin was tighter than mine and he wanted Chrissy to dance with him. He was polite about it, too, which made it more annoying, and I knew he was the favorite of a bunch of the old women who watched him and nodded and thought he was just great. I could see, too, that he tried to figure me out. He thought maybe I was with Chrissy, but she was a lot younger, and so it mixed him up to think about an old ram like me wanting to hold on to her.

But it didn't matter anyway because Chrissy wanted to dance with him, too. She did. And he put his hand on her ass once, and that surprised me, frankly, because he was the old ladies' darling and I didn't think he'd want them to view him that way. But Chrissy didn't shoo his hand off. She let it stay there, and maybe that was the beer, or maybe she thought it was just a custom in a place like that, but I thought about getting punched to stop it. That didn't seem like a good idea, though. They danced three dances and he clamped his hand on her ass each dance.

"Why don't you just fuck him then if you like him so much," I said to her when she came back to sit with me. It was an ugly thing to say. I was drunk but it was still an ugly thing to say.

"Maybe I will," she said.

"Go ahead. You can use the truck."

"He has a truck."

"Did he already tell you that?"

"Well he drove here, didn't he? And he doesn't look like the kind of guy who drives a fucking Mitsubishi."

"Whatever," I said.

She looked at me once, then she went over and found Bo Bob and got him dancing again. He knew, by this time, that he might have fallen into something pretty nice. He looked t me over Chrissy's shoulder a couple times. And I thought, you poor fucking sap. And I knew she might go to bed with him out of the same impulse that made her buy the cow horns for the truck, or, for that matter, go to bed with me.

I followed her out when she left with Bo Bob. They walked around the town square, his hand on her ass. I kept a safe distance behind them. I told myself that I was looking out for her safety, that she couldn't trust someone she had just met in a bar, but I was watching, too. My stomach gnawed at my ribs. I wondered if she'd really go through with it. I kept waiting for her to duck off into another bar, to pull him into a coffee shop or something, but they didn't stop until they reached a public parking spot. He had a truck, just as she said. It was painted with camouflage and had three hay bales in the flat bed. He held the door open for her. Then he came around and climbed in and I figured I'd lost them, figured they'd head off to another honkey-tonk. But she swung up on to him, straddling him, and they started kissing. I could see it all. I watched when he put his hand up her shirt and I watched when she pulled the shirt off, her small breasts bouncing as she humped him up and down. I knew she liked the feeling of a blue jean zipper against her when she fucked a man, liked taking it quick and hard, using as much as being used. I couldn't move. I knew she had her skirt up, her underwear off, and knew that she had him bucking. The windows started fogging. Someone made a line on the driver's side, and I realized it was her elbow inadvertently whacking a black gash as she grinded on him.

I wasn't really asleep when she came back. I heard her lower the tail gate, then a minute or two later climb under the sleeping bag. She left the tail gate down. The night was warm for October and the air felt good. I stayed quiet, but it was the kind of quiet you remember from being a kid when your parents fought downstairs, their voices muffled mostly, but occasionally ripping up through the walls. She smelled like beer.

It started to sleet in the dark and I woke to see the tail gate covered with white. I sat up and dusted the snow off, then closed the gate. She rolled next to me when I lay back down, her head tucking onto my chest. I realized, then, that she was crying. I hadn't ever seen her cry. I thought of her bucking up and down on Bo Bob and I wanted to push her away. I also wanted to fuck her. For a time we just stayed together and it was dark in the truck, the sound of the sleet ticking on the roof like sugar poured through a corn broom.

In the morning she was up before me, perky and filled with good humor. She said she'd treat me to breakfast before we went to the airport. I said fine. We drove into town and went to the Bunnery, one of the best breakfast places in the world. We had to wait in line and I kept finding myself looking at her. She looked beautiful that morning, fresh and kindly looking, a niece on a terrific summer holiday. She made me play "slaps" while we stayed in line, the game where one of you puts his hands under the other's palms and tries to slap the other's hands before she can pull them away. She was good at the game. She had my wrists stinging before a young waiter in mountain boots and a pony tail said we could go in and sit.

We ordered right away. I asked for an omelet and home fries. Chrissy had oatmeal topped with strawberries. After the waiter poured coffee, she spent ten minutes at least telling me the saga of a friend of hers who had dated a professor. She said the friend liked being with him because he was an expert on the Romantic Poets and could recite from memory Byron, Keats, Coleridge and all those other guys. She said what her friend liked was laying on the professor's chest and listening to him recite, that the words, resonating in his lungs and ribs sounded like time.

"Like time?" I asked when the waiter brought our orders.

"That's what she said," Chrissy said, eating a strawberry. "She said because the words vibrated in his chest it was like listening to an old movie reel, the kind that went around a sprocket."

"When I lay on your chest I hear your phone," I said. "I hear an episode of Friends."

"You don't lay on my chest."

"Would you if you had to listen to Friends?"

"You're hung up on this age thing, you know. You're not that old."

"I'm forty one," I said. "How old was Bo Bob?"

"I don't want to talk about him."

"Why not?"

"I just don't."

"What should we talk about then?"

She ate a strawberry and said, "Tell me where you're going to go from here."

I shrugged, said, "I may go up to Union Pass in the Winds. I know a place."

"Aren't you ever scared to go alone into these places?"

"Not really."

"That's one of the things I like about you. Young guys are scared. They don't think they are, but you can see through them. Older guys aren't scared of much."

"Except our prostates."

She reached across the table then and covered my hand with hers. She said she had had a nice time, that she'd remember the trip all her life. She said she was sorry about the other night, that it was beer, that it was a lot of things, that she didn't like thinking about it, that maybe I had goaded her into it, that it was something she was going to look at, something she had to get to the bottom of, that she had a history of choosing inappropriate men, that she sometimes put the momentary thrill ahead of the long term understanding, that she wondered, in sex, was she giving or taking away, and if she was taking, what was she taking, why was she taking, what was it that she hoped to gain.

And I told her a story about how once, when I was a young man, I had taken a job in the Stanley Hotel in Estes Park, Colorado, and how the cook came out one night and told the staff that no one could have butter for bread until whoever put the cigarette out in the butter confessed to doing it. And the whole table of staff people looked around at me because the cigarette was a Newport and I smoked Newports and everyone in the place knew I had done it. But I looked around with them and shook my head and said it was disgusting that anyone would put a cigarette out in butter, wasting food like that, and it was only seven, eight, fifteen years later that I woke up one night and knew that I had put the cigarette in the butter, that I had repressed the knowledge as soon as I had seen the cook with the butter dish, that I had answered in good faith, that I had believed sincerely at the time that I had nothing to do with the cigarette.

"So you're saying time will explain things to me," she said.

"Sometimes it not really explaining," I said. "Sometimes it's like memory shoves it in your face and makes you look at it. It isn't always fun."

"So why did you put the cigarette out in the butter in the first place?"

"Damned if I know," I said. "I'm still waiting on that one."

We laughed about that. Then out in the parking lot of the airport she climbed on top of me and fucked me the way she fucked Bo Bob. I knew it was a pity fuck, or a set the equation even fuck, but I didn't fight. I always liked her sexually and I was old enough to let her decide how she had to arrange things. Afterward I carried her bags into the airport and bought her a pack of Juicy Fruit, her favorite.

"See you," she said when they finally called her flight.

"See you," I said.

Watching her go, I thought she was probably the last young woman I would ever date. I thought that I probably needed slower currents. Then I thought about Union Pass and how I would park at 12,000 feet and walk the ridges until I came to a lake I knew, one with a million cutthroat waiting for my flies, and I realized I was done with something and that something else was beginning.

THE MOTH'S DESIRE FOR THE STARS

YOU KISS YOUR WIFE BY the chicken coop, this long love of yours, this woman you have known eight years, maybe more. And you kiss as you did the first night you dated. On that night you made out in the pickup, both of you lifting from the seat to get traction, to get closer, and you slipped your hand under her shirt and felt her breasts, beautiful breasts, and you kissed until one of your knees hit the radio knob, or the button, and you pulled back as though her father had caught you. Then you kissed harder, and she rubbed her hand between your legs, grabbed your cock once, hard, squeezed and looked in your eyes, then made you take her back to the bar. She drank two Cosmos while she let her foot dangle against your thigh, but that was long ago, years, and tonight, in January, you kiss her like all the Friday nights you've ever known, kiss her and put your hand on her pussy and she lifts the shelf of her entire body and rests it in your palm. *I love you*, you say, and you can't help it, you do, you love her more than any woman before or after, there will be no after, so you kiss her again, then push her, hard, against a birch tree. She tackles it, puts her shoulder to it like an absurd high school football player, and you reach around and undo her belt. You push her pants down, and she wiggles to get her panties lower, and you enter her and grab your hand around the white crust of birch bark. You smack her ass, just once, just enough to make her think, and then she is wetter, and more there, less tree. You lift away from her and check back at the house, but it's quiet, the children asleep. You fuck her hard, both of your breath getting jiggly, both of you straining, and the dog, Charlie, swings by, stops to inspect, and you lift a leg off the ground and nudge him to get him moving. He roams away, and you pull her pants down farther, pull your own down, and you don't care, you sit on the fence stile and pull her toward you. It's awkward, you know it's going to be awkward, but you don't care. She puts a knee on either side of you, strangles her crotch with the forgotten pants leg, then lifts up and slides out of the left leg. She stands for a second letting you see her. All of her. Then she sinks and takes your cock up inside her and rocks, her ass freezing in your hands, her chest a warm puff inside her jacket. You kiss. You kiss harder and it almost feels, way back in your head, that you are ghosts, that you can pass through each other, that the entire point of sex is to pass through your partner and continue. Then she reaches down, nods to you, and you pull out. She begins to shudder and her hand, in reflex, rubs your cock and you come on her thigh. White droplets, eighty-one degrees from freezing.

You don't pull your pants on, or even help her with hers, not at first. You grab her and swing her closer, drawing her body up so that it doesn't touch the ground, rests on you alone, and she tucks her arms smaller, makes squirrel arms, and kisses your neck. The moon stands like a "C" turned on its open end, its core colored in by one of your kids. January, the coldest week of the year. You kiss your wife fifty times, a hundred, just one kiss, or maybe many, and you hold onto her as though you could keep her somehow wrapped on you. Your personal vine. Behind you the chickens cluck. Four of them, Rhode Island Reds, deep, chuckle throated things. Maybe they think you are a fox or a weasel. You know inside the chickens sit like dull boxing gloves on the roost, their drinking water turned to ice, their yellow feet locked on the maple branch you slid in there months before. You wonder if there are eggs, but before you can pursue the thought you slide your wife's sweater up, her coat, and you put your mouth on her right nipple. She rises, kneels on your legs, and puts your head in her chest. She pulls her sweater over you, your head, and for a second you smell her scent, the scent you know and can hardly separate from air. Then quickly she shucks you out, stands, her bare ass red at the farthest behind, the last of her, and she slides her panties up. Snugs them against her pussy. She runs one finger through your come that still lingers on her thigh, holds it up, shows you. Then she reaches to the sheep fence, the wire grid behind you, and rubs it along the top metal strand. For an instant you hear the metal vibrate, a hum starting as if a finger had swung around the circled rim of a wine glass. But the sound does not come from the fence. That would be impossible. It's the wind, you realize, sanding the snowy field between you and the house. It blows hard and lifts your wife's hair, makes her cross her arms, makes you spread your legs wider to give the winter whatever it wants to take. The chickens make sounds like Japanese samurai on bad television shows, low, deadly, nasally surprised.

In the house, the world is asleep. You carry wood and follow your wife, who slips out of her jacket and goes to the children's room. Two girls. Eight and ten. You kneel next to the woodstove so you won't drop the logs and wake them. The hunks slide out anyway and rattle into the old wine crate you use for a wood box, but you can judge sounds and you know it's not enough to wake them. You open the woodstove damper, open the woodstove door, and throw in a fourteen inch oak log. The heat from the opening is almost too much and you close it quickly, happy to have the door between you and the flames. A second later your wife backs away from the bedroom and points at the kitchen. You nod. You hear the refrigerator open, close, open again. The water turns on. You are still on your knee beside the stove, maybe colder than you realized, but also grateful for the sounds reaching you. Wife, children, heat.

She comes out of the kitchen carrying a plate of cheese, pepperoni, Wheat Thins. She loves Wheat Thins. She puts the plate down on the coffee table, steps closer to the woodstove. She reaches in the pouch of her University of New Hampshire sweatshirt, pulls out a Bud. She twists it open, takes a long drink. Then passes it to you. You make room for her beside the stove, not hogging the heat, and you drink a slosh, drink again, once more. Then you put your right hand on the ram's curl of her hip and keep it there. You hand back the beer. The Austrian wall clock bongs 9:30, and you suddenly feel hungry. You leave your wife's side and sit on the couch, ravenous, and you eat a cracker, cheese, pepperoni sandwich. Mini sandwich. Twice you stack the ingredients, stack them like poker chips. Your wife rocks forward and grabs a handful of Wheat Thins. For an instant you see her as she must have appeared as a girl. Sweet, and pretty and a little tentative. Watching her, it hits you that you never have to leave her. You never have to go on another date with someone new, never have to plan to be away from her, never have to split your life from hers. Somehow you had never fully understood that before, but now you do.

Hammers hung like woodpeckers, all facing east. Brooms, dustpans, bow saws, tool belts, padlocks, drill bits, screw drivers, light switches, plastic buckets, paint scrapers, face masks, duct tape, flashlights. Saturday morning, wood floors, the scent of a woodstove going in the center of the store. Popcorn, too. You walk behind your two girls, gabby geese, both of them looking for Mabel, the store cat. Lonnie, the littlest, keeps saying *kitty kitty kitty*, but she only looks where her older sister, Naomi, looks, the line of her sight like a fiddle bow playing over the line of her sister's sight. Naomi is fast and moves ahead without waiting, convinced she will discover the cat.

Kitty kitty kitty, Lonnie says, but doesn't believe the power of her calling any longer.

"Mabel is over by the woodstove," the woman who stands behind the checkout counter says. She's an older woman with gray hair and a blue smock that says, Drake's Hardware. "I saw her there a while ago, anyway. She likes the heat."

Naomi knows she mustn't run, but she schooches her hips down, extends her legs, and begins moving faster. Lonnie can't keep up. Lonnie turns to you and says, "She's running," but it's too late, Naomi circles around the end cap – a display of sawhorse braces – and nearly collides with a man carrying a hose. She side steps quickly, and then spots Mabel. She can't prevent herself from running now, and she bolts forward, puts her hand on the old calico, and says, *Hello, Mabel.*

In triumph she turns her head to Lonnie. But Lonnie, clever in defeat, heads off to the popcorn table. The possibility that her prize may have been meaningless, that the cat is not as important as she thought, causes panic to appear on Naomi's face. She stretches, one hand remaining on the cat, her body wanting to jump ahead of her sister, but she doesn't quite know what to do.

"Come on you two," you say, "let's get some popcorn."

The cat rolls onto its back, its belly straight up at the ceiling, the weight of Naomi's hand lost to the pulsing heat of the tall, Ben Franklin woodstove.

In the rearview mirror, you watch your girls eating popcorn. Charlie rides in the way-back with his head between the girls' shoulders, a gargoyle, a popcorn monster, a silver dangle of drool hanging from his right flew. Now and then the girls lift a kernel to him and he eats it with a gentleness that makes you believe he understand the girls are small. You look Charlie in the eye, man-to-man, nod. But the dog holds your eyes for a mere second. Instead he watches their small hands arcing toward him, two girls throwing salt over their shoulders to the pink dog tongue that darts out to take the food. Dog communion. When you bump over the ditch heading into your driveway, the dog bounces down and then up, and the girls tell him the popcorn is gone. They make a show of cleaning their hands in demonstration. *See*? Naomi says. Then she sees the drool and screams, says, ewwwwwwwwww, and leans against the door. Charlie turns his head to see her and the drool slaps up against his muzzle. *Grooosssssss*, Lonnie says, and beats it out of the car as soon as it stops. Charlie leaps the seat back and lands in the back, his nose rooting popcorn kernels, his tail flapping against the car roof like a twig hitting the house on a rainy night.

You slip into bed against your wife, nap time, Saturday, cold and windy. You spoon and she pushes into you. You hold her for a while, the woodstove downstairs ticking nicely around three chunks of maple, the weathervane on the barn turning in its holder. Wind from the north, an Alberta clipper. At the push of wind you wrap your wife closer, and in time your chest moves with her chest. You reach a hand under her shirt, lazy, wondering if she is interested. To your delight she takes your hand and shoves it down, down to her pants, down to her pussy, and holds it there. She covers your hand with her own, then, like a piano teacher, presses your middle finger down just so. Slowly, quietly, she moves against your finger, moves against your hand, and you realize that maybe your hand could be any hand, or maybe you are a fantasy, or maybe you're are an old boyfriend, but it doesn't matter. She rides your hand, fucking it and squeezing it between her thighs, moaning just a little, her head back in your chest. The down comforter is over you both and you press it tight around you. Everything is else is other. Everything else is nothing at all. You rub your cock against her ass each time she backs into you, each time she uses your hand, and you kiss her neck. She builds toward an orgasm, a good one, and you let her use your hand anyway she likes, harder, softer, your mouth sliding on her neck. At the end she pushes your hand hard against her, clamps her legs, and arches. You almost come yourself from fluidity of her movement, the pure femaleness of it, but then she reaches and kisses your hand. She rolls into your body and puts her leg between yours. *Go ahead*, she says, *use me.* Before you can start, Naomi's voice comes from downstairs. You cannot even make out the words, but it is a child's question voice, a lilting girl's voice, wondering at the house, the afternoon, the wind. Your wife climbs on top of you, kisses you with everything, then whispers in your ear that she is yours tonight, that her pussy is your toy, that there is not a thing in this world you could ask her to do that she will not do, and gladly. She rubs her hand across your cock as she climbs out of bed. The sound of her going down the steps is lost in the wind hitting the lilacs in the front yard and pelting them with snow.

I'll call the baby sitter, she says.

The movie is over. She stands next to you, both of you waiting to file slowly out of the theater. You carry an empty box of Raisinets, Mike & Ikes, a pot of soda. Credits roll down the screen as the theme music blasts. At the garbage can on the way out, you unload the trash, the tiny garbage gate gobbling up the cardboard. You wife stops near the wall and uses her phone. You slip past and duck into the men's room, and by the time you come out she has hung up. *All set*, she says, *the girls are asleep. No problem.* You put your arm around her, say goodbye to the theater manager, a tall man with a broad push broom. *Night folks*, the man says to different clumps of people as they pass. Outside the wind has calmed, but it is still cold, bitterly so, and you both hustle to get to the station wagon. You let her in the passenger side, circle around, and jump inside. *Jesus*, she says, and lights a joint. She takes a drag as you start the engine, then she passes it to you. You join her, taking the smoke deep inside, letting the car idle. The smoke puts a soft edge on the evening. On the third pass you raise your hand, that's enough, but she keeps smoking. She is an old pothead anyway, likes it better than drinking, while you still enjoy a stiff Scotch. She puts out the joint as you slip the car in gear, and she slides over next to you. She always rides next to you, something you love more than you can tell her. She slips her hand onto your thigh, then leans forward to find a radio station. She fishes out Brown-Eyed Girl, an oldie, and she dances on her butt, swaying, happy on a Saturday night. No problems, no worries. The kids are safe, the house is solid, the night is quiet. The old Honda SUV runs on a solid chug through the small streets of Lincoln, past the Old Mill, a corny tourist spot, past the Motherboard, a ski shop, past the Army & Navy depot. You swing past the bar entrance, Bobby's Girl, and you hear music swelling inside. *Hop out*, you say, *I'll park it. Grab me a beer.* She doesn't hesitate, no false protests about wanting to walk with you through the cold. She is gone in an instant and you pull the car up a small hill to the parking lot. It's crowded tonight. You ease the car into a slot, careful not to skid it into the vehicles around you. Then you close the door, step quietly over to the corner of the lot, and pee. If feels oddly exhilarating to pee outside on such a cold night. Your backbone shivers and you look up to see the Big Dipper stretching its cup to draw water from the horizon. You follow the last two stars to the cup lip and there's the north star, nothing special, but true north, the north to guide anyone needing it. You pee a while longer, watching the stars, and the night vibrates with cold. When you finish you hustle across the lot, thirsty now, hungry for your wife now, and you turn your shoulder to slip past the crowd at the door. You look around. The place is jammed with skiers and you smell the faint odor of wet wool and cologne, cigarette smoke and beer. You work around toward the bar, figuring you will see her, but she isn't anywhere you can predict. Maybe the ladies' room. You luck out and find standing room close to the waitress station, catch the bartender's eye easier than you dared hope. *A Bud and a vodka tonic*, you say, nearly shouting over the music. He nods and moves off and you go up your toes, looking. You see her then. She is out on the dance floor, her hands above her head, her hips swaying. It takes her a second to see you. You raise your hand, but she looks dead in your eyes and ignores you. Instead she turns to a tall guy, a youngster, and moves toward him. Your stomach suddenly flip-flops and you feel your cock go hard. *The little tart*, you think, and smile. The guy dances at her, his crotch forward, ready to grind. She turns and grinds with him a bit, her legs spread on his thigh, but just for a second. Then she turns and catches your eye again. She makes a kissing motion at you. Then she turns back to the guy.

You drink your beer and watch her. She enjoys this. She gets caught in a sandwich between two guys and she lets them dry fuck her, her butt out, her eyes toward you. She screws her body down in pantomime, as though she's sinking to swallow their cocks, but then she comes up. She looks at you. It's sexy with the drums and the beat and heat of the bodies on the dance floor. You down the rest of your beer and then drink a little of her vodka tonic. She's playing with the guys, presumably a pair of friends. Ski bums, youngsters, boarders, but they would fuck her in a second if she gave them a chance. On one beat she reaches behind the tall guy, her first dancer, and grabs his ass. She makes sure you can see her hands move across his butt and you watch and can hardly breathe. Then she turns him, lets him grab her, and she makes a quarter turn so that you can watch. The kid's hands go over, shy, then they rub her ass, her pussy, and she lets him do it for half a second. Then leans back against him, whispers something in his ear, and heads toward the ladies' room. The kid looks at his friend. He makes a fucking motion, talking about your wife, but you don't care. It's a game. She's a cock tease. And when she suddenly shows up she is at your elbow before you knew she was there. She laces her arm under yours, grabs the vodka tonic, and takes a long drink. She sticks her tits in your back, leans up on her toes, and whispers in your ear that the boy wanted to take her to his condo. *Do you want me to take him outside and suck him off*, she asks. *How about both of them?* She slides her hand on your cock and looks you in the eye.

But it's you she takes outside. She is drunk, tipsy at least, and you grab her hair and shove her mouth down on your cock as soon as you start the car engine. You lift to make sure she takes all of it, every bit, and she puts her hand on your thigh to steady herself. She sucks you through the light in Lincoln, past the tire shop, past the Porto Italiano Restaurant, past the Lincoln Police station. You shove one hand way down her pants, past her ass, down until you can fit a finger in her pussy. She is wet. Wet from the other guys, wet from grinding, but it doesn't matter. You tell her to get on your cock, to kneel and take it, and she does, hurrying to get her pants off. She strips and throws a knee over your lap, straddles you, and takes you inside. You slide into her, out, in again, then she settles down, holding her head to one side, her lips on your neck. *I love you*, she says. *I love you.* The trees pass white and the wires are white and the mountains are cut off by fog. She stays on your cock as you put on the blinker, lets you turn, then fucks you hard a few times. She kisses you and makes you pull over. Then she makes out like a mad thing, kissing you and humping you and tells you to come inside her. But you hold off. You take her hand and put it on her pussy and tell her to touch herself. Then you drive slowly, stately, letting her masturbate and use your cock. *Did you want to go outside with those boys*, you ask when you think she is close to coming. And that sets her off. She grinds against you a few more times, her hand goes fast, and then she moans. She buries her head in your neck and you let the motion of the car be enough, let the car moving slowly through the pines and slopes of the White Mountains be enough, let the warmth of her body bring you off. You pull her down hard against you and kiss her, stop in the middle of the road and kiss her until your cock stops coming. Then you put her head against your shoulder and you drive home, your penis leaving her in pulses from your heart.

Boston Globe spread out on the breakfast bar, sports pages open. You drink coffee and cook slab bacon in a black iron skillet. A dozen eggs wait on the sideboard, brown and ovoid, pure potential. The stove makes a nice hissing sound as it grabs the bacon fat. Jazz station on the radio, juice ready for the girls. They have already slept longer than you expected, but maybe they stayed up a little late with the babysitter. It doesn't matter. You have no place to go, nothing you have to do. The cold will keep you close to the house, will keep visitors away, will keep the woodstove busy. You turn the page from a Red Sox preview to an update on the Celtics. The air formed from the turning newspaper page carries bacon smells up to your sleeping girls. You imagine Disney smoke, suddenly animate, rising, turning into creatures. You are midway through a Peter Gammons column when your wife comes out of the bedroom, still sleepy. She scurries on her socks, whispers that she has to pee, and disappears into the bathroom. Charlie decides he should be a dog, and he barks once, quickly, and the morning teeters toward noon. You hear Naomi say, *Charlieeeee*, and then Lonnie, the popinjay, copies her. A minute later, presto, you have three girls sitting at the breakfast bar, all of them sleepy, all of them waiting for eggs. You pour out juice while your wife slides the comics out for Naomi. Then she pulls out the crossword for herself, and for a moment, as you pour, Lonnie appears bereft. She has no comics, no crossword, and so you ask her if she wants to play, Guess Who? She slides off her stool in a shot, comes back carrying the game. You tell her to set up while you rustle up grub. She puts her tongue in her cheek and takes her time. It's a simple game. You try to guess the other player's mystery identity by asking things like, do you wear glasses, do you have a moustache, do you wear a hat? Lonnie loves it and she starts asking before you have selected an identity card. You play the game, the egg bowl in front of you, a little cream, some pepper, then into the skillet. You answer that you don't have a hat, that you are a girl, that you have red hair. Your wife asks, shortstop, Brooklyn Dodgers. You stir the eggs, ladle them, fold them, and in time they begin to harden. *Pee Wee Reese*, you say, *if it fits*. Then Lonnie says, *Are you Ernie*? And you are. *Darn*, you say, *you got me*. And they all have you. Three girls. All beautiful. All hungry.

You take Charlie for his last walk, the nightly routine, and the stars could not be brighter. The temperature has dipped below zero, and it falls through your clothing, into your sleeves and pants legs. Even Charlie knows it's cold. He lifts a leg a few places, but he seems distracted, tentative, as if he cannot trust his urine not to freeze and anchor him to the ground. You walk behind him, letting him go, and you feel the cold stretching your skin. Over by the brush pile Charlie suddenly pounces, propping on his legs and jamming his front legs down, trying to flush something. Nothing moves. He watches for a moment, then flexes his legs and puts his nose to the snow. He stands for a long time, his front right leg curling resolutely into a point. *You faker*, you say, then immediately regret it when a rabbit suddenly arrows out of the brush and takes off across the snow. Charlie's entire body convulses before he understands he has actually had success. Then he shoots off after the rabbit. His rush is too late, it is a snowshoe, and it goes like thistle over the snow. *Good boy*, you say when Charlie returns, emptyhanded. Empty pawed. You turn back to the house, the wind full on you now, and you hurry to get inside. As soon as you slip through the door heat rushes you, and you have a moment of wanting to be outside again, to be a rabbit, to be light enough to run over snowfields, big footed, agile, the hollow of bushes and snow mounds all the insulation you need. Instead you load the wood stove one more time, wait while the wood catches a full burn, then damper it down for the night. The clock bongs 10:30, and a board creaks somewhere, contracting with the cold. You slip into your children's room and make sure they are covered. Naomi sleeps on her back, trusting, but Lonnie, younger and more vulnerable, has gone back to the fetus position. You put your hand on each, wish them good dreams, then mount the stairs and find your wife already in bed. She has a hot pad going under her feet, a hoodie sweatshirt on under the comforter. *Get in here*, she says, *it's freezing.* You shuck off your clothes, even your boxers, and dive in. She shivers against you, the sweatshirt a funny sort of padding, and her white socks rub against your legs. You kiss her. Then you kiss her some more, and there is no use playing, no more games, you pull off her panties, roll between her legs, and fuck her. Just that. Just kissing and slow fucking and you move with her, against her, in her, the wind hitting the roof above you, the cold creeping along the floorboards. You don't even speak, there's no need to speak, you keep kissing instead. *With me*, she says. And it has not been a marathon, nothing spectacular, but you dig deeper into her, farther, until you are not sure what is more important, your cock inside her or your kiss. Then you come, and she does too, and your skin turns inside out. For a moment it feels like you have spilled something vital, something you will never recover, and that you will run out into the meadow beyond, into the cold night and wait for spring. But your wife gathers you. She kisses you and clings to you and then, like branches letting the snow free, her legs gently collapse. She slides out from under you, spoons, and you tuck your body as close as you can get. You kiss her neck, her ear, then hold her. It takes no time to fall asleep. You fall into her, able at last to walk through her, your breath her breath, night, winter, cold.

HUNGER MOON

THE DAY OF YOUR DIVORCE you wake early, 5:30, and slip your hand down to D Dog. D Dog is curled in a ball, a black lab puck, who sleeps at your feet these last seven years. When you touch her she grunts and stretches. You lay for a while longer, listening to bird song, listening to spring wedging in to the March cold outside. You cock your head to see if Clay Brook has started to run, pushing free of the ice that has held it stiff, like a mountain staircase for moose going through the New Hampshire woods. But the brook is silent. As you listen, D Dog lifts her head and sniffs at the cracked window beside your bed. *What is it,* you ask her. *What do you hear?* She looks at you and yawns, pink tongue, pink gums, her belly a tunnel for biscuits.

You eat breakfast at the Sidewalk Cafe in Bristol, a tiny town near Newfound Lake, the old woman of the place, Laurie Jane, hustling you along with raisin French toast. Laurie Jane has one bad eye so you can never be certain she is looking at you. Her hair is as white as dice. She wears a pale blue waitress outfit, the front stained by tides of eggs and juice. *Everything okay*? she asks several times, appearing at your elbow with coffee and ice water. *Fine*, you say, *thanks.*

The Boston Globe rests in front of you, NBA scores, stocks, furniture sales, auctions. You turn the pages without reading, your mind bouncing. The flap of the page makes a few grains of salt slide across the table. You turn your fork this way and that, cutting through the soggy bread, the maple syrup brown tree blood. Behind you a girl says to a boy, *Because, that's why.* They are sixteen, seventeen maybe. You smell the girl's perfume, think of her perched beside the boy, close, his hand loose on her knee, her reaching forward to the radio, hair swinging free, his hand steady on the wheel as he peeks down the holster of her shirt. And as she straightens she checks herself in the rearview mirror, happy, both of them thinking this is how it will be, this is how it will always be.

"Oh, God, it's snowing," Laurie Jane says from behind the counter where she holds a Pyrex coffee pot in her right hand. She shakes her head. Behind her, through the cook's window, a man's hands push a plate of omelets onto the pick-up shelf and the voice behind the hands says, "They said half a foot or better."

"Oh, I can't take any more snow," Laurie Jane says.

She says it loud enough so a few people turn in their seats. The snow has started falling, white, the small flecks drifting in a way that means it will come all day. Then the people turn back to their meals. You look out the window a long time, your fork poised like a drum stick on the skin of your plate. Not until your vision clears and pulls back inside your skull do you notice D Dog sitting straight up in the passenger side of your truck, watching you. She has been watching you all along, you realize, her face expressionless, the snow falling between you.

You bring the D Dog a piece of bacon and a square of toast, and she eats it from your open palm, her soft tongue a pink toad that slips out of her mouth, recedes, returns. The cold has taken a place in the truck, a passenger, and the whirring engine doesn't chase it. You prop the styrofoam cup of coffee in the cup holder, tighten your seat belt, adjust the radio. You sit for a second, doing nothing, thinking of cigarettes. You'd like a cigarette, you decide, but then cancel the craving. Not the way to go, you think. The snow is folding over the hood of the truck and suddenly you picture your wife, soon to be your ex-wife, sitting at her kitchen table, the one that used to be yours, too, sipping herbal tea. You wonder if she will wonder what to wear on a divorce day. You wonder if she thinks of you at all, wonders how you will spend the day, but then realize that is the way to self-pity. Of course she will think of you, it's unavoidable, and so you close your eyes and send a beam of thought to her. *Don't do it*, the beam says. *Don't divorce me.* But when you try to add to the thought, to say why she shouldn't divorce you, you are lost for cause. *Because* is all you can come up with and that, for Bobbie, has never been enough.

A small pin of pain starts in the middle of your forehead and you cut the beam off, let it die in the snow that is collecting on the road and on the trees and in the lilacs beside The Sidewalk Cafe. Bobbie, you think, but it comes out half comical, like the shout of Marlon Brando for Stella, except that you are thirty-seven, sitting in a 2017 Dodge Ram, not a t-shirted Marlon Brando with blazing eyes and a muscular back. You reach forward and flick on the wipers, then bend, snake humped, to see through the expanding arc of vision. D Dog bends with you, her breath tinted with bacon, her breath making a white vapor on the windshield that disappears like water sinking into sand, gone before it becomes the white evidence of her breathing.

You make the first run up your parents' driveway at noon, the snow six inches deep, the plow skipping on the old ice. Your chains dig in and you have a sense of accomplishment. This you can do. You can make black lines in the white snow, and although there are no prizes for such things, you are a superb snow-plower, always have been. Itis not as easy as it looks. D Dog beside you nods when the force of the truck is cut by the increasing load of snow spilling away from the plow.

Up, up, up, you say under your breath, goosing the engine. You have spent the morning saddling up, loading sand into the flat bed of your truck, setting the plow. The weather report is for ten to twelve inches, maybe more, and it doesn't help that it's near spring, that ice out on Winnipesaukee is only weeks away. When you round the house, the snow chiggering the bushes on either side of the drive, you spot your old man working his way down the steps. He has a walker in front of him, the four-footed kind, and for a second you have an image of him young again, carrying something, maybe an up-ended roof rack down the stairs. But it is only the snow giving you these visions, and when you turn and pile the snow against the back edge of the drive, you pause and roll your window down.

"Jesus Christ, dad, what you doing out in this? You're going to take a fall."

"Wanted to get the garage door for you," he answers.

"I can get it. Why don't you stay inside?"

But he keeps coming. And you understand he has waited all day for this, for this moment, for this one simple chore. What can you do, really? You relent, busy yourself shoving snow toward the rear of their drive, then slowly bring the truck around for a back drag. You watch your dad bend away from the walker and reach for the bottom handle of the door. He wears a pair of Dickie corduroys, red suspenders, a green flannel shirt. He bends better than you expected and lifts. The door comes up, it's always been smooth, and you wait while he pushes the walker in front, steps, pushes, steps, pushes, steps. Then he turns on baby feet and watches as you edge forward, taking the lip of snow that has built on the door of the garage and drag it backwards. It's not a novice move. You slush it back, then shove it away, the glint of the blacktop coming through in wet sparkling streams. Your dad raises his hand to guide you, keeping you away from their New Yorker that is parked in the garage, but you don't need him. Still, you pretend his help is necessary, and when you pull back the last time, the tire chains making a sound like a slave galley, or a team of horses, you honk your horn and give him a big wink.

"The rest will melt off," the old man says as soon as you flick off the engine and step out. "Who's that good looking girl you got with you?"

D Dog jumps out, runs to your dad. Your dad reaches down and gives her a rub and you tell D Dog it's okay, she can do her business out in the yard. She jumps over the bank next to the sidewalk and finds the bird feeder. She begins eating sunflower seeds, her tail going back and forth.

"Your mother has lunch," you dad says.

"Okay," you say.

You take his arm and help him up the stairs. His arm is thin, a pipe of old blood, and it trembles as he climbs. The steps are clean, though, shoveled, you know, by your mom. She has sprinkled salt, too, the grains occasionally making the old man adjust his walker, setting it back and forth to get it solid.

"It's going to be a foot," your mom says. "That's what they're calling for."

She stands at the sink, watching the birds fly to her morning's scraps. From where you sit at the kitchen table, you try to see the birds along with her. But she is in the way and the birds make black streaks against the dusky sky, your mother's head the center of a swarm of electrons. The sound of the tv breaks into the room, finding a pause in the water pant of the dish washer. Your dad is watching Judge Judy, a tv judge who gains rating points by roughing up the litigants in front of her. Your mother looks a little like Judge Judy, although you wouldn't think of telling her so.

"They might not have court today," your mom says absently, turning to you. "I hadn't thought of that. How will you know when you're divorced?"

"They'll have court," you say, tilting your bowl and eating the last of the Campbell's chicken noodle. You crack a white saltine and snap it between your teeth. D Dog hears the sound and moves closer to the table. You don't feed her from the table, never have, but she is eternally optimistic. Someone, someday will feed her. She's probably not wrong about that.

"You should see these idiots," your dad says from the tv room. You lean far enough to one side to see past the hallway sideboard to spot the tv. The defendant is shouting at the plaintiff. Judge Judy has lost control of the proceedings. Your dad glances at you and catches your eye, then gestures toward the tv as if he's introducing you. The Penny Saver is open on his lap. He reads the Items for Sale column religiously but never buys anything.

"It's just odd, I mean," your mom says from the sink, riding the hum of a gear change in the dish washer. Her words, when they reach you, seem to surf on the surge. "Not knowing the exact hour or time. Or even if, really. I mean,it might not happen today."

"It'll happen, mom, don't worry."

"I'm not worried," she says, putting her hand to her chest. "It's just so sad, is all."

When she looks back to the window, she says, "A cardinal. A nice red one."

"I should go," you say. "Thanks for lunch. I'll swing back if the storm doesn't lighten up."

"Are you doing your usual run?"

"I'm covering for Lenny," you say, "he's off."

"Well, no one expected this."

You carry your bowl to the sink, run water in it. D Dog follows you. Your mom stands aside and you watch the flurry of birds whisking at the scraps. The jays appear to be covered in fur, warm blooded among the shivering birds. You watch a grackle hop on the ground, its feet forming Y's in the fresh snow.

You slam your boots twice on the pine floor and then bend your knee and kick the right toe straight down, vertical. The last huff of snow falls free and you try to close the door as quick as you can. A few bulletins flare up and down on the tack board, and you spy the Amounousuc Snowmobile's End of the Year Bean Dinner notice, the five Warrant articles for town meeting, a notice of a lost dog, GeeGee, brown with a red collar, Andy Seller's plowing ad ,and a request for bids to cut the cemetery grass.

The papers ruffle again as you pass, your elbow brushing the last sheet, and Sylvia looks up, her glasses glinting for an instant in the florescent light. She might have shot a ray with the glint, but then the light pulls back and you see her staring straight at you, her finger lumped into a pile of tax notices. She is fifty, maybe sixty, as sexless as a shoetree. Her hair is sprayed auburn and matches her lipstick. She is the only woman you know who still wears a plastic rain bonnet on wet days, a synthetic hair bra, you think, to keep her hair from flying to heaven.

"Well, well, well," she says, "if it isn't our road agent, Mr.

Frechette."

"You still looking for someone to mow the cemetery grass?" you ask to have something to say.

"The cemetery trustees are," she says with a high voic eshe employs when making necessary divisions, "I'm not. They need someone to mow the dead, but no one's good enough."

"What's it pay?" you ask, not really interested.

"Ten twenty-five an hour if you use the town's machine. Twelve if you use your own mower."

"Can't they find a kid to do it?"

"They don't want a kid," she says, "the dead won't like it."

"Is that so?" you say, then to change the subject: "You hear from Jiggy?"

"You trust Jiggy with the sander?"

"That's right."

"Not so far. I went out for a few minutes and saw him up on Milldeer's Road. That's about where he should be, isn't it?"

"I guess."

"It's two," she says, glancing at the large white faced clock on her east wall. "He's doing okay."

"Any complaints? Any calls?"

"Not a thing," she says. "Nobody expects it to stay around. Arnie wanted to know if this will put you over bid."

"Not yet," you say. "Close."

"You wouldn't be the first," she says.

You say good-bye and head back out, trotting to the truck. The exhaust is white, red where it slips past the brake light. You swing your butt in first, click your shoes together to free them again of snow, Dorothy of Oz tapping to take her home. You cut two swipes through the parking lot, edging around Sylvia's Kia. You back drag a long walkway so she can get to her car without sinking into snow. You tap your horn twice and see her knicking her head under the shade to see if you've plowed her out. Her hand raises a little when you pull away.

D Dog stares straight ahead. You stop halfway up Joseph Patch Road and run two tires up onto the bank. After checking the road, you pop the door and let D Dog hop out. She needs a drink, you figure, and maybe another chance to go. You follow her over the snowbank, the knuckled bolts of large plows, then sink up to your knees on the other side. Suddenly, though, it's quiet. DDog knows where she's going and you simply follow her track. She otters through the snow, breast deep, and stops at the edge of Cold Brook.

Go ahead, you tell her when she turns to gaze at you. She's black in all this white. The only other black you see is the actual water, stream cold, when she flexes to bring her pink tongue against it. You try to imagine what it's like to drink from such a cold stream, then say the hell with it, the hell with it all, and you fall on your belly next to the stream. D Dog skippers a little to one side at the explosion of snow you make, but quickly resumes drinking. It's a different world down here. You are almost under the snow, almost, except for where your head sticks out above the stream. You are a snow tortoise, you think, your carapace a white taffy that stretches for miles.

You duck your chin for a second and stick your tongue in the black water, the cold creeping up and locking your jaw open. A white feather pokes at your brain, cold cold cold, and you do little except put your tongue back in the water. Again. Once more. The pines on the other side are tunnels, you realize, sluices, the portals of the deeper woods. When you lift your head the last time, the snow has taken a place on the back of your neck.

Jiggy's got a rooster tail going which means he is probably plowing too fast but you decide not to tell him. You spot him on the crest of Capplegate, an orange square with mist, sand, snow flying out both sides. He is going heavy on the sand, probably, but the hell with that too. In places the plow has taken the snow down to the road bed. In other places it has scraped to the tarmac, black gashes, as if the road were a creature in a pet travel box, the blacklines air it needed to live.

You see Jiggy spot you in his side mirror. He lifts a hand out and waves, then steams the plow to the right, deep on the side of the road. You hop down and he does too, a cigarette in his mouth as soon as his feet are on the ground. State Law says he's not supposed to smoke in a government vehicle, but you know Jiggy smokes as he likes. He's big, six-five, and wears a Carhart canvas cover all. He lights the cigarette and shakes his head before you reach him.

"Ain't this a frog snow?" he says. "Hope to God this is the last one. Shoulder's soft as a girl's."

"It's March," you say.

"Don't I know it. Saw Abe Littlefield sugaring and I wanted to laugh. Too damn late."

"He'll still get a run."

Jiggy concentrates on smoking. You walk over to the rear of the sander. It's a huge orange vehicle with a sand hopper on the back. When you were a boy, you sometimes rode on the back and stuck the wood end of a shovel down the maw so that the sand would feed. Now you're the agent and you have to know sand a different way. Two more loads, you calculate, and you will go over bid. That means you will have plowed through a New Hampshire winter for no return whatsoever except the salaries you, Jiggy, and Lenny drew.

"Jesus, Jiggy," you say when you spot the deer.

It's hoisted up on the back of the truck, just on the corner of the cab, its throat slit and its body caved out. He's field dressed it at least, but you wonder at the sand. You can imagine the calls if certain people see the deer. It's out of season, for one thing, and it's not something a plow man should be doing from the truck.

"By Jesus," Jiggy says, "wasn't she just telling me she'd like to be my dinner? I passed her twice with the plow and she didn't move, stayed right on the edge of Juvenal's orchard, the old one, and I shot her right through the window. Rolled down the window like I was taking a snap shot and plunked her."

"You can't be shooting things out the window of a plow truck, Jiggy. People won't stand for it."

"People aren't putting food on my table, as I see the thing."

He's finished his cigarette and flicks it into a snowbank. He coughs and shakes his head. Jiggy's a man who likes a conspiracy, likes the pressure of government, because it gives him something to lean against.

"Won't the sand get in her?" you ask.

"Naw, we'll hose her out. She'll be apples."

"Well, get it out of the truck as fast as you can. Don't come back to the yard with it."

"All right, boss."

You hardly feel like a boss, but Jiggy claps you on the shoulder and heads back to the sander. He reaches up and dangles for a second on the throbbing flank of the truck. Then he grins and up he goes, snow swirling, exhaust. The gears rattle and he stirs them for a moment before catching them. Then he's up and off, cresting the hill, the deer, or the shadow you imagine to be the deer, strapped and staring up into the snow.

By five the divorce is probably done but the snow isn't. You pull into the Town Hall parking lot and switch off your engine. You have plowed sixteen driveways in all, three lots, the smaller dirt roads. The taste of the snow is wetter and you know that this will be the last of the season, things go as they might. The auction has already begun by the time you push in to the Town Hall. It's hot inside, steamy, too, with the wool and fleece pulling itself dry.

A few people turn to look at you. You nod. You tell Mary at the refreshment window that you want a cheeseburger, the works, and snitch a bag of chips from the metal snack tree while you wait. You pop them open, decide on a Lipton Real Iced Tea, hold it up so Mary can add it to your bill, then turn back to the auction. Pope Summers has his voice going, *and a half, a half, you're out of it, a half, any takers, last chance,* with the gavel knocking on top of it. In the space of three minutes he sells an Anna Lee doll, a coffee table, an old scythe. It's too close inside after being out all day, but before you can leave your best friend, Edward, steps through the men lingering in the back of the room and comes toward you. You've known him since grade school, his wife friend to your wife, and you realize, watching him approach, that he's one of the few people in the room who might actually know what's happening today.

"Hey, there he is," Edward says.

He wears a red mackinaw with a black stripe. He wears too

much after shave, too, always has, and you can change the odor around you by simply turning your head. On one side is the hamburger smells, the other Edward's cologne. It's a funny thing to be able to do, but you perform the trick twice, just to check it.

"How you doing, Wedward?" you ask, using the old name between you. "You selling anything?"

"Doing pretty well," he says. "That lot we took out of the house up on the River Road? We did okay with that. That old secretary sold for one-seventy-five."

"Not bad."

Mary calls you to say your cheeseburger is ready. You take it and add ketchup, a few extra onions, a jot of relish.

When you turn back, one bite into it, Edward says Bobbie is over at her house, your house, and that his wife, Gail, went over to keep her company.

"Done then?" you say. "I wasn't sure with the snow."

Edward nods. The cheeseburger feels large and solid in your mouth. Maybe it was a mistake, you think, not to have put in an appearance at the court house. But there was nothing to contest, no fight left. You had asked Edward if a divorce falls in the court house, and no one hears it, is it still a divorce. Both of you had laughed at that, but now it doesn't seem funny and you finish chewing with difficulty, your stomach flip flopping. Edward puts his hand on your shoulder.

"Well, that's that," you say.

"I'm sorry. Gail, too. She wanted to make sure I told you that. It's one of those things. She's friends with Bobbie but she doesn't hold anything against you. You're always welcome in our house."

"Thank you."

"You are," he says.

"Well, thanks."

You nod at him, nod again, then carry your burger, the chips, the iced tea outside. On the steps of the Town Hall, you glance up. The moon is large and heavy in the sky. The Hunger Moon, you remember from Scouts. That's what the Native Americans called it, the last moon of winter.

You know the driveway, of course, in your wrists and hands. You knock straight up the side part, pushing the snow back, then tuck it hard up against the lilacs. Then second gear, reverse, second again, and you T the straight away, inching around to give a parking area. Gail's car is there, a Bronco, and Bobbie's Jetta, both of them packing down the snow in white tire smears. You go close, nipping the snow away, then shove it hard up against the back pile. The pile has softened, you understand, spring already digging into the snow. The moon is sharper now, making shadows, and you bank the snow around the small oak in back, then one more push up against the stand of birch.

Back dragging away from the garage door, you realize, almost in surprise, that this is no longer your house. Not by law, not by custom. Bobbie owns it now, you taking most of the expensive plow equipment, the half-ton, the paint equipment, scaffolding, brushes, power wash. You wonder, as you tuck off the last of the garden bank, what it was that pushed you apart. Hard to say, you think. Something like snow, like the fall of it in rock sized crystals when its pushed over a bank. What you hate to think about most is the possibility that you were always getting divorced, that the divorce is the real thing, the rest simply waiting for it.

That's one thing you would like to talk to Bobbie about, just that, but when she comes to the porch light, standing behind the storm door, you can barely breath. You'll go to Florida, you figure, or maybe out west, because you're not sure you can stand seeing her around town. Or maybe she'll move, maybe that would be the best, but right now it's too soon to know. So you raise your hand and wave. And what you mean is that all is forgiven, that you're sorry, that the blame is probably yours. You watch closely to see if she raises her hand in return, but you think not, you're pretty sure not, and you put the truck in low, the plow knocking a straight black line in the white snow as you pass the last window.

GIRLS

FRANCIE USED TO TALK ABOUT the Wailing Wall, Israel, life on the kibbutz. She had gone there once and picked weeds for a summer. She showed me a slide show her parents had put together of a family trip to Jerusalem. She shot the slides against the white wall of the play room, bright squares of light and desert, and afterward let me work through the zipper of her jeans, gold teeth clawing the back of my hand. This was in New Jersey, a long way from Israel.

Marie cocked her thumbs in the sides of her panties and stepped out of them. Beside her bed, on a rainy afternoon, she lay down and spread her legs, her right knee propped on a Kermit the Frog doll. Other dolls spilled to the floor and the white, puffy curtains breathed in and out with the damp wind. When I stood to go to the bathroom afterward the dolls stared up at me.

Later, she made tea and loaded it with cream and sugar. She sat on the back yard lawn furniture, though it was April and chilly, and watched leaves collect in the corner formed by the barbecue grill against the patio door.

You'd go to Friendly's, order a milk shake, park around back. Three or four guys in the car with you, waiting. Then the girls showed up, their cars smaller somehow, gum, cigarettes, barrettes scattered on the dash, birch inch worms coating their windshield.

"Hey," you'd say.

Then out in the darkness leaning against the car, the engine warm, the painted lines on the parking lot smooth under your bare feet, and you'd notice she has painted her toenails, maybe for you.

Up and down, up and down, faster, faster, her hand yanking and swirling your penis, her head against your shoulder, her eyes closed against this courtesy.

"Hmmmm?"she asks and when you say "nnnnnn" she works her hand faster, her face somewhere else, thinking about her outfit, about her mom, about the slow steady beat of the Beatles' Norwegian Wood. When it starts she steps away and holds your penis out, introducing it to the large maple you had been leaning against, letting you finish anywhere, anyplace, as long as not near her.

Everyday Mary Bitticini sits exactly across from you in the discussion circle. You think Mr. Masteller, the U.S. History II teacher, has noticed her legs, too, the white glimpse of her crotch you sometimes see when she crosses or uncrosses her legs. She wears a black skirt one day, a sundress another, and a plaid jumper when parents visit.

She dates Jimmy Corposara, the tread head, car mechanic, VokeTech, hard ass. You picture her sliding those legs in his jacked up, ass high Pontiac GTO.

In eighth grade, Chris Lambla's played the same song five times on the turntable, Never My Love, by the Association, and we danced in the basement of her parents' house. Her breasts lived in the soft wool pouch of her angora sweater. She told me that her mom had gone with her to pick out the sweater, the skirt, too, and that she hated shopping with her mom. Once, she said, she had gone shopping with her mom, had fallen asleep on the way home, and had come awake, hours later, in the vault of the garage. She thought she had been buried alive, something she had been learning about in Tuesday afternoon catechism. The saints, she meant, they had sometimes been buried alive. And she danced against me, the lights dim, the music syrup, and I moved my hand to her bra strap, to her waist, and once, at the end of the night, to the round hump of her ass, weighing it like a farmer judging soil.

Cindy: "If you love me then you won't ask me to do anything I'm not comfortable doing. Do you really like me? Do you? Because I like you, I do, but it's not all about what we do right here. I mean, in a car like this. I mean, what do you really think of me?"

She chewed cinnamon gum, the kind with the liquid center. *Cum gum*, she said, laughing at the way the gum squirted when she bit into it. That was when she wasn't talking about love and respect.

In the school hallway, we tried to spot Jane Ritzo, who supposedly went on the pill her sophomore year. She went on the pill for Grady Whittle, lead guitarist in the Balloon Farm. The Balloon Farm played at every high school dance, every Teen Canteen, every back yard Sweet 16. Jane Ritzo went on the pill as a gift to Grady, is what we heard. She put a bow on the pill cylinder and gave it to him. They were seniors. We had never heard of anything so fine and generous. When we managed to spot her in the hallway, we speculated about those pills. We pictured them, one by one, on her tongue, going down.

Once we snuck over to find the girls sleeping out on Sue Pope's trampoline. She had a big back yard. The girls had spread out sleeping bags, pillows, snacks on the trampoline. We climbed on, tickled, rubbed around, one move jiggling other moves.

After a while we lay quiet, all of us, the girls smelling like powder, the boys hot, all of us barefoot. Cousin Brucie, the WABC DJ, played the Beach Boys. We watched the oak tree catch the higher winds, peaceful, all of us kids together.

Later, Sue told me, the girls painted their toes, and eventually fell asleep. They sagged together, four girls ending up in a hole the size of a child's plastic wading pool, huddled against the chilly New Jersey nights.

"Did you nail her?" Bobby asked.

We were shooting hoops in his back yard. Horse. He made a right handed hook, a banker, and bounced the ball to me.

"No," I said.

I made the hook.

"Come on, you did too."

"No, honest."

"Bullshit. She puts out like a grocery clerk."

He grabbed the ball from me and held it under his arm. Then he slipped it down and humped it for a second. He raised his eyebrows up and down, laughing.

"What is that supposed to mean?"

"You know," he said.

Snack bar cook, you grill hamburgers at Echo Lake Swim club. Mrs. Staub has a plain piece of lettuce with cottage cheese glommed on top. A slice of pineapple, if one is available. She wears a white visor and comes to the snack bar in her bathing suit, bends to rub her foot free of sand or bark bits. You peek down the top of her suit, feel you must keep your distance from the counter. She pays with red nails, her purse snapping primly when she puts the change inside.

"Thanks," she says. She walks to the picnic table and sits, eats with knife and fork balanced carefully in her hands. She is brown as pine ship lap, her lipstick pale pink. You see her legs sometimes under the table, watch as they live what seems a life separate from the one her hands live.

At the end of the summer, at the pool dance, you kiss her daughter, Sally, who is small, timid, a ghost of Mrs. Staub. You put your hand on Sally's breast fast, faster than you should, and she lets you. She knows she is a ghost, a daughter ghost, and finally you dry hump on a pool pad in the towel room at the back of the men's locker room. Through movement, she becomes her new self, is no longer a ghost, and you kiss a lot, kiss like crazy, Sally becoming a new Mrs. Staub.

On Point Pleasant beach, you tuck into a sleeping bag with Joanie and grope in the flannel heat. The inside of the bag has pictures of hunters shooting at mallards over retrievers. Duck hunters. This trip to the boardwalk is a date. In the sleeping bag, you imagine, you resemble a slug creeping out of the ocean, creeping up the beach, to the boardwalk, up to the carnival rides, inching, a furrow of sand marking your passage.

Afterward you molt and slip out of the bag, shake yourself, wade into the ocean. She stands in the water, knee deep, kicking at waves. She washes you off her hands, splashes water on her face. You step behind her, take her breasts in your hands, rub your spent penis against her ass.

On the boardwalk later you buy her cotton candy not because she wants it, or you want it, but because this is supposed to be the fun, kicky side, the counterbalance to what happened in the sleeping bag. She eats the cotton candy and her chin turns pink. When you kiss her you taste spun sugar. When you try to win her a stuffed animal she grabs your arm and laughs, squeals, your elbow wedged between her breasts.

She left a note in my locker, slipped it through the vents, the note all curlicues, circle-dotted-i's, red paper.

Hi! it said. *I had a great time last night!!!!!! See you in Chemistry, 3rd period!!!!!!!!*

I rode Sarah on the bar of my English racer bicycle, my arms braced on either side of her. She sat sideways to me, her hair smelling of Prell, my thighs stropping against her body as I pedaled. She turned to me and kissed me and closed her eyes.

She closed her eyes even though I pedaled and steered.

Skip and I once took this girl Carol out and we had her sit between us in his truck, and we both fiddled around with her crotch, our hands touching sometimes. She let us.

She put her hands on our crotches, too, arms out like she was flying, like she was holding our wankers as handles and leaning away, a hood ornament, a bowsprit. Even then, I wasn't sure what she got out of it.

Janie smelled like something sweet, something made up, like a candy store with the door closed too long. Claire smelled like a lawn product, hazy, aerosol, capped. Only Molly smelled of the outdoors. She kept crickets in the top drawer of her desk all winter. It became a ritual with her: In autumn, before the first frost, she captured a dozen crickets, carrying them to a Hellman's mayonnaise jar with hollow hands. She dumped them in, screwed on the top, and later put them to graze in the top drawer of her desk. They lived in grass clipping and cedar and maybe that's why Molly smelled so good. At night, after we had turned to spoon, I put my nose against her hair. The crickets rubbed from the desk, summer, winter, spring, and cedar baked into the air at every breath.

If you give a girl an ID bracelet, or something that she can show to her friends, then she gives you better sex.

Coach B said girls can drain you. Before the game, for a few days, he said stay away from them. *Keep your head on the game*, he said. I used to meet Sue at the 7-11 in Mountainside. She wasn't my girlfriend so it really wasn't against Coach B's rules. We stood on either side of the comic kiosk and spun it back and forth. I liked Silver Surfer, she liked Spiderman. In the buggy florescent light outside she smoked cigarettes and told me about her boyfriends. We pretended we were friends, that I was just listening, but we always ended up kissing in a group of beeches a block from the store. I used to put my hand on her breast and let it rest there, afraid to go further, afraid I wouldn't keep my head in the game. Her nipples, though, felt like buttons into some place I wanted to go.

They would place the rubber on the tip of your penis, check it for size like a mechanic checking a nut, then roll it forward. They did it while they looked up, or kissed, or did anything in the world except look at what they were doing. Some of them made you do it yourself, so you felt like a fireman suiting up or a surgeon fitting on gloves.

The slow wrap of the thing squashed your penis like the muscle movement that lets a boa walk slowly over a dead rat. Afterward, when you saw your mom put shelf paper in the cupboards above the washing machine, you understood: no unsightly rings, no mess, always spongeable, always hygienic.

Girls took home-ec I used to pass by the class room and peek through the doorway, trying to catch Deidre's eye.

More often, she came to shop class with notes from Mr. Speaker, the principal. Pink notes. She handed them to Mr. Fellmen, the shop teacher, and flirted with him for a second. Then she said she wanted to talk to me about an assignment, and she stood next to the drill press, giggling, saying, *Isn't this all just incredibly dorky?*

She had a way of cocking her hip, thrusting it out, that made me stop whatever I was doing. She liked coming into that shop, the only girl in a roomful of guys.

In the Lido Diner on Route 22, Paula reached her barefoot under the table and put it squarely on my crotch. She gazed at me and let her eyes go slack. We both pretended that was the first time anyone had done that to me, pretended, too, that she had never done that to anybody else, either.

Boys think from sex to sex. Girls think about what's in between.

One summer night, in the heart of heat, you walk with your best girl out onto Echo Lake golf course. You don't dodge the sprinklers at all. You let them go over you and see her skin showing through her shirt, the hint of her skin, and you get water on your hair. You start kissing and you pull her down, or she pulls you down, and you get her out of her clothes fast. You too. Naked, with the water whipping you once every twenty or thirty seconds, you screw like mad, like wild things, grunt, shove, dig into the dirt, grass, sky, the sprinkler, her, shove shove, and kisses, kisses like maniacs kiss, like dying people kiss, you love her, love everything, love that she likes the sky above you and the sprinkler, and you keep going. Then she says she's cold so you lead her to a tall bank of grass, both of you carrying your clothes, and under a tree, out of the sprinkler whips, you make love, kiss more, talk to each other, say you love one another, and when you come it starts somewhere down deep, far away, and it arrives like a sound you have been waiting for, like a key in the door. You feel like crying and she holds you, and that starts you again. This time more simply, gentler, and you kiss until you know it is late, very late, and then together you gather your things, dress, cut through Wittingham Place, over to Baldwin, and you can't stop kissing. You wonder why you can't sleep beside each other, what would it hurt, why is the world like this, and you kiss her one last time at her door, see the lights go up her house as she makes her way to her bedroom. You run for the holy hell of it back toward your house, roses out, stars up, the maple leaves throwing puppets of shadows from the streetlights. A part of you knows it will never be like this again, not quite, and you smell honey suckle, hyacinth, soil.

You sit at the kitchen table of your house and eat a bowl of Cheerios, it's late, the smell of her on each spoonful, milk, oats, sugar. You put the bowl in the sink, run water, splash it around. Your mom has left you a note telling you are the last family member in, lock the door, so you do that, turn out the lights, climb the stairs.

It is hot upstairs, coolness just outside, and you lay in a single bed, a childhood cowboy lamp beside you, your hand absently on your crotch. You think of her, remember her pulling you closer, using gravity to draw you to the center, and you fall asleep like that, one white sheet over you, your left leg out to get the last of the air on a summer night.

THAT LINE WHERE WATER MEETS THE LAND

YOU SEE A LOBSTER BELOW you, gray black, its form barely discernible among the red stones of the Gulf of St. Lawrence in July.

Ohhhhohhhhhhh, you call through your snorkel, signaling to Peter, your buddy, pointing at the same time. But Peter doesn't hear or he isn't there. You take one look out to sea, out to Prince Edward Island, and you see nothing but green water, seal lands, cold depths.

White sharks could live there, could mistake you for a seal yourself, but you chase the thought from your mind. Instead you dunk down a little to let Nellie, your Golden Retriever, pass above you, her feet paddling. She catches your back with one paw, scrapes it, then continues on, fetching tennis balls on the lapping surf, her mouth and nose huffing as she propels herself forward, your back her last touch of land.

You rise again, take one breath, then dive through the mellow light, deeper, deeper, the lobster still in sight. You are armed with a trout net, a stave from a snow fence, and you swim with your arms out, a warrior, diving for the bottom. You hold your breath and feel pressure rinse you, close you, at the same time wondering if you are a god to this lobster, a creature out of heaven. Then you see Peter, diving twenty yards away, his own trout net ready, his hair flowing upward as he swims vertically through the water. *Pearl divers,* you think. But you kick harder to the bottom, waving the stave to get the lobster's attention, the net swirling innocently behind. Then the lobster catches on and it begins to back in earnest, its claws raised mechanically, a bulldozer hoisting a load. Everything is quiet. The mask presses against you nose and top lip, magnifying the lobster. If the white shark should take you, it should take you now, bite you in half, carry your ruptured body like a gouged tube flailing streams of blood in the cold bars of light.

Kill me, you think, as you scoop the net behind the lobster, voila, scoop, scoop, and lift. Sand and kelp come with it, but the feeling at the bottom of the net is live, trapped, a creature tied to you. You kick toward the surface, your lungs impatient, your hands along your side. And before you can break free you see Nellie again, her paddling feet an endless bicycle motion. She senses you, or has been searching for you, because she sticks her head under water, the yellow tennis ball a clownish smile, her ears straight out on the salt.

"Got one, Josh," Peter yells to you, his snorkel dangling to one side. He lifts the net, shakes it, laughs. He has a large nose. He treads water with his flippers, pushes Nellie away when she comes too close. He is a State Representative in Vermont.

"So do I," you say. "A big one."

"Lobsterville," Peter yells at the three women back on the beach. "Lobster time."

You wait until Nellie swims close, then reach out a hand and hook your fingers through her collar. She chugs. *Cwaaaaa, cwaaaa, cwwwwaaa* her breath goes around the tennis ball, through the water, her tail a furred rudder. You stretch out, the cold water taking a position down in your core. But Nellie's hairy body rubs against you, warm despite the frigid water, and you kick to help her pull you.

Riding up and down, the surf lifting you slightly, you see the woman in yellow chairs, their baseball hats down tight over their foreheads, magazines open on their laps. Behind them the red cliffs of Doll's Beach, Port Hood Island, Nova Scotia, rise in a sheer wall.

"Let me see, let me see," Jonah says as soon as you touch bottom. He is seven, not your son, and blonde enough so that even here, in Nova Scotia, he must wear a t-shirt against the sun. He is not Peter's son either. He is Nancy's boy, and Nancy is the third woman in the group, the divorced one, the one with children. She lifts out of her chair and comes over to inspect the lobsters with him. She wears a blue and white tank suit. Her blonde hair is clinched in a pony-tail. She has blue eyes, with yellow flecks in the irises. Almost every day she wears saddle shoes, one pair each summer.

"Two pounders?" she asks, then sees for herself.

"Let's get them in the cooler," Peter says from somewhere to your left. "If the freaking lobster men see us, they'll shoot us dead."

"Don't tell Bertie," Nancy says to Jonah, mentioning the only full-time resident on the island, the fix-it guy, the caretaker, the Canadian. "It wouldn't be funny. Not even a little bit."

"Okay, okay, okay," Jonah says, shivering from the water, from excitement. You put a hand on his shoulder and give him the net. He carries it, duck footed, to the red and white Coleman cooler. He lifts off the top, then pauses.

"Mom," he says and nods his head.

Nancy understands immediately — there is too much in the cooler, no room for the lobsters — and she hustles to make it right. *Right there, go ahead, right in there,* she says, guiding him, her voice a little frustrated. Then he runs back and grabs Peter's lobster, carries it over. He looks down at the cooler, a pirate checking on a treasure chest, and flips the second lobster in. Nancy quickly shuts the lid, yelping a little about the lobsters squaring off to fight.

"I hate to think of them fighting to the death in the dark," Debbie says.

She is Peter's wife, short, blonde, diminutive.

She is the youngest of the women and probably the prettiest. Her feet are buried in the sand. Her hat says Bennington College.

Abby, your wife, says, "Is it time for a gin and tonic? Who thinks it's time for a gin and tonic?"

You stretch out on a red rock, the surface rounded perfectly to your chest and arms. It is like hugging the back of a dinosaur that has dipped under the crust of the earth. Shadow cuts the rocks, turning the day suddenly to afternoon, but this rock remains directly in the light. Itis warm and you stretch completely, hugging the heat up to your core. If you put your ear to the rock, you can hear a thousand miles of ocean calling you.

You must have dozed, because when you wake your wife is climbing on top of you. Abby is wet, cold, and she climbs on top of you without asking, knees, chest, hair dragging like kelp across your back. A sea creature, you think.

"You're so warm," she whispers.

She keeps moving until she has covered you exactly, her body matching yours. She stretches, takes your fingers in hers and knots them together. *Star fish,* you think. You are star fish and you are locked together, sucking nutrients out of bare rock. Her pubic bone pushes into your tail bone, the hint of sex just lingering. But she is only after your warmth, you realize. Her breath smells of gin and lemons.

For a moment, you doze again. Her weight is good weight. You match your breathing to hers, or she does to yours, and for the time it takes the shade to find you both ,you breathe in synch. You both sleep that way until Jonah runs up. His younger sister, Joanne, who had been napping by her mother's chair, is finally awake. Joanne is blonde, too, and sand-eyed from sleep."

"There's the Green Monster," Jonah tells Joanne, pointing at you.

"He's asleep."

Joanne cocks a hip and looks at you. She is ready to run, not sure how fast you can move from your position. You listen with your eyes closed, letting them come closer. You think of stories you've heard of sea crocodiles in Australia, their eyes watching the land above them, waiting for deer and unwary creatures coming to drink. That's what you will be, you decide, a croc. You concentrate on not moving, though Jonah kicks a little sand in your direction. Abby stirs on your back. Nancy, from somewhere that sounds far away, says, *You will not wake people up to play your silly games.*

But you growl. And whatever power their mother had over them disappears. You have played this game fifty times, a million times, with them already this summer. You growl again, and this time Joanne shrieks a little and runs a few feet away. Through your nearly closed eyes you see she enjoys the feeling of running in sand, the sure traction, as she jams her feet in to stop and look back at you. Suddenly the rock is hot, your wife's body is hotter. You move your shoulders to inch Abby off you, and she accommodates you by lifting and moving to your right.

That leaves you uncovered, your body slick with sweat.

Grrrrrrrr, you say, coming awake.

Jonah says, "You can't catch me, Mr. Monster."

Grrrrrr, you say.

"Yeah," Joanne says, and wiggles her butt.

"Joanne, stop that," Nancy says.

"Dumb old monster," Jonah says.

You slip into the water without first standing. You slide off the rock, surprisingly pleased to be able to ooze into the water. It's cold. It takes your breath for a moment, then you adjust. You loll in the water five feet out, cleaning the sleep from you. Then, with a roar, you come out of the water, standing and falling, churning with your arms to claim the children for the deep.

"Green monster, green monster," Joanne says.

You roar again, then slowly pull yourself toward shore with your hands. You linger in the water, the gentle lap of the waves rocking you, your hands ready to grab the spindly legs if they come close.

"I won't hurt you," you say, which is a ritual in the game.

"Can't catch me," Jonah says, sticking one leg in the water not too far from you. If he can get close to you, without being caught, he has somehow won. Joanne, less sure, sticks her foot in farther away, impossible to catch unless you were a dolphin. You dunk down, trying to get your feet under you, ready for a surge. But before you can move, Peter grabs Jonah and snatches him into the air. Jonah screams that it's not the game, not the game, that's not the game.

He doesn't like it, you can see, but Peter can't watch the boy's face. What you want to tell Peter is that the game has gone on before his arrival, that he can't come in so quickly and confuse things, but that's too much to say about such a small thing. But it doesn't feel small, and as Jonah kicks, you must support Peter, so you rise up, Green Monster, and prepare to carry Jonah, your captive, out to sea.

Walking back to the house, the cooler propped on your shoulder, you watch Nellie chase a tennis ball Jonah has thrown. The dog bounces off her front paws, rises on her back legs, scans the tops of the Queen Ann's Lace, the Beards Tongue, the purple sedges. She is bred to retrieve ducks, but settles for this, yellow tennis balls, and now pogo's off the path, trying to see where they have gone.

"Get them," Jonah says, "over there, Nell, over there."

Nellie looks back at you. Then she looks at where she suspects the ball has gone. Then, again, to you.

"Don't look at me," you say, "find them. Find the ball."

"Yeah, find them," Joanne says.

Joanne wears little girl sunglasses, with Bugs Bunny faces on the corners of the frames. She carries her towel around her neck and stands, undecided, between the women, who trail, and you and Jonah. Peter brings up the rear, behind the women, the lawn chairs loaded on his back.

Nellie bounds off, her tail a white cockade. You watch the tail wag through the grasses, the fields taking the first coolness of evening. You hitch the cooler higher on your shoulder, feel the drinks and ice slosh inside. The lobsters scuttle. You hear their legs and claws scratching for purchase.

"She found them," Jonah yells. "Look! See, she found them.

"Nellie returns with two balls in her mouth. She pushes through the grasses, chugging still. Then she stops suddenly and lets the balls drop. She sits and chews at a spot on her belly, then on her hip, then farther back. She is eager to get at the itch, you can tell. You slide the cooler onto the ground and call her. She is reluctant to give up on the itch, reluctant to give up on the tennis balls. Finally she decides, snatching up the balls and carrying them toward you. When she reaches you, the problem becomes clear. She is coated with burrs, scores of them, matted and tangled in her hair.

"Aw, Nell," you say, "not again."

You kneel and pull her into a sit beside you. You reach down along her tail and start the process of pulling out burrs. You have performed this same task a hundred times. Nellie puts her chin on your shoulder, a baby to be burped, a dog you have known longer than any of the people with you. She tries to lick you once, but all you feel is the yellow, resin glide of tennis ball skin.

Then she puts her head back on your shoulder and you realize, in the summer evening, that she smells of bayberry and moon thistle. As the others file past you, she keeps her chin on your shoulder and gives you her paw, the oldest trick in the book to earn a biscuit.

In the evening dimness, without turning on a light, you feel up your wife, Abby, in the doorway to the sitting room. A strange thing. You aren't sure how it happened, but suddenly, with the sun on your skin, the salt, the fresh air, you kiss her as you dump the cooler down and she kisses you back.

She kisses you hard, puts her hand momentarily on your buttocks and pulls you closer. Uhmmmm, she says.

You kiss her again and again, then slide your hand up under her baggy t-shirt. She arches and you reach around behind, snap, the top of her bathing suit sags in your hand as if shot, as if dead, falling toward the floor but trapped by the complication of clothing and pressure. You both lean against the door frame of your house that is too expensive, that is draining your teachers' salaries, and you make out. You kiss her thinking of lockers, of high school classes and the odor of Mr. Elder's chemistry class curling through corridors.

Bunson burners, bunson burners, bunson burners, you think.

And you kiss your wife more, kiss her until you feel you are hard and ready for her. She slips her hand down in your bathing suit, cups you, then pulls away. Neither of you say anything. Walking away, she maneuvers out of the bathing suit top, her arms working under the t-shirt. Elbows, hands, shrug, the t-shirt molding around each movement until you think of a cat moving under a bed spread.

"You have to put some restriction on welfare," Peter says at his dining room table, a lobster claw at his mouth. "That only stands to reason. You can't provide for people indefinitely."

"Bull," your wife says, her chin shiny with traces of butter. "The amount of wealth in this country, and the way we've spent it, is an absolute scandal. It is."

"The whole history of this country," Nancy says, "is the richer classes, the more powerful classes, beating up on the poorer classes. I remember a history teacher of mine in college saying that Europeans didn't get from the east coast to the west coast in this country by being nice to people."

"What in the world does that have to do with welfare?" Peter says, then looks at you. "Help me out here, Josh, what do you think? Because, let's face it, we're all good liberals, okay? Every one of us here. I am too, despite what you might think. But our government can't continue to provide for everyone all the time in all cases. It can't. Say what you will, but that's the bottom line."

Nancy grabs her gin and tonic, says, "It sure as hell provides for the military. And has provided for the military for the entire history of our country. Do you realize we haven't been attacked in over fifty years?"

"Because no one wants to fuck with us," Peter says, then glances to the kids, who sit behind you all on an old green love seat, drowsy over coloring books, their skins pink from the sun. Peter raises his eyebrows to say he's sorry. Debbie, his wife, gets up from the table and disappears into the kitchen. Nancy, in charge of drinks, begins slicing more lemons for gin and tonics. She is shaking her head even as Peter finishes.

"You know," she says, then stops cutting and lowers her voice, "I could be in the same position as a lot of the women you're talking about. I could need welfare. I've just been lucky that John's been fair about the divorce settlement. But it wouldn't have taken much to put me on assistance. I could see it happening like that."

She pretends to snap her fingers, but the knife is in her hand.

She goes back to cutting lemons. Joanne, dangling her coloring books at her side, comes in and squeezes onto her mother's lap. She puts the book onto the table, spreads it carefully with her tiny hands, then begins to color. Nancy has to cut the lemons around her, her arms brackets. Peter goes back to his lobster. From inside the kitchen, Debbie says, "Who wants coffee?"

You stand to help. Nancy has started in again, talking about the military as a make-work program, and so you point to Abby, coffee?, Nancy, coffee?, Peter, coffee? Only Peter nods.

You go out and find Debbie standing beside the stove, waiting for the kettle to boil. She has one hip cocked, her eyes vacant, a dish towel over her arm. Ironically, you know she doesn't like political conversations despite being married to a politician. Years ago, she used to throw pots. You can never see her hands without thinking of them curved over clay. You wonder, when she picks up a cup or bowl now, if she still sometimes tests their shape.

"One coffee for Peter," you say, "that's it."

"I'm going to have tea," Debbie says, "you sure you don't want any?

""I don't think so. It will keep me awake."

"Nothing keeps me awake on this island," Debbie says, shifting the tea pot slightly so it is centered on the burner, "I sleep like the dead."

"It's all the sunlight and salt."

Your voice brings Nellie from her spot on the porch. She looks through the lower half of the door, through the screen, and you hear her tail thumping against Adirondack chairs on the porch. You don't like leaving her outside, but it's a warm night and Peter is mildly allergic to dog hair. You take a step toward her and her tail moves faster. It beats against a wood box now, and you take a step back to hear the tail slow. Then forward, then back.

"Way down upon a Swaney River," you whisper to Debbie.

You step forward, Way, back, down, forward two steps, upon, and Nellie's tail keeps beat, giving you the proper rhythm. Debbie giggles.

"Do the Star Wars theme," she says.

Before you can start, the tea kettle goes off. It rises in pitch until Debbie chokes it off, lifting it onto a free burner. Stay, you tell Nell. Then you get spoons out for Debbie, check to make sure there is sugar and cream. Debbie carries the tray in front of you, her arms surprisingly muscular. Her head reaches your breast bone exactly. As she pushes through the door to the dining room, you hear Abby saying, "But if you're going to do that, you have to enforce the laws to make sure the dead beat dads pay. You have to. You can't leave women stranded without any support. Ultimately you hurt the children, and the children end up being a bigger burden on society, then the cycle continues."

"And how are you going to enforce that?" Peter asks, looking over to see you both enter, and you can tell this is the way he looks in the House, arguing. "Are you going to jail every dad who misses a payment or two? How do you do it? It's not going to be easy and you can't pretend that most of the dead-beat dads have tons of disposable income. They don't."

"So what's your solution?" Abby asks him. "You say we're wrong, what's your answer?"

"Kill them," he says. "Annihilate them all."

"Oh, Jesus," Nancy says, apparently not sure how to take this statement.

"It's a line from a movie," Peter says.

"Or from a book," Abby says. "Try Joseph Conrad."

Peter puts his hands in front of his forehead, shapes them to be two wings, thumbs connected. It forms a W and he says in a voice taken straight from tv, "Whatever."

The last thing you remember before you wake is the feel of your wife's body next to yours, spoons, a light breeze coming in through the window. The window needs painting. The house needs painting, too, but you push that back and kiss her shoulder once. Then you lift slowly away, reaching down to pat Nellie, who is asleep on the foot of the bed.

Shhhhh, you say and her tail thumps twice.

You put your feet onto the cold floor and pick up your watch from the bed side table. It's 5:13. Shhhh, you say again to Nellie. She watches as you dress, t shirt, sweat shirt, jeans, sneakers, watch cap. Light is already coming off the sea and it fills your window, fills the air with gulls lifting to catch the tidal change.

"Going fishing, Nell," you say, "you stay."

Her tail thumps again and her brows go up and down, mirroring her hopes. Stay, you say and put a flat hand toward her.

Stay.

Then you go out, climbing carefully down stairs in the fish light, your joints greasing themselves slowly. In the kitchen, you slap together a peanut butter and jelly sandwich and tuck it in a plastic bread bag. You take a bottle of water from the fridge, then head outside, light and dew all over the grass. The sun is coming up pink in the east, its light shoveling the gulls off the water and tossing them in the air.

The water is calm, oil calm, as the islanders say, only they pronounce it in one word: *oilcam.* At the 17 foot skiff you have rented for the summer from Alex Tobey, a lobsterman, you check your fishing gear, then stow the sandwich and bottled water. You know a place to get cod, but it is seven miles out and you don't have that in you today.

Instead you rig a large Mepps lure, perfect for mackerel, then putt out of the docking area, giving the throttle a twist as you clear the breakwater. The boat fights to plane and barely holds it, heavy as it is. Sunlight rests of your left shoulder, which means you are going sorth.

At a point intersecting Tullman's Bluff and the bowling alley on the mainland, you cut the engine and drift. It is always a surprise to be without an engine on the open water. If you can't start it again, you will drift to Prince Edward Island, then farther, drifting until the seas climb over your gunwales and drag you below. And back in your mind you remember an account you read, this supposedly true, that a white shark once leaped aboard a skiff in Nova Scotia and dragged the fisherman under. It was reported in a book that had a green binding, the glue coming off, that you found in the local library in Port Hood. It was published in 1923, the account a retelling of an ancient story, witnessed, the book said, by Abe Littleton, a fisherman manning a second boat. Nothing but a glimmer of white and then the man was gone, his boat rocking as if the victim had placed his foot on the side and performed a straight dive into the water.

You make your first cast into the ocean and the lure makes a sound like a fork dropped in dish water. The line goes down, down, the drag set free. Then the Mepps hits bottom, or what you take to be the bottom, and you click the drag on, begin to reel. Every cast is a hope, but when the line is halfway up you feel nothing. You know you won't catch a fish, not this morning. Sometimes they're there for you, sometimes they're not, is what Bertie always says when you return emptyhanded. And you cast again, again, three more times, each time checking the land behind you, wondering how far you've drifted. You think about the island coming awake, Jonah and Joanne padding down to the living room to watch Aladdin for the thousandth time. And Nancy turning in her single bed, the sheet outlining her form. Maybe Peter is awake, maybe Debbie, and they are in their kitchen drinking coffee while you are out here, on the sea, watching the light scatter over the island and pull against the first shadows like a hand searching a drawer of clothing. You know what your wife's hair looks like against a pillow, how it spreads and coils, and you wonder if she is looking out the window now, if she thinks of you as her man, the one she dreamed about when she was a girl and played dolls and made Barbie kiss Ken until their mouths buckled in plastic dents, toothless heads mouthing everlasting love.

That's what you wonder as you cast again, this time following the line with your eyes more closely. It's somewhere along the line of the cast that you see something moving in the water, a wake forming, and you think shark, then you think black fish, a whale, the harbor porpoises you've heard about from islanders. They visit the island every ten years or so, harbingers of great fortune, driving mullet and mackerel before them.

You squint to see, feeling your heart gathering, wondering if you, among all the sleeping, will be the one to recount their passage. You begin to reel in, leaning forward, the line a distraction to what the morning has brought you.

And somewhere in the reeling you realize Abby is standing on the dock, waving, and your hand goes up to wave before the truth of what you see falls suddenly on you. Nellie is there, a mile to sea, swimming toward you. Oh, no Nellie, you say, *no, honey.* She has cleared the break water and is paddling toward you, her true heart killing you both.

Your hand goes to the pull cord, fumbles for it, then you realize you haven't finished reeling. The line will get curled around the prop, break the sheer pin, and she will be dead for certain. So you try to make yourself calm, insist on it, but your movements have tremors and you reel in a herky-jerky motion until you have the lure jammed up against the last ferrule. You throw the pole in the bottom of the boat and then turn, carefully, trying to coordinate your movements. And you twist to make sure you can still see her, trying to judge how long she can swim in water this cold.

Not long, you figure, not even a Golden can swim forever. You yank on the cord and the engine sputters, kicks, then sputters. That's okay, it's an outboard after all, and outboards are notorious for behavior like this, so you steady yourself in the boat and try to breathe properly. But you have trouble keeping your eyes from turning to Nellie, trouble keeping from finding her wake, and it is only with effort that you force yourself to check the choke, prop your feet wide enough, then yank with a good, smooth pull. The engine almost catches. You pull again. It takes three pulls to get the motor going and you goose it, circling away for a moment before banking a turn.

When you finally face the land dead on, you see Abby pointing and jumping up and down, her hands occasionally going to her face and covering her eyes. But what you don't see is Nellie. The water is empty except for the black backed gulls and you think it's impossible, nothing can disappear so quickly. As you throttle the boat forward, rushing to nothing you can see, you picture her down in the water, drifting in currents too deep to imagine.

Your Nellie. Oh God, you say.

And you stand in the rear of the skiff, scanning the water, hoping to catch a glimpse. Abby points to the left, toward the

Bluff, her arm emphatic. And you know how this happened. You know that Nellie slipped through an open door, ran down the wide meadow, and did not hesitate when she came to the water. You know she did not hesitate, but swam with her eyes on you, fetching her heart to you for the millionth time.

You throttle down the engine and triangulate between Abby's pointing and the emptiness of the water and your own position. Right, left, back, right, left, back. You know you will look for a long time, circling the water until nothing remains but your own wake. And you know that your heart was taken below the bright, glistening waves on this day, and that summer is finished for you and fall just beginning.

THAT SUMMER

MY MOTHER WAS DEAD, MY father worked in New York, and the house was often empty when I was eighteen. Hostas that year threw white beads up into the shade on a New Jersey summer. I slept on the screened porch most nights and read. I smoked, too, something my dad didn't know about. I slept on the porch cushions, in boxers, the plastic cushion covers sticking to my legs. I had a Kharmen Ghia, a brown egg of a Volkswagen. It had a stick. The seat covers stuck to my legs when I drove. The pedals played patty cake with your feet, short, quick, baby hands slapping against my bare feet. I wore my hair long, a beard, listened to Cat Stevens. I dated Joanie for a while in early summer. On the Point Pleasant Beach we wrapped a sleeping bag around us and felt each other up. Cold and rainy. The tide came in. Seagulls hung like clothes hangers, triangles, paused in air. Joanie wore Love's Baby Soft. She had blonde hair that she shook when we talked. She beat me at bowling one night. Afterward, in the parking lot, she reached inside my overalls and jerked me off. Joanie went away to camp for the summer. She sent me letters written in lilac ink. She colored in the round parts of her script.

At night, from the screened porch, I watched fireflies dangle over the grass. At dawn I believed the fireflies died. They could not tolerate the sun's strength. But the last light of the day struck birch bark and produced more fireflies. Fireflies were sparks, blind tinder. They would have set the earth on fire except for the dew that quenched them.

Mrs. Goos hired me to work at the Tomaques playground. She was the Director of Parks and Rec. She paid me air. I got a t-shirt and a whistle and a clipboard. Mrs. Goos worked in the town office surrounded by gray concrete floors. Two fans sprayed wind at us. They lifted papers on her desk as if they were curious, as if Mrs. Goos denied them secrets.

Rachel had worked three years at the playground. She was a college sophomore at Lehigh. She had black brown hair and dark eyes. She wore blue jean shorts, fraggled at the thighs, and tennis sneakers. Her socks had white pom-poms above the heel. Peds, she called them. Because Rachel was older, and because she had seniority, she was my boss. Rachel had a lanyard that held her whistle. The lanyard dissected her breasts into east and west.

Joanie wrote and said she had met someone. Not serious. Just a guy. It wasn't serious. Honest. She said she still thought of me all the time. She couldn't wait to get home. But fair was fair. We said if we met someone, we should tell. That was the deal. Besides, we weren't going steady, if anybody used that absurd word any longer. You know, she said. She did not color in the o's and u's and c's of her letter, and that meant she was being level. She asked me to please write back soon and not to be mad. She wondered if I had met anyone.

On a party boat with my father, I watched blue fish shine like fluorescent bars of light under the surface of the waves. The sun pushed us south, toward Cape May, toward the Chesapeake, the Caribbean. Later, on the screened porch, I thought maybe the blues resembled knife blades or swords. Maybe, I thought, the fish were the edge of blades as creatures dueled below us.

At eight in the morning mothers dropped off the kids. Cars formed a chain that opened, door by door, into the playground. Rachel and I sat on the picnic tables and watched the kids hurtle toward us. Rachel kept a sign-in list. She made lanyards and potholders and Popsicle calendars with the quiet kids. I took the frog legs around my hips, the kids jumping, attacking, swinging from the monkey bars. In the afternoon we all slept around trees, fairies, head-on-belly-head-on-belly-head-on-belly. At three I coached the softball team. The kids ran bases and churned sweat on their sideburns. Then Cisco arrived with the Mr. Softee truck, the sound of the ice-cream music a carnival. Kids stuck their heads in the coolers. Cisco smoked cigars. He gave Rachel and me free ice cream. He offered to take Rachel away, anywhere, and that became the joke. Ready today, he would ask her. And she said, no, I can't leave my guy. Meaning me. We ate bomb pops and licked and looked until finally we saw each other.

She came home with me one day for lunch. We ate peanut butter and jelly. I poured her a glass of milk in a mason jar. We thought about kissing. We both knew it but we couldn't do it. I have a boyfriend named Brad, she said, who was an engineering major. He was working with his father for the summer in Pennsylvania. He was really busy. Brad called sometimes, but not that much. She didn't know how serious it was or wasn't and she was tired of thinking about it. When her friend, Cindy, visited, we all went out together. We went to a movie then ended up in a diner. I sat across the table from them. Cindy and Rachel talked to me but looked at each other sideways. They knew what they knew what they knew. I was being evaluated. Cindy ate French fries from my plate. She dipped the fries in ketchup.

Blue jays called from the forsythia bushes that wrapped around the porch. That summer I learned to identify a cardinal's song. It went: *Birdie, birdee, birdeeeee.* The jays made a metallic sound, something like a bolt coming loose under pressure.

We threw a square dance. Mrs. Goos made every playground in town throw a function so the parents could see what their kids had been doing. We put on music and taught the kids the Virginia Reel. We got the custodian, Mr. Gorman, to open the faculty kitchen the afternoon before and we baked cookies and cupcakes. We bought cider and ice. At seven the kids appeared wearing bandanas around their throats, ready to dance. The parents joined in. We played the music and taught the parents the proper steps. They ate cupcakes and hooked their children with their arms and hoisted the kids into the air right on cue. Do-si-doe. Swing your partner. Allemande, left. Rachel wore a peasant skirt that swirled up when she spun.

You want to climb in back, she asked. We necked in the front seat. The night had been a success. Mrs. Goos had complimented us. The parents applauded when the kids presented us with two cheap straw cowboy hats. Now Rachel pushed away from me and slithered over the seat, into the far-behind, the tail section of her parents' station wagon. I climbed after her. It took a moment to rearrange ourselves, but our mouths stapled us together. We spread out. I lifted my hand under her skirt but she clamped her legs and put my hand on her breasts instead. I touched her breasts, pinched her nipples, then laid still when she climbed on top of me. I pulled her skirt up until her panties rubbed against my cock. She let me put my hands on her ass and she clamped her legs, finally, around mine. Then we pushed our breath into each other and we kissed while she clamped harder and harder on my leg. She angled until she had it right. She put her hand on my cock, flat, like someone shoving a drawer into a chest. Slowly our movements fit together and we kept kissing, thigh, hand, hands on ass, hand, thigh, until I felt her lips go up to my ear and say, I can, can you? So we did. Afterward we drove home together and sat in the car. She told me Brad wasn't a good boyfriend, but I knew, didn't I, that she was a sophomore in college. She said she thought I was terrific. She thought I would make some girl, someday, happy.

FIGURE 8

NO ONE KNEW IF JOHNNY Waverly meant to kill himself. Mrs. Waverly found him in his closet, a noose around his neck, his feet just inches from the scattered shoes on the floor. She spent an hour looking through the house before dinner, calling his name, wondering where he had got to, then opened the door and discovered him. She screamed and didn't stop screaming for days.

That's what people said. I didn't see how anyone could scream for days. I heard all of this, of course, as children hear about things: imperfectly.

I played with Johnny the afternoon he died. I was the last person to see him alive. I was a celebrity as a result. At a meeting of our scout troop two days later, we wore black arm bands. Mr. Merrill, our scout master, had us stand in a circle and give the cry of the wolf for Johnny's absence.

We stood together, all seven of us in olive uniforms, and blended our voices in the trembling, pre-adolescent warble that we thought sounded authentic. Like wolves across the arctic, we said to one another. I pitched my voice higher, called louder, than the other boys. I had the right by virtue of my proximity to Johnny's death.

The night before the scheduled service for Johnny, my father took me to the Waverlys' home. It was autumn, mid-November. We lived in New Jersey, the suburbs of New York, a bedroom community where the moms still stayed home and the dads went into the city. It was only a short walk to the Waverlys'. On the way to their home, my father told me to be honest, to answer Mrs. Waverly's questions directly, that she was in a great deal of distress. He told me no one would hold me accountable for anything that might have happened. Everyone knew it was a sad accident. He said it would help the Waverlys to get to the bottom of it all.

I stood beside him when he rang the doorbell. It played a chime sound that I knew belonged to a clock in England. My father smelled of tobacco and the single scotch he drank each night. He still wore his wing tips and his good gray suit.

A woman I didn't recognize answered our ring. She walked very quietly and backed up from the door as if carrying it by the doorknob. *She's resting*, she said. My father nodded. He put his hand on my back to let me go in while the woman carried the door back to its frame.

I'll tell her you're here.

People in the living room looked at us, grew a little quiet, but didn't say anything to us directly. My father nodded to a few of the men. Then the woman who had answered the door returned and said Mrs. Waverly would see us in the study. Mr. Waverly, I knew, was hurrying home from Japan where he had been conducting business. Mr. Merrill, our scout master, had volunteered to meet him at the airport at 3:30 in the morning. *That's what scouts did,* he told us.

Mrs. Waverly had on a black dress. Her eyes were red. She wore her hair swept up, as she always did, and she held a handkerchief in her hands. I had overheard my mother saying that Mrs. Waverly was under a doctor's care. She was on a sedative, according to my mother. Now she sat in a wing backed chair and looked at us as we entered.

"Hello, Joan," my father said. "I've had a chat with Billy here and he's going to tell you what he knows."

Mrs. Waverly didn't invite us to sit. Neither did she use the flat tone that adults sometimes adopt to talk to a child. She said it turned out that I was the last person to see Johnny alive, that she knew we had played most of the afternoon in his room, that she had been down in the kitchen cooking and wondered now, thinking back, what had occurred.

I told her. I told her we had the HO scale electric cars out, the figure-8 track, and we had been doing collisions. All the boys I knew did collisions, which meant you roared around the figure-8 track, giddy to watch the cars nearly crashing at the intersection, satisfied only when they did. I had a car called a roadster. Johnny had a Porsche. We had played it all afternoon.

She asked if Johnny had seemed sad, or distraught, or if he had been having a bad time at school. I told her I didn't think so. I said he seemed normal to me. She asked me very specifically how I had left him.

My father, I noticed, looked at me when she asked this. I didn't meet his eyes. I said Johnny was still playing with the electric cars, the figure-8, but that we had evolved into setting up army men and mowing them down with the cars. I said she had called up that I should be getting home to dinner myself. I told her I had said so long to Johnny, then went out of his room and headed home.

Did he have a rope, she wanted to know. Where did the rope come from? Did we go near the closet together?

No, I said. He was just sitting on the floor, playing with the cars. Then she asked me if we had dared each other to do anything. Anything at all. Anything that might have resulted in an accident. I shook my head. She looked at me. We were silent for a little while. Then my father asked if there was anything I could add to the whole situation that might shed light on it. He said he didn't want to scare me, didn't want to put me through anything painful, but this was a terrible tragedy, a terrible accident, really, and sometimes it helped adults to understand what someone was thinking when an accident occurred.

Mrs. Waverly just watched me. When I didn't say anything, my father nodded to Mrs.Waverly, said he was sorry for her loss and that he would see her tomorrow. He put his hand on my back to escort me out. He said if there was anything he could do, or help with, please not to hesitate. He said my mother, Mildred, sent her profound condolences.

We went out the same way I had left the day Johnny killed himself. That day, the day Johnny died, the house had smelled of pot roast and potatoes. Now it smelled of macaroni and baker's rolls. But the two vases on dining room sideboard still chattered when we passed through the room and the carpet on the floor still seemed tremendously thick.

My father again nodded to the people in the living room, then we were outside, the leaves soft and wet underfoot. My mother was unusually attentive when she put me to bed. She sat on the side of the mattress and rubbed Vick's VapoRub on my chest because I had been fighting a cold. She said school was cancelled the next day so that the children and teachers could attend Johnny's funeral. Then she told me to close my eyes, to just relax, to put everything out of my mind. She left the door cracked so I could see the pale nightlight in our hallway.

I turned on my side and looked away from the closet. In the near darkness I pushed to the far side of the bed, then slid my hand between the mattress and box spring, pushed it farther in until my fingers closed on the rope. It was the same length as Johnny Waverly's rope, half the cord we had found tangled around an abandoned oil drum in Pete's Woods. Johnny had cut it with his Kamp-King pocketknife and together we had smuggled it into the tedium of the pot roast afternoon, had tied it around the closet bar, ready to hang like bells. Johnny first. In the loop of the rope his face blossomed, turned red while the flesh at his neck ate the rough coil, and I stood, astonished, hearing him gasp, while his toes searched for the shiny maple flooring. Then he was dead. I walked away quickly that late afternoon, in my terror believing that to be apart from something would make it disappear.

CROW DANCE

MY FATHER, JIM WALKS-ON-ICE, MADE it through the first night of the Sun Dance without difficulty. This was in September of 1967 on the Crow Reservation in the south-eastern corner of Montana. My mother didn't take me to see him the first day because it fell on a Thursday and I was still in school. She heard from Aunt Lucy Bird-in-the-Ground that all the men had come through and that only one of them, fat Harry Crow, showed any sign of weakness.

"Harry is a fool," my mother, whose name was Harriet Windy-Boy, said after the phone call from Aunt Lucy. It was something we all understood about Harry, so she was not maligning him. He was overweight and soft. He had no business entering the sun lodge, where, as custom demanded, he would fast for three days and go without water for the same period. Once he entered, naturally, he could not come out before the prescribed time. Harry, my mother said twice that night, should have known better.

On Friday night, she packed the pick-up with food and sleeping bags, then we waited at Gilly's Service Station near St. Xavier on the Crow Reservation until Aunt Lucy joined us. Aunt Lucy had received her stamps and the cab of her Ford F150 was loaded with children and junk food when she arrived. She climbed out of the truck as soon as she pulled up to Gilly's, the corners of her mouth dusted by flecks of Fritos. She burped a long, wheezy burp, which pollinated the air with caramel and carbonization. Her teeth were bad and sometimes her voice whistled when she talked.

"Your old fucking man is dead on his feet," she said to my mother before she had even reached our truck. "You better bring him plenty of tobacco."

My mother didn't ask Lucy what she meant. Lucy talked too much, always had, and was quick to take pleasure at other people's misfortunes. Now she leaned into our truck window, suppressing another burp, and smiled. Her shirt near her right nipple was stained with something. Wind shifted her hair around and blew a paper bag from the back of her truck. One of her children yelled to grab it, but she ignored everything they did.

"Ricky and I will follow you," my mother said, deliberately including me so that Aunt Lucy would remember she was talking about my father.

"Better get gas, Harriet. There's nothing up there, you know?"

"We've got a full tank."

Aunt Lucy looked down the road and said nothing. My mother flicked the car keys. The key fob was a white rabbi foot. The fur on the foot was matted. It resembled the sweaty baldness of a boy's sideburns on a hot summer day.

Aunt Lucy turned back and said something fast in Crow, lowering her voice deliberately so I couldn't hear. I pretended to fix something on the floor of the passenger's side, hoping I could bring my ear closer. Aunt Lucy was too smart and quick, though, and she finished talking before I understood. She concluded in a short burst, then walked away and left my mother to start the truck.

We drove fifty miles to the base of the Big Horns, the sacred mountains of the Crow. We drove a mile or more behind Aunt Lucy the entire trip so we wouldn't breathe her dust. I watched the sun most of the way. My father would have to dance until it was gone and I worried about what Lucy had said. It was a long time to dance. Sometimes the men danced in the middle of the night, but it was the sun they honored.

On the last five-mile stretch into the Sun Dance, traversing White Horse Pass, we caught up with the drummers from the Pretty-On-Top family. They rode in Tom Handel's truck, a new High Sierra with a custom bed. The men sat on benches around a drum, their collars high against the wind. They played 49er songs, mixing English with Crow, jerking around because of the potted dirt road. I recognized Tommy from the mission school. He was fifteen, older than I by five years. His voice was pitched high and his face was pimpled. The old men let him sing over them because his voice was perfect. All of them waved to us, although their voices remained united.

We listened to their drumming and got lost in the dust and without knowing it arrived at the Sun Dance. The spot was well chosen. It was deliberately located in an obscure section of the Big Horns so that the feds would not bother us about the ceremony. My mother parked beneath a cottonwood tree.

"Leave everything," she said, "we'll see to it later."

A chain saw blasted on and off almost the instant we turned off our truck, and it was not until silence drifted down from the mountains that I realized the Pretty-on-Top family was no longer in earshot. In any case, the sun was almost gone so we wanted to hurry. My mother didn't wait for Aunt Lucy even though Aunt Lucy parked beside us. The only thing my mother carried with her was a carton of Camels.

The lodge was located on a small rise and pitched precisely where a notch in the mountains would allow the sun to reach the eastern gate as early as possible. I had heard in St. Xavier that the lodge was a good one; the lodge poles were built from beech and fir, collected from the elk meadows in the Big Horns. Stalks of maze were tied to the poles. On the center pole, gifts of tobacco, small sacks of Drum and Borkum Riff, dangled from rawhide strings. These moved in the evening breeze, which was now picking up off the western slopes.

I saw my father at once, almost, really, without looking for him. He wore a pair of black eyeglasses and leather breeches. His feet were bare and his stomach, fattened from years of school teaching, jiggled as he danced toward the center pole, blowing an eagle leg whistle. He did not look bad. His eyes were dazed, but that was to be expected after dancing for two days without food or drink. He needed rest, that was all, and when I glanced at my mother her face seemed to relax. I followed her closer to the lodge, though we avoided passing the eastern gate, where the men would stand ready to receive the sun the next morning. My father looked in our direction but made no sign he recognized us.

He danced next to Fat Harry Crow, both of their feet barely moving, their bodies painted almost identically in the manner of our clan, Walks-on-Ice. I counted twelve men beside my father and Harry. The Woman-of-the-Dance sat on a wooden bench inside the lodge. The men danced back and forth, moving toward the center pole in unison, then dancing back to the perimeter of the lodge where they continued to move their feet, waiting for the sign from the Dance-Leader, a medicine man named Yellow-Shirt, to come forward again.

They did this three times as I watched. On the last time, I saw my father's feet slip and, when I looked closely, I knew his knees had buckled and he had been lucky to catch himself. His face frowned and his head tilted slightly to one side, almost as if he listened, without anger, to hear the sudden break in his internal engine.

Then the dance ended. The sun went behind the mountains. The men moved back to the perimeter of the lodge and fell down on pine and beech rushes to rest. My father, I saw, lay flat on his back and looked at nothing at all. He breathed heavily, however. His chest beat up and down. His bare feet were gray. My mother went forward and handed the carton of cigarettes to Ben Horse-that-Laughs, the BIA agent for the reservation. He took it without a smile and put it on a table beside a pile of other contributions.

Aunt Lucy arrived at that point and told us she had to make dinner for her kids. She had already sent the older ones off to collect wood. She told us the Pretty-On-Top men were going to play to entertain the dancers later that night. She said there might be push dancing, an old style missionary dance that allowed men and women to dance together palm to palm.

"Come on, Ricky," my mother said to me, "we'll make our camp."

It was not much to make. We had lodged an old foam rubber mattress in the bed of our pick-up. On this we placed a lawn chair, then draped a tarp over the ridge the chair made so that we had a tent. It was the way we always camped. I rolled out the sleeping bags while my mother went to help Aunt Lucy prepare dinner. Then I went to collect more wood.

When I returned with an armful of scrub pine, Aunt Lucy asked me to open ten cans of Dinty Moore stew. She cut onions into the stew as I poured each can into a large pot. When she finished, she made two pots of coffee and perched them on rocks next to the fire.

"You see your father yet?" she asked me, her fat triceps wobbling as she opened a can of Colt 45. It was malt beer and smelled like boiling corn.

"Just for a second," I answered.

"How'd he look? He look like a school teacher dressed up like an Indian?"

She laughed and drank off a little beer.

"He looked all right," I said.

"Oh, he'll be okay," she said. "What choice does he have? He's got to be okay, right? Either okay or dead, right? Now, can you get those lawn chairs out of my truck? They're stuck in behind the sleeping bags. Be quiet as you can, because the little one's asleep in the cab."

I arranged the chairs for her, four of them, in a half circle around the fire. Then I left. About twenty campfires burned around the Sun Dance lodge, all of them set back enough so the smell of cooking food wouldn't torture the dancers. I looked for my mother, but she was off visiting, I guessed. I stayed away from the Sun Dance lodge and skirted the different fires, seeing who was here. I knew most of the families, although two, from the plates on their trucks, had come from as far away as South Dakota. Sioux, I figured, maybe Cheyenne.

A half hour later my mother found me. She came from the other direction, away from our camp, and raised her hand, signaling for me to wait. She appeared nervous. I knew that look when it was on her. It was a look of unpaid bills.

"Take these to your father," my mother said, handing me a prescription bottle of pills. "Don't go through the gate. Go around to the back and let him know you're there and what you've brought. Do you understand?"

I nodded.

"Don't torture him right now with a lot of questions. He won't be in the mood, Ricky. Just give him the pills, then leave him alone. Tell him we will be around all day tomorrow. Tell him I have a share in the buffalo they slaughtered. Tell him that."

"I will," I said and went off. It was getting dark. The camp fires around the edge of the area seemed to burn the darkness out of the sky. A few dogs barked, probably at early deer leaving their beds. It was too soon for elk.

I circled north around the sun lodge, hoping to be as inconspicuous as possible. I wanted to read the label on the prescription, but I had a notion that I should not show other people I carried pills to my father. I kept the pills in my pocket, my hand closed over the bottle.

I smelled the dancers as soon as I reached the western end of the sun lodge. They smelled of sweat and urine and something else, something I didn't understand. One of them smoked, because I saw the life of his cigarette as it went back and forth to his mouth. It was too dark to see where the various men were positioned inside the sun lodge. I had no choice but to get down on my knees and push forward, butting my head through the thick stalks of maize, turning my shoulders to get through the widely spaced struts of the lodge. Without meaning to, I put my hand on one of the dancer's shoulders and he said, "fuck," but didn't say anything else. Someone else, very near, said "Wasichus," which was the Sioux word for white man. It was unusual to have Sioux dancing with Crow, but the dance was sacred and all were welcome. I made a note that the men I had disturbed probably belonged to the South Dakota license plates.

I stopped after the Sioux word, my body half inside, and tried to see around the lodge. It was darker every second and the light from the camp fires was not much help. I remained in the same position, not sure what to do, until my father called my name in his dry, breathless voice.

"Over here, Ricky," he said. "To your right. I'm over here."

I raised my eyebrow at the voice, hoping he could see my indecision. It was forbidden to enter the sun lodge unless one was invited, so I wasn't sure if my father actually expected me to crawl to him. His voice came again, this time somewhat exasperated and tremendously weary. Carefully, in order not to upset the Sioux, I crawled to my right and found my father reclining on one elbow, his glasses still fixed on his nose. Fat Harry Crow snored next to him. They both smelled sour and dangerous, like water snakes beside a small stream.

"Showdagi," he whispered to greet me in Crow.

"Showdagi," I answered.

"Did your mother send you here?" he asked quietly, his voice solemn and far away. "Does she need something?"

"No," I said, pulling the pill bottle out of my pocket. "She sent these pills. She thought you might need them."

"What are they?"

"I don't know," I said. "I didn't read the bottle."

"Well, it doesn't matter. She knows I can't eat anything. It was silly for her to send these. Tell her not to bother with things like this."

"Maybe they're for energy," I said.

He didn't say anything for a little while. I followed the line of his vision to the eastern gate. Right now, the glow of camp fires circled the lodge, but soon, in twelve hours, maybe less, the sun would reappear. While we sat there silently, Harry Crow raised on his elbow and tried to throw up. He was too dry, though. He coughed and hacked, but nothing came. When he lay back down, a tortured grunt came out of his larynx.

"Fucking-a," he said.

"Not so bad, Harry," my father said.

"We got to dance another fucking day," Harry said. "I'm not going to make it, Jim."

"You'll make it," my father told him.

"Fuck I'm tired. Where the fuck is the divine hand, huh? Where's that at?"

"Go to sleep, Harry. Be quiet now."

One of the Sioux said, "Hetchetu aloh," which meant, "Indeed it is so." Apparently Fat Harry was a problem to all of them. Nevertheless, my father leaned forward to see who had spoken. Harry was our clan. It was my father's obligation to help him. When the Sioux said nothing else, my father put his hand on my shoulder.

"Go back now and take these," he said, handing me the pills,

"I don't need them. Tell your mother I won't embarrass her."

"All right," I said.

"Go out this way," he said, his breath on me suddenly. It was dry, terrible breath. He hadn't taken any water for two full days now. It smelled of chalk and stale classrooms.

I got to my hands and knees and crawled away as quickly as possible. When I made it outside the lodge, I took a moment to breathe carefully. I didn't want to carry my father in my nose. When I finished breathing him out, I went back to Aunt Lucy's camp fire and returned the pills to my mother.

"He didn't want them," I said.

My mother, sitting on one of the lawn chairs I had arranged earlier for Aunt Lucy, simply took the pills and slipped them into the jacket of her coat. Aunt Lucy laughed softly but didn't say anything.

Aunt Lucy had an open beer balanced on her knee. Beside her feet a bag of chips had tipped and left white, mushroom shaped holes around her chair. Now and then they shattered under her feet, breaking into triangles and reshaping the earth surrounding them.

I ate some of the leftover stew. Then, after staying beside the fire for an hour or two, watching the people do the push dance in a clearing before the lodge, I went to bed. As I undressed in the truck bed, my mother asked if I wanted to leave the next day. Her question confused me. I knew she had already arranged for bison meat. I had been with her, in fact, when she had discussed the price with Frank Hard Tail, who was in charge of the buffalo pastures in the northern end of the Big Horns. The meat was due to arrive the next day, no later, Frank Hard Tail had assured her, than early afternoon.

Without actually saying it, I knew she had planned the bison meat as a celebration for my father's successful completion of the Sun Dance. She hoped to cook a traditional meal, one to escort him back to life and to repay him for dancing blessings on his family.

"I don't want to leave," I said as I watched her slip into a sleeping bag beside me. "Do you want to leave?"

"No, I was just checking," she said.

"I'll go if you want to."

"He didn't want the pills?" she asked, though I knew she was thinking her own thoughts. I pushed the tarp away from the bed of the truck beside me, letting the air in. Far away, I heard the Pretty-on-Top drummers singing a love song. Tommy, the fifteen-year-old, sang the highest range, while the older men, his clansman, carried his voice in theirs.

My father had already danced four hours by the time I woke the next morning. I heard the dancers' eagle whistle seven before I climbed out of the truck. The day was bright. I put my hand to my eyes as I rolled back the tarp to air out the sleeping bags. Aunt Lucy's camp fire was gray. I carried my towel and toothbrush to Sheep Creek, a small feeder stream from higher in the mountains, and washed my face and brushed my teeth. The water was terribly cold. Splashing it on my face, I felt it push numbness into my temples. I squatted and looked at the sun. It was merely nine o'clock.

"Showdagi," someone said behind me. I turned to see Tommy, the chubby singer for the Pretty-On-Top family, coming toward the stream with a towel over his shoulder. He wore jeans and a baggy t-shirt. The t-shirt was ripped under his right arm pit. He squatted about ten feet away to my right and began splashing water on his face. He blew into the pocket of his hands and bubbled the water. When he finished, he tilted his head to one side and blew snot out of each nostril.

"Your fucking clan is whipped, man," Tommy said to me around his toothbrush, his arm gouging back and forth, back and forth. "It looks like they're going to die or something. You been up there yet?"

"No, not yet," I answered.

"It's all fucking crazy, you ask me. Everyone's into this heritage thing until it actually comes down to it. I mean, our ancestors were fucking wild men, you know what I mean?"

"I guess so."

"There were some guys last night, they wanted to kill the fucking Sioux families. They said the Sioux is the mortal enemy of the Crow. They said the Crow were guides for Custer and the whole Sioux nation hates the Crow because of it. That all took place two hundred years ago or something."

"Not that long ago," I corrected him, knowing, from conversation with my father, that what he said about the Crow being guides for Custer was true. One of my great-great-great grandfathers, White-Man-Runs-Him, was a Custer scout. My family was not certain whether to be proud or ashamed of the association.

Tommy stood and kicked dirt to cover his toothpaste. He dried his face on the towel. I stood and did the same.

"You and I will be dancing someday," Tommy said, his voice suddenly serious. "Crow Dance. It's crazy, isn't it?"

"I guess so."

"Does it scare you?"

"No, I don't think so."

Neither of us said anything for a little while. Small trout popped on the water. I looked up the stream and watched them. The circles they made, for no reason I could think of, reminded me of the yellow holes in the dirt made by Aunt Lucy's potato chips the night before.

"They're going to do a piercing," Tommy said, coming back to himself. "As soon as Ben Horse-That-Laughs leaves. The BIA would go crazy if they thought we were getting into piercing."

"Who is going to do it?"

"One of the Sioux. A man named High Horse. You've seen him already. He's dancing like a show-off."

Then Tommy headed back. I followed him up the small footpath. Aunt Lucy was at the fire, feeding sticks into a struggling flame with one hand, while she fed her baby girl a bottle with the other. She said good morning to Tommy, told him she enjoyed his singing the night before, then turned her attention to me as Tommy left for his own camp fire.

"You hungry?" she asked. "I can cook up some bacon if you like."

"I'm not that hungry," I said.

"Your mother is up by the dancers. Your dad's not doing so good."

I knew from her concern over my breakfast that it must be bad. It must be embarrassing. I wasn't certain I wanted to see. I stood beside the fire and watched her work the flame back to life. Then I went to the pick-up and pulled on a fresh sweatshirt. By the time I made it back she was seated in a lawn chair, her baby, Sean-Peter, burrowed in her chest. I ate an orange, sipped a little black coffee, then threw the peels in the fire and went to see the dancers.

My mother, I saw, sat in a lawn chair, her baseball hat pulled down low over her eyes. The sun was straight on the eastern gate. Even as I approached, two of the dancers came to dance in the full sunlight at the open gate, their bodies white with sweat, their hands outstretched. They sought visions, I knew, and later blessings. Yellow-Shirt, the Dance-Leader, came and captured the two men. He led them back toward the center pole, taking them carefully in the grip of his large eagle feather before their souls could escape and fly to the sun. Near the eastern gate the Dance-Woman watched impassively, apparently not frightened she would have to abandon her body and fly with the souls of the men to the sun, as custom dictated.

I went and squatted next to my mother. She turned and put her hand on my shoulder. At the same moment I saw my father. Everything about him had changed. He was more than fatigued. He danced deep in the recess of the lodge, far from the sun, his right leg so tender it could not support him. As a result of his leg's weakness, he circled aimlessly, turning mechanically as though he did not have sufficient wit to approach the center pole. His skin was water. Every move he made sent a shower of sweat and condensation into the atmosphere. He melted, that was the sense I had of him.

"Where's Harry Crow?" I asked my mother.

"Resting," she said.

"Asleep?"

"He fainted and he was pulled to one side. In the old days he would have been killed."

"These aren't the old days," I said.

My mother didn't say anything. I stayed beside her until it became apparent that my father did not suffer from a temporary abdication of will or desire. He was stuck in a rut, instead, his weak leg forcing him in increasingly small circles. He did not blow the eagle whistle, though he kept it to his mouth. When other dancers tried to pull him into their dance — as they did on two occasions as I watched —he simply ignored them and continued in his tight circle, entering his fifth hour.

Fortunately, we were distracted by the arrival of Frank Hard Tail with the slaughtered bison in his truck. Three of his boys rode in the back, each with a willow frond in his hand to push away the flies already gathering on the meat. The bison was good sized. Frank drove past the sun lodge so the dancers could see the bison. One of his boys, a drunk named Johnny Wind Ever, let out a short war cry. He stood in the back of the truck as it rocked and banged over the uneven ground, holding his willow frond as a spear. He turned to the Sun Dancers and called again. They didn't answer him. He remained standing, however, until Frank Hard Tail parked the truck on an incline so that blood would run out of the flat bed.

Everyone, I think, was happy to have a distraction. Frank Hard Tail was a funny man and he made the business of parceling out the meat a good pastime. My mother, for tradition sake, came forward with a wooden bowl to receive her allotment. Frank Hard Tail stood next to the huge bison carcass, one that required four men to hoist it into the back of the truck, and told her loud enough for everyone to hear that he had meat for her lodge. My mother looked down, then held out her bowl. Frank gave her ten strips of tenderloin, a section of the tongue, and told her she could return for sweetbreads if she decided to prepare them. He reminded her to hang a strip of suet in the trees for the western chickadees, who were, as she knew, friend to the Crow.

With slight alterations, it was a performance he went through with each woman who stepped forward. I watched it through the end of the morning. At one point, I was given a willow frond to help with the flies. The sun was dead on the meat by then, and to pass my frond over the flat bed was the equivalent of sketching with iridescent flies.

I might have remained there, avoiding my father, if Tommy did not come by to inform me the piercing was about to take place.

He also mentioned the dancers were eating stones, sucking on them and rolling them in their mouths, which was permitted by custom at the close of the Sun Dance. Frank Hard Tail did not try to keep me. The meat was nearly gone. Only the hooves, head, and shaggy skin remained. The bones had slid to the bottom of the flat bed and now remained there, locked together as intricately as a beaver dam.

I walked back to the Sun Lodge and looked inside. My father was not standing. I turned my head away and saw my mother in her lawn chair beside Aunt Lucy. They didn't notice me. When I turned back I saw Harry Crow sitting up, his back propped against the northern wall of the Sun Lodge. He looked pale and withered. He seemed to concentrate on each breath. His mouth moved over the pebbles he sucked against his lips. It was not until Harry's head moved slightly that I saw my father. He had been blocked from my vision by the three men clustered around the Sioux. The men were busy administering the piercing. My father no longer danced, nor even pretended to. He walked slowly in a circle, his arm still bent to hold the eagle whistle to his lips. His steps were absurdly small, an infant's steps, and he seemed entirely oblivious of everything around him. Perhaps this was his vision quest, I couldn't say. Studying him, I realized he was not at all an infant, but had somehow been introduced to advanced senility. He could not think or see or take care of himself. He simply wandered inside the lodge, his teeth moving to find moisture in stones.

Suddenly the men who had been clustered around the young Sioux backed away. They had pierced his pectorals horizontally with two six-inch arrow shafts, then had hooked a twenty-foot long, rawhide tether to each arrow. Both of the rawhide tethers had been tied to the center lodge pole. It was now up to the Sioux to run forward and back, jerking his body against the tether when it reached its outer orbit. By custom, he had to jerk hard enough to snap the arrow shaft through his skin.

The sight of the Sioux, blood dripping down his chest, did not distract my father. He continued his slow shuffle around the perimeter of the lodge, no longer part of the dance in any real sense. His belly jiggled. Next to the Sioux, a dangerous looking man with a flat gut and muscular arms, my father appeared a TV Indian. The Sioux, named High Horse as I had been told, took all the air out of the Sun Lodge. He screamed as he rushed toward the center pole, then screamed even louder as he charged back, the tether bringing him up in a convulsive jerk. The skin of his chest warped and bubbled outward. Then, in a sickening jolt, the skin and resistance of the rawhide recovered their elasticity once more and pulled him forward. He quartered the center pole, passed it by, and repeated the same jerk against the restraint on the other side.

Again, the skin on his chest heaved out, but again the rawhide held. It tightened until High Horse could not hold against it any longer. The rawhide twanged, then remained for an instant quivering. High Horse charged forward again, his waist shiny red from his blood. The leather breeches he wore soaked up the blood and collected dust from his footfalls. Johnny Wind Ever, son of Frank Hard Tail, began to whoop. Johnny had made the sound a thousand times before, at ball games, dances, even Pow-Wows, but finally his call found its place.

The Sioux, High Horse, returned his call. I moved to one side to find my father, my heart rising, but he was in the deepest section of the lodge, his body obscured by shadows. Now he was simply one of a dozen men, all secondary to High Horse. I went to my mother. She put her hand on my waist, but didn't invite me to sit or talk. Aunt Lucy leaned forward in her chair, watching High Horse. None of us had ever seen a genuine piercing before. We watched High Horse's skin, the bloody bulge his chest made each time he reared back against the weight of his own orbit, and hoped it would break easily for him. He stumbled several times, dashing to his knees and running up onto his feet again, his mind filled with adrenaline and sun visions. No one doubted he would eventually pull the arrows free and in time he did, bursting both in a red spray of blood just as the sun placed its southern rim on the base of the western mountains.

My father walked out of the lodge when the sun went down. He brought Fat Harry with him. Both hobbled and as soon as they passed the threshold of the lodge, my mother rushed forward and helped them. She squeezed between them and let them use her for support. My father, I saw, could not move as a normal man moves. He danced forward in his slow, creeping way, his feet never leaving the earth.

"Come and help, Ricky," my mother said, but over her shoulder I saw my father's eyes and didn't come closer. I stayed, instead, to watch High Horse leave the Sun Lodge. A group of people stopped him to examine his chest wounds. The wounds were bright red and looked like two mouths in the final evening light. I imagined the mouths opening and devouring the rawhide tethers. His chest, it seemed in that blue light, had eaten itself free.

An hour later, when I returned to our camp fire, my father was already asleep in the flat bed of our truck. He had eaten nothing except a small cup of bison soup. He had consumed three glasses of water, the last at a slow and steady pace. His feet, according to my mother, were more painful to him than anything else. He was accustomed to wearing shoes. Dancing in bare feet had been a grave mistake.

"He's a school teacher," Aunt Lucy said beside the fire after my mother finished telling me these things. "What did anyone expect?"

"Where's Harry Crow?" I asked both of them.

"They took him down to Sheridan," Aunt Lucy told me, reaching to her side for pretzels. "He's in a dangerous condition. His heart was racing and his head was ringing. They think he may have had a stroke."

"Did the Sioux boy get medical attention?" my mother asked me.

"I don't think so," I said.

She shook her head. I couldn't say if she was disgusted at the lack of medical attention or admired him for his stoicism. Later, near ten o'clock, my father called me to the back of the truck. He had held a whispered conversation with my mother. She had brought him more broth when he had called for it and had rubbed his feet with lotion. When I reached him he sat against the cab of the truck, a blue pillow behind his neck. A small camp light illuminated him from underneath his chin. His face was drawn. His hair, uncombed for three days, lay flat against his head. His feet were bandaged in several places. Both feet appeared swollen and brown, as though, I thought, he could not rid them of the dirt he had trampled for three days.

"You'll sleep in the cab tonight?" he asked me, which was the usual arrangement when we camped. He slept in the back with my mother. I nodded. Although I stood outside the truck, only a few feet separated us. He didn't turn to talk to me. He stared at his feet, apparently amazed to find them so deformed by dancing. The bandages were white and painful looking in the florescent light.

"We'll go home tomorrow," he said. "Do you have schoolwork?"

"Not much," I said.

"Well, you should get it done for class on Monday. I have papers to correct myself. I think I can go to school on Monday. We'll have to see how my feet mend."

"Are you all right otherwise?" I felt obliged to ask.

He shrugged. He shifted his feet. Back near the Sun Lodge, the Pretty-on-Top drummers began to play. Tommy's voice started them and led them through a song. It was short, just a warm up. Tommy's voice seemed chased through the song's rhythms.

I stayed and listened with my father until my mother came and made up her own bed. I dragged my sleeping bag and pillow into the cab and slept there, the windows open to let in some air. In the morning, we packed and drove back to St. Xavier. My father sat on the passenger side and stared out the window, a plastic bottle of water between his legs. Now and then he drank, but mostly he kept his eyes closed and rested his feet, as lightly as possible, in the well of the cab.

DRY STRIKE

IT WAS LATE AFTERNOON AT the end of a warm week in July when Dr. James Hydock, from the University of Washington, stood on Australia's Great Barrier Reef and watched the tide suck in over the brain coral and giant clams. Hydock was a thin man, slight and nervous, who was a specialist in moss and fungi.

Despite the week in the sun, he was still remarkably pale. He had used sun block throughout his time on the reef, painting his lips and nose like a clown. On top of the sun block he had sported a wide brimmed hat, a safari hat really, which he felt somewhat self-conscious about wearing. It was not that the others did not have hats. It was, instead, that he suspected the hat of being too dashing or him to carry off. The hat tried too hard, and was too obviously a parting gift from a wife. He would have been better off with a baseball cap, or even a floppy fishing hat. The stiff brim of the safari hat — not a pith helmet which might have been all right — made him seem more of an adventurer than he really was. The hat was a poor choice and had opened up a whole range of nicknames. Botswana Joe. Tarzan. Indiana Jones. Hydock had never had nicknames before, and he did not know how to carry one.

Now standing on the reef, the strength of the water surprised him. The tide had just changed but already the water ran all the way up, linking the small channel behind him with the darker ocean ahead. The plastic reef shoes he wore skidded a little on the bony coral. A million colors changed and refracted with each wash. He could not tell the difference at times between a shadow and a small depression in the structure of the coral.

He considered diving in and swimming to the glass-bottomed

launch where five or six of the other biologists waited to be ferried back to the research yacht. They already had drinks in hand and had already called an end to the day. The effect the tides had on the reef fascinated Hydock too much to leave, though he also stayed from a sense of duty. He was more dedicated than the others, who took the entire trip as something of a lark. Hydock could not rid himself of the habit of being a plugger. He was an academic at heart, not a particularly gifted one, and if he had a talent at all it was in his tireless assault on information. He was a grind, always had been, and he accepted this character trait as his one defining feature.

Nevertheless, he smiled at the boat in case his colleagues watched him. He thought to wave, then decided against it. He looked back down at the reef. The giant clams already filtered the first probing waves and, just at the edge of the reef, a few small fish splashed up into the pools. He stepped carefully over some brain coral and steadied himself when a wave lapped up. The ocean pushed in, covering the reef more quickly than he would have believed possible. When water rinsed back, it was like watching gravel being panned. Sunlight glittered everywhere he looked.

As the next tidal surge came someone yelled from the boat, but Hydock only waved back and held up five fingers to indicate he required a few more minutes. He walked diagonally across the reef, his arms out for balance, until he could peer over the edge into the deeper ocean. This was a sight that always thrilled him, yet also made him nervous. Sharks sometimes patrolled there. Flauson, the specialist on wheat hybrids, saw one earlier in the week. It had been a white tip coming in to harvest the tidal change. It had been large, nearly six feet, and it had rolled once to examine Flauson, its eye a black glint.

Standing on the edge, and timing his balance to the next push of the tide, Hydock leaned far out and saw the sheer drop off directly beneath him. A ray passed twenty feet down. Three schools of minnows, all different colors, all striped in an outlandish show of diversity, flicked back and forth as the ray's shadow touched them. Hydock watched, completely enthralled, until he found his sight wandering even deeper, skimming by the ray and dropping to the depth sof full open ocean.

The color and shifts of light mesmerized him. Sand and light and coral and wide dark forms which moved just out of range of eyesight — he saw them all without noting any one thing in detail. His breath came faster and he felt a tiny web of panic drop over him. The boat was merely a hundred yards away, nothing at all for him to swim, yet the ocean suddenly appeared intensely active. To swim over it demanded a conscious effort. He did not like to look down once he was in the water. He feared what he might see; it was that simple. He would have to dive off the reef, enter the water, and swim strongly to catch the boat. He would become another shadow, his form blocking light from the minnows, yet he would also be cumbersome and loud, a foreign element in a world of perfect order. It was that dive that worried him. It was the entrance.

"Hydock, you better get swimming," Gleason yelled. "The pub is open."

Hydock nodded, his arms still extended for balance. He didn't particularly like following Gleason's orders. Gleason came from the University of Rhode Island and had been to the Great Barrier Reef twice before. During the summers he ran graduate seminars off Point Judith on the university's boat, spending three months working with fishermen to determine quantities of ground stocks — cod, flounder, menhaden. Gleason, Hydock understood, had become the spiritual leader of the group. He was fit for the outdoors, and was always dropping the hint of some adventure into the group conversation. His skin had not tanned in the last week, but had simply grown darker, as if this last layer of pigmentation was only a varnish applied to a lifetime spent in the sun.

"You see any sharks?" Hydock yelled back, turning his shout into a joke as it left his mouth. The water was up to his knees. Two more biologists stood up in the back of the glass-bottomed launch and hoisted their beers at him.

"Come on," another one, Ford, yelled. Then Ford pointed to his right. "That wasn't a shark, was it, men? Those sharks blend in, don't they?"

This was a joke, the kind of joshing Hydock had tried hard

to master all week, but never felt comfortable using. Still he couldn't keep himself from glancing over to the pale blue water on his right. No sharks, but then, who knew? He had seen a shark come straight up once, down of fthe Grand Cayman, a hammerhead rising like a thresher's blade from a hundred feet down.

Hydock reached to the top of his head for his facemask, spit in it, rubbed it clear, then slipped it over his eyes. It was too tight, but at least it didn't leak. He put his snorkel in his mouth and blew through the tube, sending a small stream of water onto his back. The water was tepid. As soon as his snorkel cleared, his mask fogged again so that he had to pull it a few inches away and let the air in once more. He was somewhat blinded by the mask when the next wave came and knocked him backward.

It was not particularly forceful. It pushed him back only a step, but as he regained his balance he felt a small prick on the top of his instep. It was little more than a prick and he thought he had knocked his foot against a sharp piece of coral, but when he looked down he saw a snake moving away, flowing through the water with remarkable ease. The snake was so quick, and was so closely matched to the jaundiced hues of the brain coral, that at first, he could not trust his eyesight. He leaned to one side to cut the glare from the sun, and with this small adjustment he caught a last glimpse of the snake as it slipped over the other edge of the reef and disappeared.

A snake, Hydock told himself. *A reef snake.*

He tried to collect himself but he knew, as a biologist, that reef snakes were extremely venomous. He stood on one leg and tried to see the top of his foot, but the clumsiness of the mask and snorkel, the way his reef shoes slipped on the coral, made it all but impossible to see clearly. He put his foot down and concentrated on feeling his body, but he felt nothing unusual except his own fast heart. He knew he was beginning to panic, and he knew panic would only serve to pump the poison more quickly through his blood stream.

But it didn't matter. He could not control himself and he began yelling in a wild, jagged voice that carried a terror that seemed almost disembodied.

"A snake just bit me!" he yelled as loudly as he could to the launch. "A reef snake!"

"What?" someone called. A few men touched each other for silence. He saw them repeat his words down the line, so that more men turned to look at him.

"A snake," Hydock yelled again, trying to enunciate. "A reef snake!"

He tried to calm himself, but it was impossible. He waved frantically for them to bring the launch closer, but of course they couldn't risk slamming into the reef. He took a breath and leaped in, his heart going, his body flushed. Once he was in the water it was completely silent and he was shocked to discover he was making a moaning sound through his snorkel. He told himself to stop it several times, but he continued to moan, not even halting when he lifted his head out of the water to spot the boat.

Gleason waved for him to come faster. Another biologist, the city environment expert from the University of Denver, held out a boat hook, as if to offer a tow. Hydock put his head back in, trying without success to regulate his breathing. He was aware of his arms splashing wildly, almost spastically, but he could not get his mind to slow down his movements.

He was twenty feet away from the launch when he heard a loud splash and saw a wedge of bubbles erupt near him. It was Gleason in the water beside him, pulling him through the gentle chop. Hydock felt Gleason's quick, determined strength and wondered if he had been failing in the water. Was that it then, he asked himself? Had he been struggling? Was the poison already working?

"Get him aboard, get him aboard," Hydock heard people yell. Then he felt himself lifted, but they were awkward, not strong men, and his head hit the side of the boat. The mask slipped down and rammed against the mouthpiece of the snorkel, jamming it into his gums and teeth. Hydock threw the mask forward in the boat, and could not help seeing the rest of the biologists staring at him, their drinks still in hand.

"Holy shit," someone said.

"Where did it bite you?" Ford asked too loudly, too excited.

"On the foot," said Hydock, sitting on the back gunwale and holding up his right foot. He was ashamed, but his eyes had begun to water.

"Where?" Ford asked, inspecting it.

"On the instep. On the top."

Hydock now saw part of it himself. A short red gash, more like a scrape than a bite. It was on the outside of his foot, and he could not turn his ankle sufficiently to see it clearly. He tried to stand and turn his ankle more, but Ford still held his leg. He hopped absurdly for an instant on one foot, then fell back against the gunwale again. Something, a snorkel he thought, snapped against his buttock.

"Just hold on," Ford said.

"Did you see the snake?" Gleason asked. "What did it look like?"

Hydock hadn't seen Gleason climb into the boat. Suddenly he appeared, dripping, ready to take over. Hydock felt a momentary relief at his appearance. Hydock wiped his eyes and looked straight westward into the sun. It was nearing sunset and he knew he was dying.

"It was a reef snake," Hydock said.

"You're sure? You're a botanist. Are you positive you recognized the snake?"

"It was mottled color. I don't know. I saw it," Hydock said.

"How big?" Gleason asked, now taking the foot from Ford and inspecting it himself. Until Gleason examined it, Hydock realized, no one else's opinion mattered.

"About four or five feet long," Hydock said, trying to sound clinical, but still not removing his eyes from the sun. "I know what a reef snake looks like."

"I guess it doesn't matter. They're all venomous. They hunt eels so the venom has to be strong," Gleason said. "It's trouble."

"It was a reef snake. I'm sure of it."

"It doesn't even look like he bit you."

"Did it break the skin?"

"The skin is broken, but it could just as easily be a gash," Gleason said, holding up Hydock's foot for anyone to see.

"Will the poison attack nerves or tissue?" Hydock asked.

Hydock felt Gleason release his foot, almost discarding it. Hydock slowly eased it to the deck and looked again to see the small red gash. He could not believe that a gash that simple could mean his death. But the cut had taken on such significance that he could not look at it for very long.

"Nerve toxin," Gleason said, his voice taking on a lecture tone. "The reef snake has a neurotoxin which will eventually go into the spine. It will block messages to the involuntary muscle systems. Your mind won't be able to send messages out."

"So I won't breathe?" Hydock asked, knowing the answer before he asked but wanting it clarified anyway.

He looked at the sun again.

"If we could get you to an iron lung, you'd be okay. Otherwise your diaphragm will give out and you'll suffocate."

"What about a tourniquet?" Ford asked. "Can't we at least slow it all down?"

"Not after that swim," Gleason said. "He had his blood moving. No, a tourniquet is no help."

Hydock took this last piece of information as stoically as he could. He did not feel anything in his lungs or spine to indicate that the venom was at work. But it didn't matter. He knew snakes well enough to understand that a neurotoxin would take an hour to work on a body his size. It would not be immediate and it would not be painful —nothing like a rattlesnake bite which gradually destroys connective tissue and turns you into a bag of blood. The reef snake's venom would be like a fan turning off.

Hydock put his hand over his eyes, rubbing the sockets hard. He felt someone place a palm on his forehead, testing for temperature. Hydock almost pushed the hand away, but he felt increasingly concerned about his behavior. He was not a man of action. He had never wanted to be a soldier; he did not take pain well. And now here he was, bitten by a snake and forced to behave in some appropriate manner so that he would not disgrace himself. It seemed an unfair expectation.

Hydock grew aware of them watching him. He looked down at the deck, the ocean beneath them. He felt the boat rocking and thought for a moment he might be sick. Distantly he heard someone talking about radioing the coast, but they were hours from Queensland, and even a plane could not bring any sort of antidote in time. For that matter, he doubted there was an antidote. Bites by reef snakes were rare, he imagined.

"You know," Gleason said, speaking to the group as much as to Hydock, "reef snakes dry strike sometimes. We don't know why they do it, but they bite and they cling, but they don't pump the syringe. It's not profitable survival behavior, but they do it. They do it about half the time."

"You mean he could have bit Hydock and not injected the venom?" Ford asked.

"That's what I'm saying. That's the book on it. There's about a fifty-fifty chance that way," Gleason said. "And maybe Hydock wasn't even bit."

"I was bit," Hydock said, too loud he knew, but he couldn't help it.

"I'm just thinking in the water, splashing around and everything. It must have been hard to tell. The water was close to knee deep, wasn't it?"

"You think I'm making this up?" Hydock asked, feeling in the question an old accusation he had never been able to answer. He felt too nervous and frightened to make sense of anything, but he didn't want to have to defend the bite. He had seen the snake. Now, thinking back, he was certain he had felt the fangs tick through his skin.

"No, we're just trying to see a way out of this thing," Gleason said. "We're just gathering data."

Hydock put his head in his hands once more. He had one hour to live and he couldn't think of a single thing he should do. It was some sort of macabre game, a late-night riddle asked in a dormitory bull session. What do you do if the sun blows up and you have approximately nine minutes to live? What if the bomb goes off? You are given one year to live? But this was one hour, and his mind would be clear for every detail of his death.

He came close to crying again. He pinched a fold of skin on his knee. He had a son, Jonathan, who would miss him. He had a wife, Susan, and a little girl, Marie, not even three, who probably would forget him in a year. She would grow up and not know he had lived. Susan would marry again, and he would be some sort of ridiculous figure who had died by stepping on a snake at the Great Barrier Reef.

Finally, he looked up, only to see the collection of biologists studying him. No one said a thing. Someone coughed. A few men looked away. Hydock felt someone put the safari hat on his head. He had no idea how the hat had appeared in the boat.

"What time is it?" Hydock asked to break the silence.

"Almost six fifteen," Gleason said after glancing at the thick, rubberized watch that seemed suckered to his wrist. The dial glimmered blue.

"So what then?" Hydock asked. "Until seven?"

"I guess you have until seven unless he dry struck you. We'll know what's what after seven."

Another man, a biologist from Toronto whose name Hydock could not recall, stepped forward and offered his notebook and pen.

"I assure you it will be kept entirely confidential with me and I'll arrange to send it to anyone you name," the man said.

Hydock failed at first to understand what the man offered. But then it became clear. He should write a note to Susan, to his children, telling them whatever he could think to tell them. It was the only thing to do, of course, but he realized he couldn't handle a pen or organize his thoughts. He turned to Gleason and nodded at the notebook.

"Would you write a few things for me?" he asked.

"Certainly," Gleason said, taking the notebook from the other biologist. "Let me just dry my hands, then go ahead."

When Gleason was ready, Hydock closed his eyes and tried to think. He began to speak several times, and each time he felt such an enormous pull of emotion that he could not pronounce the words. His breathing felt stalled in his chest, and he wondered if this was not the beginning of the venom having its way.

"Dear Susan...my beloved, Susan," he said, bending close to Gleason and whispering. "I have only a short time. You were in my thoughts. I have always loved you and the children."

He spoke a little while longer, then found himself unable to end the message. Where do you stop, he wondered? His last word turned into a near sob and he could no longer control himself. He reached and touched Gleason, holding his arms up. Gleason, after a moment's hesitation, hugged him. It was such a welcome feeling that Hydock felt his breathing relax slightly. Gleason's body was firm and strong, and Hydock whispered, "I'm sorry. I really am. I guess I'm not behaving very well."

"You're doing fine. Whatever you need to do is fine."

"I'm scared."

"It's okay. You have a right to be."

Finally, after the boat had gone up and down three or four times, Hydock nodded against Gleason's neck. Gleason pulled back, his whiskers scraping Hydock's temple. Hydock looked around, panting, his eyes blurred and watery. No one said anything, and he wanted desperately to make a joke, to break the tension somehow, but he was incapable of it. He looked from one to the other, watching them rise and fall as they stood on the deck of the launch. One or two turned away, but others continued to stare.

Hydock said, "What time is it?"

"Six-thirty five."Twenty-five minutes."

Hydock tried to sense any failing in his body, but it was impossible to do so. Any twinge sent his mind racing around his limbs. He could not concentrate on a twinge before it was lost to another sensation, then another. But a headache began to pound in his forehead and his legs felt tremendously weak. He continued to pant. Someone brought him a glass of freshwater and he drank it, but had to break away repeatedly to catch his breath. He sat and watched the main boat, the research yacht, wading up and down. An Australian flag fluttered above the main cabin. Now and then a flying fish broke the water, and occasionally he saw small schools wheel up through the water and spin down, like leaves falling through pure sky. Minute sounds and sights he had not previously noticed pulled his attention: the hollow suction slurp of a boat just before a wave lifts it; the thrum of an anchor line stretching to hold the coral bottom; the wink of sunlight on a well polished cleat as the boat rose and settled with the lap of the waves.

"Do you want to lie down?" Gleason asked.

"How much time do I have?"

"Ten minutes maybe. But that's just a guess."

"My chest hurts."

"Maybe you should lie down."

Several men scattered to make room for him. Someone arranged a few boat cushions on the deck. Hydock began to get up by himself to make the swing to the cushions, but Gleason and Ford jumped to either side and held him. He partially fell onto the cushions. His legs gave out and he viewed this with a dispassion that astonished him. Suddenly, he was looking straight into the sky. Beneath him he felt the boat riding the waves, measured and calm. His lungs tightened. He put his arm over his face and rested the crook of his elbow over his eyes. He felt his breath pulling through his throat and he had to open his mouth wider. It was not a full hour and he was dying. He came close to tears again, his voice sometimes shuddering in choked sobs he could not catch in time.

"Breathe as smoothly as you can," Gleason said over him.

"Thank you," Hydock said with difficulty.

"No, don't thank me."

Hydock felt Gleason take his hand. He closed his eyes and waited. Someone lit a cigarette and another person said a prayer, something like a Hail Mary but Hydock couldn't be positive. *Now at the hour. I pray the Lord to take me. Into Thy Hands, I commend my spirit.* Hydock waited. People said there was peace once you accepted death, but he did not feel it. Rescued victims talked of it; heart attack patients, called back to life, spoke of lights waiting for them. He felt nothing of this. Instead he felt panic growing and he began to roll on the bottom of the launch, slowly at first, then gradually faster, thrashing back and forth until two men held him. He imagined his body decaying, turning slowly to rot beneath the soil. It was a curse to know too much, to be a scientist, because he could not kid himself now. Transmutation did not seem wondrous. It was hideous, the worst of all events, and he found himself saying aloud, "I don't want to die. I don't want to die."

Someone put a cool cloth on his head. Shadows passed over

him, and he knew they were formed by men leaning forward to watch. He felt damned by their detachment, biologists watching with their insatiable curiosity, bastards all. He was nearly hysterical, he understood that, but he could not keep his body still. He thought of himself becoming a legend in biology departments around the country, his fate part of shop talks during late afternoon beers.

That guy Hydock bought it out on the reef, they would say, his name evoking a sort of glamour he had never felt in life.

But even as Hydock thought this he realized his breathing had loosened. This became clear in slow beats of blood and pulse. His lungs were not as tight as they had been even a moment before. He finally lay still, examining each breath. By the tenth even flex of his lungs he knew that whatever had caused the shortness of breath had passed. He wondered what that meant. He began to consider that perhaps he had been dry struck after all. Or perhaps the snake had given him a small dose of venom, the flutter of his lungs a temporary reaction.

"Is he gone?" someone asked.

"I can't tell," someone else answered.

Hydock felt a finger touch his eyelid, pulling it back. He could not prevent his eyelid from flicking up and down, fighting the finger trying to pry it open. Finally, he relaxed his muscles enough to let them open his eye. He stared at the sky and the ring of faces above him.

"I think it's passing," he whispered.

"What is?" Gleason asked.

"The tightness."

"You can breathe all right now?"

"I think so."

Hydock saw Gleason look at the other men. He hated Gleason's calm expression, the cocky mustache perfectly flecked with gray and gold. Hydock covered his eyes again.

"You just stay where you are then," Gleason said. "There's no rush."

But Hydock felt the tension on the boat relax. It was a subtle thing at first, but he was confident he felt it. Some of the men began talking quietly. One man said softly,"Coowee," in imitation of the Aussies. Another opened a beer. Hydock rolled to the bulkhead, his face away from the men. Wind moved softly over the boat. Someone — he didn't see the man — placed the notebook beside him. The wire ring of the notebook grated on the fiberglass of the boat. Hydock stared down through the glass-bottomed boat, waiting for the tightness in his lungs to return.

GRIS-GRIS

I WAS SHOOTING IN ARLY, THE National Reserve of Burkina Faso, West Africa, when I received word that a rogue elephant needed to be put down near Tenado. The usual story followed: the elephant had gained a taste for village millet; a few *anciennes* had discharged their muskets in the elephant's flanks and ears, only serving to enrage it more. A telegram from the local Prefet arrived a day or two later. Would I come to Tenado? Men would be available. I could state the terms. Famine would result in the villages if the elephant continued pillaging unchecked.

I had a small window between hunting clients, so I went. I left my vehicle at the last piece of paved road in that region and set out on foot, carrying my rifle and an ample supply of cartridges. The growing season stood in full bloom; millet stalks, many twice as tall as a man, made navigation difficult. It proved impossible to see any distance or to gain perspective as to the landscape one traversed. I followed *pistes*, the dirt trails the villagers used, and stopped often to make sure I took the correct route.

Of course, by inquiring of the locals I had *spoken to the grass*, as the saying goes in Africa. In no time, a whisper passed in front of me and surrounded me. *Nassarra*, the word for white man, was coming. Small children suddenly appeared at odd intervals, stepping out from the forests of millet to regard me with solemn respect and sometimes an expression bordering on fear. Old women, I understood, whispered to their children to be good or the *Nassarra* would come and snatch them away. A remnant of the slave trade, I had been told, but disturbing nevertheless.

Tenado stood at several thousand feet of elevation, a welcome rise in that flat land, but it was a full day's march to get there. The temperatures by mid-morning reached well over one hundred degrees. I halted at noon and slept. Flies collected on my eyelids. I placed a handkerchief across my face and breathed the hot air, my head on my backpack. When I woke a young girl squatted next to me, fanning me with a frond and keeping the flies from lighting. She appeared to be eight or ten. Her face, quite beautiful, had been ritualistically scarred, a custom outlawed but still followed in the bush. Seeing me awake, she stood and disappeared, a small infant on her back. Other children waited in the millet stalks to collect her.

The Chef de Village met me one kilometer from the village. He brought a large retinue of older men, a traditional body called in most villages the *sage* – or the wise. Children and women banged drums and danced; my arrival caused celebration, but the drums also alerted the elephant that the air had changed and it could not come and go as it liked. The Chef, a sturdy looking man with gray hair and an exquisite posture, introduced himself as Adama Zurungo. He welcomed me and nodded to one of the *sage* who stepped forward with three chickens tied by the feet into a bouquet of squirming flesh. I accepted the chickens gratefully, then handed them to a woman who had been designated as my cook. Together we headed back to the village.

The cheerfulness of the greeting belied the true state of the village. The rogue had obviously trampled the granaries, lifting the tops as neatly as a child might open a jar of peanut butter. Everywhere evidence of the elephant's passing pressed on one's awareness. The Chef narrated. Here, he said, pointing at one granary, the elephant had stood half the night shoveling millet grain into its mouth; over there, the elephant had charged three men who came to fire their muskets at it; here a young boy had thrown a spear at the elephant, only to have the elephant chase him back into his mud brick compound. At night the villagers stayed inside, their doors latched and bolstered by thickets of acacia thorns. The elephant had killed no one in this village, but a man had been trampled in the bush. He had been a traveler on a bicycle. From what the tracks revealed, the man had ridden directly into the elephant. The elephant had run him over, its large feet gouging the body into half-moons of mud and offal. Now the villagers could not go out at night for fear the dead man would whisper into the elephant's ear that he desired company in his rest. Unfortunately, the result was that the latrines had been moved closer to the village, making it an unhygienic situation.

Chef Zurungo offered me a small compound to use as headquarters, but I told him I preferred my tent. He knew not to insist with Westerners. The better part of the village went with me to raise my small Eureka tent; the children marveled at the tension rods as they snapped into place. In minutes, I had erected the green nylon structure. Chef Zurungo sent a squad of men off and in minutes they returned with several logs to form benches outside the tent. Then a woman brought a calabash of dollo, the beer made from millet, and the Chef and the *sage* drank my health. I drank with them for politeness sake, spilling a drop of dollo on the ground to honor our ancestors. After a while the men grew drunk and told story after story about the elephant. I listened. The elephant would return at nightfall, I suspected. Until then we remained in the shade and waited.

The night passed without a glimpse of the elephant. Midway through the darkness I walked the perimeter of the village to make sure I had not somehow missed it. It sounds absurd to believe one could miss an elephant, but the night was dark and the millet pressed on the village. When I satisfied myself that the elephant had not attacked the granaries that night, I returned to my tent and slept the last hours until sunrise. I woke to the sound of women bringing me a breakfast of saga bowl, a millet pudding the consistency of Cream of Wheat. They had also brought with them a young man named Franklin. At first glance, I knew Franklin was what passed for a *ye-ye* in the bush. A *ye-ye* is a man, never a woman, who travels to Paris or Abidjan or Dakar, gains a taste of French culture, then returns to his small village and finds himself absurdly out of place. Typically, he affects a continental style, though the clothing is betrayed by the poverty that undermines the attempt.

Nevertheless Franklin, I knew, passed for a poet or at least an educated youngster, one who doubtless considered himself too good for manual labor. He wore bright lilac pants and cordovan colored Bataka plastic sandals. He carried a transistor radio tuned to a French music station, often pressing it to his head to hear the news that, by implication, still interested him more than his immediate surroundings. His head was shaped like an old-fashioned bicycle seat; his visage was virtually tri-cornered, the chin forming a pedestal upon which the wider, heavier section rested.

"Enchantez," Franklin said as the women finished preparing the last of the saga bowl. "Chef Zurungo suggested I might be of use to you as an interpreter."

"I speak French," I said.

"Yes, of course, I see."

He said nothing else. He meant that he was to serve as a cultural interpreter, but he was reluctant to expand. I invited him to eat. He set on the food avidly, all cultural pretense vanishing. We ate as is customary in the West African bush. We used our right hand to cup some of the saga bowl millet into a clump, then dipped the glob into a sauce which we then carried to our mouths. The sauce tasted of the chickens given to me as I entered the village. As we ate, Franklin informed me that runners had already come from Lati, a village five kilometers to the southwest. The elephant had attacked the granaries at Lati, and would not flee even after one man threw a string of firecrackers at the animal. Two *anciennes* had shot the elephant with their muskets, both having no effect.

"Does the Chef want me to go to Lati?" I asked when Franklin finished his report.

"No," Franklin said, "the village is safe while you are here. That is the understanding. If we can finish the harvest we will survive. He has asked that you stay and stand guard."

"I can hunt the elephant as easily at Lati as here. Why not track it and kill it?"

"The Chef prefers that you are here."

I obliged. The elephant stood as much chance of returning to Tenado as remaining at Lati. With luck, it might simply move away, returning to the grazing fields farther south. I found a convenient spot on the granaries and stood guard while the village worked. It was a magnificent scene. The flamboyant trees had cast red flowers and the baobabs bloomed to the east and north. Nothing can compare to the African pagnas, the bright cloths women wear as dresses. Everywhere one looked the men cut millet while the women bound the fallen stalks into sheaves. Afterward the women sang and walked in single file back to the compounds where I knew they spread the millet heads to dry. Now and then I heard someone shout, "Viper!" and the commotion of a cobra's passing would ripple through the millet like the wake of a canoe, but the elephant made no appearance. The Chef supplied me with fresh water and food; repeatedly throughout the day Franklin stood beneath me and checked to find if I was satisfied with the harvest. I said that I was each time and Franklin went off to report back to the Chef. The day passed.

At nightfall, I encouraged the villagers to remain quiet. They had nearly finished the harvest and they were in a mood to celebrate, but noise and drumming might serve to scare the elephant away. Quietly I assumed a position near the most south-facing compound. If the elephant arrived from Lati, he would come from that direction. I positioned my back against a portion of an old well and settled into wait. I kept a large flashlight beside me, ready to illuminate the elephant at the first sound of its approach.

The elephant failed to appear. The night became a parody of a hunt, I jumped at the rise of a pair of mottled pentards, and sighted in on two antelopes tapping their boned hooves on the nearest laterite *piste*. By the time Franklin fetched me for breakfast, I felt grumpy and tired of the entire process. Immediately he reported that the elephant had again raided Lati. This time, he said, the damage was even more extensive. I tried to read his expression, but he guarded himself closely.

I determined to go to Lati. My thought was that in passing from one village to the next I might encounter the animal. I thought, too, that after eating the elephant would want water. I could sit up for him over a drinking place. When I informed

Franklin of my intention to travel toward Lati, he appeared displeased.

"The harvest is not finished here," he said.

"I appreciate that, but I should get back to my own affairs. What does it matter where I shoot the elephant? It could raid your village as easily as it raided Lati."

"No, Lati must find its own solution. You were summoned to help this village."

"That's nonsense."

Franklin shrugged. I packed after he departed, lowering the tent and strapping it to my backpack. To my surprise, the Chef did not come to argue with me. He did not appear at all. Only a few children followed me out to the farthest meadows. It struck me that they did not seem to fear the elephant now.

I had traveled only a kilometer when I spied the first shaman. He wore nothing but a rawhide band around his waist; he carried in one hand a bright shield with white figures crudely painted on the surface. In the other hand, he carried a spear. It took me a moment to realize he did not look toward me; he had turned his back. The face that I saw watching me was formed of a rounded calabash. A child might have drawn the details of the face. Square eyes, square nose, square mouth. But stationed as he was well back in the millet, he called to mind a corn spirit, or a creature living among the weathered strips of agriculture. It did not surprise me to find other shamans stationed at intervals along the trail. Each had turned his back to me. The message could not have been more elementary: I was being shunned. It was my payment for shunning the village by my departure.

I knew this kind of gris-gris. I knew, furthermore, that although it might be directed at me, it probably had more to do with a rivalry between Lati and Tenado. Perhaps by my arrival I had sent the elephant to Lati. Perhaps the people of Lati blamed me for scaring the elephant into their laps, so to speak. In any case, someone was unhappy with my travel between the two villages. The corn men flanked me for two kilometers before the elephant fortunately interrupted the display.

The initial sighting of the elephant provided nothing dramatic. It stood perpendicular to the trail, contentedly chewing at a pile of harvested millet stalks. A few bloody holes bled slowly from its trunk and hindquarters, obviously the product of the *anciennes*' musket fire. Flies followed each movement of the creature, almost as though it had taken its own shadow and cast it into the air above it.

Killing it looked to be a simple business. I knelt and positioned my rifle on my steadied hand. I aimed directly for its spine, a foot behind the round knob of its skull. As I sighted, however, the elephant turned to face me. Its ears pushed forward. Then it charged.

I had hunted elephants before, and had observed them in the bush countless times, but never had I seen one charge so abruptly. My nerve faltered. For a moment, my hand pushed the rifle in small circles of indecision. I yearned to run, but I knew that would be fatal. Instead I spoke to myself aloud and said to concentrate. The elephant crashed through the dry stalks, its feet shuffling forward in the awkward gait elephants use, the sound of the stalks breaking like kindling being eaten by flames. I fired. The bullet struck the elephant square in the face and staggered him. Then I shot another round, then another. Before the elephant had approached by ten strides I had stitched a fine lace of bullet holes in his forehead.

The animal sank to its knees. Remarkably, the wind of its charge spilled over me. I smelled his strong odor. I smelled his blood and the wash of his anger. The millet stalks near me wagged in one violent shake. The creature's spirit, I felt, had passed by me, carried forward by its hatred of men. I shot the animal three or four more times to ensure its rapid death.

It is the custom in Burkina Faso to deliver to the Mora Naba – the tribal head of the entire country — the foot of any elephant shot within the country's borders. To prepare the elephant hoof, the villagers hang the amputated limb in an acacia tree where the sun dries it and the ants hollow it out. The process requires a month. When I received word that the hoof had achieved its proper shape and form I had no choice but to travel once more to Tenado to retrieve it. I could not hope to continue my guiding service in the national parks if I alienated the Mora Naba. No one else could deliver the elephant hoof except the hunter. The elephants of Burkina Faso belonged to the Mora Naba. Killing one required the proper homage afterward.

I dreaded the trip. The image of the shamans shunning me disturbed me still. Relating the story to several friends to get their opinions, they had warned me that I had blundered into the middle of a tricky business. My arrival in Tenado obviously had sent the elephant to Lati; if a shaman had been protecting Lati by spells and incantations, I had undermined him in the most public manner. To make things right, he would have to settle the score on my return. My friends joked that I should be careful about what I ate and that I should protect my hair and nails from theft by women or children.

The harvest had finished by the time I arranged to retrieve the elephant hoof. Already the sun had withered the remaining stalks, turning the fields into brown striped prison yards. Many of the stalks had been bundled and left near the *pistes*, readied, I knew, for use as mats and roofing. I walked most of the morning with the sun on my back. At noon, I slept under a baobab, my handkerchief again across my face. I slept deeply. Heat pushed out of the earth. I woke damp with sweat. No little girl fanned my face this time. I had seen no one since I entered the bush.

I reached Tenado by mid-afternoon. This time no celebration greeted me. I had resolved to gather the elephant foot as quickly as I could and depart. I preferred to sleep in the bush rather than the village, but the decision, I understood, was only partially mine. Chef Zurungo sent the contingent of old men, the *sage*, to greet me. Franklin came with them and stepped forward immediately to welcome me to the village. He spoke in a ceremonial manner without warmth. The entire situation made us all uncomfortable. By custom, they were obliged to be gracious hosts; by custom, I was forced to appear grateful.

"How is the road behind you? Have you eaten today?" Franklin used the ceremonial greeting and touched his chest.

I told him I had eaten and the road was long. I explained that I hoped to leave as soon as possible in order to return to my truck by nightfall. Franklin nodded and explained my comments to one or two of the *sage* who spoke no French. They murmured at hearing my intent. It was unusual for a man to leave the village so late in the day. They could not ensure my safety in the bush at night. The next morning, if I liked, they would provide me with runners. The hoof was heavy, filled as it was with warm stones to keep its shape. Could they not dissuade me?

I realized, watching them, that they simply followed protocol. They did not want me in the village any more than I wanted to remain. To follow form, I thanked them profusely for their invitation but insisted that I had business elsewhere. They made me sit and drink a calabash of dollo while they prepared the elephant foot for transport.

Before we had properly finished one measure of dollo, two young men appeared with the elephant hoof. Somehow the Africans had taken up the European notion that an elephant foot made an elegant umbrella stand. It was a particularly absurd notion for such an arid country, but I had never seen a foot turned to anything else. The foot could be sold by the Mora Naba, I supposed. If it were not turned to something useful, it would remain nothing more than an odd curiosity. It saddened me to think of the animal's foot resting in a hallway, its life rendered into a decorative antique.

I examined the foot when the boys presented it to me. It was gray and large, as tall as my thigh. The sun and ants had done their jobs. The thick epidermis, bagged and stiffened by their drying, had been burned with sticks until it contained pictures of antelopes and birds. An elephant rib, somehow made supple, served as the stand's handle. Egg shaped stones filled the interior; the yellowed toe nails, each as wide as a coffee cup, had been filed flat and even, and a varnish had been applied to give the nails gloss. For its type of artifact, it was quite handsome. The Mora Naba would be pleased.

As I examined it, I realized carrying it was going to be more difficult than I had anticipated. I considered remaining the night and accepting the *sages'* offer to provide me with runners the next morning, but the awkwardness of our greeting, the relative silence of the village, reinforced my desire to be away. Something had changed – for reasons I couldn't hope to understand – in the village's attitude toward me. They regarded me with fear, as though they detected doom lingering about my person. My exact perception was that I was contagious, a leper, a person to be excommunicated. Resolutely I thanked the *sage* and Franklin, and shook their hands. They wished me well and watched me prepare to pick up the hoof. I could not rid myself of the impression that they waited to see me assume a burden.

I forced myself to concentrate on the practical problem of lifting the hoof in a manner that would make walking possible. Had I been an African, I might have balanced the foot on my head, but lacking that skill, I clutched the umbrella stand to my chest. The skin felt as dense and unpleasant as rotted wood. I shuffled the load in my arms until it felt reasonably comfortable, then began to walk. The *sage* did not accompany me to the outskirts of the village. Neither did Franklin. In moments, I had cleared the last compound and had entered the rough bush terrain.

A simple hand truck or wagon would have made transporting the hoof an easy task, but burdened as I was, the going proved difficult. Sweat became a pulse that worked over my body. The weight of the hoof was obstacle enough; the size and awkwardness of the shape made it annoying in the extreme to carry. Additionally, the putrid stink of the hoof, pressed as it had to be to my chest, made my breathing short. Several times in the first minutes of my walking I smelled again the hot rush of the elephant, the same phantom breeze that passed over me as I killed it. The odor choked me. I was forced to turn my head to one side and that made following the narrow *piste* all the more difficult.

I had not traveled a half kilometer when I was forced to put the hoof down and rest. I found my heart beat quickly not merely from exertion, but also from an unnamed fear. Why was I so troubled by this entire incident? And why had the shamans pointed their powers at me? I had done the village a favor by ridding it of the elephant. I had not contacted anyone from Lati, but, surely, they were as relieved as the people of Tenado to have the rogue removed. Sitting on a raised mound of earth with the elephant hoof in the middle of the footpath, I could not imagine who would benefit by working *gris-gris* on me. My business and daily activities were located well to the south of Tenado. I had been merely an exterminator at the behest of the regional government.

Before I hoisted the elephant hoof again, I cautioned myself that I was thinking somewhat irrationally. Once one gave into the possibility of *gris-gris's* exsistence, one had already granted it power. That was the great trick of it. In defiance, I grabbed the elephant hoof and hugged it to my chest. The smell struck me as overpowering still, but now, at least, my body had warmed to the labor. I set off at a great rate, determined to get this work finished and behind me. My resolve lasted only a short while before the weight of the foot began to work against me. I staggered a little as I climbed a short hill. My inhalations began to choke with the noxious smell. I set the foot down again. The sun had moved perilously close to the western horizon.

Despite what I had told Franklin and the *sage*, I did not fancy a night in the bush. The hoof smelled sufficiently to attract the attention of scavengers. Although lions were scarce in that portion of Burkina Faso, they were not unheard of. Jackals, too, might come around at night. Perhaps even a pack of hyena. I could not safely keep the hoof in the tent with me. I would have to hang it and then sleep well away from it. The hoof might be injured, which would be a great insult to the Mora Naba, one that I couldn't afford. I might be able to sit up with the hoof if I could make a fire, but even that could be risky. The thing to do, I knew, was push on back to my truck.

When I clutched the foot again to my chest, a strange fear entered me: I resolved that I must not look into the hollowed core. The egg-shaped stones, gray as wolves, clicked and rattled as I began again to walk. But now the stones and noises took on greater significance. I feared what I might see inside the leg. I kept my face averted. Despite my best efforts to persuade myself that this was all nonsense, I could not overcome the fear. I imagined a cobra had crawled into the hollowed leg and now rode on the hot stones, ready to strike at my eyes if I let them peer over the rim of the interior. I wondered if anyone from the village had checked the hoof before passing it on to me. After all, snakes often found their way into hollow containers. They frequently turned up in calabashes and water bowls. A friend had once woken in the morning to a cobra curled in the springy bulge of his mosquito net, the viper contentedly asleep inches from his chest. Common sense would have dictated that I put the foot down to examine it, assuring myself that it was merely a bowl of desiccated flesh, but I did not do so. The rational part of me understood that nothing could be in the foot and that to give in to such imaginings was more dangerous in the end than even the most venomous snake might be. I carried the hoof against my chest, hugging it even harder to prove to myself that I did not fear it.

When I halted again, this time at a shorter interval than the last march, I placed the hoof down and moved away from it. My arms and legs ached; the weight of my backpack seemed extraordinary. For an instant, I wondered if I might be having a physical collapse. I lay my hand flat against my chest to feel my heart. It beat strongly but in time it leveled into a consistent drumming, a dull thud in the core of my body that echoed into my temples. With my hand still pressed to my chest, I doggedly scaled a termite mound and looked around. The sun now hung its lower lip on the edge of the western horizon. A flock of millet sparrows spun against the bright orange blank of the sun's face. Under other circumstances, it was my favorite part of the day in West Africa. It was time for a long cold drink, then a cocktail, then dinner. But now the sun seemed deliberately to sink. The scattered stalks of millet sent long, worried shadows pointing at the east. A nick of panic entered me as I stretched my fingers to arm's length, an old trick I used to calculate the margin before true sunset. I used my hand as a sextant and counted each finger width between top of the sun's round hump and the flat cord of earth. A half hour until darkness, I judged. I could not be certain that I would reach my truck before nightfall. And once darkness surrounded me, navigation on such a large, blank terrain would prove impossible. I could pass within meters of my truck without seeing it. I might walk parallel to the paved road all night without striking it.

The thing to do, I understood, was to hurry onward. But when I turned to regard the foot once more I felt such revulsion that I could not bring myself to move. I remained on the termite mound, consciously avoiding any second glance at the foot. What in the world was happening? I considered the possibility of abandoning the foot altogether. I could make up any manner of story. Lions had stalked me, I could say. Or I might say that I felt my heart straining alarmingly, and when I went for help the foot was stolen. But the grass talks in Africa, and I knew the Mora Naba would not believe me. I deliberated for a moment longer, then rushed down the mound and tackled the foot to my chest. I lumbered forward, the elephant skin chafing my own. The gray stones clicked and rubbed in the interior; my shadow stretched before me, and in horror I realized that I seemed to be attempting to pour my silhouette into the hollowed center of the leg. A ludicrous image, but one that remained with me nevertheless. I turned my head and carried the foot faster, veering off the *piste* at times and knocking into random stalks of millet. Each time I regained the *piste's* level surface, I vowed to remain calm. But in moments my speed increased.

I fell. The foot slapped to the ground with the heavy, dull plunk of an antelope shot and stumbling to the earth. I cast my body to one side, narrowly avoiding a direct landing on top of it. The gray stones rolled out of the core and dripped like dice into the dust. The loss of the stones caused the shank of the ankle to sag and bow, a deflated balloon at the end of a child's birthday party. For an instant, I lay like a bed mate next to it. Then I rolled away, pushing to my feet so that I would not have to see its gruesome outline. I glimpsed faces in the sinking flesh, masks of horrible devilish anguish tightening as the skin sagged.

Blindly, I scrambled forward ten steps, my heart now rising in grief and fear, my only hope to escape the foot. The absurdity of my fear, the cowardliness of my desire to flee, could not restrain me. For one primal instant, I convinced myself that by running I would be free of the damned thing. But I could not escape the stench of the rot as it clung to my skin, and in twenty strides I slowed. By thirty strides I halted. I turned and faced the foot where it lay like an empty grocery bag on the trail behind me. I returned to it.

The sun had now gone into the earth. The only light remaining lingered for one last partial rotation of the globe. Night already crouched on the trail behind and before me. It was too late to continue. I knew that I would have to sit up over the hoof through the night. Oddly, the decision brought me a measure of calm. I felt satisfied to have a plan. I had sat up over game many nights, though usually with a group of bearers. At least, I reasoned, I would not have to touch the foot again until daylight. That filled me with greater confidence. I had been carried away. That was all. I had been like a child in a windstorm, my mind turning one thing after another into malevolent creatures. For the next ten minutes, careful not to wander too far from the *piste*, I gathered millet stalks. I moved attentively, because nightfall is the moment that snakes, many of them cobras, begin to hunt in the bush. I purposely made noise before shifting the grass. I let my feet fall forcibly on the ground, so that my vibrations would alert any snakes of my approach. In time, I had a pile of stalks nearly as high as my waist. They would burn quickly, I knew, but if I fed them scrupulously to the fire, they might last the night.

From my backpack, I withdrew a candle and a box of matches. I made the fire quickly; the millet was dry from the long harvest season. Immediately my situation seemed much improved. When the last light finally pulled back from the sun, I had a cheerful fire burning. I fished a wedge of cheese and a stack of crackers from my pack. I leaned against the backpack as I ate, feeding the millet like stiff rope into the fire. Beyond the illumination, five meters away, the foot remained as I had left it. The gray stones extended toward me in the dust. I could glimpse into the interior of the leg, but could see nothing except darkness.

I slept. When I woke, sometime deep into the night, it took me a moment to recall where I was. As I looked about me, gradually coming to my senses, I realized I could not recall when or how I had fallen asleep. I had been awake one moment, then unconscious. Fatigue, I told myself. But it was not prudent to sleep in the bush, especially now that the fire had died. I had always prided myself on my ability to endure long periods of sleep privation; now I had fallen asleep as easily as a child, surrendering my security to blind luck.

I stirred the fire and began feeding it again. The flames built easily; the millet stalks cracked as dry as kindling. I glanced at the hoof and saw its position had not changed. The gray stones remained in the dust. My exhaustion had dulled me. I could not conceive of the malevolence I had attributed to the foot hours before. How curious it all was. How foolish. The leg again resembled a dull grocery bag, tired of sustaining its ovoid shape. I felt impatient with myself; I was impatient for morning when I would finish my annoying task and be returned to my compound by nightfall next. As I brought my attention back to the fire, a large grasshopper flew into the fire and burnt. Before I had time to wonder at it, another burst into flame, then another. In moments twenty or thirty grasshoppers flickered above me, their wings whirring like chiggering fans, their bodies dropping suddenly into the heated coals. Now and then one crawled out and began to fly again, carrying flame on its scalded back like a candle drifting into the night. I tried at first to catch them before they could ladle flames onto the brittle millet fields, but they were too many. I stood and stamped on the few nearby. Others disappeared into darkness, but none seemed to ignite a fire. For a time, I tried to keep the unharmed grasshoppers out of the fire, swatting at them as they neared the light. I spent a futile ten minutes hitting at the insects until at last I gave up and returned to my seat against the backpack. For the next half hour, the grasshoppers landed in the fire and lifted away. It was as I followed the flight of one particularly large insect that I glimpsed the first rays of sun saw across the horizon.

In the same instant, a hyena appeared next to the leg. It came directly along the path, its face pointed toward me. Its cousins, I suspected, ringed the fire, though I did not hear them. The hyena did not falter or hesitate. It took the foot in its mouth and began pulling it back toward Tenado. The stones clattered and for a moment frightened the creature away. Then a second hyena dripped free from the millet fields and began assisting the first.

They growled solemnly, but without rancor. In the glimmering light, I squinted to see them. That they might have been men dressed as hyena, I had no doubts. But their movements were authentic; they stayed low to the ground, betraying the illusion not at all. By the time they had dragged the filthy leg twenty paces away, more and more creatures fell on the amputated limb. They did not quarrel, as blood hungry hyena would do. Instead they worked collaboratively, and in moments had disappeared into the rapidly disappearing darkness.

I knew what I must do. I stood and ran at the fire, jumping it easily. I reached and threw a handful of millet stalks onto the flames. They flared up instantly, and as I backed away from the fire I doubted that I might clear it. But I again ran at the fire, this time leaping through white heat and yellowness until I landed on the other side. I was aware that my leg hairs had singed; my shirtsleeve glimmered red. But I ran again at the flame, leaped, and landed. Again. I ran and leaped. Like the grasshoppers, I carried flame with me at times. At other times, I went quickly through the hottest portions of the fire, leaping effortlessly over everything. My clothes tarred. My boot souls became soft as bread. But when I jumped the final time, the sun had cleared the eastern horizon and ran like a bright red triangle from the earth into the stars and back.

A STORY ABOUT NEW JERSEY THAT INCLUDES BOWLING, FRENCH FRIES, AND A BUICK 225

THE FIRST TIME I TRULY noticed Roxy LeHeulier, the head majorette for our high school marching band of Fighting Blue Devils, she held the huge paper ring that marked the symbolic birth canal for our entire football team. It was Thanksgiving Day, 1970. A photograph of her appeared in the local newspaper the following afternoon. It fixed her in time, forever, and would have made as splendid an anthropological portrait as any done of, say, Sitting Bull or Crazy Horse. It was a testament to cultural relevance. Her hair, in a fashion set by Sonny and Cher, hung perfectly straight. Her make-up was dark and heavy, particularly around the eyes, where she had liberally applied an iridescent green the shade of a dragon fly's belly. Her majorette costume was obscenely short. Holding the paper circle, with the "Blue Devil" pitch-forking her in her alabaster thigh, she leaned forward enough to reveal the blue hint of her majorette panties.

It was fitting, too, that she held a paper hymen — one ready to be smashed by the entire Fighting Blue Devil squad, football players who, incidentally, held a certain resemblance to sperm with their wide heads and slim bodies — because she appeared as fertile and young as a spring corn field. Her huge cockade, a phallic tom-tom stick stuck erectly to the front of her majorette hat, cast a shadow onto the magnificent Blue Devil end zone. The grass beneath her white marching boots glimmered the finest suburban green.

A second later, naturally, the image was shattered forever. Roxy, grinning broadly as the spermy young men smashed through the tattered paper circle, quickly carried the circle away when they finished and returned with her baton. Taking center stage, or what she believed to be center stage — most of the crowd's attention was on the football team, after all — she blew a whistle at the band, then leaned ridiculously backwards and proceeded to prance through the goal posts herself, her baton a feminine tommy gun under her muscular right arm.

Oh, Roxy! She was radiant! She was glorious! Sitting in the grandstand myself, Loraine, my steady girlfriend beside me, I was transfixed. Baked on a good gram and a half of hash, smoked, surreptitiously in my father's Buick Electra 225 amid the horn honking and egg throwing of the arriving game crowd, I watched Roxy as though she were an alien creature. I knew her, of course. I had seen her at every pep rally, at every football and basketball game for four years of high school. For an entire semester, she had once reigned at the front of my history class, answering questions in a determined, serious voice, while I, generally high on wacky-tobaccy, perused Rolling Stone or High Times, scoffing at the sincerity with which Mr. Broward, our earnest instructor, approached World War I. While I wore T-shirts and jeans, she dressed each day in Fair Isle sweaters and carefully coordinated skirts. While I held down my position in the Elephants — a rock band I had helped to found — she was a majorette for the Fighting Blue Devils. We had nothing in common except hormones. But that, as it turned out, was enough.

Irony was in the mix too. Why else would Loraine, who never attended football games, much less take seriously what was going on in front of her, chance to look up from the book of poetry she held on her lap and see Roxy? Loraine, who was baked also on some good Moroccan, shook her head and said, "Oh, wow." I knew immediately she was gawking at Roxy. And, in fact, Roxy was worth gawking at, for at that moment she was in the process of throwing two bright swords into the autumnal sky, only to spin beneath them and snatch them from the air as they threatened to impale her. It was show biz! It was a pot smoker's dream come true, and Lorraine, always amused by the visual aspects of our drug use, set aside her volume of poetry and leaned forward to watch.

"Oh, wow," she said a few minutes later as Roxy sprinted fifty yards, fully half the gridiron, with her feet pointed straight ahead and her body leaning backward. It was a tradition (I later discovered) for the out-going majorette to do the "final strut" on Thanksgiving Day, so that all the past majorettes could compare their accomplishments to their current embodiment. In short, Roxy was part of the long- tasseled line, the rich tradition of female exhibitionism that had marked our high school football games for several decades. Cantilevered backwards, her muscle-ridged thighs kicking in front of her, she resembled a young filly so full of itself that it threatened to kick down the white Kentucky fencing. Even in my drugged state, I knew she represented something. Youth, innocence, pride, hunger, virginity – a thousand things and more. And when the entire crowd rose to its feet as Roxy pranced into the end zone one last time, only to turn and give an incredible, almost poignant blast on her whistle, I stood with the rest and began to clap. She was a majorette for the ages! At least she appeared so as she bid the band break into "The Star Spangled Banner." She trembled from emotion and held the baton in front of her, nestled across her notable breasts, its small white head lending it an oddly human appearance. When the band shifted and raised its voice even higher, breaking into the "O Say does that star spangled ban—n—er—ah wa-ah-ve?" portion of the anthem, Roxy, timing herself perfectly, and sensing the crowd's emotion, leaned slowly forward in a lunge that left her front leg bent, her back leg trailing, her face pointed up at a hopeful, wonderful, possible future.

Hurrah, America! Hurrah, Roxy! God bless us, everyone!

Then the drums reclaimed the afternoon and the football captains waddled out to the center of the field for the coin toss. Roxy — I watched her — was loathe to yield the field. She turned, blew her whistle shrilly once more, and, to the tom tom tom of the drums, marched out the back of the end zone, the fifty members of the Fighting Blue Devils Band caught helplessly in the gravitational pull of her splendor.

"I'm hungry," I said to Loraine. "Do you want anything from the snack bar?"

"No thanks."

"Are you sure?"

She nodded and looked down at her poetry book. I stood beside her and waited a moment. I even reached out my hand and pushed back her hair behind her ear. She reached her own hand up and touched mine. The familiarity of the small exchange proved almost enough to make me want to sit down again, because what I planned, almost despite myself, was a quest to find Roxy. I was high, remember, and perhaps wanted to do nothing more than to mention to Roxy that I found her a majorette for the ages, but I felt guilty nonetheless. I knew, in some part of me, that I was done with Loraine. Our relationship might not end at that moment, or even in the next weeks, but it was fated to expire, to be rubbed away as some stone steps are rubbed away at public institutions by sheer foot traffic.

A number of students — males — called my name as I descended. I had a small reputation myself from playing in the Elephants, one which, by careful nurturing, I had turned into a rebel persona. At the sound of the beckoning voices, therefore, I deliberately turned in the wrong direction, slightly askew, so that those calling to me could not fail to realize I was high. I worked a dreamy, somewhat bemused expression onto my face. Heavy-lidded, dopey, a deliberately languid air about me, I merely smiled when one of my buddies called, "Munchies." Yes, they were right. Yes, I was high. Yes, it was impossibly droll that I was here, at the weenie football game, but here I was, and the world should know no one as cool as Arnie McNally could get through the game without serious — in our vernacular at the time — bong-ification and hotdog-ification. What a goof! To walk right through the grandstands, surrounded by teachers and parents, while being totally bong-ified, was a form of victory. It was the ideal teenage state. Better still to wave, as I did, to some of the surrealistic teachers in our school, to wink at Al Bobel, the sunny, hippo-cheeked principal of Westview High, to give the peace sign to Mr. Guttmacher, the woodshop mad man who ate vitamins constantly and whose forearms were so muscular his hands appeared to be marionettes connected by stout cords to his elbow. Hello to Mrs. Ketchum, the typing teacher, who taught five generations of typists by saying in a sing-song chant, "Locate the E, strike, E, strike, E, strike space. Locate the A, strike, A, strike, A, strike space." Hello to Mrs. Vicadomiti, the fiery math teacher who still believed, despite all evidence to the contrary, that math was fun. And when, finally, I reached the bottom of the bleachers, and a friend named Kenny Rider stood in the middle of the student section and shouted, "Arnie!" I was able to turn back to the entire wedge of my community and smile with a wifty, druggy smile, giving one final dope-eyed nod that suggested, I hoped, I was off to inhale lemon furniture polish from a paper bag and seek new highs in my relentless quest to find meaning.

Instead, of course, I was off to find Roxy. I was hungry, too, which gave me an excuse to work toward the snack bar. Half way there, I stopped for a second to watch the kick off. By chance I was lined up precisely with the deep back who circled under the end-over-end kick, and I had a moment's understanding of what it might be like to wait for the ball in a big game like this one, the opponent's squad hell bent on crushing you, your lone ally illusion and speed. Then, following the trajectory of the ball, my eye happened to pass over the waiting running back – Donny Knoblock, I knew him — to light on the object of my search, Roxy LeHoulier. It was fate. It was destiny. The ball, tumbling its way down between us, descended from the heavens and stitched our lines of sight together. It was not my imagination, either, because when Donny Knobloch finally caught the ball with a small huff, then started his perilous journey up field, our eyes stayed locked together. Only out of my peripheral vision did I see Donny get slaughtered by a huge Plainsview man, his grunt one of strangled surprise.

Roxy's eyes did not follow Donny up the field. They stayed on me, intently, relentlessly, boldly. An instant later, when it was evident to us both that something had clicked, she looked down and began polishing one of her batons with a silver-polish soaked rag. The band struck up a fight song, "Cheer, cheer for old Notre Dame," and I, ridiculously, found myself walking to the corny beat. A slight boink of adrenaline hit me, and I moved through the crowd as though through an oncoming football team, my steps springy, my intentions clear. I wanted Roxy. I wanted to meet her. I turned once to spot Loraine in the bleachers.

She was there, head down, her eyes forever fixed on a book. Au revoir, my pet! May God keep you in his hand! I almost blew a kiss to her, but instead continued walking, soaking in the atmosphere, inhaling the fatty odor of hot dogs boiling too long in their own juices, pretzels burning under heat lamps, mustard pocked by countless flies' feet. It smelled delicious, all of it, especially when mingled with the overwhelming scent of dying leaves and the faint, distance odor of Atomic Bomb, the muscle relaxing balm popular among the athletes of that era. I smelled cigars, heard lawn chairs yawn under the weight of wealthy suburban bankers and lawyers, watched as the first play went for ten yards on an end sweep, the colors of the jerseys painfully bright. The grass was green, preserved all summer and fall for this last contest. The players' cleats threw up small clods of dirt, so that their legs appeared swarmed by dark, blistering beetles.

Roxy ambushed me. When I began to pass by her — because she still existed only in my imagination, so to speak, I may have timidly ignored her and simply purchased a hot dog — she suddenly hopped up from where she sat among her fellow band members and bustled to the snow fence separating the field and cinder walkway.

"Go Blue Devils!" she shouted in a voice, frankly, unpleasantly nasal. After the shout, she jumped. It was a short, petulant little pout of frustration at something, apparently, the Blue Devils did or didn't do.

"Damn," she whispered, then turned back to her band compatriots. She puffed her annoyance out in a little, breathy pant, then waved one hand over her shoulder, as if to dismiss the entire football team. She was the leader, clearly. The other band members didn't take their eyes off her. And yet, what a crew to command! The band was filled with chubby, four-eyed, boys and girls. Butter-eaters, butt pinchers, pen-pockets, teachers' pets, Audio Visual Squaders, model train fanciers, accordion players, and Eagle Scouts. In short, the Fighting Blue Devil Marching Band consisted of the great unwashed of high school society, a leprous caste of untouchables. In a glance, I saw geeky Nellie Potter, the chubby-wubby girl who worked the ticket booth at the local movie theater on Saturdays nights, a barrel of popcorn at her side, her lips oiled and salted. And Keith Selgeman, a junior Shriner, who, on more than one public occasion, dressed up in a Shriner's uniform, a replica of his dad's, and performed dare-devil precision driving tasks with cars the size of Golden Retrievers. There were more. Fifty, sixty, seventy more. Roxy was the queen, or, more accurately, a female Satan fallen from the heavens and abandoned to an unthinkable fate. Perhaps she felt it better to rule in hell than be governed in heaven, because she obviously enjoyed the attention she received. She flounced out of frustration at something on the field again, then swirled back to the band members, sitting exactly in their center, her knees spanking together.

"Oh, fiddlesticks," she said and everyone laughed. Everyone! Hell, I laughed too, because I realized I wanted to climb up there as well, sit in the uncomplicated world of model trains and tuba practice, suffering nothing more than Roxy's inane jokes. Why not? Her world seemed enviable to me. It seemed simple and understandable, a Norman Rockwell version of my life. Her days were full, I was certain, of slumber parties and taffy pulls.

I was still thinking these things when she suddenly turned to me, and in a voice loud enough for her entire entourage to hear, asked: "What do you think you're looking at? Hmmmm? Cat got your tongue?"

"Nothing," I answered, startled by her directness and unaware I had been staring at her in a druggy, stupefied state.

"I have blue panties on, if that's what you're wondering," she said, which brought on an hysterical response from her buddies. She looked around, beaming, as they laughed at her "good one." It seemed likely this was an old, tried and true line. They were delighted I had fallen for it and were pleased I seemed disquieted by her frankness. She was a wild one, their looks confirmed. A card, a cut-up. She was like a favorite niece, not skinny or particularly bright, who is doted upon by her backward uncle and aunt. She was indulged, pampered, adored. Who cared if she shined only out of the dimness surrounding her?

"I have white panties on," I said, recovering. "In case you're interested."

"Wo ho," a myopic clarinet player said from the third row. "Har de har har."

"I wanted to talk to you," I said to Roxy. "If you have a minute, I mean."

"Maybe a minute, but that's all."

She stood. The band made a "whoooooooo" sound, indicating it thought we were coupling up. Seeing her come at me, however, made me wonder if this hadn't all been a bad idea. She was tall and more physically fit than any human I had ever met. Her muscles were toned. The bodice of her baton outfit nearly burst with her vitality. Her hair was blonde, her brows brown. A huge beauty mole perched on her upper lip at the right corner. It was as wide and as dark as a nail head, and I could not look at it without imagining a carpenter sinking his final nail of the day, setting it home with particular relish. It was, in fact, her defining feature. Any caricaturist worth his or her salt would have given prominence to the beauty spot, making it the hub of her otherwise average looks.

"What do you want?" she asked as she came to a stop near me.

"I just wanted to tell you I thought you were great. As a baton twirler, I mean."

"I'm not a baton twirler, you space-o," she said, then turned to see if her buddies in the band were catching this, "but thanks anyway."

"Are you thirsty? I wanted to get a soda, if you wanted to."

"You mean you want to buy me a soda?" she asked without a blush.

"Yes, I guess so."

"You guess so or you mean so?"

"I mean so."

"You have a funny way of talking," she said.

"So do you."

"All right. You can buy me a soda."

I turned once again to spy Loraine. It was difficult to see her, trapped, as she was, in the rows of student fans, but I managed to pick her out. Her head was still bent over her book. She looked, from that distance, as calm and comforting as an easy chair, whereas Roxy, beside me, was unmistakably of the carnival world. A circus performer, that's what she seemed to me. I could easily imagine her dangling from the big top by a tether, her teeth clamped to the pliant leather, her knees forming a perfect figure four. Ta da! Even walking beside her seemed to demand some sort of muscular energy. She turned and waved to her followers, the four-eyed band members, then turned to me and said she was hungry. Really hungry. That twirling always made her hungry, it was true, she could eat like a horse, a real horse, not just a pretend one, people said that all the time, but she was serious, seriously serious, a real palomino, that's what she was, a palomino, but no, really, she had calculated, well, it wasn't really her who had calculated, she had read it somewhere, a girl's magazine, she thought it was, and they said in there that twirling was extremely beneficial as a means of exercise, it was, although jogging and bike riding was better, were better, she meant, burned more calories, but she thought they didn't take into account the fact that twirling tightened your upper arms.

It was jabber! It was terrific! I stayed beside her, listening raptly, amazed that anyone could carry on so. What's more, her lips did not completely close when she spoke, so that, in some manner I couldn't quite identify, she resembled a person who had swallowed something hot and tried to talk around it. She lisped frequently, though not in any discernible pattern, so that I found I had to bend forward to catch her drift. Her words were a bath. They were incredibly welcome after the times of dry quietness with Loraine. Not to have to struggle for conversation! Not to search for meaning in the things we said! It was liberating to listen to her, to merely nod and pull out of my pocket the appropriate bills to pay our check — she wanted a hotdog after all — and to watch as other people detected her passing and looked with admiration at her first class body, her huge tom tom hat, her spectacular beauty mark.

"Thanks," she said when we backed away from the concession stand, both of us holding hot dogs and sodas. "Now tell the truth, Arnie. It's Arnie, right? I remember you from history class. You never talked, did you?"

"Not much, I guess."

"Well of course I talk enough for three people. That's what my dad says. He says I talk because I can't stand silence. Imagine that? But that wasn't it. What I wanted to ask was why you came over like that? I mean right up in front of the band and all?"

"I just wanted to meet you."

"That's all?"

"Well, yes, I guess."

"Don't you have a girl friend? Aren't you seeing Loraine?"

"Sometimes," I lied.

"Sometimes? Like every night is more like it."

She ate rapidly, watching me over the barrel of her wiener. Then she sipped her soda. It was my move. I liked her and she knew it. I felt slightly dizzy at her cool acknowledgment of my interest. I stared at the beauty spot perched on her lip, trying to center myself. I imagined what it would mean to kiss those lips, aware the beauty spot lingered underneath each peck. Could it fail to give a gritty flavor to a kiss? I shivered, then concentrated on eating my hot dog, wanting her to speak, to keep talking as she had before. But instead she leaned back against the refreshment stand, no longer a circus performer, but a TV western bar girl instead. She was Kitty of Gun Smoke fame! Marshal Matt Dillon's long-standing love! She watched me with wise eyes, knowing full well what I was after, knowing why I had singled her out of the pack, knowing that something illicit had already been established between us. But she didn't blanch. She was a coquette, but a steely-eyed one. It startled me to realize that the tables had turned. I wasn't doing her a favor by asking her to have a hot dog with me. Just the opposite. She might appear somewhat ludicrous prancing down the gridiron with a cockade sticking out of her majorette hat, but that was a public performance. This was something different, clearly, and she was in control in a manner that suggested this was not the first time she had been approached for a date.

"Would you want to do something tonight?" I asked finally. "I mean it's Thanksgiving and all."

"My family eats early," she said.

"So does mine. Would you want to do something at about seven or seven-thirty?"

"Sure," she said.

"What do you like to do?"

"We'll figure that out later. I have to get back now. I'll see you. Do you know where I live?"

"No, I don't think so."

She gave me her address and directions to get there. Then she hurried back to the band. I watched her go. When she was back among her compatriots, I searched the distant grandstands until I spotted Loraine. She sat with her head up, her eyes searching. Whether she looked for me, or merely wanted to watch a play, was impossible to tell.

At seven fifteen I stood in front of Roxy's house, stunned to find myself ready to knock on a door other than Loraine's. The house was a low, inelegant affair in a part of town I knew was not the best. The yards were small. The trees were young. An entire row of houses boasted circular driveways, all of them made from crushed white stone, all of them too large and elaborate for the tiny yards they circumnavigated. Roxy's address was written out in script above the door, so that it was not 534 Barchester Way, but instead Five Hundred and Thirty-Four. The script was an attempt to render the house elegant, when, in fact, the entire structure appeared ready to be outfitted with tires and pulled away by a muscle truck displaying plenty of chrome.

The doorbell played a chime, a tune I didn't quite catch. It was either "Winchester Cathedral" or "Strangers in the Night." A moment later the door swung open. Roxy stepped outside, closing the door quickly behind her.

"Come on," she said, "before you have to meet the whole crew."

Then she grabbed my arm and pulled me off the stairs and out toward my father's Buick Electra 225. My first impression was that she wore enough perfume to make me breathe through my mouth. Air had to be filtered around her, not merely drawn inside one's lungs. I started to go around to her side in order to let her in, when she tossed my hand away and said, "Don't bother with that right now. Just get in." She hustled around the front of the car, making it to the passenger seat beside me before I started the engine. She slammed her door shut, washing me with perfume.

"God, don't you hate holidays?" she asked, reaching forward and flicking on the radio. "I do. I really, really do. I want to live in Las Vegas or someplace where nobody gives a good doody about holidays. It's all so crazy. We had this really terrible turkey, Swanson's or some doody brand, and it was just ridiculous. I mean, what's the big deal? Indians and pilgrims, about a thousand years ago. It's crazy. Seriously, in Las Vegas nothing shuts down. Not for Christmas or Thanksgiving, not for anything. I like that. I really do. And it's in the desert, so you don't have to get all misty about snow storms and pine trees and all of that doody. Just go through your day. That's what I want. I just want one day to be like the next and the next and the next. None of this doody."

"I hate it too," I said, overwhelmed, and trying to remember if I had ever met someone who used the word "doody" so confidently.

"Oh, but you probably do the whole thing. The turkey and everything. Real turkey, I mean, not the doody we had. I bet your house is sort of like Andy Hardy's, you know, your dad smoking a pipe and a fireplace going. Isn't it? That's how I picture it, anyway."

"No, it's not really like that."

"Well, what do you want to do? How about bowling? I love to bowl."

"Bowling is great. We can do anything you like."

"Well, let's start with bowling then. I could use a good bowl."

Bowling was a particularly good choice because it was not something Loraine and I would ever do. Loraine wasn't the bowling type. I nodded agreement, then drove the stately Buick 225 down Barchester Way and up Winnadotta Trail, catching sideways glances of Roxy the entire trip. Up close, as a flesh and blood entity in my car, she was almost more impressive than she had been in her majorette uniform. She wore a brown sweater, tightly fitted over her torpedo breasts, and blue jeans that seemed cruelly strained by her lovely curves. The mole on her lip stood out with remarkable prominence. As she chewed gum, the mole performed a small dance, a gum drop above a red crescent of lip. Meanwhile her hand flew over the radio, stabbing buttons, nodding her head at the first few bars of any given song, then moving relentlessly onward. She demonstrated no particular interest in me. In fact, when we arrived at the bowling alley, Rip Van Winkle's Bowl-o-Rama, and I came around to help her out of the car, she bumped into me and said it was just a date, silly, not a royal wedding or anything, and I didn't have to open all the doors and pull out chairs and any of that doody.

"Okay," I said.

"Do you pull out Loraine's chair all the time?" Roxy asked as we walked up the ramp toward the lanes. "I'm just curious."

"Sometimes, I guess."

"It's weird. I think it's just weird, that's all."

What was weird? What was any of this about? I felt angry at myself for allowing this date to occur. What had I been thinking? I had traded in — metaphorically, at least - - a fine old Mercedes Benz for a ride in an electric golf cart. I missed Loraine! As I pushed open the wide Glass doors to the lane, I saw myself reflected in the printed "O's" of Rip Van Winkle's Bowl-o-Rama. I was a loathsome, terrible creature. I was below contempt. How could I throw away Loraine, mistreat her so treacherously, and squander our years of love on a doody head like Roxy? It was insane.

I followed her to the reservation counter, my eyes scouting the walls for a pay phone. I wanted to call Loraine. I wanted to ask her if she would meet me later, it didn't matter when, so that we could talk and kiss and reestablish our relationship. But Roxy was a step ahead of me. She had already requested a lane, shoes too, so that it would have been ungentlemanly to ditch her. I pulled out my wallet and paid, then followed Roxy to lane 34, red and green bowling shoes in hand, her perfume an olfactory beacon dragging me forward.

"Did you ever just close one eye and sort of watch the balls going up and down the lanes? Ever do that?" asked Roxy as she sat at the scoring table. "If you look just right, the balls look like they're going up and down instead of on a level. Like big yo-yo's. You have to tilt your head, of course."

She pulled on her shoes. Her socks, I noticed, came to her ankles and were trimmed with lace. It seemed an interesting extravagance, one Loraine would have shunned. Despite my discomfort at being with Roxy, despite the feeling that I was lower than dirt at stepping out on Loraine, I nevertheless felt sexually stirred. She was the naughty girl of my dreams, the fantasy woman of my years and years of boyhood masturbation. When she left to find a bowling ball, only to return a moment later with a marbled confection cradled against her chest, I watched her as I had never watched Loraine. And when she stood at the bowling line, ready to heave the ball at the pins, I stared at her round rump, listened to her crackling gum, inhaled her over powering aroma. I half closed my eyes, blood engorging my Mister (as my mom, Sally McNally, called my tiny toddler penis), imagining Roxy performing unthinkable acts, ones to which Loraine would never consent.

"Your turn," she said when she finished chucking her ball at the pins. She had knocked down eight on her first ball, then nailed the spare.

"You're a good bowler," I said.

"My dad used to take me all the time."

"Did he?" I asked, trying to picture my father at the lanes, chucking the ball. The image wouldn't jell.

"Sure. Bowling is one of the nation's favorite family sports. It is. I'm not making that up."

"I didn't think you were."

"Well, the way you look at me sometimes, I hardly know what you think."

She stared at me, then sat at the scoring table and flicked on an overhead light. It was a device used for tournaments, one which broadcast the score card on a small movie screen suspended near the foul line. With a clunky, childlike hand, she wrote: Roxy & Arnie. Then she drew in a big heart around both our names. She glanced at me and smiled. Is that what she thought? That we already constituted a couple? I opened my mouth to say something, then stopped.

"We have to go," I blurted an instant later. "I'm sorry, Roxy, but I don't feel right about this whole thing. I feel like I'm cheating on Loraine. It's not right. I'm really, really sorry."

"You want to go? Right now? Just like that?"

"Yes. It's just not right. It's nothing personal. Seriously, it's not. You're great. I mean it. You're really beautiful. You're so beautiful it scares me a little, but this whole thing was wrong right from the beginning. If I break up with Loraine, then I can date you. If you wanted to, I mean. If you'd do this again. But not before I break up with her. You wouldn't respect me, would you?"

"I guess not, when you put it like that."

"It's just slimy. Really. I mean, imagine if Loraine went out on me. I'd feel like, well, like doddy."

"Doody."

"That's what I mean."

"Okay, if you're sure."

"I'm afraid I am. Sorry. Do you forgive me? It's a lousy thing to do to someone. I appreciate you being such a good sport about it."

What a swell, understanding gal she turned out to be! She didn't protest as we slipped out of our bowling shoes. I felt calmer immediately. I had made a mistake, that was all. Anyone could make a mistake. In fact, I imagined telling Loraine the entire story, laughing it off with her, explaining that it was bound to happen, dating as long as we had. Then I would give Loraine a chance to confess anything she wished to confess, any flirtations, any *affair de coeurs*, no recriminations, make a clean breast of it, start fresh from here. By the time we had our street shoes on and were headed toward the door, I was near to congratulating myself on revitalizing Loraine's and my relationship. Naturally things happened. It was to be expected. Did we think, seriously, that we would go along forever, our love entirely untested? That would have been unnatural. Roxy was an unlucky third party, fortune's fool, as it were, but I felt a genuine warmth toward her. She deserved my affection, certainly, and going out the door, it was mere instinct to put my hand on her back. And it was kindness, really, to stop as I helped her in the passenger seat and give her the smallest kiss of appreciation as we stood by the door. Why not?

"Thank you for understanding," I said. My breath somehow caught in hers, however, and in the next inhalation she sucked toward me, her mouth on mine, her body, so different from Loraine's, driving into me as relentlessly as an ancient ivy-covered wall waking in spring.

"Yes, yes, yes," she whispered, kissing me feverishly.

"Yes, yes, yes," she said on our second smooch, rubbing her body into mine, apparently lamenting, as I did, that our worlds would remain apart.

Agony! Forbidden fruit! We continued to kiss, each moment cementing us closer and closer. An instant later she reached down and cupped my Mister, massaging it masterfully, knuckling its wadded thickness, shaking hands with it hello and good bye.

"My god," I said. She pulled away her hand and looked at me regretfully.

"I'm sorry," she said. "I'm just a really really passionate person. I always have been. I'm sorry. I didn't mean to get carried away."

"No apology necessary."

"Okay, but I'm sorry. I am. I guess we should get going then. I just get carried away. I'm sorry, genuinely sorry."

She tucked herself into the Buick 225, looking up and waiting for me to shut the door. She appeared warm and frazzled. I leaned down and kissed her again. I whispered, "This is wrong, isn't it?" She nodded but continued kissing me. Mister, as thick as a terrier's paw now, pressed into my jeans. I wanted Roxy to touch Mister again, but this time she controlled herself and merely rubbed my upper thigh.

"We should go," she said. "This is crazy."

"We should."

"We should go. Really."

"Okay, I'm ready."

I closed the door. Roxy put her palm flat against the window. I met her palm with mine, a Dr. Zhivago moment of tenderness and longing in the parking lot of Rip Van Winkle's Bowl-O-Rama. I hurried around the back of the huge Buick, my hand wrestling Mister into an acceptable public tumescence. Loraine who! I pulled open the driver's door and dove into the greasy smell of Roxy's perfume. Roxy leaned over at once, her pliable body wrapping around me, her voice saying, "No, we shouldn't."

Au contraire, said Mister Mister. We kissed. I put my hand on the side of her breast and she didn't stop me. Not a peep! I rubbed her left breast, and, like a genie's lamp, rubbing there succeeded in encouraging her hand back to my lap. She kissed me harder. Her mouth opened. She rolled slightly to one side, giving herself to me, succumbing to my desire.

"It's wrong though, isn't it?" she asked in a breath between kisses.

"I don't know, I don't know, I don't know."

"This can't be wrong. Not and feel like this. It can't be wrong."

"I know, I know, I know."

It was good teenage dialogue. We kissed harder, deeper. Then a car door slammed nearby and someone, a male, made a whooping sound that announced he had seen us necking and admired what he had seen. We both sat up. My lips hurt. My skin smelled of perfume. I took a deep breath to steady myself, then reached forward to start the engine. Roxy, straightening her clothes, then bending forward to see her hair in the rear-view mirror, finally turned to face me.

"I have to tell you, Arnie. I was really excited when you asked me out. Really. I don't know what you think of me, really......"

".....I think you're great....."

".....but most of the guys I date are so....."

".....terrific...."

".....idiotic, and then I ran into a college guy, this guy named Tyler...."

"Who is Tyler?" I asked, ladling the Buick slowly over the speed bumps that cross hatched the parking lot.

"Oh, just this guy. This guy I sometimes date in college. He's at Seton Hall, a junior. He's just a mad man and I hate him in a lot of ways, but, I don't know, it was just so healthy to be dating someone my own age."

"Your own age?"

"You, I mean."

"So, are you like on a rebound or something?" I asked, trying to get this straight.

"Not a rebound. I hate that word. It's just that we're seeing other people now."

"I see," I said. "Tyler is seeing other people too?"

"Sure. You know, at college and everything. He went to Union Catholic high school, that's where I met him. I guess what I'm saying is that I understand about Loraine. I do. This love stuff is all pretty confusing. Isn't it? Sometimes I get so sick of it I don't want to date anyone. But I like you. It impressed me the way you came up to me at the game and everything."

"Well, I liked the way you led the band and everything."

"Thank you. I really value that. A lot of people don't appreciate a good majorette," she said, then turned back to face forward. "Would you mind if we went to Gino's for a hamburger? I'll treat. I'm just really hungry. Then you can take me home, swear to Roy Rogers.

I had never heard anyone say "swear to Roy Rogers," nor did I particularly understand where she and Tyler stood, but I didn't mind driving her through town, the Buick 225 as wide and as comfortable as a carriage, the September night filled with the dingle starry. Her perfume had subsided somewhat, or perhaps I had grown accustomed to it, because now she smelled delicious. I reached over and put my hand on her knee. Instantly she slid across the wide Buick console and tucked herself next to me. Then, thinking better of it, she leaned away and looked at me.

"Do you mind?" she asked, and when I shook my head, she squeezed even closer. She put her hand on the inside of my thigh, kindly and lightly, said something about it just being friendlier this way, just buddy-buddy, then reached her free hand to the radio and resumed stabbing buttons. We listened to "Satisfaction" and George Harrison's "My Sweet Lord." At a stop light at the intersection of Madison and Freemont, we kissed until a Ford Maverick behind honked to let us know the light was green. Roxy smiled when we broke apart. She held my hand as I wheeled the stately Buick into the Gino's parking lot.

"Remember, it's my treat," she said.

"No, the least I can do is buy you a hamburger."

"I insist," she said.

She insisted, perhaps, because she knew the dimensions of her appetite. Standing at Gino's metal counter, Roxy examined the menu boards with no little attention. "Hungry, hungry, hungry," she said to no one, her knees bent to press against the frame of the counter. She ordered a large Double Gino Burger, a Large Fry, a "Vanilly Shake" (she was being witty on that item), and an extra hamburger just in case. Then she slid down the counter and said that should tide her over. She wasn't joking. I ordered a hamburger, small fries, and a small coke.

We sat in the vast Buick front seat, our drinks lined up on the dash, our laps spread wide to hold the wax paper wrappers. We ate silently, our creaking jaws accompanied by the occasional sound of an onion or pickle slice escaping for its life and plopping on our napkins.

Roxy ate with abandon, dabbing her French fries into the ketchup, twisting the top off her hamburger so that she could squeeze more mustard onto the roll. It was a marked change from the meals I had experienced with Loraine. Whereas Loraine had picked at everything, and preferred things fresh and low in fats, Roxy consumed caloric foods on a grand scale. She made no secret of her enjoyment, and seldom used her napkin. I finished before she did. I sat behind the large Buick steering wheel, watching her work her way through the last fries. She didn't offer to share. In fact, she hardly looked up at all. When she finished at last, she poked her index finger at the wrapper and dotted up a few final crumbs. Her lips were shiny silver, and her fingertips salty as pretzels.

"Good?" I asked.

"Hmmmmm," she said, wiping herself clean. "It was great. But food always makes me sleepy."

"Are you sleepy now?"

"Not really. Let's just sit awhile. I've got to digest. I wish we could have gone bowling. I mean, you know. I understand everything, but I wish we could have gone. I need the exercise. If I don't get exercise, I just don't feel like myself."

She crumpled her wrappers and stuffed them in the carry sack. Then she leaned over and kissed me, and I couldn't shake the impression that I was the second course. She smelled like a Gino's special, but so did I, and we blended together in an oniony, pickled pall. We kissed for a while, her tremendous strength pulling me deeper and deeper inside her mouth. I felt, hopelessly, like a Gino Burger myself, a victim of her appetite, prepared, sans condiments, to be devoured in large, sudden bites. At other times, she seemed to want to climb inside my mouth, because she pushed up almost to her knees and butted her teeth against mine.

"Oh," she sighed at various intervals. Her eyes remained closed. I know, because I checked. I watched through our windshield as the nightly parade of high school notables make its way toward the Gino order counter. Who cared that we had all consumed a full turkey dinner that afternoon? We were hungry, insatiably so, all of us burning with reckless hormonal juices. Watching them, with Roxy gnawing at my mouth, I had a dizzy sensation that I was in a plane, a speedy little Piper Cub, looking down at the glassy reaches of the Jersey meadowlands. I surrendered to an imaginary aerial view, one in which the cars and lights were speeded up to maddening alacrity, so that the streets become veins, the houses corpuscles, the airports huge pumping aortas. Everything in the world dissolved to simple biology. The musky sparrows winging their lives away above the polluted rushes outside Newark Airport, the cranky skunks that patrolled the far reaches of the Watchung Reservation, and even Roxy and myself, intertwined in the luxurious upholstery afforded by my diligent father — it was all biology! It was not a bold new insight, not at all, but it was argument enough to give in when Roxy's hamburgered hands reached for Mister. And it was sufficient rationalization to allow me to reach for her own biological goodies, to inch my fingers down the front of her pants until she sat up and ground her pelvis away.

"Stop, oh, stop, honey," she said. "Just hold on a minute.

Easy, easy, just hold on."

"What is it?" I asked, my body pounding, the pressure in my groin the stuff of high school fables.

"Oh, my, you've got me so worked up. You're a good kisser. You really are. Tyler just mauls me, but you're gentler. I like that."

"Well, come back here and let me kiss you some more."

"Now hold on," she said. "We don't know each other that well, do we? Now let's just get this in proper perspective. I've got to tell you a few things."

"Right now?"

"Yes, right now."

She sat straighter. She looked in the mirror and patted her hair. Then she moved away far enough to swivel and face me. By the high school code of Union County, New Jersey, Roxy was perilously close to being responsible for bringing about my seminal discharge. She obviously understood. That was why she had called a halt to the proceedings. We panted for a few moments, sending searing glances at one another. Then Roxy heaved a large sigh, and finally launched into her speech.

"I intend to remain a virgin until I marry," she said. "I know, I know, a lot of people think that's funny. They think it's old fashioned. But I don't. My mother was a virgin when she married my father. It's a tradition in the LeHoulier household. We don't have much, but we have our pride."

"I see. Forgive me for saying this, Roxy, but aren't we getting a little ahead....."

"Let me finish, please," she said, holding up her hand to stop me. "I guess I'd have to say, though, that I'm not a goody-goody. I like physical embraces. I don't think my future husband would hold some kissing against me, do you? I mean, I can't be completely innocent. Not in this day and age. No one is. That's what my mom says. So where does that leave us? Is that what you're wondering? I know how important sex is to men."

"I don't want to force you into....."

"You couldn't if you wanted to, Arnie," she said with no little passion, her oniony breath adding to her sincerity. "I mean that. I'm very strong in mind and body. I am. So let's be real respectful of that. Okay?"

"Okay," I said, wondering if she thought she could beat me up.

"I didn't mean to take all the fun out of this. It is fun, isn't it? Do you like being with me?"

"Sure I do."

"Well I like being with you too. And there are other things, aren't there? Things we can do that are just as much fun as the horse and pony. I'm pretty good at certain things. You'll see. And you'll be happy with it, too."

With that she leaned back and cuddled next to me. She nibbled my neck, then slowly, expertly, unzipped the fly of my jeans. Evidently this was a demonstration of her abilities. I pushed my butt deep into the seat in order to give her sufficient room to seize Mister Mister. She brought him out slowly, her hand guiding him gently into the florescent Gino's parking lot lights.

"Oh, there he is," she said. Then she began to pump. Tyler, or whoever she had accommodated before, had apparently liked his sex somewhat spirited. She continued nestling her chin in my shoulder, simultaneously working my penis like a child making Mr. Potato Head dance on a table top. Or, perhaps more accurately, she put my penis through a series of calisthenics, bending it right, then left, up, down, then in a circular gyration. Her approach was that of a man taking a brisk walk around a ship's deck. But no matter. I felt the tide of my private ocean rise in me. Roxy sensed it too, because at the critical moment she snatched a paper cup off the dash board, flipped off the top, and turned the spout of my penis into Gino's soft drink container.

"There," Roxy said, snapping the top back on the soft drink cup. She jumped out of the car and crossed the parking lot, her butt swaying, her hair yellow-white, her step athletic. She turned to me as she held the cup and let it drop in one of Gino's large, football shaped garbage cans. She winked. I winked back.

Villainy! Treachery! I walked the halls of Westview High School the following Monday knowing I had done something as shameful as our high school code of ethics allowed. What did

I want? I had no idea. I had spent the weekend in Fair Haven, New Jersey, pulling my uncle's boat out of the water. It was not something I was originally interested in doing, but after my rendezvous with Roxy I had to get away.

Returning Sunday night, I had deliberately not answered the phone so that Loraine couldn't get in touch with me. But it was impossible to avoid Roxy. After third period chemistry class, she came toward me through a crowd of sophomores who had just emerged from a morning of PSAT's. She appeared, in that morning light, as purposeful as a jackal searching the butcher grass for a desiccated zebra haunch. Her head, blonde and gleaming, turned this way and that until she spotted me. Then, focusing on my eyes, she came at me with her mouth turned in a half smile, the mole on her lip giving it an insouciant naughtiness. She was glad to see me. Once, while blocked by the migratory sophomores who rolled their eyes and complained about the difficulties of the PSAT's, she raised her hand and waved, alerting me that she would be just a moment longer. Finally reaching me, she raised up on her toes and kissed me on the mouth, her tongue flashing for an instant against my gums, her breasts scraping two tingling channels in my chest. Then, thinking suddenly of Loraine, Roxy turned her head back and forth, searching the halls, her hand still on my shoulder for support.

"Is she around?" she asked. "Loraine, I mean."

She was good. She actually appeared concerned, though, of course, anyone who had been genuinely concerned wouldn't have kissed me in public. I told her Loraine had driver's ed, which meant she was probably out on Rahway Avenue somewhere, listening to Dr. D'Andrea scream at her to find the brakes.

"Oh, I hate driver's ed. I think it's demeaning, don't you?" Roxy said, her hand squeezing my arm. "Now, where are you going? Come with me for a second. I have something to show you."

"I have to get to class."

"It will just take a second, silly."

She grabbed my hand and led me to the balcony section of our high school auditorium. I had been there a thousand times before and didn't get the point until she pulled a key out and held it in front of me.

"Johnny gave me this," she said. "He plays tuba in the band. He is also like the king of the AV squad."

Of course. It made perfect sense. I knew Johnny. Everyone knew Johnny Cremechi, because he was famous for arriving in class pushing a 35 mm projector, his pocket loaded with pens and miniature screw drivers, his orthopedic shoes squeaking. But who knew he had entered the black market of Audio Visual Squad keys?

"He can get in anywhere. He's got masters to everything. It's really pretty cool."

She said this as she opened the door of the projection booth. Here was Johnny's throne room! It was a small, dark room, illuminated by red bulbs. From his seat here, Johnny could watch the performance stage while still remaining hidden in darkness. It was the Great Oz's station behind the curtain, without Oz to run the levers. Roxy grabbed my hand again and pulled me inside. Immediately she turned and began kissing me. Our skin, due to the lighting, was red. Her teeth gleamed pink, as though she had just devoured a small creature, ripping apart its stringy flesh with her pronounced incisors. For an instant, as she surged toward me, I viewed her as a devil. I had been correct after all. She was Satan, a fallen angel, a devious shape-changer who could seduce me and drain me of my life's fluids. In fact, I had once read a pornographic novel called "The Succubus" about a woman who seduces men, then continues, through her insatiable sexual need, to boff them to death. Naturally it was a male fantasy, the nympho from the centerfold of Playboy come to life, but Roxy was not a bad approximation. She ground against me, urgently pulling me deeper into her arms. The late bell rang. I tried to wrench myself away, but she continued kissing me, whispering that it would be all right, no one really cared if I was late, and she just had one more thing she wanted to do.

With quick, sudden hands, she pulled my penis out of my pants. Despite myself, I found it tremendously sexy. The chance of discovery, the dark, grappling violet hue of the light, the heated residue of old projection camera bulbs, all added to the excitement. What's more, my penis, when it dodged out of my jeans, appeared a fiery dragon, a red bolt of inflamed flannel. Communion with the devil! Why not! Roxy, taking my penis in hand, led me gently to the small sink that Johnny undoubtedly used to rinse off his wall-eyed glasses or the skeet of his slide rule. No Gino's 25 cent cola cup this time. She aimed my penis at the glistening interior of the sink, cranked vigorously for a minute or two, and viola! An instant after I finished, Roxy abandoned my penis and directed the water nozzle at the damnable spots.

She cleaned everything as if silently answering a command from Johnny to keep the place clean, then turned back to me.

"Better?" she asked.

Better than what? I wanted to ask, but merely nodded instead. I wanted out. Roxy had other plans, however. She wanted to know if I could drive her to something that night. She didn't want to say what it was, because I might think it was silly. Would I? Please? I agreed, remembering, with no little concern, the image of Roxy drawing a heart around our names at the bowling alley. Why not have Loraine and these small adventures on the side? Who did it hurt?

At six thirty that evening I picked up Roxy. I had spoken to Loraine in the afternoon, covering my trail for the past couple days with phony excuses, but obviously she sensed something was wrong. She asked repeatedly if I was all right, if I wanted to tell her anything, if I was coming by to see her? I lied about everything, surprising myself with my talent for prevarication, hating myself as I effortlessly concocted one story after another. As a rationalization, I repeated to myself that this wasn't about Loraine, that it had nothing to do with her, really. This was simply a case of a man sowing his oats, Roxy merely a fertile field. Loraine would have to understand. After all, hadn't she occasionally hinted that the fabric of our relationship was wearing thin? Hadn't she — incredibly — marveled more than once over the biceps and buttocks of Billy Hasbro, Westview's first state champ — 178 lbs – in wrestling in the past twelve years? She even attended two of his matches, because, she claimed, she had taken algebra class with him and admired the Greek notion of sound body, sound mind, embodied in Spartan Billy Hasbro. What was that if not a flirtation? As a matter of fact, it was a flirtation of the same sort —minus the physical contact — that I had experienced with Roxy LeHoulier. Loraine lusted in her mind, which was, as Jimmy Carter told the American public a few short years later, as sinful as carnal investigation.

Naturally I didn't believe any of this, but it suited my purpose at the time. Roxy charged into my car that evening carrying a large duffel bag. She smelled as floridly as ever, wearing a scent that screamed of the death of ten million lilacs. Although I didn't know her well, I could tell she was unusually keen this evening. Her make-up was cut and sharply applied; her hair stood at imperial attention at the top most point of her skull. She had gained seven inches as a result of her hair-do, and she was obliged to slump in the wide Buick seat in order not to glue herself to the soft, dove gray felt of the Electra ceiling. When asked about the duffel bag, she merely smiled and said, "You'll see."

Afterward she busied herself with the radio, flicking through the buttons and directing me toward Scotch Plains, an adjoining town, her chatter inconsequentially significant, like brush around a quail.

"Did you talk to Loraine?" she asked, five minutes into our journey. "I heard some interesting things about her, you know? She's seeing someone. That's what I heard, anyway."

"Come on, Roxy," I said, taking the news like a short rabbit punch to the gut. If she was making things up, then she demonstrated uncanny insight. "I'd prefer you didn't talk about Loraine."

"Why? Are you still stuck on her?"

"I don't know. No, I'm not, actually. But Loraine's not like that. She wouldn't rush into anything just to spite me."

"You'd be surprised what a girl would do."

"Maybe some would, but not Loraine. Besides, she doesn't even know about us. I talked to her this afternoon. She didn't say anything."

"What do you expect her to say? How goofy you men can

be, jeezum. But don't believe me. I don't care. Turn left here. Right in there."

I followed her directions into a wide, graveled parking lot, though my hands and brain felt paralyzed. Loraine seeing somebody! Immediately my mind said impossible, though part of me knew otherwise. Loraine possessed, after all, a broody, poet's heart. If she knew I had been with someone new, she might conceivably sacrifice herself on the altar of sexual communion. Spite might suit her very well indeed, containing, as it did, a churning, vengeful energy all its own. Yes, Loraine would respond to spite. She might even find it romantic, a form of teenage self-immolation in the tortured flames sanctified by Sylvia Plath. Everybody had a hungry heart, and Loraine's, regardless of its quiet consistency, was no less ravenous for all of that.

Roxy understood. In fact, as I pulled to a stop next to other cars busy parking, she swooped over, smothered me for a moment with her perfume, and kissed the side of my neck.

"Don't worry," she said, "you've got me."

Then she squeezed my hand and grabbed her duffel bag from the back seat.

"Come on, slow poke," she said and jumped out into the darkness, car doors slamming all around us. She hollered to someone, then laughed. I waited behind the steering wheel, my heart splintering. I wanted to shove the Buick into reverse and gun out of the parking lot. Loraine! It was one thing for me to be playing the oat field, quite another for her to be doing likewise. What if she, right this moment, was cranking somebody's penis into a Gino's twenty-five cent Cola cup? A horrid thought! Or worse, suppose Loraine — more expert and sexier than Roxy would ever be – were in the process of seducing an older man, say a college guy, introduced to her by her poet contacts. Maybe now, as I heard Roxy tapping on my window, sweet Loraine was in a New York high rise, letting some never-will-be Dylan Thomas slip his intellectual Mister into her good graces. And who could blame her? It was my fault, all my fault. Even as I climbed out to follow Roxy, I understood I had to call Loraine immediately. Fate was afoot. Perhaps it was not too late to snag

Loraine from the clutches of her own treachery.

"Have you guessed what it is yet?" Roxy asked when she corralled me outside the Buick. "Can you tell?"

"No, I can't. What is it?"

"Oh, come on, silly. Don't you see? It's all girls, for one thing. And we're all pretty. See? Oh, gosh, sometimes you're dense, Arnie. It's a beauty pageant! Miss Teen New Jersey! It's just a rehearsal, but wait till you see. You won't believe it."

"I don't know if I'm up to it, Roxy. Listen, we should talk."

"We don't have time! This is dress rehearsal night. The show is on Saturday, so it's very tense right now. Two girls, Miss Essex County and Miss Monmouth County, already dropped out. They couldn't stand the pressure. It's too bad, too, because Miss Essex County was a very fine vocalist."

Roxy handed me her bag, then led me into a large, yellow brick building. It was American Legion Hall, Post 74, Scotch Plains, New Jersey. She greeted everyone as we walked, a mayoral candidate attending her local Fourth of July Parade. She was a glad-hander. Hello to Julie, the piano player from Neptune, New Jersey who played Chopin for the talent portion of the pageant. (A bitch, Roxy said to me in an aside.) Bonjour to Rene, the French-Canadian girl who did a can-can. (It's an authentic dance, but she does it to show off her butt, Roxy whispered.) Hello to Margaret, the knock-kneed girl who specialized in modern dance, favoring choreography first established by Isadora Duncan. (She's aiming for the arty-farty vote, Roxy said. I mean, who can tell if she's good or not? Anyone can wear a black leotard and put a serious expression on her face and jump around the stage awhile. It's doody.) A compliment there. A nod here. A kind word yelled across chair backs. Occasionally she linked her arm in mine, bumped her shoulder against me, then yawned in a phony smile that, as Darwin first observed, was a human adaptation of a primate bark. She would have chewed out their throats in a dark room, but she sublimated the impulse instead, choosing to vent her aggression through her venomous asides to me.

She finally parked me down near the orchestra pit of a small auditorium, bent to give me a kiss on the cheek, whispered an endearment and a promise of things to come — "Handy Andy can't wait to come for a visit to Arnie's house," she said, an only slightly veiled reference to yet another hand-job — then shot away, toting her bag behind her, her politic face seized once more into a smile. If the pageant awarded a Miss Congeniality prize, Roxy was a dead lock. But she obviously wanted more.

As soon as she made it behind the curtain, I hopped up and went outside in search of a phone. I found one next to a model howitzer. I dialed Loraine's number. She picked up on the fifth ring, her voice soft and comforting after Roxy's nasal honk.

"Where are you right now?" Loraine asked almost immediately. "I called your house and your mom said you took the car and went out. Arnie, tell me the truth. I've heard some rumors going around. Where are you?"

"I don't even know. I'm just out. I've just been driving around," I lied.

"Arnie, we've known each other too long to start lying now."

"I'm not lying. Let's not make a federal case out of this. You never had to go out for a ride or something?"

"Where are you? Because if you're where I think you are, we're finished. Are you with Roxy LeHoulier?"

"Oh come on."

"Are you?" she asked.

"I heard you were out with Billy Hasbro."

"Billy Hasbro asked me out. He thought we were finished because he said the whole school knows you're seeing Roxy. She's been blabbing about it to everyone she knows. You're a feather in her cap."

"This whole conversation is ridiculous."

"Are you seeing Roxy or not? I can't believe it! That absurd girl with the batons? She was a joke to us! What does she do that I don't do?"

"Look, Loraine....."

"Jesus Christ, you are seeing her, aren't you? I thought it was all a big mix-up. I thought you couldn't possibly do something like this to me. Not to me. How do you sleep at night, Arnie? If you wanted to see someone else, you should have at least told me. How could you not tell me? Are you trying to hurt me? Is that it?"

"Loraine, I'm sorry."

She hung up. I stood beside the phone for five minutes, close to tears, my stomach grinding. How could this have happened? What a detestable, low-life creature I was! I had wounded my first love! I had smashed our innocence, a gift we are given but once in a lifetime. I returned to the auditorium resolved to break it off with Roxy. Unfortunately, the rehearsal was in full swing. I found my seat in the darkness, my mind conjuring images of Loraine walking the halls of Westview High with the muscular Billy Hasbro. What tender looks she would give him! How devoted she would be! I well knew how serious her attention could be, how delicious her concern, how wide she opened her life to people. And sex, of course. Loraine was no Roxy LeHoulier, no Handy- Andy! She enjoyed sex, craved it, required the closeness it brought frequently. She saw it as a natural part of our relationship, not a sedative to be administered to overheated men. What an expression her sexual side might find in the washboard solar plexus of Billy Hasbro! The thought made my stomach flip-flop. If the pageant girls had not been lined up in their opening parade, smiling and waving in their evening gowns as each county representative was announced, I might have told Roxy it was finished that instant. But I was paralyzed. I sat in the dark, sunk in my own misery, moved not at all when Roxy, finally, shot onto the stage in her sequined body suit and proceeded to wow us all with tumbling catches of her swords.

Even when she twirled two flaming batons, an overweight stage manager standing in the background with a red canister of extinguishing foam cocked ready to plug her, I wasn't interested. Little did I know, in my pain, that I had established a destructive pattern with women. As reprehensible as my behavior had been with Roxy, it was the heartbreak of losing Loraine I had been after all along. That was the understanding I gleaned in the dim light of the Miss Teen New Jersey Pageant sometime in 1970.

VAMPIRE

THE VAMPIRE'S HOUSE STOOD ON a small knob of New Hampshire granite. Pine bushes pressed against the house and ate the paint. The bushes needed clipping and the house needed scraping. The house also needed a pound or two of nails to hang the shutters back in place, to put the soffets right, to hang the numbers of the address over the front door again. The steps to the front porch had cracked. Frost had found the cracks and widened them. A drainpipe on the south side of the house had come free and dangled against the clapboards, bumping in the afternoon breeze. The empty pipe matched the beat of a tire swing, hung from an oak branch that twirled enough to twist the support chain. November had stripped the oak and a scarecrow's worth of leaves had collected in the belly of the tire. The rest had made a leafy mat along the front weed patch.

Vampires aren't much on home maintenance, I thought.

A Goth girl answered the door when I knocked. She looked to be twenty-five. She liked black. She wore three studs in her nose, ten in her ears, one in her bellybutton, five in her eyebrows. She probably had more you couldn't see. She made you want to grab a kitchen magnet and plunk it on her. She had been pretty once, but now she wasn't.

"What?" she asked.

"I'm Detective Poulchuk," I said. "Does Alan Pemi live here?"

"Why should I tell you?"

"Why not?"

"You're a cop," she said. "Cops suck."

"Right," I said.

"Don't you need a warrant or something?"

"I'm not here to search anything. Just want to talk to Mr. Pemi."

"He doesn't talk to people until sunset."

"Because he's a vampire?"

She shrugged.

"But you're not a vampire," I said.

She shrugged.

"You must be in training," I said.

"Fuck you."

She closed the door.

I drove over to Java the Hut's, bought two coffees, then drove to Wentworth Park and pulled up next to the statue of a Boy Scout. The Boy Scout posed on one knee, his hands stretched out to give drinks to passing animals. During the summer water dripped out of his hands into a drinking bowl for dogs. Now, without the trickle of water, the Boy Scout looked like a kid asking for a handout. Not the intended effect.

Wally Hoyle, my deputy, slid into the passenger seat.

"You don't think it's cold," he said, "and then it is."

"November in New Hampshire," I said.

"Tell that to the freaking kids," he said.

He pushed his chin at the usual collection of kids, early high-schoolers, pre-drivers. Girls and boys. They smoked cigarettes and played hacky-sack and sometimes did drugs. They asked older kids to pick them up a six-pack or two. They didn't do much that other kids didn't do except that they did it in the center of town with the municipal bandstand as their headquarters. Today, from what I could see, they seemed determined to kick their skateboards into the air and slide on them along a sidewalk railing. Nothing new there, either.

"Coffee for me?" Wally asked.

I nodded. I stirred my coffee with a wooden stirrer. Wally took a sip of his. He hardly looked much older than the kids collected around the bandstand. He wore a red mackinaw and musher's fur cap. His pistol formed a small bulge under his jacket, but you wouldn't notice it if you didn't look for it.

"Anything?" I asked.

"They're not talking," Wally said. "When I mentioned the

vampire, they all shut up. They're scared of him."

"They admit he's been down here?"

"They don't say yes or no. You know kids. They don't want to give anything away."

"The vampire is still sleeping," I said.

Wally glanced at the late afternoon sky.

"Of course he is," he said.

"Do what we said then," I said. "Tell them someone sold Ricky Adelar some dirty ecstasy and that Ricky's brain may be scrambled. Tell them that Ricky said it was the vampire, but that we're still investigating. Tell them to be smart. If they want to turn anything into us, no questions asked, we'd appreciate it. Tell them Ricky's parents are completely devastated."

"Okay," Wally said.

"And try to sound like Jimmy Stewart when you do it," I said.

"Okay," Wally said.

He climbed out of the car. He took the coffee with him.

I swung by Speare Memorial, got Ricky's room number from a young nurse in a cardigan sweater, then went up in the hospital elevator. As soon as the door opened I spotted Mr. Adelar. He sat in an easy chair reading a Farmer's Almanac someone had left in the waiting room. The TV behind him broadcasted Granite State Challenge, a quiz game that pitted one New Hampshire high school team against another. I heard Manchester's Trinity high school mentioned, but then Mr. Adelar looked up.

"Afternoon," I said. "How's Ricky doing?"

"Better," Adelar said.

He put the almanac aside and stood. He was a tall, thin guy with an outsized Adam's apple. You couldn't look at him without thinking about blue herons. He worked for the state's agricultural department. Something to do with lumber production, out of the Fish & Game Department in Plymouth.

"Still disassociated," Adelar said. "Really it's just wait and see. He recognizes us, knows where he is, but he's not sure of the day of the week, the president, stuff like that."

"Does he still maintain he took ecstasy?"

"He isn't that precise. Have you talked to this vampire fellow he mentioned?"

"Not yet."

"Are you going to search his house?"

Trinity High School buzzed in on a question. What Caribbean country's volcano recently erupted, causing the population to evacuate?

Trinity's team captain said: *Bermuda.*

The quizmaster buzzed. Wrong answer.

"Guys like this fellow," I said, "never have the stuff in their houses. A guy up in Rumney buried a school bus in a retired stockbroker's field. Turned it into a pot factory. Little generator, the whole thing. Grow lights. Made it through three seasons before someone finally spotted him going through a manhole cover into the ground. Most we'd get if we searched the place would be a little pot, maybe, if that."

"So then what do you do?" Adelar asked.

The other team buzzed in, said, *Barbados*, and got buzzed, too.

Monserrat, the quizmaster said.

"I'm going to see him right after this," I said. "We'll make it uncomfortable for him."

Mrs. Adelar stepped out of Ricky's room and nodded at me. If Mr. Adelar was a heron, Mrs. Adelar was a trout. Her feet and neck had about the same thickness. She was as balanced as a throwing knife. She wore jeans and a sweatshirt that had a black dog on it. The black dog promoted beer and a certain bar.

"He's asleep," Mrs. Adelar said. "He drops off so suddenly it terrifies me."

Mr. Adelar slipped his arm over his wife's shoulders.

I reached down and picked up the farmer's almanac. Sunset, according to the chart, had already happened five minutes ago.

The Goth girl opened the door.

"Is he awake yet?" I asked.

"He's awake but he says you need a warrant."

"Tell him he watches too many TV shows about cops. Tell

him he doesn't really want to make this more difficult than it needs to be."

She looked at me. The streetlight caught the speckle of her studs.

"Stay there," she said.

I did. I turned around and looked at the street and thought about vampires. If I were a vampire, I figured, I'd live someplace warmer. Maybe Florida. Maybe Louisiana. New Hampshire seemed like a hard place to be a vampire. People stayed indoors in winter and wore turtlenecks.

I turned back to the door when I heard it open.

"Come in," she said, "but he hasn't fed yet."

"Fed?"

She nodded.

"You don't want to anger him," she said.

"I wouldn't want that," I agreed.

She shrugged.

"What's your name?" I asked.

"Wolf," she said.

"Wolf?" I asked, "like the dog?"

"Like the wolf."

"As in bay at the moon?"

She nodded.

"Got it," I said.

I followed her down a very ugly hallway, past two doors that might have led to sitting rooms when the house had a different spirit, then into a large ell kitchen. The kitchen, in the dim light, looked as though it had last been renovated during the 1950's. Linoleum floor, vinyl counters, red plastic kitchen chairs. It was retro without having a clue what retro meant. A chicken shaped clock clicked above the sink. Or clucked. The chicken hadn't cleaned the dishes below it in some time, and neither had anyone else in the house.

Wolf turned around and left.

The vampire sat at the kitchen table smoking a cigarette. He wore black. He had a horse-head, a long, thin skull that made his chin hang too far out from his chest. He had as many studs in his face as Wolf. He looked slack and thin, but, I considered, maybe he would look better after he fed. He might have been thirty. He resembled a guy who came back to the high school reunion and still couldn't figure out why everyone still wanted to shove him into a locker.

He stood. He was short, maybe five-nine. He wore a chain around his waist. Someone had bolted the chain into the wall behind him. A leash. He offered a chair. I sat. He sat. The kitchen table sat between us. The vampire jabbed out his cigarette and folded his hands.

"We have a kid named Ricky Adelar who says you sold him ecstasy," I said. "The kid's in a hospital acting a little unglued."

"Kids says the darndest things," the vampire said, "don't they?"

He smiled. Now I got the full dazzle. His upper teeth had been filed into points. He had a shark mouth. If you were fifteen years old, and escorted into this room, the combined vampire effect would have been pretty good

"Kids do say funny things," I said. "But he says he bought it from you and that's not all that funny."

The vampire spread his hands.

"Yippee," he said.

"If the kid died, it could be murder."

"Everyone dies," he said.

"Not vampires."

"Christians drink the blood of Christ for eternal life. We drink other blood. Different strokes."

It was a prepared speech I bet he gave it all the time.

"You always wear the chain?" I asked

"Always," he said. "Except when I don't."

He smiled to say I couldn't ruffle him. And to show me his teeth.

"Here's the thing," I said. "I could get a warrant and come back and search the place and maybe I'll still do that. Or maybe I could hear that you stopped coming around the kids and that maybe you even decided to leave town. Either way, you're on notice. If you decide to stay, it will probably be a matter of time before you get picked up. Meanwhile, Ricky may remember more about what went on with his purchase. We may even get a few other kids to remember a few things. It might take a little while, but your string is going to run out. That's the way these things go."

He looked at me. Smiled.

"And your name is Alan," I said. "Alan Pemi. And you come from Berlin, New Hampshire, where your dad is still a logger and your mom does hair. They said to say hello and wondered when you would be home to visit."

He nodded. If having his true identity presented to him made any impact, it didn't show.

"Your problem is," he said, "trying to link me to the kid. And you can't do that. So buzz off. As to the rest, it's police harassment. So buzz off again. I don't sell dope to kids."

"Maybe I'll give the kids Crucifixes."

"Maybe you should."

We sat for a while. He lit another cigarette. He had me and he knew it. I couldn't prove much. Ricky Adelar, especially in his current condition, wouldn't make much of a witness. The vampire leaned back and crossed his legs. The chain rattled a little.

"Anything else we need to talk about?" I asked.

He shrugged.

"Do you think you're a vampire?"

"I am a vampire," he said.

"How about Wolf?"

"Not yet," he said. "These things take time."

"If I took a mirror and held it in front of you, would you see your reflection?"

"Sure," he said. "I'm not Bela Lugosi."

I nodded and stood.

"Up here in New Hampshire," I said, "the turtlenecks get in the way?"

He shook his head.

"Not too bad," he said.

I picked up Wally from the town square.

"You give the kids the talk?" I asked as he climbed in, the cold air following him.

"You bet."

"They buy it?"

He shrugged. Ice had formed on the top of his hat and on the collar of his mackinaw. He rubbed his hands together in front of the heater vent.

"He hangs around the cemetery," Wally said. "That's kind of his big thing. Hanging at the cemetery."

"The kids tell you that?"

He nodded.

"Could have the stuff buried there," he said. "Not a bad place to stash things."

"The dead keep their secrets," I said.

He looked at me.

"I can't tell if you're joking or not," he said.

"Maybe issue garlic to the kids," I said. "And wolfbane. What is wolfbane?"

Wally shrugged again and stopped rubbing his hands.

"How'd your talk go with him?" he asked.

"He's not stupid. He knows we have to connect him to Ricky Adelar somehow."

"Won't be easy," Wally said.

"He's a small time pusher. Maybe if we could figure out who supplies him, they would put the vampire out of business. Wolfbane him."

"Do you know what wolfbane is?" Wally asked.

"No idea," I said, "but I like saying it."

"Does it work against vampires?"

"It must," I said. "Garlic can't be the whole protection system."

"You're having fun with this," Wally said.

"Always wanted to hunt a vampire," I said. "Now I can."

Two days later I saw Steve Sweeter pruning trees. He stood on an apple ladder in front of the Simon's yard. A sign on Sweeter's red truck gave his phone number. He didn't have a company name or a yard service rig. You only called Sweeter if you wanted the best and you only got him if he felt like your plants merited his attention. Apparently the Simon's had an interesting tree.

I pulled over and stepped out. The weather had turned colder. The noon sun did what it could. Sweedler wore a fleece, jeans, and a pair of earmuffs. He nearly always wore earmuffs. This day he wore bifocals, had saggy khakis tucked into a pair of outsized boots, and wore a black back brace the size of a heating pad across his beltline.

"Wolfbane," I said.

"Monkshood," he said, not looking at me.

"Keep vampires away?"

"Poisonous," he said. "Keep just about anything away. Hooded flowers, look like a monk's hood. Aconitum genus. Also known as aconite and wolfbane."

"Why wolf?"

"Why elm? Why birch? Who knows?"

"Werewolves?"

He stopped trimming and looked at me over his bifocals.

"You're a strange man," he said.

"Given the source, I'll count that as a compliment."

He went back to picking at the tree.

"Monkshood probably had various uses. Abortion. Killing your mother in law. Love charms. I'm not an expert on its uses. Might work against vampires and werewolves."

I watched him work for a while.

"What kind of tree?" I asked.

"Metasequoia. Cousin of the coastal redwoods. Also known as a dawn redwood. They thought this was extinct until about 1938 when a Chinese biology professor wandered into a valley and found a shrine built below one. Big race to bring back the seeds. Harvard versus California."

"Harvard win?" I asked.

"Depends who you ask," he said. "Tree came back from the dead. Propagated all over the world. This one isn't happy this far north."

"Can you save it?"

He looked at me.

"Do you have anything else to do?" he asked.

"Not this minute. Where would I find some wolfbane?"

"On the internet, where else? The entire world is on the internet, didn't you know?"

"Any website?"

"Google wolfbane, you'll find it. You could check the health food store."

"I'll let you know if it works against vampires," I said.

"Is there one hereabouts?"

"Some say."

"Well, well, well," Sweeter said. "Vampires don't like dogwoods, either. Christ was executed on a dogwood."

"You see why I stop to talk to you?"

He looked at me. His glasses flicked light at me as he returned to his work.

The temperature turned twelve degrees at 9:37 p.m., one minute before I saw the vampire in the graveyard. I knew the time because I checked it on my Timex Expedition watch. It has a glow feature. I knew the temperature rang down at twelve because I used my night vision glasses to check the tiny L.L. Bean thermometer on the zipper of my parka. I sat against Caleb Potter's headstone without much else to do. My haunches had frozen and my back felt the thick click of cold dropping into my spine. And I was bored because after sitting up for six nights in a row, the vampire hadn't shown.

Until he did.

You could not film it better. He came from the south end of the graveyard, moving slowly through fog and mist, headstone to headstone. Without the night vision glasses, I wouldn't have spotted him. He wore black. No surprise there. But I hadn't been quite prepared for the precision of his movement, the graceful way he glided through the mist.

I reached in my pocket. Garlic, wolfbane, a small Crucifix. Then I took out my cell phone and called Wally.

"He's here," I said softly.

Then I turned it off.

Alone in a cemetery with a vampire. I had to smile.

I watched. I sat in the old part of the cemetery, up where the founding families had been buried. That section of the cemetery had been built on a small rise. From Caleb Potter's grave I could watch most of the newer portion of the cemetery. The newer sections had a dozen mausoleums, attractive, I figured, to the living dead.

I felt pretty good, pretty smart watching him until he disappeared.

Just like that.

I stood. He hadn't moved behind a mausoleum, nor had he slid down behind a gravestone. From all appearances he had been walking along and had suddenly vanished. I couldn't help admiring him. It had been a neat trick.

But when you have eliminated all the possibilities, whatever remains must be the truth. He wasn't a vampire. He hadn't flown or turned invisible. That meant he had slipped into a hiding place. The fog and mist had made it more convincing than it would have been on a clear night. I pushed up my glasses. They didn't help much in the fog.

I drew my revolver and walked down the hill to where he had disappeared. I wondered if I needed silver bullets. If he didn't go up, he had to go down, I figured. I looked back at Caleb Potter's gravestone to calculate distance and line. When I arrived at the spot I had last seen him, I stopped. I used my flashlight and searched the ground. It took a few minutes. Next to a clump of winterberry I saw the trapdoor. The vampire had done a good job with it. He had covered the lid with sod and had placed the hole back among the plants so that no one strolling through the cemetery would step on the trapdoor. He could disappear quickly and he could reappear when he liked. It would freak kids out to see him suddenly materialize in the cemetery when no one had seen him coming. Maybe Wolf walked kids nearby, escorted them to a fixed point, and then the vampire would appear magically.

I was still admiring his work when he suddenly snorkeled a periscope out of a breathing hole. Again, a pretty slick feature. He could scan the area to make sure no one was around. He probably told himself that he was smarter than anyone else and no one could catch him. The periscope scanned slowly in a circle.

I put my hand over the periscope lens.

I resisted the impulse to say peek-a-boo.

Out on Millcross Road, I heard Wally arrive in the department Cherokee.

I pulled some wolfbane out of my pocket. Garlic, too. I pushed the periscope back in, then dropped the wolfbane in and the garlic. I stepped on the trapdoor.

"Wally," I yelled, "bring the wooden stake and the holy water."

The vampire started yelling under my feet.

Two days later Wally gave me the report. The vampire's hideout had been an old refrigerator, enlarged at the foot and head with two plastic boxes. It had been tight, but he had been able to go inside, fish out whatever he needed, then tuck it into his jacket. He had three flashlights, a PVC air stack, and a blanket. He could sleep in there to hide out. Maybe it made him feel like a vampire.

He also had a small pharmacy.

"Did you watch a lot of vampire movies as a kid?" Wally asked.

He sat next to my desk in the rolling chair. He liked the rolling chair because he could push back and glide to his desk. He delivered the report by sliding to me.

"As many as I could."

"I always thought they were stupid," Wally said. "All that hypnosis. The bats in the eyes."

"The vampire could control Frankenstein. That's something."

"But didn't the Wolfman kill the vampire?"

"In Abbott and Costello. Real vampires would never let that happen."

Wally looked at me.

"You meeting the vampire's parents?"

I nodded.

"You think they can get him to admit selling the stuff to Adelar kid?"

"Doubt it."
"Then what's the point?"
"You never know until you know."
"Is that Zen?"
"If it's not, it should be."

The vampire didn't look great in orange. His Concord State Prison jumpsuit sagged around him. His pointed teeth looked merely old and decayed. When he sat down across the table from us, his mother reached for his hand. He let her hold it. She was a gray woman who wore a gray raincoat. She wore Merrills on her feet. She made no sound when she walked. She reminded me of smoke.

"You have to stop all this nonsense," his father said. "No more of this vampire crap."

His dad wore plaid. Plaid coat, plaid shirt, plaid hat. He looked like a Scottish potato. He was no taller than his son, but twice as broad.

"My lawyer said not to say anything," the vampire said.

"You don't have to," I said. "But you could help yourself. Tell us who supplies you, who else is selling things. All you need to do today is agree in principle. We can talk about the details later."

"Alan," his mother said, "you listen to Chief Poulchuk."

"I can't squeal on other people. It wouldn't be good for my health. I'll tell you this much, though. Ricky Adelar helped himself to whatever drugs he took. He used to sell the stuff all the time. One of my competitors."

His dad blew air between his lips. His mom kept the vampire's hand in hers. She looked at my expression to see if her son's confession had any impact on me.

"Interesting," I said.

"So he got a little nutty from the stuff and he had to blame someone. So he blamed me," the vampire said.

"Might make sense," I said.

"Put me out of business and cover things with his parents."

"Got it," I said.

I stood. Mom and dad remained seated.

"What was that shit you threw down at me?" the vampire said. "Into the hole, I mean."

"Wolfbane."

"Thought so."

"And garlic."

"Cut it," his dad said. "Just cut it."

PYTHON

MRS. SHEFFIELD HAD THE KIND of house that makes you buy a lottery ticket at the next liquor store you visit. It was a class New England Cape, freshly painted, with a stone wall bordering a wide, well kept lawn. She had coaxed ivy up the chimney, decorated her porch with three barrels of pansies, and hung a hummingbird feeder near one window. But it was the view from the front yard that made the house spectacular. Halfway up the sidewalk, I turned and studied Mrs. Sheffield's ten acres of Squam Lake, New Hampshire. The lake stretched for miles east and west. The surface of the lake was flat, mirroring the clouds' reflections.

I walked the rest of the way to the door and rang the bell. Mrs. Sheffield smiled as she opened the door. I had expected retiree, but I was wrong. Mrs. Sheffield wore shorts and no shoes. Her legs were tanned and tight. I put her at thirty-seven, maybe forty-two. If she had been a dog, I would have said she had a glossy coat.

"Detective Poulchuck?" she asked.

"Yes, m'am."

"Thank you for coming so promptly."

"Slow day," I said. "You have a beautiful home. A wonderful view."

"We love it."

"Hard not to."

We didn't shake hands. We should have shaken hands; we both knew we should have shaken hands; we didn't. Then she turned and nodded toward the kitchen.

"Coffee?" she asked.

"I'll pass."

"Do you mind if I do?"

"Not at all."

We sat at the kitchen table. It was a marble topped table. I took out my notebook. I hardly ever write down anything worthwhile, but I found it soothed the people giving me reports. At least it told them they could begin.

"It's embarrassing," Mrs. Sheffield said, pouring coffee out of a kitchen thermos. It was the kind of thermos people use when they spend a lot of time dripping coffee through filters. "I gave a dinner party last night and someone stole something."

"What did the person steal?"

"A ring."

"Value?"

"Expensive, Detective."

"Approximate value?"

I wrote a question mark. She watched me write it. I wrote another one for the hell of it.

She said, "Maybe ten thousand dollars? I don't know. It was a gift."

"Do you suspect someone from the party?" I asked and wrote ten g's. I underlined the g's.

"Yes, I know it was someone, actually."

"How do you know that, Mrs. Sheffield?"

"He's done it before. Lots of times. Lots of places."

"Who would that be?"

She stopped. She drank some coffee, put down the cup, lifted to see if it left a ring on the table, then put it down again. From an open window somewhere I smelled the lake. I also smelled the lawn and the leaves turning.

"It's embarrassing, as I said," Mrs. Sheffield continued. "I wouldn't even say anything, but my husband gave me that ring. And it's somewhat valuable."

"I understand. Did you see the person take it?"

"No, I didn't."

"Then how would you know he took it? It is a he, isn't it?"

"Yes."

"How would you know?"

"He's done it before. He has a reputation."

"And you still invited him to your party?"

"He's very wealthy. He comes from a prestigious family. That's why people don't press charges."

"You want to give me his name?"

"Gil Wilson."

"I know the name. It's a big name in New Hampshire."

"He eats them," Mrs. Sheffield said. "That's what I didn't tell you."

"Excuse me?"

"He eats things. Metal. That's what he does."

"So you think he ate your ring?"

"Yes."

"You want to explain?"

"That's what he does, Detective. It's a standing joke, though of course no one mentions it to him. He attends dinner parties, then excuses himself and goes to the bathroom. Then he'll slip into the master bedroom and swallow something. He usually shows better judgment. And he finds a way to make it up to the host."

"He swallows metal?"

"Yes. Jewelry in particular."

"Do you know why?"

"Sexual pleasure, I guess. I don't know."

"But this time he swallowed something more valuable than usual?"

"Exactly. It was probably a mistake."

"You sure about this, Mrs. Sheffield?"

"Yes. They call him the Python."

"Who calls him that?"

"Everyone," she said. "Everyone in this crowd."

"And you still had him to dinner?"

"His family is very prominent in New Hampshire, Detective."

"I understand."

"What will you do, Detective?"

"I'll talk to him."

Mrs. Sheffield bit her lip. She sipped her coffee. She debated. Then she shrugged.

"The ring meant a lot to me," she said. "Otherwise, I wouldn't bother. My husband gave it to me for an anniversary."

"I'll get back to you."

"Would you? Can you make it look as if you're just checking on things?"

"That's all I'm doing."

"But you know," she said and looked out the window.

From a parking lot out of a Pay & Go, I called Dr. Jill DuFresne. We had worked together several times over the years. She was a Ph.D. from Harvard, now teaching at Plymouth State University. She told me more than once that she could have taught at Dartmouth or Yale, except she preferred teaching to publication. I said that was okay with me. Her assistant didn't recognize my name. She buzzed Dr. DuFresne anyway. No one picked up. The call bounced back to the assistant.

"Do you know when she will be back in?" I asked the assistant.

I watched a kid with a jittery hair cut jump off a curb on a skateboard. The metal wheels made a loud clacking sound, then gave way to the old roller skate sound.

"She's supposed to be in now," the assistant said. "She has office hours scheduled."

"It's summer. She keeps office hours in the summer?"

"It's late summer. Pre-registration. Classes begin next week."

"Okay."

"Do you want to hold and see?"

"Hold for her to get back? Not knowing how long that could be?"

"Wait a second," the assistant said. "Here she is. She's in the copy room."

The boy went down the curb again. I saw a manager or someone watch him through the store window. A younger kid, a boy about the skateboarder's age, knocked on the window with his knuckle. The boy inside made a cutting motion across his throat. The skateboard kid nodded and kicked the skateboard up into his hand. He sat on the curb and waited, spinning one of the skateboard wheels with his finger.

"Detective Poulchuck?" Dr. DuFresne asked, the sound of a copy machine still going behind her. "Long time no hear."

"It's been a while."

"You have something to ask me? I'm in kind of a rush."

"I want to know if you ever heard of someone swallowing metal objects on purpose."

"Sure. It happens. Everything happens."

Dr. DuFresne covered the phone for a second

"Both sides," she said to someone, then uncovered the mouthpiece.

I asked, "Why would someone do that?"

"Who knows?"

"You're the psychologist. You tell me."

"It's always the same thing. Someone is trying to fill something up."

"That's the whole thing?"

"Was that a pun, Detective? Whole thing?"

"Not mean to be."

She took a breath, said, "Why do people love to wear plastic bags? Or fornicate with rubber dolls? Or be kicked by men in sweat socks? I can record the phenomena, Detective, not necessarily explain it."

"A woman thinks a man she had to dinner swallowed her ring."

"It's possible. Nothing new under the sun."

"She says he does it regular. Wouldn't he die pretty soon?"

"I'm sure he eliminates a lot of it. Might be part of the ritual."

"I guess."

"It's a strange world, Detective. I don't have to tell you."

"But you did anyway."

"I thought you needed reminding."

She covered the mouthpiece again.

When she came back on, she said, "I have students waiting, Detective. Anything else?"

"No, Doctor, I appreciate it."

"You should," she said and hung up.

Mary, a female butler, escorted me into Mr. Wilson's house. I knew her name was Mary because she told me. She was tall and dark and gave the impression of never having been a little girl. She wore a sedate tuxedo, stylish, that possessed a feminine cut.

"I'll see if he's available," she told me when I asked if Mr. Wilson was around.

She asked if I had a card.

I probably did, somewhere, but I told her I didn't. I showed her my name badge instead. She left me standing in a hallway with a checkered floor while she padded away in Doc Martens. She walked on her toes.

She walked back to me on her toes three minutes later and asked me follow her. I did. She led to the only private library I had ever visited that boasted its own set of authentic armor. At least I assumed it was authentic. It stood by a fireplace and appeared short enough to have once belonged to a knight of the middle ages. The library had books around three walls and windows from ceiling to floor on the fourth wall. The windows looked out on a perennial bed. The perennial bed picked up the red hues of the oriental carpet. Taken together, it was the kind of room that made you think drinks on the lawn and croquet might comprise an interesting afternoon.

Wilson came in a few minutes later. He wore a blue blazer, tan slacks, and black penny loafers. His shirt had a red strip and appeared starched; the cuffs seemed to know just when to pop out from his jacket sleeves for a second. He had a tan and an almost bald head. He looked rich. He looked like a hundred other rich guys except that his mouth was wider than normal. I couldn't look at it without thinking it was a whale's mouth, a baleen, a gap in his head that sifted plankton and smaller people until he had taken nutrition from them.

"Detective Poulchuck?" Mr. Wilson said, coming forward to shake my hand. "I hope I have your name right. Are you Polish?"

"Hungarian."

"Ah, Magyar."

"Mostly American."

"Of course, of course," he said.

His handshake was firm, but the rest of his arm seemed to hang limply so that I had the weight of it in my fingers. He was the type who liked to look you directly in the eye until one of you had to look away. I looked away. He let go of my hand.

"Won't you sit down, Detective?" he asked. "Would you care for something to drink? An iced tea?"

"No thank you."

I pulled out my notebook.

"Well, at least sit."

"Thank you."

I sat on a leather couch that made sounds like a cowboy getting off a horse whenever I moved. Wilson sat on a cloth rocker. He didn't say anything for a moment. Somewhere in the house I heard a vacuum going. It buzzed louder for a second, then seemed to drift away. I heard it bump into a wall and heard a cord drag across the floor. Wilson didn't seem to notice.

"I'd like to ask you a couple questions," I started. "I'm curious about a few things. I have an odd situation, I'm afraid."

"Questions?" Wilson said. "Well, dear me. I suppose I can answer questions. Nothing to hide, as they say."

"They say that," I said, figuring there wasn't any way to ease into the necessary line of questioning. "I wonder if you could tell me anything about a missing ring at the Sheffield's house. You attended a dinner party there last night, didn't you?"

"At the Sheffield's?"

"You were there at dinner last night."

"No, of course I know the name. I made the connection, I mean. They're missing a ring?"

"So it seems."

"Dreadful," Wilson said and seemed to mean it.

"Funny circumstances," I said. "You can understand her desire to be discreet."

"Certainly. Friends to dinner, a ring missing. Well, I can understand."

"She thinks you might have taken it."

"I?"

The vacuum went off, then started again. I wrote something in the notebook. It was the name of my fifth grade teacher, Mrs. Isaacs. I wrote the name of my third grade teacher, Mrs. Lindstom, and waited some more.

"I suppose I'm offended," Wilson said after a moment. "Am I

supposed to say something?"

"Understandable that you might be offended. Can you guess why she might think you took the ring?"

"I have no idea."

"She thinks you ate it," I said, and this time I met his eyes and he turned away.

"Ate it?"

"Swallowed it."

"Swallowed it?" he said, but his color changed. "Why on earth would I swallow a …what was it again?"

"A ring."

"A ring then."

"The psychologist at the college thinks it's to fill a sexual void. If you did swallow it, I mean."

"Detective, this is insulting. I don't know anything about Mrs. Sheffield's ring. Surely I'm not the only person you're interviewing. There must have been ten people at the party."

"You married?"

"What's that got to do with it?"

"Just curious," I said. "What I'd like to do is to bring you to the emergency room and get an x-ray. That would prove it one way or the other."

"If you think I am going to accompany you to the hospital, you are sadly mistaken."

"Did you eat it?"

"Of course not."

"You eat other things at other parties?"

"I'm going to stop answering your absurd questions, Detective. I think you are being deliberately insulting now. I think this interview is finished."

"I'm trying to find a ring. No insult intended."

"Perhaps you don't realize I'm not without a certain amount of influence in this area."

"Is that a double negative?" I asked, then tried to bluff him. "Would it matter if you knew we had your finger prints in the master bedroom? On the dressing table?"

"You can't have them because I wasn't there."

"Okay," I said, "thank you for your time."

"Who is your superior, Detective Poulchuck?"

"Just about everyone," I said, standing, "but the woman you want to talk to is Chief Libby. Call her in Plymouth."

"I will do that."

Mary showed me out.

I called Chief Libby, told her what had occurred with Wilson. She said she'd wait for the call. I asked her if she had any brainstorms about how to proceed. She said she'd buy a big magnet and stick it on Wilson's stomach. That was a joke, she said.

Afterward I ate a hamburger at Burger King and bought a lemonade from two kids at a front yard stand. The kids had a hose under the table. I suspected maybe they watered down their drinks, increasing their profits if not customer satisfaction. The lemonade tasted like wilted vase water. The kids put my two quarters in an old fashioned purse that poked out with turtle lips to take the coins.

I called Mrs. Sheffield and asked her if she could tell me where Mr. Sheffield worked. She said he did private investing, but also ran a small gallery in Sandwich. The gallery hours were ten to two, or by appointment. It featured water colors, Mrs. Sheffield told me.

I drove to Sandwich. The town was mossy and green with lots of shade and windows open. Mr. Sheffield's gallery was called, suitably, The Sheffield Sandwich Gallery. The gallery was as big as a breakfast restaurant, with bare birch floors and white walls covered with water colors. Mr. Sheffield sat behind an architect's desk, his glasses propped on his forehead. He was a few years older than Mrs. Sheffield, but not by much. He wore a pale blue dress shirt, a tie that tried damn hard to be interesting, and top siders without socks. He smiled when I stepped inside, but he didn't say anything. A book lay in front of him. It was big and wide, an art book.

"Mr. Sheffield?" I asked. "I'm Detective Poulchuck."

"Congratulations."

"Funny. Your wife call you to tell you I was on my way?"

"Yes, Detective."

"She tell you I have been over to see Mr. Wilson?"

"Yes," he said and finally closed the book in front of him, keeping a finger in it to mark his place.

"Your wife thinks Mr. Wilson took the ring. What do you think?"

"Swallowed it, you mean?"

"Maybe."

"It's almost a metaphor. A man swallowing things. He prominent in New Hampshire. In the Republican Party, particularly."

"Your wife wants the ring back."

"Insurance will cover it. I didn't think she should report it to the police. I advised against it. But she went ahead anyway. She does that. She hates the idea that he might get away with this. With doing this over and over at people's houses."

"You'd have to report it to the police to collect on the insurance."

"You're probably right, but I wanted to report it missing and leave it at that. It wouldn't matter to the insurance company how it disappeared."

"If I ran a check on your finances, what would I find?"

"You think I might have taken the ring?"

"I guess I didn't say that."

He looked at me. The glasses still hung on his forehead. He lowered them slowly, letting them fit to his nose. He seemed to consider how to answer me.

"You'd find," he said, "that I'm a very rich man."

"Congratulations."

"Touché."

"So where would you like me to go from here?" I asked. "I can't make Mr. Wilson give back the ring. It's not a bad way to steal something when you get right down to it. That is, if he stole something."

"Just file the report. The insurance company will take care of it. We can say it's missing, as I said."

"Who is your insurance agent?"

"I really don't know."

"What company?"

"Mathewson and Brothers," Mr. Sheffield said. "It's a local company."

"Okay," I said. "I'll file the report."

"Thank you, Detective."

He put his head back in his book. He didn't look up as I stepped outside.

I drove back to Mrs. Sheffield's house. She was in her yard, gardening. She wore the same shorts she had worn earlier. She wore a straw hat that was old, but appeared to have been beaten by an angry sales person to make it look old. She had a large brass fork in her hand and a couple day lilies halves in front of her. Transplanting.

"Not much luck, I'm afraid," I said. "You may have to file an insurance form. Your husband says your agent it with Matewson and Brothers."

"Did you go to Mr. Wilson?"

"Yes, I did. He says he didn't take anything."

"Well, you wouldn't expect him to admit it, would you?"

"I'm not sure what you would like me to do. You want me to give him the rubber hose treatment?"

"No reason to be glib, Detective."

Her smile hardened just a bit. It wasn't easy to catch it, but it was there. I looked at her eyes. She hated Mr. Wilson and she hated me for letting him off the hook. She hated a lot of people, actually. That's what I saw in her eyes.

"You don't like Mr. Wilson much," I said, turning to look at the water. "Funny you would bother to have him at your house."

"I told you, Detective, he's an important man in this state. I'm sure you know that."

"People are only important if you want something from them. What did you want from him, Mrs. Sheffield?"

"Not a damn thing. Remember, I didn't take his ring, Detective."

"Why have him to your house, though?" I asked. "That's what I can't figure. Just a social engagement?"

"Yes, just a social engagement."

"So you won't have him again," I asked. "He's pretty much off the list?"

"Yes, he's off the list."

"Well, I'm sorry I couldn't be more help."

I turned to go. Then it clicked. It clicked because she turned back to her gardening too quickly. It clicked because she had known all along what the outcome would be and wasn't disappointed at losing her ring. It was the only thing that made sense. The ring wasn't gone unless she had taken it.

No, what was gone was Mr. Wilson's support. Maybe he did eat things. Maybe he had a reputation for it. And maybe Mrs. Sheffield had heard the rumors, found them titillating, and discovered in them just the right way to alienate Mr. Wilson irrevocably. No reason to do that unless you had a husband who had political aspirations in the New Hampshire Republican Party and you hated those aspirations. Gil Wilson wasn't coming to anymore parties, political or otherwise, for the Sheffield's. Gil Wilson wasn't going to swallow her husband. Mrs. Sheffield had seen to that.

She bent back to the daylilies and jiggled one apart from its cluster. I thought about saying I knew what she was up to, but I didn't care enough to do it. I walked down the flagstone path slowly. I stood next to my car for a second and looked at Squam Lake. It was going to be a pretty autumn, with leaves filled with ants floating like slave galleys across all that water.

LOBSTER SEASON

IT WAS TOO FAR TO drive. That had always been the problem, and Meech wasn't immune to it even now. Even this minute, as he sat behind the wheel of his Jeep Cherokee and directed it along Route 9, heading north from Bangor, he tried to remember what games his family had played in order to pass the time. All of fourteen hours, was what he told people. In fact, it was more like sixteen to twenty when you counted in the stops for bathroom breaks, a chance to walk the dog, and the necessary arrangements for gasoline. Anyway you sliced it, it came down to a day and a half of driving. Besides, it had never made any sense to get to the wharf after six o'clock, because by that time Bertie, the island caretaker, had docked the lobster boat for the night and refused, except in emergencies, to be rousted out.

Meech drove thinking of the past, which was not, he felt, a healthy thing to do. He had promised Sylvia that he could handle the sale of the house without becoming too emotional. She had extracted the promise from him, he knew, because the house had always been his. She had taken pleasure in decorating it, and had cheerfully cooked up the mackerel and cod he had brought in from fishing expeditions with his sons, but she had never felt the place as he had. She had never, for example, seriously considered the possibility that they might retire up in Nova Scotia. Doubtless she was correct about that; the winters were too severe. Bertie, every year since they had purchased the house, had taken an annual photograph of the seals that visited the island during winter. There was one, left on the refrigerator at home for more years than Meech could count, of a seal perched ridiculously on their island doorstep. On the white edge of the photograph, Bertie had scribbled: YOUR NEW NEIGHBORS

COME FOR TEA. It had been a wonderful joke during the long, tame months of teaching, though Meech had caught Sylvia's eye more than once at a dinner party when he had pulled it off the refrigerator and showed it to the gathered guests.

"Our summer place," he liked to announce. "Of course that's a picture in the winter."

Boring, he supposed. Boring, he supposed, even as the house had become boring to his adolescent children. It had surprised him to discover that teenagers could become tired of sand and water and open skies. He had been warned – he wasn't a fool – but when the enthusiasm for long, listless summers had cooled in his youngsters, he had taken it personally. As always, the same familial progression held: Bobby, seventeen, had first begged to stay home in New Hampshire in order to take a summer job; he had even arranged everything, including an offer from the Mackotowiczes to allow him to stay with his best friend, John. Employed and a place to live. How could they protest?

Of course, his example had led the way. Gloria was next. Then, at long last, the family pet, Rudolph. Rudolph, the clown and daredevil, the boy who had taken most to island life. Even now, as he gave the Jeep a goose and passed a pulp truck on an uphill stretch, Meech could remember how uncomfortable Rudy had been as he broke the news. Meech had known, through various hints and rumblings, through less than subtle bread crumbs dropped by Sylvia, that Rudy was too old for a quiet summer of reading, fishing, and hikes. Rudy himself had tried to cushion the request by making it seem as if it were simply a temporary measure. Naturally, Meech could do little. *Go ahead,* he had told Rudy, trying as best he could, to keep any accusation out of his voice. *I understand, certainly, it's a quiet life up there, but we'll miss you. Maybe you'll get up for a week....fly into Halifax and I'll come to pick you up.*

By that time Bobby and Gloria lived away from home. Bobby had taken a job with a branch of the Chicago Tribune. Gloria was in her final year at Duke. For a time, they had talked about a reunion, about getting everyone up for one last month, but, well, he understood. No recriminations. He had always meant the place to be a gift, not an obligation.

He stopped that night at Antigonish at a Best Western motel. The motel was modern and a far cry better than the ones they had visited in their early migrations. He asked for a room away from the road, so that he could not have to hear the traffic flowing all night. The desk clerk, a cheery young woman with apple cheeks, informed him that some guests deliberately chose the highway side.

"They say it sounds just like the ocean," she explained. "You know, the cars like waves, I guess."

He ate a club sandwich with French fries in the dining room – he was on vacation, he told himself, and so he allowed himself the fries – and read the Scotian Sun. He skimmed the news, checked the tide tables, then turned, as had always been his habit, to the classifieds. He preferred, whenever traveling, to read about real estate and items for sale. He particularly liked reading the column on "marine supplies," despite the fact that he had not been in the market for a boat in years. Nevertheless, he found two that looked tempting. A 21 foot skiff, used, the ad said, to haul mackerel nets. Mercury 40 Horse, life jackets included. $3,500 obo. It took Meech a moment to puzzle out the "obo" as meaning "or best offer."

The other was a 32 foot ketch, complete with sails and a long-stemmed British outboard. A Seagull motor. Huge props on the motor, Meech imagined. He doubted the capacity of the boat would allow much horse power. Water could only be pushed by a boat so fast, and from the description in the ad – double keeled, rough weight three thousand pounds, self-righting – he felt the boat was probably prone to wallowing. Still, it sounded like a reliable craft, and he absently felt in his pocket for a pen to underline it. But he had removed his pen when he had settled his bags in the room, and his fingers glided in and out of the scoop of material, then continued down and turned the page.

He paid, taking note of the punch the exchange on his dollar gave him. Fifteen percent off everything, although years ago, when he bought the house, it had been nearly thirty-four percent. On his modest salary — $56,000 at top rank, plus

Geology Department Chair – the exchange had always been a secret pleasure. His money went further than his colleagues', who insisted on summering in Cape Cod or Maine.

His guilt over what he considered a long-standing bargain forced him to leave a sizeable tip. He folded the newspaper, then carried it through the lobby and up the stairs to his room. He felt more tired now than he had first realized when he had arrived; his eyes stung and objects continued to move just on the edge of his vision. He settled himself on the bed – four pillows, a small pleasure he had always denied himself in his marriage bed, although he couldn't say why – and called Sylvia.

She answered on the second ring, which told him she had probably been waiting for his call. He had made no reservation. One wasn't needed so early in the year, a week or two before the schools let out. Besides, he hadn't known how far he could drive in a day, so he had left his arrival open. He realized at her quick "Hello?" that he had been somewhat inconsiderate. He should have called before dinner, set her mind to rest. He understood something about his old age mixed in her concern for him.

He gave her the details of the trip. She asked questions as if the journey were an old friend he had gone to visit. He told her his observations. He pinched his eyes a little as he talked, because the road still came at him, turning the bedspread into something blurry and indistinct.

"I should have come along," she said. "I feel terrible, I really do. I knew it would be like this."

"Sylvia, it's just tying up loose ends, signing the papers. The house is sold."

"I know, but still. Even to keep you company."

"I'll just be a day, then turn around. With your back," he said and let it go.

He hung up a few minutes later. He closed his eyes and lay back on the pillows. He could not explain to himself how it was that he had lived his life without ever making sure his bed contained four pillows.

Meech arrived at the Canso Causeway near noon. A bagpiper played in the Tourist Information parking lot to welcome him to Cape Breton. He pulled over and called Bertie, arranging to meet him in a half hour at the Port Hood wharf.

"How will I know you?" Bertie asked, as Bertie had asked for the last twenty years.

"I'll wear a carnation," Meech answered, as was expected of him.

It took twenty-six minutes to drive the last leg of the journey. He didn't mind the time. Anne's Bay stretched to his left; the Northumberland Strait lay to the north. Prince Edward Island was some twenty miles out to sea. He drove with a pleasant view of the water and the smell of salt and seaweed coming in through the window. It was still the heart of lobstering season, early June, so that he sometimes recognized a boat out on the water. He spotted Scott Cameron's *Sea Rover*, and Willy Toby's *Laura Shell.* Although it was hardly a definite rule, he had always believed he could tell how good the lobster season had been by the painted trim on the boats. If the trims were sharp and newly colored, then the lobstering was good. This year looked to be just fine.

Bertie waited at the Port Hood Wharf.

"No carnation, but I think I recognize you anyway," Bertie said.

Meech shook Bertie's hand. Rough callouses, sturdy fingers, a handshake Meech could not help considering to be somehow more honest than his own. Bertie appeared older, although he was still, Meech guessed, in his late fifties. He wore a green coverall, a hat with a Goodyear insignia, and an L.L. Bean wristwatch, a Christmas present from Sylvia and himself. The watch had a compass built into the band. It rattled slightly as Bertie handed the luggage into the boat.

Meech left the Jeep on the wharf and climbed aboard. He grew aware, as he always had at this moment, of leaving something and gaining something at the same time. It had something to do with the chuck of the waves under the bow of Bertie's lobster boat; it had something to do with the gulls and the wharf piled high with traps, but it remained elusive so that the answer

Meech always found for himself was to step into the tiny cuddy and have at least part of his conversation covered by the chum of Bertie's Chevy engine.

The bay was calm. The breakwater, to the east, hardly spun the water white. Once clear of the dock, Bertie turned and smiled. A new tooth missing, Meech noted, but otherwise he appeared unchanged.

"They've been over," Bertie said. "They'll be coming back tomorrow."

"Is that right?"

"Got two little monkeys with them and a dog, of course. Big kind of a dog…what do you call them? A Newfie, I suspect."

"Black?"

"All black and big. Lazy as anything, though."

Meech nodded. He had heard something about the Newfie from the lawyer, Trevor MacDonald, who had handled the transaction out of Hawksbury. Meech couldn't remember precisely, but it seemed to him that the dog had been mentioned as a way of sealing the agreement. As if, he thought now, the house should be passed along to a family with a dog.

"They going to do much with it?" Meech asked, looking through the cabin window and seeing the island clearly for the first time.

"Structural things at first. Some sills rotted out in the back, where the gutter broke off. You never know. People don't understand what the sea can do to a house. They've probably got some plans, but right now it's just noise."

"Well, we've probably let it run down more than we should have."

"A summer home's never just right," Bertie said and shrugged.

It took ten minutes to cross the bay. Port Hood Island sat a mile out to sea, swimmable, actually, on a fair day. Meech went to the stern when Bertie quartered to the dock. He grabbed the line and climbed up as soon as Bertie cut the engine. Hitched it to the cleat, the loop and tug returning to him without conscious thought. Meech wondered how his hands remembered things so easily.

"Shirley made some dinner. We got a lobster feed for you, if you think you can choke it down," Bertie said when he finished handing up the bags.

"I might at that."

"Good. Now I'll run you up."

The house was there, of course. Up on a hill overlooking the bay, Meech had occasionally seen harbor porpoises from his front lawn. He sat in a small wagon attached to a 4-wheeler and let Bertie drive him up the grassy road. The minute Bertie turned off the engine, no sound reached them except the wind blowing as it always had.

Meech saw them arrive in Bertie's boat around two the next day. It was clear and the bay remained calm, but still the two children wore lifejackets. The big dog remained down in the hull of the boat until it finally figured its way onto the dock by climbing the gunwale, then onto the cabin of the boat, which was, at a middling tide, almost the exact level of the wharf.

Meech had slept the night before on the couch in the living room and his back was sore from the unevenness of the cushions. He waved down the hill at the family, using the motion as a chance to stretch. His back felt tight; too much driving, he told himself, and too little sleep. Rudy had called – put up to it, he imagined, by Sylvia – and the call had left him restless and edgy. He had stayed up until two, pulling out the items Sylvia had asked him to clear out. The furniture remained – it would have been too much, they both decided, to arrange for its transport. Besides, it wasn't worth much off island, and most of it smelled mildly of mildew and a house closed up for winter.

His pile, when he finished, was remarkably small. A book of flower pressings; a few children's report cards; a fishing and temperature record Bobby had kept one summer; a list of eagle sightings; an old-fashioned Monopoly game with the winners noted on the inside of the box top; and one battered jigsaw puzzle that had been a ritual completed each summer. He gathered other odds and ends, but they seemed, once stacked together, more bother than they were worth. In cash value, Meech figured the whole lot could not be worth more than a hundred dollars.

He waved again and walked down the hill to meet them. Bertie came up on the 4-Wheeler, dragging a wagon load of baggage behind him. Even from halfway up the hill, Meech saw a bright red and a patterned arm chair wedged on top of the load. The colors took him by surprise; it was as if, he understood, Sylvia and he had lost a feeling for such vibrancy. The chair would look good in the living room. In fact, it would look good wherever it landed in the house, and Meech imagined it sitting on the bright rug, a comfortable spot for the mother to hold her babies.

"Hello, hello," he said in a voice too hospitable. He stepped to one side to let Bertie pass.

"Hello, Mr. Meech," the woman, Claudia, answered, her voice a tiny bit loud as the engine cut off.

She walked with a baby in her arms; a second child, a toddler, straggled along behind. The husband, Jason, brought up the rear. He carried a long pole, probably a curtain rod, straight over his shoulder like a rifle.

"How was your trip? Claudia asked. "Was it a long ride?"

"Well, it was always long," Meech said, "but worth it."

"We took two days to do it. Of course, Jason has a brother in Bangor. We stopped there for the night."

Naturally, it was uncomfortable. Awkward. Meech realized, as he reached to shake Jason's hand, that this had all been a mistake. He should have left. He should have gathered his belongings and gone. His plans to show Jason the tricks of the woodstove, the old Evinrude, now seemed clearly misguided. Bertie would take them in hand. Or perhaps – he hadn't thought of this before – they were better suited to this type of summer than he had been. It wasn't a hardship, after all, to get an outboard going or to patch a few shingles.

Fortunately, Bertie came to his rescue. Bertie, could always be counted on to get to loading and unloading, made a fuss about the bags. He roped Jason into helping him, which left Meech along with Claudia and the two children. Meech found himself liking Claudia more than he bargained for; she had already taken possession of the house, and that was as it should be.

He stood with her beside the picnic table while she fished two bottles out of a canvas tote and gave them to the youngsters.

The children, he noticed, had already kicked out of their shoes, though they still wore the bright orange life jackets. The dog – she introduced him as Sir Galahad – got busy marking the line of the lawn where it gave way to meadow.

"It's a beautiful home," Claudia said, squinting slightly as she turned to him.

"Yes, we always thought so. Did Bertie tell you that you can see porpoises here? Bottle nosed whales, too, although they call them black fish up here."

"Well, he said something, but we didn't know if that was possible."

"Oh, you'll see them."

When the unloading was finished, Meech made a show of taking Jason on a tour of the house. They had all seen it before, he knew, but he pointed out a few things one could only know through long acquaintance with the house. He uncovered some wooden screens in the side shed, and then spent an unnecessarily long time permitting Claudia to reassure him that the items he had taken – the pile of rubble – was his to take, goodness sakes. She even helped him load it onto Bertie's wagon, admiring as she carried the items, that these were wonderful mementos.

Then it was time. It was happening too quickly, as he had always known it would, but he managed to keep his wits about him long enough to tell Bertie he preferred to walk down the hill. He shook hands with Jason, nodded, too formally, to Claudia. He began down the hill, the grasses blowing, and stopped only long enough to kiss the warm black down on the top of its head. Kissed him and pressed his face quickly into the fur along the dog's neck, no tears, nothing but the warmth of sunlight in the middle of lobster season.

WHITE TOAST

ABBY WORKED AT THE ST. Rumney School in High Acre, New Hampshire. That was where I had taken a job as an English teacher after my first novel, "The Wayward Ones" had been published. I was twenty-nine. Abby was a fund raiser. Shortly before I came to work at St. Rumney, in fact, she had spear-headed the capital campaign for the new library on campus. Engaging an architect from a prestigious firm, she boinked him (I learned this in our pre-matrimonial confessions sometimes later) during his preliminary visit, then engaged him to design a building without thought to cost. Six months later he returned to be boinked once more by the long-legged Abby, and to lay out the blueprints for an extraordinarily elaborate library. Within three weeks, Abby had secured funding for the eleven million dollar project.

"It's all in knowing whom to call and how to approach them, Arnie," Abby told me when she recounted her machinations to me. "People are willing to help out in a pinch."

Her people, of course, were members the enormously wealthy, White Toast class who had never known a pinch themselves. Abby herself did not come from that sort of money, a tragic flaw that provided irony in her life. She had gained her start in the world of White Toast by working as a personal secretary for a woman whose surname began with a "W" and was synonymous with small scale purchases in towns across America. Fresh from the University of Kentucky, a smiling greedy, dervish of a co-ed with a bachelor degree in Art History, Abby approached a domestic placement service in New York City and caught on immediately with Mrs. LuLu W. To nearly everyone else, such a step might have marked a deficiency in character, or at least in ambition, but not Abby. Through competency and relentless attention to detail, she rapidly became Mr. LuLu W's right hand. During days, she took care of two children, Boo and Sudie. In the afternoon, she booked travel arrangements, made sure limos waited, bags were delivered, tips provided. In the evenings, at Mrs. LuLu W's expense and insistence, she attended cooking classes. She learned the feel of a well-weighted sauce pan, learned to make ridiculously sinful desserts, learned to speak French somewhat fluently. It was a deliberate self-transformation. It made no dent to point out, as I did often, that hers was an attempt to hide her obscure origins. Nor did it strike her odd that she, the daughter of a Coca-Cola truck driver from Lexington, Kentucky, and a mom who went into trances during Baptist revivals in stifling tents around the southeast, should find such pleasure and identity among the upper crust of New York society.

Physically, her transformation was no less marvelous. Though she had carried a few pounds of extra weight through her years of U of K – her sorority photographs, when I discovered them during our third year of marriage, revealed a chunky, beer-eyed girl of nineteen, her arm around a sorority sister, her chest stained with beer slosh from an apparent keg party, the caption below written in a girly, swirling hand: "Go Big Blue!" – she peeled off the pounds the first summer in New York through will power and a rigid regimen of exercise, an aesthete at the temple of her own body.

To be fair, I engaged in my own transformation those first weeks at St. Rumney. Anglophilia was rife on that campus and I was not immune. To keep acc, I adopted a walking stick and purchased three tweed sports jackets at a men's clothing store which catered almost exclusively to the male faculty at St. Rumney. A novel under my belt, published, I might add, to excellent reviews, I bathed in the ambiance of St. Rumney's settled life. Self-satisfied, I walked the ground with stick in hand, stopping occasionally to think deep thoughts, jotting down notes and scraps of conversation in a notebook I never opened when actually composing. I let my hair grow, releasing it from the bondage of comb or brush, until it became a willful tuft which covered, like meadow grass, fecund soil beneath. I began taking long looks at Yellow Labs, calling breeders of those short, stumpy dogs – not at all like the huge, Black Labradors favored by American sportsmen – so dear to the British heart. To accompany the dog, I purchased a gleaming over-under Smithson shotgun, one which, when broken properly, could ride my forearm like a falcon as I trudged the St. Rumney meadows intent on murdering pheasants.

It was a pleasant period in many ways. I enjoyed teaching, content to be idolized by the students who thought a novelist, especially one with unruly hair, somehow understood their young, pampered hearts. I read their student essays, their attempts at short stories, their scribbled poems, handing each back with a derisive comment, a statement that they needed "to apply the seat of their pants to the seat of their chair and keep working." I decorated my quizzes – when I bothered to give them – with pithy writing aphorisms, quoting such sources as Schiller ("Who reflects too much will accomplish little.", Coleridge (Five miles meandering with a mazy motion."), and even Nikolai Nekrasov (You do not have to be a poet, but you are obliged to be a citizen.")

I carefully signed volumes of my novel with inspirational admonitions when my apprentices fetched them to me, handing the novel back to them with a serious expression of the priest to the communicant. I used the students, frankly, as a diversion from my own work. I had, as publishers call it, the sophomore jinx. On the heels of my first modest publishing success, I found a second novel impossible to write. No wonder I turned to my students. One novel in the cartridge belt, I had sufficient ammunition to gun down even the most impertinent of the lot.

Except Toshi. Nothing prepared me for Toshi. As self-involved as I was, I scarcely knew he lived in my residence hall, or that I was responsible for him, until he arrived at my door one late Monday night, crying his dwarfish heart to smithereens. He was, I knew, of Asian parentage, but whether that meant he was Chinese, Japanese, Taiwanese, or Burmese was of no interest to me. I hoped, honestly that he would leave me alone. According to school rumors, he was a math genius, his mind electronic in his precision, his interest dry and foreboding. He wore polo shirts every day, white khakis, and sandals with socks. I imagined him, when I thought of him at all, as being the responsibility of the math department, not mine. Wouldn't he be happier, I told myself, to be cloistered with some other bubble gummed-breathed boys, fingering a computer in numeric masturbation, solving problems of rocket trajectories and planetary vacillation, their conversation one long, intricate word problem? I thought so.

Yet on a night in late September, shortly before I met Abby and changed my life forever, Toshi arrived at my door, his Asian eyes squeezing tears down his highly carved cheekbones. He stood framed by the doorjamb, his chest shuddering with his sadness, his hands flat at his sides as if preparing to be shot out of a cannon. He said nothing. When I invited him inside, he shook his head and remained standing in the doorway, his large, fat tears littering his polo shirt with run-off.

"Are you okay, sport?" I asked, a brandy swirling merrily in my snifter. "You appear a little upset. Tell me, Toshi, it is Toshi, isn't it? Tell me, are you okay? You didn't hurt yourself, did you?"

"No," he said in a voice that sounded rusty with lack of use.

"Get a bad piece of news or something? Something from home?"

"No."

"Well, what is it then, Toshi? Come on, speak up. You'll feel better about things if you talk them out."

"No," he said.

Even at the best of times, I had little patience with student fragility. I prided myself on a Teddy Roosevelt bully-boy-ism, replete with monocled platitudes governing attitude and spirit. *Back up, or Buck out,* was a common saying of mine, especially when students proved inconvenient in their mopey behavior. Toshi, however, did not appear a candidate for Roosevelt-ian jingoism. I knew, vaguely, that the relationship between teacher and student was a sacred one. Toshi, whatever his country of origin, was decidedly Asian, so it was a tricky business to know how to proceed. Toshi continued crying his arms still flat at his sides, his eyes straight ahead. I glanced back at my cheerful fire, glanced at my own volume of Steinbeck, and wondered how I might whisk Toshi away. I decided it was impossible to be humane and comfortable, so I grabbed Toshi's upper arm and towed him inside. I maneuvered him until he plunked down in a seat by the fire, his eyes forward, his tears glazed snakes crawling down his cheeks.

"So tell me," I said, taking my seat, "what the problem seems to be."

He said nothing.

"Are you homesick? Because if you are, I can tell you that that is an extremely common problem. Have you ever been away to a boarding school before? It's a frightening proposition at first, but you'll get used to it. You will, I promise."

He did not reply. Despite my eagerness to boot him back into the grimy student halls with their predatory packs of boys, I found I admired him. Obviously, he was terrifically sad, yet he possessed the wisdom and fortitude not to cheapen it with gay explanations of parental indifference or squabbles with his dorm mate. Nor did he appear to want to hide his grief in any way. He embraced his worries, it seemed, and allowed them to consume the outer layers of his body while deep inside his core remained impassive.

"Well," I said.

He said nothing.

"Listen, I'm going to give a call to someone. Do you mind? I'll be just a minute."

By this time, naturally, I knew he wouldn't answer. I went into my study and quickly dialed the Dean of Students, Bill Taylor. Bill Taylor, in his booming, British voice, gave me a snapshot of Toshi's background. Toshi was Japanese. He came from an enormously wealthy family, a family which had pioneered technology along the Pacific Rim. They sent Toshi to St. Rumney in order to have a family member "Americanized for future business dealings." In essence, Toshi was relegated to a life-long undercover assignment, one which would school him in American customs so that he might, on some future date, understand better how to plunder the American market place. Meanwhile he was to learn everything he could, perform his studies scrupulously, and to remain Japanese in his affiliation and affection for his father. Billy Taylor concluded by telling me to call the student dispensary if things became too sticky. He said he was certain I could handle it, though. Not to worry.

Toshi hadn't moved by the time I returned to the living room. With Bill Taylor's ham-brained advice digesting inside my gut, I resumed my seat. It felt astonishingly comfortable to have him there, sitting passively, as rooted as a stump. In his presence, I discovered the reason for keeping fish or caged birds. I leaned forward and stared at Toshi. He maintained his indirect attention. I told him, as calmly as I could, that I wanted to be his pal, that I was willing to listen to anything he chose to tell me, that I would immediately give him my full attention the instant he needed it, but that I didn't intend to sit and wait for such an occurrence. I explained I was going to read Steinbeck and allow him time to compose himself. If he needed or wanted anything, I would be happy to provide it insofar as my meager house (I actually used the phrase, a product of too many Kung Fu movies growing up) could accommodate his request.

Five minutes later, someone knocked at the door. I looked at Toshi. He still hadn't moved, although is tears had slowed and he seemed more placid.

"Be right back," I said.

I went to the door and opened it. Abby stood in the hallway, her hand raised to knock again. What was our first glance like? Did our eyes burn for each other? I don't know. She was pretty, certainly. She was nearly my height, six feet tall, and weighed approximately one hundred and forty pounds. She was not large breasted, although she had a knack, I later learned, of showing her breasts to advantage. She wore a gray cashmere sweater, a black mini skirt, black stockings and crafty boots. Her extravagant hair, which was doubtless her most dramatic feature, clung to the top of her skull like a frightened animal. Taken altogether, she struck me as the prototypical schoolmarm who, on rare occasions, shakes out her hair, slips off her glasses, flashes a naughty grin, and finally loosens her silk blouse. Beneath it all, however, the schoolmarm was not entirely submerged. About the corners of her mouth lingered a prissiness that indicated she had taken a sip of the world's juices and found them mildly soured. Moreover, her eyes carried the conviction that not only were the juices tainted, it was somebody's fault as well. Despite that, however, one battled to gain her approbation. One wanted not to love her, but to have one's finger painting hung in perpetuity on her refrigerator door.

On this night, Abby's chief concern was Toshi. Stepping back in order to let me step in the hall with her, she quickly introduced herself and then asked, in a heated whisper, how Toshi fared.

"How do you know about Toshi?" I asked, whispering to meet her whisper.

"Billy Taylor called," she answered. "I'm Toshi's contact here. I'm his guardian, so to speak. Mr. Yakamuro, Toshi's father, is concerned that Toshi is babied at home. He doesn't want the same pattern established here. He's prone to weeping, I guess."

"Mr. Yakamuro or Toshi?"

"Toshi, of course, Abby said, her wild, rabid hair nodding as though counting out one-two-three before it leaped from her head. "Mr. Yakamuro is an extremely important friend to this school. Extremely important. I can't emphasize that enough. We have to play this one very carefully."

"You mean by 'a friend" that he's a donor? Is that why Bill Taylor was so quick to call in reinforcements?"

"I mean he's a friend," Abby said, verbally underlining the word in the best White Toast manner so there could be no mistake that she didn't want to initiate a conversation about donors. "Billy thought you might need a hand, seeing as this is your first year at St. Rumney. You know, your first year in this kind of situation. What's Toshi doing now?"

"Sitting in a chair," I said, suddenly feeling protective of the little cry baby.

"How did this all start?"

"He showed up at my door. He appeared distraught."

"Was he crying?"

"No, not really," I lied. "Maybe leaking a bit, but he's been no trouble. I suspect he's a little lonely. Everyone gets a little lonely from time to time. Am I right?"

"He probably needs a male influence," Abby said, ignoring

my question. "Mr. Yakamuro is gone on business a great deal. I told Toshi he could come to me whenever he liked, anytime day or night, but apparently he wants to be with you. He's making an obvious choice from a psychological standpoint. I guess that's good. You're the writer fellow, aren't you?"

"You could say that," I answered, then managed to slip in, "I just had a novel come out."

"I'll tell you what we'll do," she said, ignoring my publishing feat while thinking aloud. "Why don't I just stick my head in, pretend that we're friends you and I, and say hello to Toshi? I'll stay for a little while and chat with him and we'll see where that gets us, okay?"

"He refuses to talk. I don't think they'll be much chatting to do. Actually, I think it would be better if you left us alone. He doesn't seem to need anything at the moment. I can let him bunk out on my couch if he's too upset to go back to his room."

"That's fine and good, but I need to see him. Establish a visual check. Later I'll have to call Mr. Yakamuro. What time is it in Japan, do you know?"

"I may be new at this, but I don't think calling the boy's father and getting the kid scolded is the way to stop him from crying, do you? That's just my feeling off the cuff, so to speak."

"I'll call Mr. Yakamuro and say there has been a small incident. That's all," Abby said, displaying to me, for the first time, her enormous capacity to bulldoze through sarcasm. "We have a responsibility to the parents of our charges to keep them informed. In loco parentis, Arnold."

"My name is Arnie."

"Yes, of course, Arnie."

Potentially it was a stand-off. Toshi had taken sanctuary, after all, in my private quarters. I might have put my foot down, won the first contest between Abby and myself, forged a different contract. Instead I merely shrugged and let her inside. Over her shoulder, I watched Toshi bristle and tighten as Abby charged into the room.

"Oh, Toshi, you're here," she exclaimed, lying as expertly as anyone I had ever seen.

Toshi's eyes began filling again. Abby pretended astonishment at his tears, put her hand to her weedy bosom, and dashed around the couch.

"Toshi, what is it, dear?" she asked. "Oh, Toshi, you look so morose."

"He's okay," I said, but it was too late.

She grabbed Toshi and pulled his rigid body against her own. I watched her performance with no little admiration. She was worth any salary St. Rumney paid her. In fact, my earlier reservations were on the verge of being swept away by Abby's canned solicitude, when I happened to catch Toshi's eyes. Still leaning in his awkward way against her bosom, his tear ducts sprinkling incredibly large drop's on her sincere shoulder, he glanced in my direction before locking his gaze back on the distant Atlantis of his internal life.

His expression was simple: *You betrayed me.*

He knew Abby for the phony she was, knew, furthermore, that Abby intended to call his father immediately. He also knew I was a terrible faker – one even more insidious and cruel than Abby.

Abby hoisted Toshi out of his seat and promised him a milkshake at the student snack bar. Toshi, still wooden, permitted himself to be hauled away. Two hours later, shortly before I retired, Abby returned. Thoughtful woman, she carried a milkshake for me, smiling her acknowledgement that a frappe did not adequately repay me for my troubles. Her feral hair quivered cutely under a L.L. Bean rain hat. In our preposterous British enclave, she resembled a gawky Beatrix Potter just returned from vespers at the parsonage.

"So sorry to have put you out," she said, stepping inside my small living room and taking a position near the fire. "I feel as though I bullied you. But really, Arnie, I've been through these things before. Homesickness is temporary, believe me. Besides, Toshi knows me. It's likely that he's going to want some masculine guidance – and Mr. Yakamura said he was extremely relieved to hear you were in the picture – but at this stage Toshi still requires a little mothering. I'm happy to do it, believe me. And Billy Taylor is tickled the way you've stepped forward. He really is."

"I hardly stepped forward," I said, fishing for additional compliments, happily sipping, with my traitorous lips, both straws of the milkshake.

"Oh, but you did," Abby said, patting the seat of her rain coat dry, the coals hissing behind her. "You certainly did, Arnie. May I stay a moment? The fire feels so good."

"Of course."

She shucked off her coat. I offered her brandy and she accepted. She remained in front of the fire while I sucked down the last of the milkshake. Appropriate, I thought much later, that her first gift to me had been frigid breast milk. At the time, though, I was happy to be taken into Abby's confidence. She admitted, off the record and in a conspiring whisper, that Mr. Yakamuro had verbally committed to a five million dollar gift to St. Rumney's rebuilding program. It was to be used to construct the highest quality computer lab in any secondary school in the world. Part of the five million was earmarked for faculty salaries, two of whom were to come from Mr. Yakamuro's firm, Taayako Electronics.

Try as I might to be blasé about what she told me, I sat enraptured. Watching Abby prattle on, I imagined Mr. Yakamuro, out of gratitude for work with his Number one Son, sending me a small set of automobile keys for my Christmas stocking. I would resist, naturally. But eventually, and with a good-hearted shrug of compliance, I would allow myself to be lowered into the cockpit of the racy little spitfire, the Yakamuro family nodding with pleasure around me as I revved the engine. Merry Christmas to all, I might shout, wheeling away in a car with the street-hugging handling of a recent road kill.

And as if that were not enough, I also felt myself soothed by Abby's presence. How right, really, to have a woman in front of one's fire. How right to look forward to yawns and knowing glances as the evening's pleasure at bedtime approached. What more did I want than a book published, a form of steady employment, and a fine, cultured woman with whom to share my life? Throw into the mix the chance at an extravagant Christmas present from Mr. Yakamuro, and all the Yakamuros of my future, and my life, taken on balance, was an outstanding proposition.

Abby felt it, too. She glowed as she accepted a second brandy. And a third. She smiled freely when I, awkwardly, kissed her and backed her haunches into the direct heat of the roaring fire. She let out a small yelp, cutting our kiss off in order to prevent a trip to the burn clinic. After twisting in a feminine manner to check behind her, she grabbed me and kissed me passionately, her lips buttered by brandy.

"We shouldn't," she said.

"Yes, we should," I said, though the thought of tangling with Abby hadn't entered my mind until I had spoken. I left her in front of the fire and dashed around the room turning out lights. By the time I returned, she had already slipped out of her mini skirt, taking care to fold it neatly over the back of a wing chair. I jumped out of my trousers and stood, absurdly, with my penis arching like a tent pole in the paisley print of my boxers.

"Oh, Archie," Abby said.

"Arnie," I corrected her.

"Arnie," she repeated, not at all embarrassed.

When we were finally spent, we lay on the couch, the oak logs snapping, our fate together already sealed. My wife! I watched Abby in that luscious light and felt myself to be a lucky man. When we fell asleep – although she snapped to attention around three and scrammed out of there in order not to set tongues wagging around campus – I held a lock of her hair entwined in my fingers. Abby fell asleep with a kiss planted on my neck. A sweet gesture, I thought, until I realized, as she settled into sleep, that her top lips had been pulled back somehow. Whether it was caused by my own neck pushing against her lip, or whether she habitually slept in a snarl, I couldn't tell. Either way, her teeth were indisputably bared against my jugular. As gently as possible I moved away, shaken, wondering if this woman might not awaken during the night and find inside my neck the sustenance of her vampiric life.

We planned a June wedding. Abby's Kentucky mother, Betsy, the self-same woman who entered trances in Baptist revival tents, came to stay in February and did not leave, for any extended period, until well after the wedding was over. As most men do, I lost track of the reason for marry Abby in the whirlwind of preparations. Abby had no intention of entering married life quietly. She was intent on showing the world she had married well, or at least married lavishly, and she took St. Rumney over in her march to the altar. Within a week of our engagement, she had persuaded Billy Taylor to allow us to be married in the charming St. Rumney chapel, despite the fact that neither of us was Episcopalian. A week later, with a little arm twisting, she acquired a vast, Gothic reception room in Hyde Hall for our use. Everything was free, even down to the food donated by a local caterer who was intent to win more business from the St. Rumney crowd. On the odd nights when actually we spent significant time together, we made love like mad people, leaping over couches, burrowing under movie seats, groping in cars. Sex was our primary means of communication and we moved together like victims of St. Vitus' dance.

During the afternoon when Abby was off plundering the countryside, and when my teaching duties were finished, I chopped wood. Toshi accompanied me. Using one of the school's Ford pickups, we drove each afternoon down the long, dirt roads of St. Rumney's 180 acre campus, splashing through spring puddles, gliding over the last remnants of ice and winter freeze, until one of us, usually Toshi, spotted a spool of dead birches. I parked and climbed out, yanking my bow saw out of the flatbed. Toshi, his own bow saw in hand, took special pleasure in toppling the crusty birches. Jumping back, we watched the tree falling through the arms of its comrades, neither of us daring to shout, "Timber!" Working in his dwarfish squat, the bow saw busy in his hands, he might have been a Rumpelstiltskin of wood, a fairy tale creature fused from the fog and chilly spring run-off. Oh, but I loved him! I admired him! His stoic acceptance of his banishment to a life as a Japanese double agent, in the face of my caterwauling over my stalled writing career, was tonic. Although I was ostensibly the teacher, he the student, nothing could have been further from the truth. It was, in fact, after an afternoon marveling over Toshi's rhythmic dance with the paper-skinned birches, that I finally found the torch of my writing once more. It occurred on a Thursday evening sometime in early April, a night when Abby had travelled to Hanover, New Hampshire for a dinner function with St. Rumney alumni. Setting my Smith-Corona on a card table in front of my fireplace, I sat on a folding chair and tried to write. Again, the usual gibberish. I pulled my hair. I went and poured a shot of Scotch, then another, drinking them both like cough medicine. When I returned to my card table, I thought, seriously, of abandoning writing altogether. Why bother? I would soon have a wife to think about, maybe children, and life as a school master was not going to foot the demanding bills of family life. It was time to grow up. Time to get serious. Time to become rich, time to become, say, a corporate lawyer, a deadly, gray-templed hot shot who wore tasseled black loafers and killer Italian suits.

Then, shortly before quitting in despair once more, an idea for a story struck. Yanking paper violently from the platen, I inserted another sheet and began to write. Suddenly, after months of being blocked, months of bitter frustration, the words flowed. As if cresting a small dam, then a larger one, the words pooled in saucy currents, urged, urged, urged, until I could not type fast enough to relieve the pressure. I wept as I wrote; I continued typing. I did not even look up when Toshi, blessed Toshi, stepped into my apartment and claimed his spot by the fire. He carried his own books with him, but he knew, as keenly as he observed me each day, that I had finally broken free. Moving with utmost care, he brought me coffee and brandy for the remainder of the night. He did not return to his dorm room, nor did he sleep. I write through the night and into the morning, pained by the sun, wishing, futilely, that light would cease this single day and allow me to continue for another twelve hours in the delirium of my writing. Although Toshi pulled the drapes, I knew it was no use.

“Breakfast,” I croaked to Toshi.

I took him to the Millhouse Restaurant, both of us exhausted, my hands thrilled at the weight of a cup of coffee, the gritty hum of a knife passing butter to the edges of a piece of toast. A wondrous morning altogether. I had typed, double-spaced, with few errors, forty-eight pages. My night's output constituted a quarter of a novel.

"Twenty-five percent of a novel," I told Abby over the phone later that morning. "Can you believe it? I've never experienced anything like it. Isn't it incredible?"

"Good for you, Arnie."

"It was a transcendent experience. I'm thrilled. I really am."

"I have some good news myself," Abby said, sinking my hear that she did not choose to discuss my rapturous night further. "The McWilliams will chip in for flowers. You wouldn't believe how happy they were to be able to do something. They were really pleased."

"I'm glad about that, Abby, I really am, but I'm still caught up in what happened to me. It was astonishing."

"I'm sure it was. I'm pleased for you, but right now I have a small wedding on my mind, Arnie. In case you've forgotten, it's just a few weeks away. Remember? But let's not argue about this. I have to run, sweetie. You can tell me all about it when I get home. A bientot!"

What more proof of our unsuitability did I require? Any knucklehead could see we were destined to make each other miserable. On the other hand, I thought as I hung up, it wasn't her duty to share my private intellectual life. I had to be fair. Who did I think I was, anyway? I was not Van Gogh stropping a razor against his head and posting ears to his beloved. Abby had every right to view my writing as a type of advanced woodworking.

When Abby returned that night, her triumph plain, I put my manuscript aside, literally and metaphorically, and tackled her on the spot. Here was the stuff of life!

"My goodness, you're savage tonight, Arnie," Abby later said in the post coital languor, her clothes still tangled about her. "Really savage. I love it when you know exactly what you want."

"We should have a baby right away," I said, my voice somehow disembodied.

"A baby?"

"Yes, right away. I want to become a daddy. I want to rake leaves with five or six kids around me. I want to carve pumpkins and hang stockings and do all that sort of thing."

"Arnie, what's gotten into you?" Abby asked, rising on one elbow. "Are you all right? I've never seen you like this."

"I mean it. Let's start a family right now, tonight, right away. I want to sit at a kitchen table and help the kids with homework. Come on, what do you say? Let's do it again and this time we'll both try for a baby."

"Hold on now," Abby said, sitting up and arranging her clothes. "I don't know what's got into you, Arnie. Did someone die?"

"No, of course not."

"Because I've read people want to make babies when family members die."

"No, my family is fine. This isn't about them. Or about anyone except us right now. Let's see what kind of kid we could have."

"Arnie, you're scaring me now. Stop it," she said, standing and pulling her clothes around her in short, concentrated movements. "The image that comes to mind right now is a southern cracker grunting on top of his woman in a trailer park. That's how you're making me feel, Arnie. I don't appreciate this line of conversation at all."

She stomped out of my apartment and spent the remainder of the weekend with her mom, Betsy. For once, however, I didn't simply grovel after her. Instead, on Monday morning, I called to announce that I wanted Toshi to be my best man. It was a master stroke in our burgeoning animosities, particularly because she had been after me to pick someone. As soon as I uttered the phrase, she stalled deliciously. In the perfect chapel with the glorious flowers everywhere, with hundreds of important people seated in pews to witness our union, Toshi, the great cry baby, would stand at the altar waiting for Abby to make her way down the center runway. Oh, the lovely, indecorous Toshi! How Abby must have pictured him dancing with her, his head wedged into her breasts, his weepy face worried and drawn!

The day of our wedding dawned bright and blustery. Naturally I could not see Abby before the ceremony, bride that she was, but she had sent Wally, a former classmate of hers from the U of K, to supervise my costuming. Apparently I was not to be trusted to dress myself, and Toshi, who was my rightful butler for the day, was relegated to junior varsity status. Wally was gay, flamboyantly so, and understood the cut of a man's suit. Standing back, his hand on his hip, his own tie a bright purple ascot, Wally regarded me critically, then shook his head.

"You look like a great big Ken doll, I'm afraid. Oh, my."

Wally spoke the truth. I was a Ken doll, a fake, artificial concoction, sans penis, destined to escort Barbie on her Barbie Get-Away Camper, to take her to the Barbie Work-Out center. Barbie and Ken, however, excited in little girls a sense of optimism. My own appearance in the mirror, despite Wally's best efforts, excited only doom. Climbing into the purring limo, Wally behind me to keep me in order, I felt this was somehow a joke. In an hour, perhaps two, we would all have a donkey laugh at this charade and go out and drink a belly of beer. Hell, even Abby, if pushed to see it in the right perspective, would get a good laugh out of it. To combine my immaturity with Abby's social climbing, to mix my fatalism with Abby's fabulous can-do spirit, would be disastrous beyond imagining.

"You know, they have a bar in here if you need a little courage," Wally kindly pointed out. "You seem a tad tight."

"Pour me a Scotch, would you, Wally? But only if you have some breath mints. I don't want Abby to think I had to get drunk to marry her."

"Thoughtful of you," Wally answered, pouring me a good sized jolt.

"Another," I said as soon as I swigged the first.

"Steady as she goes," Wally said, peering out the limousine's smoky windows at the well-wishers congregating for the wedding. "People might notice."

"One more, Wally if there's a drop of mercy in your cold heart," I said, feeling the tentacles of the first Scotch clawing at my guts. "Tell me the truth, Wally. I hate to put you in this position, but I don't have anyone else to ask. Honestly, Wally, what do you think of Abby?"

"Don't get moribund on me, Arnie."

"Answer the question, please."

"She's a fine woman. You're lucky to win her."

"Am I?"

"Well, certainly you are."

"Can I tell you something, Wally?"

"Surely."

"I'm scared to death of her," I said, realizing this was the truth behind everything as I said it. "I think she may be a vampire."

"That's enough of the drinky-winkies then," Wally said, grabbing my glass.

"I don't mean a blood sucker, Wally," I continued, "I mean a soul snatcher. Do you think that's possible? That one person can steal another's soul? She sleeps with her teeth bared. Have you ever seen her sleep?"

"Arnie, I don't think I'm the fellow to give you advice. Definitely not sitting in the bridal limousine in front of the wedding chapel. I hate to say it, but perhaps you should have thought about this before this particular moment."

"You're right. You're absolutely correct. I'm sorry to drop all this on you."

"That's okay. You've simply got a case of the jitters. Perfectly natural. Now I suppose we should pop out and get to the front of the chapel. Abby should arrive shortly."

He dissembled, I knew, but who could blame him? He had his own misgivings about Abby. In any case, Wally jumped out, happy, I imagined, to be free of me. What a miserable, whining skunk I was. Nevertheless, as I worked my way through the amiable crowd in front of the chapel, accepting good wishes, shaking hands, laughing uproariously when I was told to break a leg, I felt my traitorous heart banging inside my chest. It continued to sing, clanking and flexing in my chest, as Wally led me around to the rear of the chapel and forced me to sit down in the choir's robing room while he went to check with the minister. Sitting amidst the bright red sacramental robes, amidst the starched white surplices with black ermine collars, I felt close to fainting.

I might have easily passed out if Toshi hadn't appeared at that moment. He stepped through the outside door, a gale of wind adorning him with a diaphanous halo of spring pollen. He waddled eagerly toward me, his lumpy legs designed for carrying agricultural products, his face screwed into an expression of solemnity.

"The Tosh-man," I said in false bonhomie, a flash of tears suddenly rinsing my eyes. "My best man, the Tosher."

He handed me a handkerchief, directing his attention away while I honked out my grief in squawks. Far away in the walls of the chapel, I heard the organ begin to moan.

"Let's do it," Wally said a few minutes later as he charged in to round us up. "Abby just arrived. Everyone's seated. It's showtime!"

I placed my hand on Toshi's shoulder. Relying on him as a cane, I walked slowly after Wally, smiling when Wally finally ducked aside at the last moment and allowed Toshi and I to pass into the chapel interior. I stumbled slightly on the lip of the door, then righted myself and tried to look dignified as I entered. Lined up in pew after pew, eyes fixed on the doorway from which Toshi and I had emerged, sat the collected rogue's gallery of my life – friends from college, friends from my bohemian life in New York, friends from magazines I had written for, my agent, my editor. I waved. Most of them, unsure of protocol, refrained from waving back. I continued waving, feeling, absurdly, that this was a sixth grade pageant and I had somehow been given a particularly difficult role to master.

Then, without meaning to, my hand still extended in a wave, my eyes suddenly halted on Abby's father, Henry. He sat beside his wife, Betsy, directly across the center aisle from my parents. Henry, whether he understood it or not, had been chucked out of his own daughter's wedding party because he was not decorative enough. He who had worked thirty years behind the wheel of a Coca-Cola step van to support his daughter in her efforts to forget him, had been persuaded by the two females in his life that his bad leg (it was true, he was gimpy) prevented him from escorting his lovely daughter down the aisle, and that he need only hobble over and buzz her once on the cheek as send-off. Obviously he had lived hard. His lower lip held a permanent bulge from the tobacco plugs he gathered – according to Abby – from plants growing beside the lush Kentucky highways. His teeth were hardened into yellow embers, as if his mouth had occasionally burst into flames, leaving behind these ivory remnants.

His eyes stared back at me, listless, troubled, serious. What did I see? I couldn't tell. I continued to stare, my hand dropping, my sight becoming oddly telescopic and falling down the channel of his returning vision. He wanted to tell me something, that was clear, and it was not merely about Abby's abandonment of him at her wedding. I cocked my head in inquiry.

In answer, he shook his head once, and that only minutely, from side to side.

It was the subtlest movement I had ever witnessed. It's doubtful Henry even knew he performed it, but he had. In nearly imperceptible movement, he had told me to run for my life. Shaken, I removed my hand from Toshi's shoulder, leaving a wet spot there. At the same instant the organ suddenly turned shrill, purled into triumph, then the back to the chapel opened to reveal my first glimpse of Abby.

In one movement, the congregation stood, a mingled sigh lifting and sucking Abby toward us. She was beautiful! Radiant! She quivered as she took her first steps forward, a bouquet of lily-of-the-valley trembling in her hands. Alone as she was, with no bridesmaids to distract from her entrance, her skirts filled the aisle. Sweeping against the pews and the long white runner, her train dangled behind her not unlike certain paper wasps' trailing abdomens. Notwithstanding, she had managed to strike the proper note of elegance through her understatement. Oh, what a lucky man was I!

I glanced again at Henry and saw he too had turned to watch. Ridiculous, I told myself, how easily I had become rattled. Henry had not tried to pass along a message to me. It was natural to be confused and anxious – every groom was. I smiled. Abby smiled back. After Henry kissed her and passed her hand to mine, I kissed the back of her knuckles and looked at Toshi. Great tears ran down his cheeks, but whether they were for me, for life, for his own empty heart, I would never know and never ask.

IF WISHES WERE FISHES

THIS IS AN OLD STORY, one we know well, but most of us prefer old stories anyway. This story has a bit of magic and an ending that may be happy or sad, depending on your point of view.

It began on a smoky day in late September, close to the end of trout season in New Hampshire. On that morning, Sam Hollins woke, cooked himself a bagel and carried it on a paper plate to the small porch outside his home. The porch overlooked Mt. Moosilaukiee, the tallest peak in the western portion of the White Mountains. There he sat to watch the morning slip quietly past the mountain and spend itself on the meadow beyond his porch.

A nice morning, altogether. Whistle Dog, his four-year old black lab, sat beside him. He had already fed Whistle Dog, but Whistle Dog-known as WD or WD40 to friends and family-had an insatiable appetite and could not be trusted around children carrying cookies. WD40 stayed beside Sam and watched Sam's hand move back and forth as his master leisurely ate his bagel.

Sam Hollins was married, but his wife, Sarah did not like to wake early. Besides, later in the afternoon she would have to travel to the Redwood Nursing Home where she worked as maintenance and housekeeping supervisor on the second shift, earning, as Sam well knew, $31,689 a year. She supplemented that salary by bringing home toilet paper, paper towels, cleaning products, tired paperback novels, outdated magazines, and around Christmas, odd treats of fruitcake, pecans, and dried figs that went unclaimed, or remained undeliverable, around the nursing home. Their only child, Shelly, now married and living in Concord, New Hampshire, always laughed at his wife's low grade thievery, though Sam, truth be told, always felt ill at ease when using the nursing home's products.

Sam finished his bagel, shook out the crumbs for WD40, then crumpled the paper plate. His fishing gear, an Eagle Claw spinning rig complete with hook and bobber, leaned against the wall. The night before, when Sarah returned from work, he had informed her that he had an unexpected three days free from work. He was a pulp rep, a paper-products salesman for Carimiso Logging Company of Rumney, New Hampshire, whose territory covered most of New England. The vacation was the unhappy fruit stemming from a horrible accident, one involving a driver Sam knew not at all, but one who had been, as Sam understood it, a well-respected employee. As is often the case in the logging industry, the accident had been chilling: the driver, operating a crane at the rear of his truck, had swung the hemlock log too far in one direction or the other, and the butt of the log had knocked the driver dead as cleanly as a croquet mallet striking a ball. Matt Stanton, the firm's owner, had related the gory details to Sam, but Sam had been in the logging business long enough to fix his attention on the bird feeder outside his kitchen, allowing the sad chapter to be pecked and pulled apart by the birds, the gruesome death growing abstract except for the part when Matt Stanton said, "We're going to shut down the business for a couple days. Kind of a half mast thing. You know. The drivers expect it and you can't blame them."

Sam might have gone on calls, but it would have appeared insensitive, a betrayal of the hard-bitten men who lugged trees from here to there, their lives one long trail of saw dust. He spent the afternoon before Sarah returned cancelling appointments, accepting condolences he hadn't felt justified in receiving, then found himself, in mid week, free for the first time in many years.

Sarah suggested he go fishing. At first, he had resisted the idea, but then, slowly, he had given in. It had been years since he had fished, though at one time he had been quite passionate about it. He suspected she made the suggestion to counteract his proclivity to spend his free time puttering around the yard, constantly beginning projects he seldom brought to successful conclusion. Besides, she said, the weather was magnificent. September in New Hampshire, she reminded him, was the chief reason for living in New Hampshire at all. Get out, she said finally, and packed him a lunch.

And so it was at 6:30 that he slapped his thigh to get WD40's attention, shrugged his old Appalachian pack basket on his shoulders, and grabbed his fishing pole. He started across the wide meadow, glad to see WD40 puppyish in his springing, goofy joy to be on a walk with his master. *I should do more of this*, Sam thought as he climbed over the small wooden stile at the base of his property, at the same time knowing he wouldn't.

In an hour, he reached the pond. It was unnamed, as far as Sam knew, its bright, weedy surface a liver of water stretched between two hills. Three mallards took to flight as WD40 ran down to the northern edge, plunged in, then swam in an abbreviated circle, his choppy black nose huffing contentedly. Sam had believed, while setting up his fishing pole, that he would remember how to fish the pond, but now it seemed a slightly foreboding, empty sheet of light. He recognized no specific landmarks and wondered, for a moment before launching his bobber and worm, how a shoreline could change so completely in the few short years he had been absent.

He flung the worm and bobber out toward the center of the pond and set the drag on his fishing reel. He rested the rod against a boulder, nicking the topmost guy against a depression in the stone. Then he grabbed a portable camp chair from the pack basket, found a banana he had laid carefully between two ribs of the basket, and sat down to eat and rest.

The banana tasted marvelous. He ate it with as much pleasure as he had eaten anything for a long time. For a moment he was able to delude himself that this was how he would eat from now on. *Good food*, he thought, *nourishing food.* He would eat properly for a change, he decided, perhaps even lose some weight. He fashioned an image of himself as a cleaner, trimmer version of himself, perhaps one not so involved with his work. He would spend more days like this, out in nature, contentedly taking in the seasonal changes. As he finished his banana, he looked down and patted his stomach—a bit broad, he knew—and wondered how much weight he needed to lose. Twenty pounds, probably. Maybe more.

He bent to one side and dug a hole for the banana peel, and when he looked up the bobber had gone under. For a moment, it bobbled like the float barrels in *Jaws*, then it wiggled and danced toward him, happily marking the struggle of a fish below. Awkwardly he grabbed the pole and reeled in too quickly. Fortunately, the fish had hooked itself well. He stood as the fish skittered over the last foot of muddy shore. Then he lifted the rod tip and saw the fish sparkle toward him, dangling like a toy magnet in an arcade game.

It was a beautiful little brookie, no more than six or eight inches. The red dots on the fish's side shivered in the morning sun. Same grabbed the trout sweetly and tried to pry the hook free of its mouth. The fish, however, had done its work well, greedily gobbling the worm. The hook laced the tongue to the top palate of the fish's mouth, the barb making it impossible to extract. Sam pried harder, but the fish did not surrender the hook. Instead the trout, wheezing and bristling with pain, made a series of squeaking sounds that seemed, in the quiet morning, remarkably like language. Sam didn't like hearing the sounds at all. He could not hold the fish more lightly in his hands while still maintaining his grip. Still, the fish grunted and groaned as if in exquisite pain. Sam paused only a moment, discounted the similarity to language as his own empathy kicking in, then tried again to release the fish.

This time the fish granted three wishes – or rather the grunts and cries from the fish blended in the breezes working through the trees until Sam heard *three wishes, three wishes,* as clear as a little boy calling uncle.

Impossible, of course. But that, incredibly, was what Sam heard. Whether the fish spoke to him, or whether he simply understood the trout somehow, is really beside the point. One way or the other, he sensed he had been given three wishes.

A child might have credited the wishes instantly, but Sam was a responsible adult, fifty-four years old last birthday, so the wishes – if they had truly been wishes—disappeared from his mind immediately. In place of any fiddle-faddle about magic, he remembered he had a pair of needle nose pliers in the pack basket and quickly fetched them out. He cut the hook free from the fish's tongue, apologized for injuring the trout in the first place, then lowered it into the shallow water. The fish reeled drunkenly to one side and Sam feared the worst. The he recalled from his fishing days that he could revive the fish by slowly sawing it through the water, back and forth, back and forth, washing the gills with oxygenated water. After one or two experiments, the fish steadied in his hand and then flicked away, its tail almost like a last handshake against Sam's palm.

Sam found himself standing on the shore, dazed, WD40 regarding him skeptically. He stared at the water. How strange he felt. Distantly he remembered the story of Rip Van Winkle, how the man had gone into the woods, drank beer, and woke up, years later, as a bearded old man. Sam did not compare himself to Rip Van Winkle precisely, but something had certainly occurred and Sam wasn't sure what it might be. One thing he knew: he was done with fishing. He reeled in whatever little line was left out, threw the remaining worms into the water, and then walked to a large boulder and sat down.

All of us have played at the idea of having three wishes, but now, on this September morning, Sam believed he had been given something strange and rare and possibly wonderful. Three wishes! He could make himself rich. Or, he thought as his mind got going, he could wish for world peace, for freedom from illness, from crippling injuries. Anything was possible! He might wish for a new life, a younger man's body, a fresh start. Then he wondered if that was permitted. Weren't there rules for this sort of thing? Didn't the wishes from storybooks have limitations?

It took him a moment or two before he realized he had been imagining – truly imagining – what he might do with his wishes. How peculiar! He stood and shook himself, brushed his clothes and then went to the water and washed his hands. The trout had not granted him three wishes and to believe that it had, to play with the idea at all, said more about his state of mind than he cared to admit. For the next ten minutes, he packed and tidied the picnic spot. Afterward, he slipped into the shoulder straps of his pack basket and headed for home, WD40 trotting in front of him.

"What would you do if you suddenly had three wishes?" Sam asked Sarah that night at a late snack Sam had prepared for her. She had been delighted to find him still awake, still marvelously awake, in fact, a warm onion quiche ready and waiting. She had approached the breakfast bar with playful misgiving, hand to her chest, her eyes roaming over the food, the glass of wine, the blue asters he had put in a glass milk bottle. She had lowered her bag beside the breakfast bar, her eyes still fixed on the food and wine, her body poised as if prepared for flight. Her performance had been an elaborate charade, a set piece, but Sam watched it and felt saddened that she should be so surprised by his expression of kindness and interest. Had their marriage really become so stodgy and boring, he wondered? But he played it through, laughing loudly and saying that he had been expecting someone else, a different date, ha, ha, ha, and then he slid a glass of wine to her and asked her to sit.

Now, watching Sarah smile at his question about wishes – she thought it was idle dinner chatter, he knew – he nearly wished he could make her understand without an explanation. But he knew that was useless. She would have to hear the story from beginning to end. And so he told her everything he remembered, everything about the fish, the odd squeaking sound it made, the grateful, human shake of its tail as it sprinted back to its weedy life. He saw her eyes cloud and twice he made sweeping motions with his hands, impatient gestures he hoped she would not take personally. He meant the gestures as punctuation, and entreaty to take him seriously. Obviously, she would doubt the story; that was expected. But when he poured her another glass of wine, his chest busy with catching breath, he saw she was at least willing to be tolerant. Maybe, he thought she simply wants to get off to bed. Either way, he felt he had a small gap of opportunity, a chance to sail for a while down wind and straight.

"Well, it's easy enough to test," she said in the voice she occasionally used when explaining a type of baking ingredient or dry-cleaning instruction she did not fully trust him to carry out correctly. "If you're serious. I mean. Just wish for something small. Wish for the dishes to be cleaned up."

Throughout the meal he had wanted to ask her about the wishes, but he worried about sounding like a lunatic. Strangely, in the hours since he had released the trout, he had come to believe more, not less, in the truth of the wishes. He had been sorely tempted to try them out, to try one on something small and nonessential, but he worried about wasting any wish. He had also resolved not to utter the word *wish* for fear of turning it into a request and he had even gone so far as to rummage through the basement bookshelves on the off chance they had a copy of *Aladdin* or the *Cat's Paw* somewhere in the house. As he well knew, wishes could have downsides, unexpected reversals that could prove calamitous. He did not intend to be foolish about his wishes.

"That would be a waste," Sam said. "A wish is an obligation as much as it is an opportunity."

"Oh Sam," she said, "you're scaring me a little. I don't know how to take you. Are you really serious? You believe you have three wishes? And that this fish gave them to you?"

Sam nodded.

She stared at him for a moment. The she inhaled and put her hands flat on the table.

She said, "Then wish for something solid and real, but something that is contained. You know what I mean. A wish without a lot of loose ends. Then if it works, we'll know."

"I don't think it should be a frivolous wish," Sam said.

"I didn't say frivolous. It needs a deadline. We have to be able to test it. Observe it. Then if it doesn't work, well, then you'll know."

"What should it be? Do you have any suggestions?"

"Sam, I'm still having an awfully hard time believing you're serious about all this. Tell me straight away. Are you really?"

"I am," he said.

"Then why not wish for a new automobile? Or wish for the house to be painted? You said we should have it done soon. Why not wish for that?

"That seems pretty mundane."

"Well, it's a beginning. Wish for it to be painted and never need paint again. That would be handy. It's not dramatic, but at least we'd know. We'd be able to tell if it worked or not."

"How would we be able to explain it to other people? Imagine if they woke up in the morning and found the house newly painted. No, I think you were right before. Let's do something small and contained. I am going to wish that our refrigerator produce any food we like. Say the dish and we simply open the refrigerator and it will be prepared. How does that sound?"

"Go ahead. Although I'd amend it so that you can get warm food from the oven and cold food from the refrigerator."

"All right, that's my wish. I wish for food to be ready at our demand from the refrigerator. Hot food from the oven and cold food from the refrigerator. Furthermore, I wish that the food be delicious."

"Wait!" Sarah said, but it was too late.

Sam understood immediately.

"Two things! I wished for two things! Oh, how stupid. How blindingly stupid."

But then, only for an instant, Sam remembered what foolishness this certainly promised to be. Wishes indeed! He stood in the kitchen, directly behind the breakfast bar, watching his wife's nervous face. Had she believed too? It was too much to comprehend. Here they stood, two perfectly reasonable adults, and they had both succumbed to this rubbish. Say what you will, he thought, they had both believed for a moment, otherwise why shriek out that he had wasted a wish?

"Are you all right?" he asked his wife. Her face hung in a dazed, worn expression. He could not tell if she appeared happy or sad.

"I would like some cherry cheesecake," she said. "You'll find it in the fridge."

Sam stared at her for some time, determined that he could not tell if she was being serious or not, then turned quietly on his heel. He put his hand on the fridge and turned back to glance at her. She nodded; he pulled. He felt the rubber suck of the gasket giving away. Then a paw of cold air pressed against him and threw the lazy fog of condensation into the room. Through the fog, he spotted a piece of golden cheesecake sitting on a white piece of dinner ware.

"Oh my goodness," his wife said behind him.

"It's here," he said, dumbfounded.

"Don't touch it," she said, hurrying around the breakfast counter and coming to stand beside him. "Don't you dare touch it."

Despite his amazement at the sight of the cherry cheesecake, Sam could not stop the thin, reedy whine in his forehead. They had wasted two wishes! On cheesecake, no less! And yes, it was an astonishing occurrence, but suddenly he grew aware of the slipperiness of what he had been given. It was not a blessing alone, but rather something mixed and complicated, a power, he suspected, that might alter the course of his life without him being fully aware of what had happened.

"We have to taste it," he said. "Don't you want to taste it?"

"I'm afraid," Sarah said.

"Oh, don't be, honey. Not of this. I have a feeling that this is not the thing we have to be afraid of. Do you know what I mean?"

And she did know. She knew exactly. He could tell she understood because she had been his wife for decades, because they understood nearly everything about each other, and because she quietly reached in for the cheese cake. She broke a piece off with her fingers and nodded at him. He opened his mouth. She fed him a piece, then broke off a second morsel and popped it in her own mouth.

For a moment, Sam thought that he had never tasted food until that moment. He merely had been chewing all these years, he decided. The cheesecake tasted like an angel wing must taste, like the candied ear of a heavenly goat. How sublime! It was nearly more than he could stand. He looked at Sarah and watched her lift one hand to prevent him from speaking. Her eyes rested half closed; her mouth moved in a sideways chaw, lingering over each touch of her tongue to the food. Then, remarkably, he watched her eyes suddenly grow animated and she slipped past him, placed the plate of cheesecake on the breakfast bar, and grabbed his two hands.

"It's true," she said, as excited as he had ever seen her, "you caught a magical fish!"

"Yes," he started to say, but her hand suddenly covered his mouth.

"No, don't speak. You can't speak at all. Don't you see? You may say I wish this or that inadvertently, then the wish would be wasted. And who knows, you might wish for something terrible by accident. You might get into an argument with someone, even me, and say you wish this or that person would die! I've read about these situations. You must be so careful, Samuel. So careful! And the other thing is, well, I'm just thinking out loud now, but the other thing is, you may have used two wishes already. Or maybe it's just one! How can we know? No, see, we have to operate under the presumption that you only have one wish remaining. That's the safest bet."

"But what…" he started again and her hand, which had dropped away from his face, sprang back in place.

"Wait. Wait, be certain. Think carefully about what you're going to say. Think it through. Don't use the word wish. Use the letter W instead. We will talk about your W's, how's that?"

He nodded and lowered her hand.

"Carefully," she said again. "Please, Samuel."

He took a deep breath. The flavor of the cheesecake lingered in his mouth. His thoughts seemed pulled and stretched like bats of pink insulation, the Pink Panther type, that he sold as one of his product lines. For a moment, he thought this must all be a terrible delusion, a twist of some incalculable psychosis, but that theory did not hold water. The cheese cake certainly tasted real enough. And yet he suspected again that they must be careful. Such a gift must not be taken lightly.

"The chief thing to decide is whether we have one W or two W's," he said. "And if we decide we can't know that, then we should make one solid W and let it stand there."

"We'll make a list," Sarah said.

"Yes," he agreed, "but they must be simple W's. I'm more convinced than ever that we must be careful. Do you agree?

"That's exactly what I was thinking."

"Then I must make a third W, immediately after the next one. We don't want to leave one W in the chamber, as it were. It could be dangerous, as you say, or even reckless. So two solid W's, but nothing too fancy. And I'm afraid they have to be about us. We can't risk W-ing about someone else. It wouldn't be fair."

"Agreed," Sarah said.

"And whatever we decide, well, let's remember that it can't be perfect. We'll always wonder if we didn't do something wrong or not W for enough of one thing or another. But that will just drive us crazy."

She nodded. Then she grabbed a piece of paper from the counter top and sat with her head cocked to one side, almost if she could listen to proposals from voices he couldn't hear. Now and then her hand reached out and broke off a piece of cheesecake. And when she put it in her mouth, she stopped writing altogether. The sight of her transfixed, her jaws moving slowly around the cheesecake, filled him with worry. Silently he vowed to be done with the wishes sooner rather than later, and he wished though he did not speak it, that he had never caught the fish at all.

Samuel passed a long and restless night. He woke early and took WD40 on their favorite walk, up past a small stream, then through a quiet pine grove. He didn't speak at all, and hadn't spoken, really, for hours. That had been the agreement, for safety's sake, but Samuel enjoyed the silence and didn't mind the restriction. Besides, Sarah talked restlessly about the wish, or wishes, and though he did not think of her as an overzealous character out of a fairy tale, he had been surprised by her avidity. She reminded him of someone who has never gambled, a granny from the Midwest, for instance, who suddenly finds herself at a blackjack table and to everyone's surprise, discovers she has a dangerously deep gambler's stripe.

WD40 chased a red squirrel up the bole of a large oak, then looked back, satisfied, awaiting Sam's approval. Sam gave it, then slapped his thigh and headed for home. When he arrived, he smelled bacon and eggs, cinnamon toast and waffles. He hung up WD40's leash and found Sarah at the large dining room table, a spectacular breakfast arranged on their best china.

"I could get used to this!" she laughed and came over to kiss him.

He kissed her back and for a moment they stood looking at each other, almost if they shared an old joke between them. Then Sarah patted him softly on the arm and told him to come eat.

What food! Sam had never tasted its equal. Sitting at the table, the plates arranged before him like the skins of a drum set, he tried to remember the very best meal he had ever eaten. But such an exercise soon became meaningless—nothing could compare to the food in front of him. He ate scones, cinnamon rolls, the most delicious, fluffy scrambled eggs. Even the condiments — an apple butter concoction and a marvelous marmalade — turned his tongue into a joyous, happy instrument. And the coffee! Each sip of his coffee made him understand he had been sipping something like boiled baseball mitts in his earlier days. He started to tell Sara exactly that, when he glanced at her and saw that she, too, had become rapturously involved with her meal. After each forkful, their eyes met. Each bite brought a new expression, each one attempting to convey that this morsel here, this exact one, was entirely unsurpassed unless, of course, you took another bite.

"Oh my," Sarah said when she finished. "We'll become a thousand pounds if we don't watch ourselves."

"We'll roll around the house like big apple barrels," Sam said.

"Shhh," Sarah said, her hand raised to cover his mouth if necessary. "What if you had wished such a thing. Shhh."

"I'm not going to go through life trying not to W for anything."

"I understand," Sarah said. "And that's why I think whatever we're going to do, we should do quickly. Not hastily but quickly. Do you agree?"

"Yes."

"Are you sure?"

"Yes, I'd like that."

Her list, though predictable in certain choices, surprised him with its thoughtfulness. She wished for nothing that might directly ease her own life. The predictable items — a perpetually clean house, including laundry; walks, driveways, and roofs that would magically shed snow; gardens that would remain fertile but weedless; a car that would run safely, and without need of repair — fell within the small category of husbandry. Obviously, she had carefully controlled her desire, selecting smaller, more solid projects than open-ended, potentially dangerous choices. She had a list, too, of friends and relatives, and acquaintances who might benefit by a well-placed wish, but she quickly edited, saying on top of her reading that she doubted such a wish would be fair, violating, as it did, their general agreement that a wish should be directed at them, not at others. That way, she explained, unforeseen consequences would rest squarely on their shoulders.

"Any of those would be good W's," he said when she finished. "I think we should just make two in rapid succession and be finished with it."

"How can you be so casual about it? Aren't you as wound up about it as I am?"

"If you really want to know," he said, "I've been wondering if we shouldn't W for life to return to the way it was."

There, he said it! In speaking it, he knew that was what had been on his mind all along. He watched her eyes stretch wide, then grow annoyed. Then her expression blended and he could not tell what she was thinking. Nevertheless, he knew, having said his thought aloud, that back to normal was where he wanted to go. He liked his life and that was a great, happy thing. Besides, something about the wish coming as it did shortly after the death of one of his fellow workers at the lumber mill, didn't sit well. True, the food they had consumed was magnificent, but who knew what consequences such W's might have? It was safer by far to wish things back as they were.

"How would you W it?" Sarah asked.

She lifted her coffee and drank it slowly, her eyes fixed on his. He still could not read her. He wondered, on top of everything else, if she had been happy with their life. Was it fair, honestly, to remove the W's altogether? What if she had not been as satisfied with their life as he had been? Certainly, her faithful kindness, her long, steady devotion, required consideration. Still, he had to speak his heart and he now understood that a wish granted might be the tick of one domino, the flip flip flip of dominoes in an elephant walk that no one could anticipate.

He spoke carefully.

"I would W for life to return to its proper course, that's all. I have misgivings, Sarah. And I have been happy with our life. I wonder if you have, too."

She nodded and said she had.

"Then are we agreed?" he asked.

She nodded again.

He took a deep breath, then wished for their lives to return to normal. He wished, secondly, that they be as happy in their lives— more, no less— as when they had encountered the fish.

As soon as he spoke the words, Sam leaned across the corner of the table and kissed Sarah. She kissed him back. Whatever they had waited for—a flash of light, a blink of thunder— failed to arrive. They held hands while they finished their coffee. It was good coffee, not stewed baseball mitts at all, but neither was it the coffee they had enjoyed earlier.

And that was how they lived their lives. They lived a contented, happy life, without great triumphs, but with much solid joy. They had done the right thing with the wishes from the trout, though few people would have been wise enough, or disciplined enough, to have refused the offer of three wishes. Sam could not know, however, that a third wish, one he was not conscious of making, had been granted in the end. He had made only two wishes deliberately, and it was not until he had been resetting a stone wall among his apple orchard that he wished for skilled hands. He became, in time, something of a local attraction, building wonderful stone walls around his property. He worked at his husbandry, just as he always did, but his efforts bore such fruit that people could not pass by his home without seeing the goodness of its old foundation, the straight peak of its roof, the shaded garden filled with hosta and Shasta daisies. Stopping in the road, visitors pointed to the features of the house and on cold days, when Sam happened to be out raking with WD40 beside him, he raised his hand to wave back. Though he never knew it, seeing him outside his home, Sarah with him, the good crispness of a New Hampshire November tucked against the house, he satisfied a longing in countless people who passed. *Home*, they thought, one after another, then drove on, their car exhaust white against a leafy road.